OLD FA

Jin Moreau had gott
leader apparently reco
chutzpah from a mere l

Jin frowned at the alien, managing to get two more steps before coming to a confused halt. "What's the problem?" she asked, glancing back at Merrick. Her hands came casually together, her left forefinger tapping the little finger of her right hand. "I said he would give it—*God in heaven*—" She broke off, her eyes going wide as she focused on the empty corridor behind the Trofts.

And as the Trofts started to turn around, she activated her sonic disruptor. The two Trofts closest to the center of the blast jerked like they'd been punched in the faces, while the ones at the edges staggered like drunkards, all of them clearly fighting to hold onto their balance. They were still trying to make their uncooperative bodies turn when Merrick lifted his right hand and activated his stunner.

Without even a gasp, one of the Trofts collapsed to the floor and lay still. He was still falling when Merrick shifted his aim to the next alien in line and again fired his stunner. Four more shots, and it was over.

"Backup," Jin murmured, nodding toward the corner where the Trofts had appeared.

Merrick nodded and headed across the lobby, his hands curled into fingertip-laser firing position, his heart thudding painfully with reaction. He'd never used his stunner outside the Sun Center practice range, certainly never against another living being.

And suddenly the old family stories and histories had come boiling off their nice, neat pages. This was real. This was combat.

This was war.

Baen Books by Timothy Zahn

Blackcollar: The Judas Solution

Blackcollar (contains *The Blackcollar* and *Blackcollar: The Backlash Mission*)

The Cobra Trilogy
(contains: *Cobra*; *Cobra Strike*; and *Cobra Bargain*)

Cobra War:
Cobra Alliance
Cobra Guardian (forthcoming)

COBRA ALLIANCE:

COBRA WAR, BOOK ONE

TIMOTHY ZAHN

COBRA ALLIANCE

A Baen Books Original

Baen Publishing Enterprises
P.O. Box 1403
Riverdale, NY 10471
www.baen.com

ISBN: 978-1-4391-3404-7

Cover art by David Mattingly

First Baen paperback printing, December 2010

Distributed by Simon & Schuster
1230 Avenue of the Americas
New York, NY 10020

Library of Congress Cataloging-in-Publication Data:
2009039505

Printed in the United States of America

10 9 8 7 6 5 4 3 2 1

COBRA ALLIANCE:

COBRA WAR, BOOK ONE

CHAPTER ONE

The warehouse stretched out in front of them, its lights dimmed, its floor and furnishings old and drab. It was obviously deserted, with a thick layer of dust that indicated years of disuse and neglect. For all Jasmine "Jin" Moreau Broom could tell as she gazed over the scene, the place might have been sitting here unnoticed since the founding of Capitalia, or even since the first human colonists arrived on Aventine.

But Jin knew better. The stacks of crates, the parked forklifts, the dangling cables from the ceiling cranes—it was all an illusion. The room had never been a warehouse. Nor had it ever been an aircraft hangar, an office floor, or an alien landscape.

All it had ever been was a deathtrap.

A shiver of memory ran through her, the goose bumps that rippled through her flesh twinging against the arthritis growing its slow but inexorable way through her shoulders and hips. Jin's own Cobra training, thirty-two years ago, had taken place elsewhere on Aventine, as befit the uniqueness of the mission she and her ill-fated teammates had been assigned. As a result, she herself had never had to deal with this room in any of its various incarnations.

But her husband had taken his turn in here. Many turns, in fact. So had both of her sons, and she could still remember the unpleasant mixture of anxiety and pride she'd felt every time she'd stood here on the glassed-in observation catwalk watching one of them in action.

The fear and pride she'd felt in them as Cobras.

Unfortunately, not all of the members of the group here today shared Jin's sense of respect for this place. "You think maybe we could get on with it?" Aventinian Senior Governor Tomo Treakness muttered under his breath from his position two people to Jin's left. "I have actual work to do."

Jin leaned forward to look at him, a list of withering retorts jockeying for the privilege of leading the charge. She picked the most devastating of the options.

And left it unsaid as the man standing between her and Treakness laid a calming hand on hers. "Patience, Governor," Paul Broom said with the mildness and assured self-control that Jin so admired in her husband. "As I'm sure your estate's chief vintner would tell you, a fine wine can't be rushed."

A flash of something crossed Treakness's face. Annoyance, Jin hoped. Politicians like Treakness, who liked to portray themselves as friends of the common folk, didn't like being reminded about their wealth. "Interesting comparison, Cobra Broom," Treakness said. "So you see this as a slow-aged *luxury* beverage?"

"The Cobras are hardly a luxury," Governor Ellen Hoffman put in stiffly from Jin's right. "Maybe you don't need them so much in Capitalia anymore—"

"Please, Ellen," Treakness interrupted, his tone cool with a hint of condescension about it. "You know perfectly well I didn't mean the Cobras themselves."

"If you disparage the Sun Advanced Training Center, you disparage the Cobras," Hoffman countered. "Without the center, there *are* no Cobras."

"Really?" Treakness asked with feigned incredulity. "I'm sorry—did the MacDonald Center burn down when I wasn't looking?"

Hoffman's face darkened—"That's enough," the fifth member of the group, Governor-General Chintawa, put in firmly from Hoffman's other side. "Save the fireworks for the Council chamber. We're here to observe, not debate."

"If there's ever anything *to* observe," Treakness said.

"Patience, Governor," Paul said again, pointing to the left. "Here they come now."

Jin craned her neck to look. Fifteen shadowy figures had appeared around the side of one of the stacks and were marching with military precision toward the section of floor in front of the observation catwalk. Keying her optical enhancers for telescopic and light-amplification, she took a closer look.

Another shiver ran up her back. The alien Trofts who occupied the vast stretches of space between the Cobra Worlds and the distant Dominion of Man had been trusted friends and trading partners as long as Jin had been alive, plus quite a few years before that. But she knew her history, and the sight of the creatures who had once been mankind's deadliest enemies never failed to stir feelings of not-quite distrust.

This particular group of Trofts were even more impressive than usual, she decided as she watched them marching along. Their gait was military-precise and as fluid as their back-jointed legs could manage. Their hand-and-a-half lasers, the size and power currently favored by the Tlossie demesne's patrol forces, were held in cross-chest ready positions. Their eyes continually swept the areas around them, their pointed deer-like ears twitching as they did their own auditory scan, and the wing-like radiator membranes on the backs of their upper arms fluttered in and out to maintain their internal temperature and distinctive infrared signatures.

They were so perfect, in fact, that they might have been real.

"They get better every year, don't they?" Paul murmured.

Jin nodded . . . because the figures marching along down there were not, in fact, living Trofts. They were robots, designed as the ultimate test of new Cobras and seasoned veterans alike.

And like all ultimate challenges, this one carried the ultimate risk.

"Finally," Treakness grumbled. "Now how long are we going to have to wait for them to get to their hiding places before the Cobras can move in?"

The words were barely out of his mouth when the brilliant spear of a Cobra antiarmor laser beam slashed across the warehouse, slicing into one of the lasers in the center of the enemy formation. "Not long at all," Paul said calmly. "This is an ambush exercise."

The robots scattered madly for cover as three more Cobra lasers joined in the attack. Two of the enemy went down in that first salvo, as did a third whose laser exploded in its face as the Cobras' attack shorted out the weapon's power pack. A moment later, the remaining Trofts had made it to cover, and the battle settled into a slower but no less deadly game of hide-and-seek.

Jin gazed down at the operation, another set of memories rising from the back of her mind. She'd fought the Trofts herself once, the only person since the First Cobras to have ever faced the aliens in actual combat. She'd taken on a cargo ship full of them on the human breakaway colony world of Qasama, more or less single-handedly. Not only had she lived to tell the tale, but she'd even managed to pull a quiet but genuine victory out of the situation.

And had then returned to Aventine and watched helplessly as that victory was snatched from her fingers by truth-twisting politicians.

She leaned forward for a surreptitious look past her husband. Treakness was watching the battle closely, visibly wincing every time one of the robots was knocked out of action. With Treakness it was always about money, and Jin could practically see the calculator tape running through his brain. Fifteen robots at roughly a million *klae* each, plus the costs of the techs running the exercise, plus the maintenance costs of the Sun Center, plus the creation and training of the Cobras themselves—

"They're not actually being destroyed, you know," Paul commented.

"No, the lasers are just chewing up their outer ablative coating material," Treakness said tartly. "I *do* read the reports, thank you."

"I just thought it might be worth mentioning," Paul murmured.

"I also know that it still costs a minimum of fifty thousand for each refurbishing," Treakness continued. "That's a *minimum* of fifty thousand. If the internal works get damaged, that bill can quadruple."

"And it's worth every *klae*," Hoffman put in. "The statistics on Cobra survival in the field have gone up tremendously since the Sun Center opened."

"You get a lot of Troft warriors in the fields of Donyang Province, do you?" Treakness asked pointedly. "I must have missed those reports."

Paul looked sideways at Jin; she rolled her eyes at him in silent reply. For some reason that she couldn't fathom, the military concept of *deterrence* still managed to elude some of the allegedly brightest minds in the Cobra Worlds. *Yes,* for most of the Worlds' existence the Cobras had served mainly as frontier guardians, policemen, and hunters, working hard to clear out the spine leopards and other lethal predators from newly opened territories so the farmers and ranchers and loggers could move in. And *yes,* the three Troft demesnes nearest the Worlds had been as peaceable as anyone could ever hope for, even if they did always tend to press their trade deals a bit harder than they should and wring out every brightly colored *klae* possible.

But *some* group of Troft demesnes had once felt themselves capable of attacking the Dominion of Man and occupying two of its worlds. If there was one thing every governor-general since Zhu had understood, it was that the Trofts needed to know that the Cobras were the finest, nastiest, deadliest warriors the universe had ever seen, and that the Cobra Worlds were most emphatically not to be trifled with. Why Treakness and some of the others couldn't understand that simple point Jin had never been able to figure out.

Perhaps it was simply the natural way of things. Perhaps when people were too far removed from immediate, visible threats they began to doubt that such threats could ever exist again. Or, indeed, that they had ever existed at all.

Maybe people periodically needed something to shake them up. Not a war, certainly—Jin wouldn't wish that on anyone. But it would have to be something dramatic, immediate, and impossible to ignore. A sudden influx of spine leopards into Aventine's cities, maybe, or a small but loud uprising among some group of disaffected citizens.

"Jin," Paul said quietly.

Jin snapped out of her reverie. There had been something in his tone . . . "Where?" she asked, her eyes darting around the warehouse.

"That one," Paul said, nodding microscopically to the far left toward one of the Troft robots moving around the crate stacks.

A hard knot settled into the pit of Jin's stomach. The robot had half a dozen laser slashes across its torso and head, enough damage that it should have shut itself off in defeat and collapsed onto the floor. But it was still wandering around in aimless-looking circles, its laser hefted across its burned torso, its head turning back and forth as it searched for a target. "I think I can get to my comm," she murmured.

"Don't bother—I already hit my EM," Paul murmured back. "The malfunction must have scrambled the local comm system."

And the techs in the control room, their attention occupied with other duties, hadn't yet noticed the problem. "You think we should risk trying to wave at one of the cameras?" Jin asked.

And then, before Paul could answer, the robot's head turned and tilted back a few degrees, its eyes coming to rest on the three men and two women standing on the catwalk.

"No one move," Paul ordered, his voice quiet but suddenly carrying the crisp edges of absolute authority.

"Don't even blink," Jin added, her mind sifting rapidly through their options. At this distance her fingertip lasers were too weak to do any good, especially since they'd first have to punch through the catwalk's glass enclosure. The antiarmor laser in her left calf was a far more powerful weapon, theoretically capable of slagging the robot where it stood, assuming she could hold the laser on target long enough to penetrate the layers of material protecting the robot's expensive optronics. The targeting lock built into her optical enhancers and the nanocomputer buried beneath her brain could easily handle such a task, but only if the robot didn't make it to cover before the laser finished its work. Neither her arcthrower nor her assortment of sonic weapons would operate through the glass, and her ceramic-laminated bones and servo-enhanced muscles were of no use whatsoever in this particular situation.

She was still trying to come up with a plan when the robot lifted its laser toward the observers.

"Stay here," Paul ordered, and with a sudden smooth motion, he ducked past Treakness and took off into a mad dash along the catwalk in the direction of the rogue robot.

"What the—?" Treakness demanded.

"He's trying to draw its fire," Jin snapped, her heart thudding hard in her throat. Just like a real soldier, the robot was programmed to see an enemy moving rapidly in its direction as a greater threat and therefore a higher-priority target than four other enemies standing motionless and unthreatening.

Only now that her husband had gotten the robot's attention, the only thing standing between him and death were his programmed Cobra reflexes. In the tight quarters of the enclosed catwalk, those reflexes were going to be sorely limited.

But there might be another way. Getting a grip on the handrail in front of her, Jin braced her feet against the catwalk floor, her eyes on the robot as its laser tracked along its target's vector. Paul was perhaps a quarter of the way to the distant door at the far end of the catwalk when Jin saw the subtle shift of robot musculature as the tracking laser found its mark. "Stop!" she shouted to her husband.

And pushing off the floor, she sprinted full speed after him.

For a terrifying fraction of a second she was afraid Paul hadn't gotten the message, that he would keep running straight to his death. But even as Jin dodged around past Treakness her husband braked to a halt.

And with that, it was suddenly now Jin, not Paul, who represented the greater threat. Without even pausing to squeeze off a shot at its original target, the robot swung its laser around toward Jin.

Jin clenched her teeth against the arthritic pain jabbing into her joints as she ran. *Well,* she thought. *That worked.*

Or had it? To her dismay, she suddenly realized that with the bouncing inherent in a flat-out run she could no longer see the subtle warning signs that would indicate the robot had acquired her and was preparing to fire. She tried putting a targeting lock on the machine, hoping it might steady her eyesight. But it didn't. She kept running, trying to coax a little more speed out of her leg servos—

"Stop!" Paul shouted.

Jin leaned back and locked her legs, gasping at the sudden flash of pain from her bad left knee. Even as she skidded to a halt she saw Paul break again into a run.

Jin focused on the robot, watching as it disengaged its attention from her and once again shifted to the more immediate threat. This would work, she told herself. It would work. She and Paul could just tag-team their way to the door, get off the catwalk and through the door into the rest of the building and yell to the oblivious techs to hit the emergency abort.

She spared a fraction of a second to glance down the catwalk. Only it wouldn't work, she realized with a sinking sensation. The closer she and Paul got to the rogue robot on their angled vector, the faster it would acquire its new target, and the shorter the distance each of them would get before being forced to stop again. Worse, since Paul was closer to the robot than Jin was, his window of opportunity would get shorter faster than hers would, which meant she would slowly catch up to him, which meant they would eventually end up within range of a quick one-two from the robot. At that point, their only two choices would be to stand still and hope the robot lost interest, or go into an emergency corkscrew sprint and hope they could beat its fire.

The robot twitched—"Stop!" Jin shouted, and started her next run.

She got no more than two-thirds her last distance before Paul's warning brought her to another knee-wrenching halt. Two more sprints each, she estimated, maybe three, and they would reach the dead-end killing box she'd already anticipated. They had to come up with a new plan before that happened.

But she hadn't thought of anything by the time she called Paul to a halt and started her next run. She watched him out of the corner of her eye as she ran, hoping he'd come up with something.

But he merely shouted her to a stop and took off again himself, with no indication that he was trying anything new. Either he hadn't made it to the same conclusion Jin had, or else he had and had decided their only chance was to try to beat the robot's motion sensors to the punch.

The robot's motion sensors . . .

It would be a risk, Jin knew. The chance that even a damaged robot's sensors would lock on to something so much smaller than a human target was vanishingly small. More ominously, what she was planning could easily throw off Paul's stride enough that the robot would finally get in that lethal shot.

But she had to try. Turning her chest toward the glass wall in front of her, gripping the handrail for support, she activated her sonic disruptor.

The backwash as the blast bounced off the glass nearly ripped her hands from the rail and sent her flying backward into the wall behind her. Grimly, she held on, her head rattling with subsonics as the weapon searched for the resonance of the target it had been presented.

And with an earsplitting blast, the glass shattered.

Not just in front of Jin, but halfway down the catwalk in both directions. Through the lingering rattling in her head, she dimly felt herself being hammered by flying objects.

But her full attention was on the robot, whose laser was even now lining up on her husband. The robot which had suddenly been presented with a hundred small objects flying through the air in its general direction.

The robot which was just standing there, frozen, its laser still pointed toward the human threats as its deranged optronic brain tried to work through its threat-assessment algorithms.

The gamble had worked, Jin realized, an edge of cautious hope tugging at her. All the flying glass had distracted the robot and bought Paul a little time. If he could get to the door and call for help, they still had a chance.

And then, the motion at the edge of her peripheral vision stopped.

She shifted her eyes toward Paul, her first horrifying thought that the shattering glass might have sliced into an artery or vein, that her move might have in fact killed her husband instead of saving him.

She was searching his form for spurting blood, and opening her mouth to shout at him to get moving, when a flash like noonday sunlight blazed across her vision and a clap of thunder slammed across her already throbbing head.

Paul had fired his arcthrower.

Reflexively, Jin squeezed her eyes shut against the lightning bolt's purple afterimage, simultaneously keying in her optical enhancers. In the image they provided, she saw that the high-voltage current had turned the robot's laser and right arm into a smoking mass of charred metal and ablative material.

But the robot was still standing . . . and with its threat assessment now complete it was reaching for the backup projectile pistol belted at its side.

Jin could do something about that. Keying for her own arcthrower, she lifted her right arm and pointed her little finger at the robot. The arcthrower was a two-stage weapon: her fingertip laser would fire first, creating a path of ionized air between her and the robot that the current from the arcthrower's capacitor could then follow. She curled her other fingers inward and set her thumb against the ring-finger nail.

And broke off as a pair of human figures appeared, sprinting into view from behind different stacks near the damaged robot. The two men leaped in unison, one of them hitting the robot at neck height, the other at its knees, unceremoniously dumping the machine at last onto the floor. The dim overhead lighting abruptly shifted to bright red, the signal of emergency abort.

It was finally over.

"About time," someone said.

Jin turned to look at the other three members of their group, still huddled together in stunned disbelief a hundred meters behind her. She wondered who had spoken into her ringing ears, realized it must have been her. At the far end of the catwalk, behind the politicians, the door flew open and a line of Sun Center personnel came charging through.

It was only then, as Jin wiped at the sweat on her forehead, that she realized she was bleeding.

Paul and Governor-General Chintawa were deep in conversation in the waiting area when Jin emerged from the treatment room. "You all right?" Paul asked, bouncing to his feet and hurrying toward her, his eyes flicking over the fresh bandages on her forehead and cheeks. "They wouldn't let me come in there with you."

"I'm fine," Jin assured him as he took her hands in his, gripping them with that unique combination of strength and gentleness that she'd fallen in love with so many years ago. "They had to use cleansing mist to get some of the bits of glass out, that's all. By the time you'd have gotten suited up, it would have been too late to watch anyway."

"I'm glad you're all right, Cobra Broom," Chintawa said gravely, rising from his own seat in old-provincial politeness as Jin and Paul came over to him. "That was quick thinking, on both your parts. Very impressive. Thank you for risking your lives for us."

"You're welcome," Paul replied for both of them. "After all, protecting civilians is what we're all about."

"Indeed." Chintawa's lip twitched. "Unfortunately, some would say otherwise." He gestured toward the door. "But we can discuss that on the way back to Capitalia."

Chintawa's aircar was waiting on the parking area where they'd set down four hours ago. "Where are the others?" Paul asked as the driver opened the rear door for them.

"They left an hour ago," Chintawa said, gesturing Jin into the car ahead of him.

Jin shot a frown at her husband as she climbed in. The group had only brought two aircars: Chintawa's and Treakness's. "Governor Hoffman was actually willing to get in an aircar with Governor Treakness?" she asked.

"Neither of them wanted to wait for you two to get patched up," Chintawa said. "It was either share an aircar or one of them was going to have to walk."

"It's so nice to work for grateful people," Jin murmured as Paul sat down beside her.

"Sarcasm ill befits you, dear," Paul murmured back.

"Unfortunately, in this case sarcasm is a close match for reality," Chintawa said as he sat down across from them and signaled the driver to take off. "Did Governor Hoffman tell you why she wanted you to join us in observing today's exercise?"

Jin pricked up her ears. She and Paul had been trying to figure that one out ever since Chintawa issued the invitation the previous afternoon. "No, she didn't."

"She's submitted a proposal to have a second advanced training center built in Donyang Province," Chintawa said. "Her argument is that it would be closer to the expansion regions where the Cobras are needed. And of course, it would also be closer to where most of the recruits these days are coming from."

Jin rubbed her fingers gently across one of the bandages on her forearm, feeling the brief flicker of pain from the cut beneath it. She'd been looking at the recruitment numbers only a couple of weeks ago, and had noticed the ominous downtrend in new Cobras coming from Capitalia and Aventine's other large cities. "We could certainly use another center," she said. "I understand Esqualine and Viminal still haven't gotten the quotas the Council voted them."

"Not to mention Caelian," Paul added.

"Yes, let's not mention Caelian," Chintawa said darkly. "At any rate, Governor Hoffman wanted you two along to add a little weight to today's proceedings. She was hoping that a particularly impressive showing might help convince Governor Treakness that moving the center out there would be a good idea. Now, though—" He shook his head.

"Actually, what happened was far more impressive than a simple by-the-numbers Cobra exercise," Paul offered mildly. "It showed Cobra initiative, courtesy of Jin and me, as well as the quick assessment and response on the part of Cobras Patterson and Encyro."

"You're preaching to the choir, Cobra Broom," Chintawa said sourly. "I doubt most of the rest of the Council will see the event much differently than Governor Treakness, either. We'll be lucky if we don't lose a few more Syndics to his side of the argument."

At her hip, Jin's comm vibrated. Pulling it out, she keyed it on. "Hello?"

"I just heard the news," the tight voice of their younger son Lorne said without preamble. "Are you and Dad okay?"

"We're fine," Jin assured him. Paul was looking at her with raised eyebrows; *Lorne,* she mouthed silently at him. "A few scrapes and cuts. Nothing serious."

"Are you sure?" Lorne persisted. "The prelim report said the whole observation catwalk had been destroyed."

"Since when do you believe prelim reports?" Jin asked, keeping her voice light. "No, really. Some of the glass got broken, but the catwalk itself held together just fine.

"*Some* of the glass?" Lorne retorted. "Come on, Mom—they *had* pictures."

"Okay, maybe more than just some," Jin conceded. Out of the corner of her eye, she saw Paul pull out his own comm and quietly answer it. "But your dad and I are okay," she went on. "Really."

There was a pause, and Jin could imagine that intense look on Lorne's face as he sifted through her tone and inflection. Of their three children, he was the one most sensitive to the quiet currents underlying people's words. Back when they were children, both his older brother Merrick and his younger sister Jody had occasionally been allowed to stay home from school solely because Lorne had thought he'd heard pain or sickness in their voices. Usually, the sibling he'd fingered had wound up running a fever within a couple of hours. "Okay, if you say so," he said at last. "But I'm coming in."

"That's really not necessary," Jin protested, wincing again. The thoughtful, sensitive type Lorne might be, but he nevertheless had a bad tendency to drive way too fast, especially when he thought there was trouble in his family. "Besides, aren't you on duty?"

"I'll get Randall to cover for me," Lorne said. "They've postponed the spine leopard hunt again, so it's not like I'm really needed."

"In that case, you might as well stay for dinner, too," Jin said, conceding defeat. "We should be back home in a couple of hours. If you get there first, let yourself in."

"I will," Lorne said. "See you soon. Bye."

"Bye." Jin closed down the comm and put it away, noting as she did so that Paul had also finished with his conversation. "Lorne's coming to the house for dinner," she told him.

"I hope he's learned to cook," Paul said. "We're going to the Island tonight."

Jin frowned. "That was Uncle Corwin?"

"Merrick, actually," Paul said. "He said Uncle Corwin had called and invited all of us to dinner."

A tingle went up Jin's back. Uncle Corwin never called dinner parties on the spur of the moment this way. And if he had, he would have called Jin, not Merrick, to make the arrangements.

Which meant this family get-together was Merrick's idea, with the Uncle Corwin connection having been thrown in simply for cover.

Jin looked at Chintawa. He was busily leafing through some papers, but she could tell he was listening closely to the conversation. "Sounds good to me," she told Paul. "All I have at the house is leftovers anyway. I'll call Lorne and let him know."

"No need," Paul said. "Merrick was going to call both him and Jody as soon as he got off the comm."

"Okay." Settling back against the cushions, Jin closed her eyes.

And wondered uneasily what was going on.

It couldn't have anything to do with today's trouble at the Sun Center. Merrick had inherited his father's cool unflappability, and he wouldn't have even started worrying until he had something besides an initial report to go on. He'd been planning to stop by the house today and drop off some of Jody's new azaleas—could something have happened to their house?

But then why hadn't he just said so? Surely he wouldn't have worried about either Chintawa or the two governors hearing that the plants were dying or that someone had driven a car into their living room.

"Think of it as an early Thanksgiving," Paul said into her musings. "It'll be a nice treat to have the whole family together again, even if only for one evening."

"Absolutely," Jin murmured. "And you all know how much I love surprises."

CHAPTER TWO

Merrick Broom closed the comm and looked across the desk at the silver-haired man sitting there. "They're coming," he confirmed. "Dad said they'd be home in a couple of hours. Add in time to clean up and change, and they should be here by six or so."

"Good," Corwin Moreau said, thoughtfully fingering the paper Merrick had brought to him half an hour ago. Those fingers, Merrick noted, were thin and age-stained, but still strong and flexible.

As was Great-Uncle Corwin himself. Eighty-seven years old, he was still hale and hearty, with every indication that he still had ten to twenty years of good life left in him.

A hundred years, or even beyond, whereas Merrick's own grandfather Justin, five years Corwin's junior, had barely made it to sixty. A sobering reminder of how drastically the implanted Cobra weapons and equipment shortened the lives of all those who committed themselves to that service.

A list which included both of Merrick's parents and Merrick's younger brother Lorne. Not to mention Merrick himself.

"What do you think she's going to do?" Corwin asked, lifting the paper slightly.

Merrick pulled his thoughts back from the dark future to the equally dark present. "You really think there's a question?" he countered. "She's going to go for it, of course."

"I'm afraid you're right," Corwin conceded. "Your mother's always been the damn-the-consequences sort."

Merrick raised his eyebrows slightly. "I understand it runs in the family."

Corwin's wrinkled face cracked in a wry smile. "Don't believe everything your mother tells you," he warned. "Even at the height of my political career I never took a single step without making sure the floor was solid beneath me."

"I'm sure you didn't," Merrick said. But he knew better. The last step of Corwin's political career, thirty-two years ago, had been made knowing full well that the planks beneath that step were riddled with dry rot. Corwin had taken that step knowing it would destroy him, but also knowing that it was the right thing to do. Outsiders who remembered the Moreau family at all tended to forget that part of it.

But Merrick hadn't forgotten. Neither had the rest of the family.

There was a hint of sound somewhere behind him. Merrick notched up his auditory enhancers, and the sound resolved into a set of soft footsteps on the hallway carpet. "So I guess the question is whether or not we're going to let her," he said, lowering the enhancement again.

Corwin snorted. "You really think you'll be able to talk her out of it?"

"*I* won't, no," Merrick said. "But I think Dad can." He raised his voice. "Hello, Aunt Thena."

"Hello, Merrick," Thena's voice came from the vicinity of the footsteps behind him. "Corwin, in case you missed it, the timer just went off on whatever you had running downstairs."

"Oops," Corwin said, looking at his watch. "Thanks, dear—I'd forgotten about that." He stood up and came around the side of his desk. "Come on, Merrick. As long as you're here, I might as well put you to work."

"What have you got cooking this time?" Merrick asked, standing up as well.

"It's a new ceramic the computer simulation says should be as strong as the stuff you're currently wearing," Corwin said, gesturing toward Merrick's body. "It's also supposedly less reactive than standard Cobra bone laminae, which may help delay the onset of anemia and arthritis."

"Sounds good," Merrick said. After his stormy departure from politics, Corwin had gone back to school, earning a degree in materials science and launching into his own private crusade to try to solve the medical problems that had been shortening the lives of Cobras since the very beginning of the program a century ago.

Though even if he succeeded it would do Merrick himself no good. He had the same equipment that had sent his own father to an early grave.

"I wouldn't get my hopes up *too* high, of course," Corwin warned as he walked past Merrick. "But you know what they say: fifty-something's the charm."

Merrick fell into step behind him, noting the hint of stiffness in his great-uncle's gait. His own parents, three decades younger than Corwin, had that same stiffness, especially first thing in the morning. Another sobering reminder, if he'd needed one, of how rapidly the clock was ticking down for them.

"Before you take Merrick away to the dungeon, never to be seen again," Thena said as Corwin reached her, "I wonder if I might borrow him for a quick menu consultation."

"Sure," Corwin said, his hand brushing hers as he passed. "Come on down when you're finished."

"I'll be right there," Merrick promised. "Oh, and I need to call Lorne and Jody, too."

"Take your time." Corwin headed out into the hallway and turned toward the stairway that led down to his private lab.

Merrick stopped beside Thena and raised his eyebrows. "The *menu*?" he murmured.

"It seemed plausible," she said, handing him a pad.

"I don't know why you even bother," Merrick said as he took the pad. "You know he's not fooled in the slightest."

"No, but he enjoys playing the game."

"If you say so," Merrick said, running his eyes down the list she'd made. Drogfowl cacciatore, sautéed greenburrs, garlic longbread, and citrus icelets for dessert. Nothing he couldn't handle with his eyes closed. "You have everything, or will I need to go shopping?"

"It's all here," she said. "I've got the drogfowl defrosting, and the longbread dough should be finished rising in half an hour." Thena lowered her voice. "Merrick, you can't let her do this."

"Have you ever seen my mother in full gantua mode?" Merrick asked dryly.

"Actually, I have," Thena said grimly. "But I'm not talking about the inherent danger of this whole insane thing. You have to stop her because she'll be doing it for the wrong reason."

Merrick frowned. That was not where he'd expected Thena to be going with this. "You mean she'll be doing it to justify herself?"

"Not at all," Thena said. "I mean she'll be doing it to justify Corwin."

Merrick winced. Thena was right, he realized suddenly. His mother had never truly forgiven herself for her perceived role in wrecking her uncle's political career. The fact that everyone else in the family—Corwin included—agreed that she didn't bear any of the responsibility was completely irrelevant. "Is that what Uncle Corwin thinks, too?"

"I don't know," Thena said. "But if it hasn't occurred to him yet, it will soon enough."

"And of course, he can't mention that to Mom, because she'd just dig in her heels and insist he was imagining things."

"Exactly," Thena said. "In case you hadn't noticed, there's an incredible streak of stubbornness in your family."

"Hey, don't look at me," Merrick protested. "*I* was drafted for this outfit. *You're* the one who volunteered."

Thena smiled, a whisper of fondness penetrating the taut concern in her face. "Willingly, even," she said quietly. "I don't know if you ever knew, but I was in love with your uncle for many years before he finally figured out there was more to life than politics."

"The public spotlight can be pretty dazzling sometimes."

"And the Moreau family has somehow always managed to be in that spotlight," Thena agreed. "Right in the center of Cobra Worlds history." Her smile faded. "But you've paid a huge price for it."

Merrick sighed. "Mainly because so many of us over the years have chosen to be Cobras."

"And because even those like Corwin who haven't have usually ended up directly under the fallout from those decisions," Thena said. "Don't get me wrong—I'm proud of the family I married into. Immensely proud. You've done great things for the Cobra Worlds, whether anyone else remembers or not." She looked away. "I just don't want to see that fallout claim another victim."

"I agree," Merrick said. "Let's see how the evening goes." He pulled out his comm again. "Meanwhile, I need to touch base with Lorne and Jody."

"Go ahead," Thena said. "I'll go pull out the spices and measuring spoons."

"And don't worry," Merrick said, reaching out to touch her shoulder as she started to leave. "You never know. Mom could decide to be reasonable."

The twitch of Thena's cheek told Merrick what she thought of that possibility. But she merely nodded. "Let's hope so," she said.

Lorne Broom put away his comm and turned to the sandy-haired man standing a couple of meters away. "Mom says they're okay," he told the other. "Of course, she'd probably say that if she and Dad each had a limb hanging on by scraps of skin."

"Yeah, my mom hates it when I worry, too," Randall Sumara agreed. "You'd better get going if you're going to beat the Capitalia traffic."

"You sure you don't mind?" Lorne asked. "I know you and Gina were planning to make a long weekend of it."

"So we make a short weekend instead," Randall said with a shrug. "She'll understand. I'll have her drive out early tomorrow and we'll take off as soon as you're back."

"Which will be tomorrow evening at the very latest," Lorne promised. "Sooner if I don't see any actual blood."

"Take your time," Randall said. "Like I said—"

Across the room, the intercom warbled. "All Cobras: assembly room," Commandant Ishikuma's voice came tartly.

"Uh-oh," Randall muttered. "You think they've changed their minds about the hunt?"

"I hope not," Lorne said, wincing. The spine leopard hunts were vitally important to the citizens out here in Aventine's expansion regions, and being a protector of those citizens had been his main reason for joining the Cobras in the first place.

But his parents' health was important, too, and for his own peace of mind he needed to personally make sure they were all right.

The other seven men in their squad were waiting when Lorne and Randall arrived at the assembly room. Ishikuma was standing behind the display table, flanked by four civilians Lorne had never seen before.

And laid out on the table in front of them all were four rifles.

Not just any rifles, either. They were high-tech, super-advanced gizmos: top-heavy with lightscopes, darkscopes, and needle-sensors, bottom-heavy with dual power packs and redundant emitters, and topped with an ominous-looking double walnut shape nearly buried beneath all the hardware.

Lorne sighed. *Not again,* he thought wearily.

"Have a seat, Cobras," Ishikuma said briskly, nodding Lorne and Randall to a pair of vacant chairs. "The gentleman to my left is Dr. Emile Belain, from Jaland City's Applied Tech Institute. We've been asked to assist him and his team in their final field test of a new scheme for hunting spine leopards. Dr. Belain, perhaps you can give us a quick thumbnail of your technique."

"Thank you, Commandant," Belain said, and launched into an enthusiastic description of his new guns and their computerized ability to identify, target, and fire at the number-one scourge of expansion-region citizens.

Lorne and the other Cobras had often speculated as to when the bulgebrains in their nice safe ivory towers would figure out that none of the elaborate weaponry they kept coming up with could replace live soldiers. The recognition software was too iffy, the range of spine leopard physiques and colorations too variable, and the simple inertia of the guns worked against the kind of quickness that was critically important to the gunner's survival. Not to mention the fact that the combat and hunting abilities of the citizens who were supposed to use the guns were literally all over the map.

The bulgebrains knew that, of course. Surely by now they knew it. But they kept hammering at the problem anyway. There were just too many people in the civilized regions of Aventine who disliked or feared the Cobras, and who would grasp at any straw that might lead to their ultimate elimination.

Still, even if the visiting bulgebrains never had the right answers, they could always be counted on for a good dog-and-pony show. Belain waxed bafflegabbily poetic about the capabilities of his new guns, with plenty of reasons why they were so much better than the efforts of those who had gone before. Lorne listened with half an ear, trying to put the image of maimed parents out of his mind.

At least that latter task was made a little easier when, midway through the briefing, his comm keyed in with a message: Merrick was inviting the whole family to Uncle Corwin's estate for dinner. That was a good sign, Lorne knew—if they were gathering at the Island instead of the hospital, his parents must genuinely be doing all right.

Finally, after ten interminable minutes, Belain ran out of superlatives and wind. "All right, Cobras, listen up," Ishikuma said. "As you know, the usual procedure is to start these things in the practice cage. However, Dr. Belain has requested something a little more realistic, so we're going to head to Sutter's Creek and the glade where Dushan Matavuli reported signs of a way station. Questions? Then get to the transports—we're taking One and Three. Broom, stand clear a moment."

Silently, the Cobras got out of their chairs and headed for the door. Belain and his civilians joined the stream, their new superweapons resting in the crooks of their elbows and pointing proudly at the ceiling. Lorne stayed out of the crowd, and as the last of the group vanished out the door, Ishikuma left the table and came over to him. "I hear there was some problem at the Sun Center this afternoon," the commandant said.

"Yes, sir," Lorne confirmed. "But my mother says she and Dad are all right."

"The aftermath film looked pretty nasty," Ishikuma said, watching Lorne's face closely. "I also hear that you've arranged with Sumara to take the first half of your weekend shift."

"Yes, sir, I have," Lorne said, wondering how the hell Ishikuma always knew so much about everything. He must have the whole station wired. "He said he'd log it for me."

"I'm sure he will once we're back from this exercise," Ishikuma said. "Meanwhile, you're dismissed. Check out an aircar and get your tail to Capitalia."

"Thank you, sir," Lorne said, briefly fighting the temptation to salute, turn around, and obey the orders he'd just been given. "But we're going on a hunt. I need to be there."

Ishikuma snorted. "This may come as a shock, Cobra Broom, but we were doing just fine out here before you came along, and we'll do equally well after you leave. We'll handle the hunt. You get to Capitalia and check on your parents."

"I appreciate the offer, sir," Lorne said. "I'll head out as soon as the hunt is over."

For a moment Ishikuma eyed him. "As you wish, Cobra Broom," he said. "Get to your transport."

It was a ten-minute trip to the Matavuli spread and the section of Sutter's Creek where the rancher had spotted the spine leopard way station. Sumara and Werle put the transports down on the nearest halfway-reasonable landing area, and the group headed in.

"Did the local who reported this way station mention its size?" Belain asked quietly as the group walked through the tall grass and thickening woods toward the sound of running water. He was holding his gun in a more or less horizontal position, swinging it gently back and forth in a thirty-degree arc. All four of the civilians were doing that, and the Cobras had responded by fanning out mostly behind and beside them in hopes of staying out of their lines of fire.

It wasn't simply paranoia. Two Cobras over in Donyang Province had been seriously hurt three months ago by a different group of bulgebrains and their weapons.

"He didn't get close enough for a good look," Ishikuma said from Belain's side. "But this close to water, it's probably a good-sized one."

They had gone another ten meters, and Lorne had just caught sight of the matted reeds and splintered bones that marked a spine leopard way station, when they were attacked.

The spine leopards came in two groups, the first consisting of four males leaping from the tall grass beside a big obsidian rock, the second group of three males half a second later coming from beneath the edge of the drop-off beside the creek bed.

Lorne snapped his hands up, his eyes tracking through the sudden deluge of laser fire coming from both the civilians and his fellow Cobras. The first group of spine leopards collapsed to the ground, the black stitching of laser burns along their sides and bellies. Apparently, Belain's weapons were holding their own. Lorne shifted his attention to the second group, targeting one of the as-yet-untouched predators.

He had just fired a volley from his fingertip lasers into the creature's head when his enhanced hearing caught a soft rustling from the reeds behind him.

Instantly, his nanocomputer took control of his body's network of implanted servo motors, breaking off his attack and throwing him into a long slide-leap to his right. He rolled half over onto his back as he hit the ground, twisting his head around just in time to see another pair of spine leopards slice through the space he'd just vacated. He twitched his eye to put a targeting lock on the nearer of the two and fired his antiarmor laser, his body twisting awkwardly around as his servos brought the weapon to bear.

The laser flashed, cutting into the leopard's flank. Without waiting to see if that single shot had done the job, Lorne shifted his eyes to the second predator, who had hit the ground and bounded out into a second leap toward the party. Before he could fire, another antiarmor laser blazed across the leafy background, taking the spine leopard's head off at the neck.

Lorne rolled up onto his feet, his fingertip lasers again held at the ready as he rapidly scanned the impromptu battlefield. But the only ones still on their feet were the humans.

Minus one.

He hurried over to the group crouching or standing guard around the fallen civilian. "What happened?" he asked as he took a spot in the defensive circle, sparing a single glance at the writhing body Ishikuma and de Portola were hunched over.

"Same as always," Randall said bitterly. "The guns all targeted just fine, only they all targeted the first wave, three of them alone on the first spine leopard who poked his nose into sight. By the time the computers disengaged and retargeted, it was too late to shift to the second wave."

Lorne nodded grimly. And without a Cobra's servos and programmed reflexes to protect them, the civilians had been sitting ducks. If they'd been out here alone, all four would probably be dead now.

He looked at Dr. Belain. The other was staring down at the injured man, his face pale, his jaws tight, his hands gripping his rifle as if it was a magic totem.

Lorne turned his attention back to the woods around them. When would they learn, he wondered. When would they ever learn?

"That's all we can do here," Ishikuma said briskly, getting back to his feet. "Broom, Sumara—get him to one of the transports and take him to Archway. Be sure to call ahead and make sure they've got a trauma room prepped."

"Yes, sir," Sumara acknowledged for both of them.

"And when you've done that," Ishikuma added, his eyes boring into Lorne's face, "you, Broom, are to get yourself out of my jurisdiction as per my previous order. Understood?"

"Yes, sir," Lorne said.

"Then move it," Ishikuma said, his voice marginally less severe. "And give them both my best wishes."

"I'll be there," Jody Moreau Broom promised into her comm. "Bye."

She closed the device and put it away. "Well?" Geoff Boulton asked anxiously, his eyes flicking back and forth across the display screen in front of him.

"Merrick says they're both fine," Jody assured him. "Mom picked up a few small cuts from flying glass, but that's about it."

"I don't know," Geoff said doubtfully, fiddling with the view on the display. "Near as I can tell from this, whatever happened left a real mess."

"Merrick wouldn't lie to me," Jody said firmly. "Besides, he's already talked to Lorne, who talked to Mom. You can't hide anything from Lorne."

"If you say so," Geoff said, still not sounding entirely convinced. "So. Where were we?"

"She was showing us her new trap design," Freylan Sonderby spoke up from beside the workbench. He frowned slightly, as if something had just occurred to him. "Unless you were wanting to go to the hospital, I mean," he added awkwardly to Jody. "I mean, you *did* just say you'd be there, right? There being—wherever *there* is. Or is going to be?"

Jody suppressed a smile. That was Freylan, all right. He was the tech end of the team, with the analytical and biochemical skills necessary for taking Geoff's visionary ideas and translating them into reality.

He was also the stereotypical socially inept bulgebrain, with a sometimes astonishing lack of ability to put coherent sentences together. Another good reason why they let him do the lab work while Geoff handled the grant-application pitches that had kept the team going for the past year and a half.

Jody herself possessed neither set of skills. Fortunately, she had other things to bring to the table. "That was just a dinner invitation," she assured Freylan, stepping around the desk to join him at the table. "Whenever you're ready, Geoff?"

"Ready now." Geoff took one last lingering look at the pictures of the Sun Center damage, then shut off the feed and got up from his chair. "Ready," he said again, stepping to Jody's side. "Nice little rabbit trap, anyway," he commented.

"It *is* just a model," Jody reminded him, running her eyes over the device. It didn't actually look like much, she had to admit: a flat, rectangular tangle of mesh, thirty centimeters by fifteen, sitting in midair and supported by a pair of meter-long bars extending outward along each of the rectangle's long sides. One set of bars was currently resting on the end of the table, the other on Geoff's desk. Between each set of bars were a set of five slender crossbars with what looked like thin medicine bottles extending a few centimeters upward from their centers. To the side of the central rectangle was another rectangle, similarly sized, though the mesh in this one was neatly arranged instead of apparently tangled. "We'll have plenty of time to construct a proper one on the way to Caelian," she added.

"Assuming we ever get there," Freylan muttered.

"We will," Geoff promised. "So how's it work?"

"The whole thing gets buried under a couple of centimeters of dirt or leaves," Jody explained. "With a much deeper hole under the central section, of course. Little Rabbit Foo-Foo comes hopping along the trail—" she pulled out her comm and bounced it, rabbit-like, along the desk toward the arms and crossbars "—and comes upon a nice little morsel of food." She stopped at the first medicine bottle and nuzzled the comm against it. "Being a smart, hungry little bunny, she of course scarfs it right down."

"Question," Freylan said, half raising his hand. "How do we make sure that only Little Rabbit—what was it again?"

"Foo-Foo," Jody supplied.

Freylan frowned slightly, but apparently decided to take it in stride. "That only Little Rabbit Foo-Foo takes the bait?"

"Good question," Jody said. "We'll need to figure out how to tailor the bait to whatever animal we're after at the time. Hopefully, the settlers will be able to help us with that once we're there. Anyway, once Foo-Foo has taken the first bite, we keep her going the right direction by having the rest of the bait cups open up in sequence, one at a time, drawing her onto the main part of the trap." She bounced her comm along the bars, stopping briefly at each bait cup, and onto the main part of the trap.

And as she dropped the comm with a little extra force in the center of the rectangle, the entire structure collapsed, the tangle of mesh dropping down and resolving itself into the sides and bottom of a deep box. Simultaneously, the screen that had been sitting next to the box flipped over onto the top, forming a lid and sealing the comm inside. "And presto—one trapped test animal," Jody said, gesturing at the enclosed comm like a magician concluding her act.

"Very neat," Geoff said approvingly. "You come up with this yourself?"

"Hardly," Jody said. "The basic design's been around for centuries. My main contribution is here."

She pointed to the mesh on the sides and bottom of the cage. "Note the little cylindrical free-spinning tubes around each of the main mesh wires. That means that, instead of the animal just lying there, highly annoyed and using every claw and tooth it's got to try to tear through the mesh—"

"I get it," Freylan spoke up suddenly. "If you make the mesh wide enough and the hole deep enough, when it lands its legs will slide on the rollers and go straight through so that it ends up lying on the mesh on its belly."

"Exactly," Jody said. "For most of the animals we'll be looking at, that'll immediately put their claws out of action."

"And even if it manages to chew through the lid, it still won't be able to climb out," Geoff said. "*Very* neat."

"Thank you," Jody said. "And of course, the lifting bars let us pick the whole thing up like a sedan chair and trot it back to the lab without having to open the cage out in the open, risking those same aforementioned claws and teeth."

"Amen to that." Geoff grinned at Freylan. "See, buddy? Let that be a lesson to you. When you hire the best, you get the best."

"Thank you kindly," Jody said, inclining her head. And pretending to believe him.

But she knew better. Her ability with animal traps wasn't the reason Geoff had insisted on hiring her. Neither were her newly minted college degrees in animal physiology and management. No, Geoff had something else entirely in mind.

But it wouldn't do to bring it up. Not here. Not in front of courteous, earnest, naïve Freylan. If this worked out, the three of them would be spending a good deal of time together on the hell world that was Caelian, and there was no point in revealing to him the full depths of his buddy's deviousness.

"So how long will it take you to build a full-sized one?" Geoff asked. "Wait a second—hold that thought," he interrupted himself, pulling out his comm. "This could be it." He clicked it open. "Hello?"

Listening to his end of the conversation with half an ear, Jody unfastened the lid on her trap and retrieved her comm. She put it away, then pushed the bottom and sides up again, fastening the bottom with the quick-release hooks that had held it in place until it was sprung.

"You really want to do this?" Freylan asked quietly at her side.

She frowned at him. "What do you mean?"

"Caelian," he said, his dark, earnest eyes boring into her face. "I know everyone calls it a hell world. But most of them just say that just because everyone else says it. They don't really know what they're talking about. But I do. My uncle spent eight months there a few years ago, and it nearly killed him."

"You and Geoff are going," Jody reminded him. "Assuming you get permission, that is." She nodded toward Geoff and his quiet conversation.

"Yeah, but Geoff and I are crazy," Freylan said, an uncertain smile briefly touching his lips. "You aren't. So why do you want to go with us?"

Jody looked over at Geoff, who was now pacing the room the way he always did in the midst of deep comm conversations. "There are just over three thousand Cobras on Aventine," she said. "Roughly one for every four hundred people. You know how many Cobras there are on Caelian?"

Freylan huffed. "Some ungodly number, probably."

"Seven hundred," Jody told him. "That's one for every *six* settlers. When people say the Cobra project is too expensive and that they want to shut it down, what they really mean is that *Caelian* is too expensive."

"I know," Freylan said heavily. "I also know you and your family have a long history with the Cobras."

"Never mind the history," Jody said shortly. "We need the Cobras, Freylan. The Trofts aren't our friends. We trade with them, and we have good diplomatic relationships with maybe three or four of the demesnes. But even those three or four aren't really our friends. And there are hundreds of demesnes out there."

"And there's Qasama," Freylan murmured.

Jody felt her throat tighten. Qasama. There was a lot of family history tied up in that world, too. Way too much history. "And there's Qasama," she agreed. "The point is that we can't afford to stop the Cobra project. Ever." She ran her fingertips gently over the stainless steel of her trap. "That's why we need to solve the problem of Caelian. If we can find a way to finally tame that world, it'll knock a lot of the props out from under the anti-Cobra argument. Some of the Caelian Cobras could be retasked, the world could be opened up for new colonization, and we could start pushing out the boundaries on Viminal and even here on Aventine. It's not the Cobras themselves the public doesn't like, it's the feeling that the whole program's become nothing but a sinkhole for everyone's hard-earned money—"

"Hey, hey—steady," Freylan said, holding up his hands in a gesture of surrender. "We're on your side, remember?"

Jody made a face. "Right. Sorry."

"That's okay," Freylan said, a little awkwardly. "Passion is good. That's what Geoff always says, anyway. Passion is why people do stuff like this."

Jody cocked an eyebrow at him. "You mean aside from the fame and fortune parts?"

His smile this time was a lot more relaxed and genuine. "Aside from that, sure," he agreed.

Across the room Geoff gave a sudden war whoop. "We're in!" he shouted, lifting his comm in triumph. "That was Governor Uy's office. The project's been approved. We're going to Caelian!"

"That's great," Freylan said, his eyes lighting up. "Jody—we're in."

"Yes, we are," Jody agreed. "Congratulations."

And hoped that her own smile looked as genuine as theirs.

CHAPTER THREE

Uncle Corwin had moved to his estate at the southern edge of Capitalia nearly thirty years ago, a week after his fifty-seventh birthday and less than two years after his political enemies had forced him out of his governorship. That loss had ended his political career, a life he'd led as long as Jin had been alive, and even after all these years she still couldn't think about that without feeling a twinge of guilt for her part in the whole thing.

Corwin didn't blame her, she knew. Never had, for that matter. But knowing that was only minor consolation.

The gate opened as she and Paul walked toward it. Either Corwin had set it on automatic or else someone inside was keeping close watch. "Did you ever get hold of Jody, by the way?" Jin asked as they passed the gate and started down the twinkle-lit walkway toward the dark, looming structure ahead.

"Yes, while you were showering," Paul said. "She doesn't know what this is about, either. But I do know she's been trying to talk Corwin into coming in on her side on this proposed Caelian trip of hers."

Jin grimaced. Caelian had been the third world settled by the Dominion colonists who had come here nearly a century ago, right after beachheads had been established on Aventine and Palatine. The first two worlds, despite occasional bumps along the way, had eventually become unqualified successes.

Caelian, unfortunately, hadn't.

The planet had a hundred different bitter-edged epithets among the Cobra Worlds' population, most of them variants on the words *money pit, home of damn fools,* or *hellhole.* Out of a high-water population of nearly nineteen thousand, only forty-five hundred still remained, all of them too stubborn or stupid to give up and move back to Aventine or to one of the two latest additions to the Worlds.

But though most Worlders had written off Caelian as a dead loss, not everyone had. Every year or two some group of young visionaries would surface with a new plan for dealing with the deadly plant and animal life that was so determined to choke mankind off their world. Jody's friends Geoff Boulton and Freylan Sonderby were merely the latest in that long parade of idealists. "If she thinks Uncle Corwin's going to help her visit Caelian, she's sorely underestimated his senility level," she said.

Paul shrugged. "Perhaps."

The estate's grounds were compact but well gardened, and Jin could smell the delicate scent of budding bablar trees as they walked toward the house. Some gardens of this sort included pools, fish ponds, even small waterfalls, additions Corwin hadn't bothered with.

So why then did he call it the Island?

No one in the family knew, but that hadn't kept them from speculating about it. Jin had always thought it was a reference to the ancient *no man is an island* aphorism, but had never been able to coax a yes or no out of her uncle. Jody's theory was that it was a reference to an old Earth classic book, while Lorne believed it to be a not-so-subtle jab at the five islands in the lake west of Capitalia and their rather snobbish inhabitants. Merrick, typically, hadn't bothered with the question, declaring that his great-uncle would tell them when he was good and ready.

Jin and Paul reached the house, to find Jody waiting for them just inside the main door. "Mom; Dad," she said in greeting. She was silhouetted against the hall light, but Jin's optical enhancers were able to pick out the tension lines in her daughter's face. "I hear you had a bad day."

"It could get worse," Jin warned her, "depending on what's happening with your project."

"I showed Geoff and Freylan my trap design today," Jody said. "They liked it."

"What about your application?"

Jody shrugged. "You know governments. These things take time."

"But Uy hasn't denied it?" Jin persisted. She'd been hoping against hope that Caelian's governor would shut down the project at his end.

"Sorry," Jody said.

"I think," Paul put in wryly, "the day's just gotten worse."

"It won't be that bad, Mom," Jody insisted. "We really *do* know what we're doing."

"Do you?" Jin countered. "Do you really?"

"Yes, we do," Jody said. Her voice was low and earnest, matured and reasoned.

And grown-up. Despite all her emotional expectations to the contrary, Jin couldn't ignore the fact that her little girl had grown up.

"I imagine we'll be discussing it further tonight," Paul said. If he was feeling the same surge of emotion, Jin thought resentfully, he was hiding it well. "Meanwhile, you have your mother and father standing out in the cold Aventinian evening air."

"It's not *that* cold," Jody said, a hint of her little-girl dry humor peeking out through the adult she'd become. Nevertheless, she stepped aside out of the doorway. "Come on in—dinner should be ready soon."

"Who's cooking?" Jin asked. "Uncle Corwin, or Aunt Thena?"

"Merrick, actually," Jody said. "He said that as long as he'd called this dinner, it was his responsibility to feed all of us."

"As long as it's Merrick and not Lorne," Paul murmured.

"Trust me," Jody promised. "*No* one wants the day to get *that* bad."

When Merrick had first become a Cobra seven years ago, Jin remembered fondly, he'd sworn the whole family to secrecy about his culinary skills. Not because he'd been afraid the other Cobras would rib him about it, but because he'd been on enough field maneuvers during training to fear that he might be designated official unit cook and chained to the stove while the others dealt with the real Cobra work. So far, he'd managed to keep his secret.

The dinner conversation was as pleasant as the food. Jody, who'd always been good at taking hints, avoided any mention of Caelian, instead focusing her end of the conversation on the last few remaining details of her upcoming graduation ceremony. Lorne, after once again confirming that his parents had emerged from the Sun Center trouble mostly unscathed, shifted his part to news of the expansion provinces and the various social and business doings out in those hinterlands, peppering each story with the dry humor he shared with his younger sister.

Merrick himself, Jin noticed, was being especially quiet tonight, carefully cutting precise pieces from his cacciatore and adding little to the table talk. At the head of the table, Corwin and Thena were equally restrained.

Finally, the meal was over. "Excellent, Merrick, as always," Corwin complimented the young man as the group stacked the dishes together. "A man who can cook will always be surrounded by friends."

"Thank you, Uncle Corwin," Merrick said gravely. "Coming from someone who gets to sample Aunt Thena's cooking on a regular basis, I count such praise very highly indeed."

"Diplomatic as always," Thena said with a smile. "Do bear in mind, though, that your uncle Corwin survived on his own cooking longer than he has on mine."

"*Survived* being the operative word," Corwin said, reaching over to take his wife's hand.

Jin watched them, feeling another twinge of guilt. Uncle Corwin hadn't married Thena until his fall from power, and while Jin couldn't see anything but good having come from their marriage, she still couldn't help wondering if Corwin saw the life of a husband and father as something of a consolation prize.

Especially now that their son Rave was himself grown and out of his parents' house. All Corwin had left was his wife, his home, and his memories.

"So cooking's the secret, huh?" Lorne put in. "I've always thought the best way to keep friends around you was to owe everyone money."

"Whatever works for you," Merrick said equably. "Speaking of debts, I did all the cooking. That means it's up to you two to go load the dishwasher."

"That seems fair," Corwin agreed. "Go ahead—we'll wait on dessert for you."

"Not a chance," Jody said, folding her arms across her chest. "I know this trick, and we're not falling for it. Whatever you and Merrick have cooking, Lorne and I are going to be in on it."

"Jody, that's no way to talk to your great-uncle," Paul warned.

"It is when he's trying to send us to the children's table," Jody countered. "In case some of you haven't noticed, the baby of the family is twenty-one now. We're full-fledged members of this family now."

"Which isn't to say there aren't things that concern one member and not another," Jin said.

"It's all right, Jin," Corwin said. "She and Lorne can stay."

"I respectfully disagree, Uncle Corwin," Merrick said firmly. "Not because we're trying to hide anything from you," he added, looking back at his brother and sister, "but because we're trying to protect you."

"I'm sure we both appreciate the thought," Lorne said. "But as a twenty-four-year-old, I sort of resent the implication that I need protecting." He looked over at his great uncle. "As a twenty-four-year-old Cobra, I *definitely* resent the implication."

"Resent it all you want," Merrick said. "We're not talking about jaywalking or disturbing the peace here."

"What *are* we talking about?" Lorne countered.

"Treason," Merrick said flatly.

Lorne seemed to draw back in his seat. "What?" he asked, his voice suddenly subdued.

"You heard me," Merrick said. "What we're talking about tonight is borderline treason."

"Only *borderline*?" Jody said. "Well, that's not so bad."

Merrick turned toward her—"It's all right, Merrick," Corwin said again. "Go ahead—give your mother the letter."

For a moment Merrick hesitated. Then, with a sigh, he reached into the inner pocket of his jacket. "I was unloading Jody's azaleas at the side of the house today when a courier came to the door," he said, pulling out a long, thin envelope. "He marched up to me and said, 'Cobra Broom?' I of course said yes, and he handed me this. I'm afraid I've already opened and read it." He held out the envelope toward his mother.

"Tell her the rest," Corwin murmured.

Merrick's lips compressed briefly. "The courier," he said, "was a Troft."

Jin froze, her fingers a millimeter from the envelope. "A *Troft*?"

Merrick nodded. "A Tlossie, I think. Like I said, I thought it was for me, so I opened it. Three minutes later, I was on the comm to Uncle Corwin."

Jin shot a look at Corwin as she took the envelope from her son. She opened it and pulled out the single slip of paper inside.

The note was short, consisting of just two handwritten lines in precise Qasaman script:

To the Demon Warrior Jasmine Jin Moreau:
Urgent you return at once to Qasama. Crisis situation requires your personal attention.

There was no signature.

"What is it?" Lorne asked.

"Sort of a party invitation," Jin murmured, handing the note to Paul.

"It's *what*?" Lorne demanded. He half stood, reaching across the table and trying to snatch the note from his father's hand.

Without even looking in his direction Paul twitched the paper out of the other's reach, his forehead wrinkling as he read the note. Lorne stayed where he was, his hand outstretched, and after a moment his father handed it across to him. "Interesting," Paul said thoughtfully as Jody leaned close to Lorne to read over his shoulder. "I wonder how he got it to the Tlossies."

"How who got it to them?" Lorne asked, frowning at the note the same way his father had. "Who's it from?"

"Daulo Sammon, I assume," Paul said, cocking his head at Jin. "That *is* his handwriting, isn't it?"

"Actually, I don't know," Jin said, struggling to keep her mind focused as memories three decades old came flooding back. Daulo Sammon, Obolo Nardin and his treacherous Mangus plot, the earnest but deadly young Shahni agent Miron Akim—

"What do you mean, you don't know?" Lorne asked.

With an effort, Jin pushed back the memories. "The only thing I ever saw him write was an order at the family mines," she explained. "It was written very quickly, on a pad balanced on his arm in a blustery wind. I never saw what his writing looked like when he was being careful."

"On the other hand, who else down there ever knew your full name?" Jody pointed out. "It has to be Daulo, doesn't it?"

"There were a few others who knew my name," Jin told her. "But I doubt any of them would want to see me again."

"Except maybe for revenge," Merrick said.

"Thirty-two years later?" Jin shook her head. "Highly unlikely."

"But not impossible?"

Jin grimaced. "No."

"Let's try it from the other direction," Corwin suggested. "Any idea what the crisis situation might be that the note mentions?"

Jin snorted. "On *Qasama*? It could be any of a hundred things."

"Give us a couple of possibilities," Paul said.

"Well, there was a strong tension between the cities and the villages when I was there," Jin said. "Largely because the cities had mostly gotten rid of their mojos while the villages still held onto some of theirs."

"Using the birds as bodyguards?" Merrick asked.

"Partly that, and partly as added protection against the krisjaws and spine leopards," Jin said.

"Though if the plan worked, I would assume the mojos will have deserted even the villagers by now," Corwin reminded her. "And of course, once the local spine leopards all have them as symbionts, the predator attacks should also stop, making mojo bodyguards unnecessary."

"Lot of *if* and *should* in there," Lorne warned.

Corwin shrugged uncomfortably. "Life is uncertain," he conceded.

"Actually, I think the shift was already starting," Jin said. "But even if you write the mojos out of the equation it doesn't necessarily follow that the cities and villages will have started getting along."

"Witness the tension between our own cities and expansion regions," Merrick murmured.

"Exactly," Jin said. "And feelings and memories run a lot deeper on Qasama than they do here."

"What other possibilities for trouble might there be?" Paul asked.

"Like I said, it could be any number of things," Jin said. "Obolo Nardin's effort to subvert the Shahni with his Mangus Project might have had a resurgence somewhere. Some Troft demesne might be poking around Qasaman internal affairs again. Or someone might have been inspired by Nardin and be trying his own plan for revolt or subversion."

"So far, none of this sounds like a problem they'd want your help with," Lorne pointed out.

"Except maybe the Troft thing," Jody said. "The Qasamans can't know nearly as much about the ins and outs of Troft culture and politics as we do."

"Not necessarily," Jin said. "They've obviously made contact with at least the Tlossies." She gestured toward the paper Lorne was still holding. "Or at least Daulo has. And Qasamans learn *very* quickly."

"Yes, let's talk about the Tlossies for a minute," Paul said. "Merrick, did this courier say anything about how he'd obtained this note?"

"Not a word," Merrick said. "I had the impression he had no idea what the envelope was, that he'd simply been hired or ordered to deliver it. He did give me a card with contact information, but it wasn't for him personally."

"How do you know?" Lorne asked.

"The status curlies around the card's border didn't match those on his abdomen sash," Merrick explained. "Not nearly as elaborate, either, which means the card is from someone considerably higher in social rank."

"I spent an hour earlier trying to match the curlies to known Tlossie traders, but the search came up dry," Corwin added. "Whoever the card's from, he's apparently no one who's done serious business here."

"Have you tried contacting him?" Jody asked.

Merrick shook his head. "I assumed that whether or not we went that far would be up to Mom."

A brief silence settled over the room. Jin stared at the note lying beside Lorne's dessert fork, acutely aware of the precarious ledge she was now standing on.

The ledge *all* of them were standing on. Merrick's earlier warning that they were edging onto treason hadn't been hyperbole—the Cobra Worlds Council had imposed a strict interdiction on travel to Qasama, and they meant it. Even getting on a starship with intent to travel there could conceivably land Jin a multiyear prison term.

And the knowledge that she was planning such a trip could likewise land everyone in this room in that same prison on conspiracy charges.

But the legality of the matter wasn't really the question. The question was what was the right thing to do.

Qasama . . .

They were still waiting for her, she realized suddenly. "Well, it can't hurt to ask," she said, motioning to Merrick as she pulled out her comm. He hesitated, then slid a small business-sized card from his pocket and handed it to her. Jin glanced at the number and punched it in.

It was answered on the fifth ring. [The evening, it is good, Jasmine Moreau Broom,] a recorded Troft voice said, the alien cattertalk as crisp and precise in its way as the Qasaman handwriting on the brief note. [The voyage, if you intend to make it, will depart from Pindar three days from the delivery time of the package. All that is necessary, it will be provided.]

There was a click, and the connection was broken. "Well?" Paul asked as Jin closed the comm again.

"It was a recording," she said. "I'm to leave from Pindar in three days, at—Merrick, what time was the note delivered?"

"Just after two."

"Three days from now at two o'clock," Jin said. "He says he'll provide everything I need, which I assume will include proper Qasaman clothing and accessories."

"Sounds good," Lorne said briskly. Briskly, but with an undertone of tension beneath the words. "Three days should give me enough time to get myself on the off-duty roster. I'll collect my stuff—"

"Whoa, whoa," Jin interrupted. "The invitation was for *me*."

"So?" Lorne countered.

"So I'm going alone," Jin said firmly.

"You most certainly are not," Paul said, just as firmly. "But you *are* right about Lorne not going with you. We can—"

"You're not going, either," Jin said, forcing herself to look into her husband's eyes.

Haunted eyes. Worried eyes. Loving eyes. "Jin—" he began.

"No," Jin insisted. "You don't know the Qasamans, Paul. One Cobra sneaking onto their world is bad enough. Two of them will be interpreted as an invasion."

"So we make sure they don't see anything that jumps them to that conclusion," Paul countered. "I can stay in the background, or be your loyal servant, or whatever you need."

Jin braced herself. "What I need," she said as gently as she could, "is for you to be willing to stay behind. I have to do this alone. I really do."

"What is this, mass insanity?" Lorne demanded. "Jody's going to Caelian, you're going to Qasama—"

"*Caelian?*" Jin cut him off.

"Lorne!" Jody bit out, her stunned expression edging rapidly toward fury.

Lorne winced. "Sorry," he apologized.

"Never mind sorry," Jin said sternly, her stomach suddenly doing flip-turns inside her. "Jody?"

"I was going to tell you after dinner, Mom," Jody said, her expression managing to be repentant and stubborn at the same time. "We got the call this afternoon from Governor Uy's office. We're leaving on the *Freedom's Fire* in—" she grimaced "—in three days."

"From Capitalia?" Paul asked.

"Yes," Jody said. "But maybe I can get the time changed."

"Don't try," Jin said, feeling the heavy weight of irony settling across her shoulders. The same time Jin would be leaving Aventine . . . only they'd be leaving from spaceports a thousand kilometers apart. The universe wasn't even going to let her say a proper dockside farewell to her daughter. "They'd only want to know why, and we can't afford anyone asking awkward questions."

"I'm sorry, Mom," Jody said. "I know you didn't want this."

"No, I didn't," Jin said quietly. "But I doubt your grandfather really wanted me going to Qasama, either. Sometimes we just have to face the unpleasant fact that our children do, in fact, grow up."

She looked at Corwin, wondering if he would point up the obvious difference in their situations: that Jin's father, at least, had sent her off to Qasama with a group of other Cobras.

But her uncle remained silent, and after a couple of seconds she turned back to Lorne. "Your cue, Lorne," she invited.

"My what?" he asked, frowning.

"A minute ago you were all set to come to Qasama with me," she reminded him. "Time to offer to accompany your sister to Caelian instead."

"Go for it, kiddo, because *I'm* sure not going," Merrick spoke up before Lorne could answer. "Capitalia patroller duty may not be as glamorous as hunting spine leopards, but my commandant takes our duty rosters very seriously."

"Well—okay, sure," Lorne said, fumbling a bit. "Jody—"

"Sorry, Lorne, but you're not going to Caelian, either," Paul spoke up. "You have a duty to the citizens of the expansion region."

Jin turned to her husband in disbelief. "Paul—"

"Luckily," Paul continued, looking over at his daughter, "I just happen to have an opening in my own calendar."

Jin felt her lower jaw drop open, her planned protest strangling into silence in her throat. "Paul, you are *not* going to Caelian," she insisted.

"Why not?" Paul countered calmly. "No, let me put it more strongly: I'm not going to sit home and water the azaleas while my wife and daughter travel to the two most dangerous places in the known galaxy. If I'm not going to Qasama with you, I'm going to Caelian with Jody."

Jin stared at him, momentarily at an uncharacteristic loss for words.

And yet, as the emotional fogbank cleared away, she realized he was right. Even at fifty-three, with arthritis and anemia starting to make themselves felt, Paul was still a Cobra. Moreover, he had the maturity and experience and coolheadedness that Lorne still lacked. There could be no better protection for Jin's little girl.

She grimaced. No, not her little girl. Her young lady.

She looked at her two sons in turn. Lorne seemed midway between annoyed and frustrated, no doubt as a result of the ground being cut out from under him twice in two minutes. Merrick merely looked his usual stolid self, with no hint of embarrassment or shame at how quickly he'd refused to even consider going to Caelian with his sister.

Or maybe he'd simply realized before the rest of them that his father was heading in that direction and had made certain he wouldn't be standing in the elder Broom's way. "I guess it's settled, then," Jin said, forcing some false heartiness into her voice. "Paul and Jody will go to Caelian, I'll head to Qasama, and Lorne and Merrick will hold down the fort here."

"And try to maintain the illusion that you're still on Aventine," Merrick put in.

Jin frowned. She hadn't thought about that part of it. "Yes, good point. Any ideas on how we do that?"

"One or two," Merrick said. "But we can work on that later." He raised his eyebrows at Corwin. "After dessert, perhaps?" he prompted.

"That is the direction we were headed, wasn't it?" Corwin agreed. "Perhaps, *now,* Lorne and Jody, you'll be kind enough to clear the table for us?"

"Sure," Jody said as they both obediently pushed their chairs back from the table and started collecting the dishes.

"So is that it for the evening's surprises?" Paul asked, looking at Corwin.

Corwin cocked an eyebrow. "Isn't that enough for one night?"

"Very much so," Paul said dryly. Reaching under the table, he took Jin's hand in his. "I just wanted to make sure. *And* to make sure that everyone had a say."

"Everyone who wanted a say has had one," Corwin assured him. "For now."

The group was midway through dessert, and the conversation had shifted to Jody's plans for the Caelian study, when Jin suddenly realized that Aunt Thena hadn't said a single word throughout the entire debate.

The next three days went by quickly. Far too quickly.

The Troft recording had said that everything Jin needed would be supplied aboard ship. But she couldn't and wouldn't simply assume the Trofts knew what a proper infiltrator needed to do her job.

On the other hand, she could hardly go to the hardware store and ask the clerk to assemble a standard-issue commando backpack for her, either. Fortunately, the standard Cobra survival pack was a good place to start, and she knew its contents by heart. She bought enough supplies to stock two such packs, making sure to shop in a half dozen different stores across the city so as to muddy the backtrail a bit. Once those were prepared, she added a few other odds and ends as they occurred to her, and then decided she was as ready as she was going to be.

She spent the rest of the time she had left with her family. Those hours went by even faster.

The sky was beginning to cloud up as she stepped off the intercity transport and headed on foot toward the long, sleek Troft freighter squatting on its pad across the Pindar landing field. She'd done everything she could; had given Paul and Jody their final hugs earlier that morning, and then had called from the transport for a last good-bye as her husband and daughter watched Jody's two colleagues load the last bits of gear aboard the *Freedom's Fire.* But the farewells had been sorely inadequate for the occasion, and Jin could feel her mood filling with its own dark clouds as she walked wearily toward the ship.

The danger she had long ago accepted. The loneliness she hadn't counted on.

"Carry your bags, ma'am?"

She spun around, feeling her eyes widen with shock. Merrick was back there, smiling solemnly as he strode toward her, a survival pack of his own settled across his shoulders. "What are *you* doing here?" she demanded.

"What do you think?" he countered, stopping beside her and getting a grip on the straps of one of his mother's packs. "I'm coming with you."

"You most certainly are *not*," she insisted, trying to snatch her pack away from him. It was a waste of effort—his servos were every bit as strong as hers were. "Now get of here and back to Capitalia before someone sees you."

Merrick shook his head. "Sorry," he said. "I'm on temporary detached duty, assigned to watch over one of the legendary heroes of the Cobra Worlds."

"What legendary hero?" Jin asked, thoroughly confused now.

"You, of course," Merrick said. "In case you hadn't noticed, you've gone into a tailspin of depression over Jody and Dad's plan to go to Caelian. Lorne and I have been very worried about you, especially when you announced you were going out to the wilderness north of Pindar to, quote, think things over."

"So what, I'm a strap-stretcher case now?" Jin demanded, not sure whether she was more outraged or embarrassed by the story her sons had concocted.

"Oh, I'm sure you'll pull out of it after a while," Merrick said. "The point is that I'm on indefinite leave, and we're off in the wilderness all alone where no one's likely to notice us."

"Brilliant," Jin growled. "But your poor, aged mother is perfectly capable of, quote, thinking things over on her own."

Merrick took a deep breath. "Mom, remember back at the Island three days ago, and the talk Uncle Corwin and Aunt Thena had with you after dinner?"

Jin grimaced. Like she would ever forget. Corwin had grilled her for nearly an hour about her motives for wanting to go to Qasama, trying to get her to admit that she was doing it solely to vindicate him. Which she wasn't. "I remember it very well," she said. "And how exactly do *you* know about it? I thought you were all off in the billiards room at the time."

"I know because Uncle Corwin, Aunt Thena, and I planned the talk long before you and the rest showed up, of course." A brief flicker of grim amusement touched his eyes. "When did you think Dad, Lorne, Jody, and I cooked up the rest of this scheme? The only safe time to do it was while you were busy defending your honor."

"Only you'd already made up your mind about this, hadn't you?" Jin asked, thinking back to that evening. "That's why you were so quick to take yourself off Jody's escort list."

"Uncle Corwin and I had already run the logic," Merrick said. "Dad was too old to go with you—he's got the same health limitations you do. Lorne is too young, plus he really *is* needed in the expansion regions. That leaves me."

"Or it leaves me going by myself," Jin said. "Or don't you think I can handle it?"

Merrick sighed. "If you insist. No, we *don't* think you can handle it. Not if worst comes to worst."

"Because I might be going with the wrong motives?"

"Because you're fifty-two years old," Merrick said bluntly. "You're not exactly in prime fighting condition anymore, you know."

"Bring me a couple of spine leopards, kiddo, and I'll show you what condition I'm in," Jin retorted. "Besides, the idea is to avoid *any* fighting."

"Amen," Merrick said fervently. "But if it *does* come down to a fight, you know as well as I do that two Cobras will always have a better chance than one."

"Unless it was the presence of that second Cobra that precipitated the fight in the first place," Jin said. "As long as we're remembering conversations, do you remember *that* one?"

"Certainly," Merrick said. "But as I recall, the Qasamans are very family-oriented, and I as your son am the kind of close blood relation that even Dad can't match. The Qasamans will respect that."

He was right, Jin had to admit. Even if they discovered he was a Cobra, they would more likely interpret his role as that of his mother's protector than as an invader.

And as she gazed at the determination in her son's eyes, she realized suddenly that she really *didn't* want to do this alone. "There's no chance I can talk you out of it, is there?" she asked, just to be sure.

"None," he said in a voice that left no room for argument.

"Then let's do it," she said, turning toward the ship. She paused and let go of the bag he was still holding. "And yes, you *may* carry my bag."

Besides, this was just a friendly visit between old acquaintances, she reminded herself. There wouldn't be any fighting. Surely there wouldn't.

CHAPTER FOUR

The last time Jin had traveled to Qasama, the ship had been running on a fuel-conserving course and had taken two weeks. She was therefore somewhat surprised when, barely five days into the trip, the Troft captain announced that they would be arriving at Qasama within the next twelve hours. Even granting three decades' worth of advances in starship efficiency and the fact that this was a modern Troft freighter instead of the older models the aliens typically foisted off on the Worlds, the captain clearly wasn't all that concerned about his transportation costs. Either he had an important schedule to keep, or else the crisis on Qasama was as critical as the mysterious note had made it sound.

Not that Jin was able to find out which. The captain and crew were polite enough, as befit the long trading history the Tlos'khin'fahi demesne had with the Worlds. But the veneer of hospitality had a steel wall behind it, and five days' worth of gentle probing and wheedling had gained Jin exactly nothing in the way of new information. Merrick, who had inherited his father's calmer and more diplomatic wheedling approach, came up equally dry.

Jin had also hoped the captain might have further information on the logistics of the operation, particularly some advice on how to sneak into Daulo Sammon's town of Milika without attracting unwelcome attention. But the captain assured her he'd been given nothing but the original note, a small collection of old-smelling Qasaman clothing, and an easterly approach vector that would hopefully slip his passengers into the forest west of Milika without tripping whatever radar coverage the Qasamans had set up to guard the Great Arc region where most of their people lived.

Which meant that as far as actual penetration of the Qasaman populace was concerned, Jin and Merrick were on their own.

They made a final check of their gear, including the Qasaman clothing, and loaded it aboard the freighter's shuttle. Designed as it was for cargo transport, the shuttle had no actual passenger seating. But the cockpit was designed for a crew of four, and the captain assured them that the engineering and supercargo stations could be left open for a trip this short.

They dropped over the nighttime side of the planet, the freighter pulling up and away as the Troft pilot sent the shuttle skittering toward the dark mass below. Five minutes into the flight they hit the first noticeable wisps of upper atmosphere, and the shuttle began to shiver, then tremble, then shake as the air around them grew steadily more dense.

Jin spent the trip staring at the mass rushing up toward them and consciously forcing herself not to dig her fingers into her seat's upholstery. Occasionally, she sent a furtive glance at Merrick, noting with a small nugget of wry resentment that her son showed no hint of the tension Jin herself was feeling. The buffeting hit a teeth-chattering peak, then began to subside again as the shuttle slowed to subsonic speeds. The ground below remained a mostly featureless inky black, but as they headed eastward toward the western arm of the Great Arc Jin began spotting little clusters of lights nestled among the forests that dominated the western part of the planet's inhabited regions. She watched the lights as they went slowly past, her muscles taut as she waited for a repeat of the attack that had killed her first team.

But no attack came. An hour after leaving the freighter, they touched down in a small clearing at the edge of their planned landing zone.

Jin and Merrick and their gear were at the edge of the clearing in ninety seconds flat. Thirty seconds after that, the shuttle was back in the air, clawing for altitude. Ten seconds more and the red glow from its gravity lifts had vanished over the treetops.

Hopefully, the captain's information about this area being outside any likely radar coverage had been correct. If not, Jin and Merrick would be getting some company very soon.

But for now, at least, they were alone, and Jin took a moment to stand beneath the tree canopy, the sounds and scents of Qasama whispering through her senses and echoing back from her memory. Suddenly, the last thirty-two years of her life seemed to vanish. She was once again the young Cobra all alone on a distant and hostile world . . .

"Spine leopard at three o'clock," Merrick murmured from beside her.

As quickly as they'd gone, the lost years came crashing back onto Jin's shoulders. Activating her optical enhancers' light-amplifiers, she looked to her right.

The spine leopard was standing motionless in the shadows, its eyes staring at the two rash humans who had intruded on its territory. The quills on its forelegs were quivering as the creature apparently mulled over whether or not this would be a good time for lunch.

"So that's a mojo," Merrick murmured.

Jin shifted her gaze from the spine leopard's forelegs to the silver-blue hawk-like bird perched on the spine leopard's back behind its head. The mojo, too, was watching the humans, gazing at them with a disconcerting alertness and perception that Jin had never quite gotten used to. "That it is," she confirmed "The question is, has he figured out that we're not someone he and his companion want to mess with?"

"Maybe we can help him out a little," Merrick suggested. "Watch your eyes."

Jin switched from light-amp to infrared, watching as the images of the spine leopard and mojo shifted from pale green to flowing shades of red and orange. "Go."

Lifting his right hand, Merrick fired a brief low-level burst from his fingertip laser into the tree trunk beside him.

The spine leopard dropped into a crouch, its quills flaring outward. But the mojo showed no such agitation, merely fluttering its wings as it got a fresh grip on the predator's back. For perhaps half a second both of them continued to gaze at the humans. Then, with a shake of its head, the spine leopard straightened out of its crouch, its quills resettling themselves along his forelegs. It turned away, and without a backward glance strode back into the forest.

"Smart bird," Merrick commented.

"Luckily for us," Jin agreed, the warm scent of burned wood from her son's laser shot drifting across her nose. And luckily for the animals, too, she added silently. The spine leopard and mojo made up a symbiotic pair, with the bird functioning as the primary decision-maker of the team. On its own, the spine leopard would probably have leaped blindly to the attack and been dead by now.

Once, the mojos had served a similar purpose for the humans of Qasama, calming natural aggression with guidance so subtle that the inhabitants had never recognized it for what it was. Jin's own father, grandfather, and uncles had helped create the scheme for seeding Qasama with spine leopards, hoping that the mojos would be lured away from their human hosts and onto the more useful—from the mojos' point of view—predators.

Unfortunately, the Qasamans hadn't seen it that way. The introduction of new and deadly predators onto their world had driven much of the hatred they felt toward the Cobra Worlds.

Distantly, Jin wondered if the people here would ever truly understand that the plan had been for their ultimate good. Or whether such understanding would make any difference.

"It's about thirty kilometers east, right?" Merrick asked.

"East by north," Jin said, shaking the thoughts away. Standing in the middle of the Qasaman forest at night was hardly the time and place for deep philosophical contemplations. Shifting back to light-amp, she checked her compass. "That way," she added, pointing.

"Assuming, of course, Daulo Sammon is still living in Milika," Merrick warned as he adjusted his pack across his shoulders.

"He will be," Jin assured him. "Qasaman families stick very close to their hereditary land."

"Let's get to it, then," Merrick said.

Jin frowned at him. His expression had the same oddness she'd just heard in his voice. "Something wrong?" she asked.

"No, nothing." Merrick nodded in the direction the spine leopard and mojo had gone. "I was just thinking that Qasaman birds seem to understand the concept of deterrence better than some of our own politicians."

"No argument there," Jin agreed sourly. "But then, mojos don't have political agendas muddying their thinking. All they care about is survival." She took a deep breath. "Which is something you and I should also keep in mind. Quietly, now. And from this point on, we speak only Qasaman."

The trip wasn't nearly as difficult as Jin had expected. There were plenty of natural hazards along the way, with the complete range of tripping vines, thorn bushes, and leaf-covered roots that a healthy forest had to offer. But their optical enhancers gave them fair warning of most of the pitfalls, and even when the forest did manage to trip one of them their bone laminae and strengthened ligaments protected them from sprained ankles or worse.

More interesting to Jin was the fact that the only animals that gave them any trouble along the way were the six-limbed monkey-like baelcra, the gliding-lizard monota, and a few varieties of annoying insects. They saw a handful of spine leopards and a couple of the native krisjaws, but those larger, more deadly predators merely watched the two humans go past without interfering with them.

But then, none of the baelcra had mojos watching over their best interests. All of the spine leopards and krisjaws did.

Jin and the Troft captain had worked out the landing place and time to give them about six hours of darkness in which to cover the thirty kilometers to Daulo's village. With the lack of serious predator problems, they made it in just over five, emerging beside the main road leading to the village's high wall and closed gate. The gate itself wasn't visible from their exit point, but a bit of the wall could be seen about half a kilometer away through the trees around the next curve in the road.

It would have been convenient if they could simply march up to the gates and knock. But that was out of the question. The last time Jin had been here few people traveled the Qasaman forest at night, and none of them outside of sturdy vehicles. That might have changed in the past three decades, but it wasn't a risk she wanted to take.

Instead, she and Merrick retreated fifty meters back into the forest and settled in to grab a few hours' rest, each taking a turn on watch.

It was midmorning when Jin decided it was time. Her enhanced hearing could pick up the faint sounds of activity from Milika's direction, and it took no enhancement at all to hear the vehicles passing along the nearby road. She and Merrick cleaned themselves up as best they could, then changed into their Qasaman clothing. Their half-empty packs went into a shallow hole that Merrick had spent an hour of his time on watch digging, which they then covered with a generous helping of dirt and dead leaves.

And with that, the final stage of their journey was before them. "Remember that men are very much the dominant gender here," Jin reminded her son as she gave his outfit a final check. "Naturally, you'll show respect to me as your mother, but you're the one who'll approach other citizens, who'll ask all the questions, and who'll make all the decisions. And don't forget the sign of respect."

"I won't," Merrick said, and Jin winced a little at the slightly strained patience in his voice. They'd only been over this a million times on the transport, but he was far too polite to remind her of that. "I make the sign first to superiors, and inferiors make it first to me." He touched his bunched fingertips to his forehead in demonstration.

"And you can assume that most of the people in there will be our superiors," Jin said. She paused, searching for anything she might have missed. But nothing came to mind, at least nothing she hadn't already told him another million times already. "Okay," she said, making sure the pouch of wild *charko* leaves she'd picked during an hour of her watch was securely tied to her sash. "We left early this morning to get *charko* leaves for a stew I'm making, we had a little trouble finding a good patch, and we're only just now getting back to town. Got it?"

"Yes, Mother," Merrick said, as calm and patient as ever.

"Right." Jin took a deep breath. "Okay. Let's do it."

With the aid of their optical enhancers, the trip through the predawn had been relatively easy. In broad daylight, it was even easier. Still, Jin approached the edge of the tree line cautiously, waiting for a momentary lull in the road's vehicular traffic before she and Merrick stepped out of the woods and headed at a brisk walk toward Milika.

The last time Jin had been here, Milika's gates had stood open throughout the daylight hours, with a pair of armed guards on duty in case some krisjaw or spine leopard was foolish enough to try to attack that many people at once. That part of village life, at least, hadn't changed, she saw as she and Merrick rounded the last curve in the road and came within sight of the gates.

Still, the guards did look more relaxed than they had in days gone by. Apparently, rogue predators weren't nearly the problem they'd once been.

There was more traffic on the road now than there had been thirty years ago, too. A large number of vehicles were on the move, some of them heading down the road she and Merrick were using, with a somewhat larger number making a hard right turn just outside the wall onto a road that hadn't been there before.

As for pedestrians, the village beyond the wall was teeming with them, striding along about their business, browsing the small shop stands near the gate, or engaged in animated conversations with their fellow citizens. Clearly, Milika was prospering.

Jin keyed in her optical enhancers' telescopic capability as they approached, paying particular attention to the pedestrians' clothing. To her relief, it all seemed reasonably similar in style to the outfits she and Merrick were wearing. That had been one of her major concerns, that the Trofts might have brought them clothing that was so out-of-date it would instantly finger them as foreigners.

Keying off her opticals, she picked up her pace a little. All was as well as could be expected, certainly as well as she could make it. The goal now was to get to Daulo's house and out of the public eye before she or Merrick made some dangerous social blunder.

She had keyed her audio enhancers on low-power, listening to the nearest conversations to remind herself of the region's accent, when she heard a sudden catch in Merrick's breath. "Mom—one o'clock," he murmured. "Those two men in gray and blue."

Jin shifted her gaze and audio enhancers in the indicated direction. The two men seemed to have just started an animated conversation about animal pelts. "What about them?" she asked.

"Just watch," Merrick said, his voice dark. "There—that other one coming toward them. Watch him." The newcomer stepped up to the other two, smiled, and lifted his right hand to make the sign of respect.

Only it wasn't the same sign Jin had learned thirty years ago, the one she'd just coached Merrick on. Instead of touching bunched fingertips to forehead, the newcomer touched only his first two fingertips to his forehead and then touched his lips.

And the two other men answered, not with two fingers, but with *three* fingers to foreheads and lips.

The Qasamans had changed their mark of respect.

Jin shot another look around the people beyond the wall, a jolt of sudden panic running through her. She'd expected clothing styles to have changed over the years, and had been relieved that she and Merrick had the right versions. It had never even occurred to her that something so basic as the mark of respect might similarly have been modified.

And if the mark of respect had changed so drastically, what else might have changed along with it?

She didn't know. What she *did* know was that she and Merrick were in big trouble. There were new rules to Qasaman social interaction, and neither of them had the faintest idea what those rules were.

Merrick had obviously tracked the same logic. "Not good," he murmured.

"Extremely not good," Jin agreed tightly, focusing her attention back on the gate area. A few steps behind the two armed guards she'd already noted were four more men, two on either side, who she'd originally dismissed as common loiterers.

But now that she was concentrating on them, she realized their faces were too alert for that, their eyes lingering just a little too long on each passing vehicle as it entered the village.

Milika wasn't the haven she'd expected it to be. Milika was a trap.

And she and Merrick were walking right into it.

"We have a plan?" Merrick asked.

"Working on it," Jin gritted out, forcing herself to keep walking. One of the four non-obvious guards had spotted the two incoming pedestrians and was watching them closely. The last thing she and Merrick could afford was a guilty-looking break in their stride. "You want to try running?" she asked her son.

"To where?"

"Exactly," Jin agreed. "Fighting is out, too—way too many people around."

Merrick huffed a thoughtful breath. "So we bluff?"

"We bluff," Jin confirmed reluctantly. "Okay. Best guess, and it's only a guess, is that the number of fingers used indicates rank. I just wish I knew whether two fingers is the minimum or whether it goes all the way down to one."

"Or if women use different signs entirely," Merrick added.

Jin winced. Unfortunately, that was a distinct possibility. "Could be," she conceded. "Haven't got a clue what it would be, though."

"Well, all we can do is try," Merrick said calmly. "Let's both stick with the two-finger version. If they call us on it, maybe we can convince them we're social idiots who grew up in a barn."

Not likely, Jin thought grimly. But at the moment she didn't have anything better to offer. "Okay," she said. "But if it blows up—if they want to search us or even toss us into holding—just go along with them. Whatever happens, do *not* do anything to show who you really are."

"Understood," Merrick said. "And don't *you* forget to be a nice, quiet, submissive little woman."

Jin grimaced. Sticking with that role had been one of the toughest parts of her previous visit here. This time, with her pride and ego presumably tempered by age and maturity, maybe it would be easier.

"Hey!" a gruff male voice called from behind them.

Jin turned, forcing herself not to lift her hands into combat positions. A boxy brown car was coming up along the road toward them, its driver steering with one hand as he gestured out the window with the other. "Hey, cousin!" he called again.

Jin keyed in her enhancers, trying to cut through the midmorning glare off the windshield. The driver was a young man, Merrick's age or a bit younger, with black hair and a short, neatly trimmed beard. His eyes were locked on her and Merrick, his expression hard. "Mom?" Merrick asked quietly.

"Better answer him," Jin told said as the car came to a stop beside them.

Merrick nodded microscopically and touched two fingers to his forehead. "Good day—" he started.

"Did you run out of fuel *again*?" the man in the car interrupted. He was clearly trying for a wry tone, but the darkness in his face effectively negated any humor that might have been in his voice. "That *was* your car I saw two kilometers back, wasn't it?"

Out of the corner of her eye, Jin saw that the gate guards were watching the conversation. "Mm-mm," she grunted softly, hoping Merrick would pick up on the cue.

He did. "I'm afraid so," he told the driver. "We decided to walk instead of—"

"You have to stop doing that," the other young man said. "Get in—I'll take you in. You can send someone back for the car later."

Merrick started to look questioningly at Jin, remembered in time that he was supposed to be the one making these decisions, and nodded. "That would be most kind," he said, stepping behind Jin to the car's rear door.

For a second his fingers fumbled as he tried to figure out the mechanism. Then, he got it, pulled the door open, and ushered Jin inside. Motioning her to move over, he started to get in beside her.

"You come up here," the driver said softly.

Obediently, Merrick closed the door and started around the front of the car. Jin tensed, wondering if the driver was planning to suddenly gun his engine and try to run him down. Maybe this was some elaborate trap designed to reveal Cobra reflexes.

But the car didn't move as Merrick finished his circle and climbed into the front passenger seat. "We thank you for your hospitality," he said as he closed the door behind him.

"Save your gratitude," the driver growled. Now that the gate guards couldn't hear, he'd abandoned even his half-hearted attempt at levity. He looked Merrick up and down, shaking his head in disgust, and started the car rolling again. "I just hope that no one with actual eyes saw you in those outfits."

Jin watched the guards closely as the driver maneuvered them through the gate. The two armed men merely glanced at the driver, but sent hard gazes at her and Merrick. The four non-obvious guards, in contrast, seemed to divide their time equally between all three occupants. Still, none of the six seemed to show any more suspicion than they had with any of the other cars that had passed their positions.

And then the car was past the gate and into Milika. Jin thought about checking behind them, decided that would look suspicious if the guards were still watching, and forced herself to continue facing forward. "Where are we going?" she asked.

The driver scowled at her in the mirror. "If you can't figure even that much out, you must not be much of a spy."

"You're welcome to believe that," Merrick murmured.

The driver shot him a look, and then fell silent.

Milika didn't seem to have changed much in thirty years, Jin decided as they crossed the Great Ring Road and continued inward toward the center of town. Several buildings were clearly new, but the shops and the people seemed much as they had back then.

Of course, she reminded herself, she hadn't had *that* much time to really observe the village. There were probably a lot of smaller changes she was simply missing.

They reached the center of town and turned left onto the Small Ring Road, circling the large park area known as the Inner Green. Jin leaned forward, her heartbeat picking up as she watched for her first glimpse of the Sammon house.

And then, there it was: a high privacy wall surrounding the courtyard, with the top of the house visible beyond it. Memories flooded back: the family's unhesitant hospitality when they thought her merely an injured stranger; their cautious but firm support when they learned who she really was; Daulo's willingness to risk his life for her. Not just his life, but also his family's honor.

A shiver ran up Jin's back as the driver maneuvered the car beneath the archway into the courtyard. The Sammon family had risked everything for her . . . and now her very presence on Qasama was once again putting them at horrible risk.

Whatever Daulo had summoned her here for, it must be something incredibly important.

"He's expecting you," the driver said as he pulled the car in front of the ornate door and rolled to a stop. "Do you need someone to show you the way?"

"No, I remember," Jin said. "Thank you."

The driver didn't answer.

The house struck Jin largely the same way the village itself had. It was basically the same as she remembered it, but there were enough differences in furnishings and décor to show the passage of years and the presence of a new owner. Feeling her heart once again speeding up, she climbed the stairs and went down the hallway to the room that had once been Kruin Sammon's office.

The door to the office stood open, with no guards in evidence. Jin keyed in her audio enhancers as she and Merrick approached, concentrating on the quiet sounds of breathing ahead of her. There was only one person in there, she decided. She started to step ahead of her son—

His hand brushed her arm. "I'll go first," he murmured. Before she could reply, he lengthened his stride and crossed in front of her through the doorway. Grimacing, Jin followed.

She rounded the door jamb to find Merrick standing a little to the right just inside the room. Seated at the desk across the room, his eyes steady on his visitors, was a heavyset man with a roundish face and white-flecked black hair. He wore an elaborate red-and-silver robe, with a dual-patterned scarf tied casually around his throat.

Jin took a deep breath. "Hello, Daulo Sammon," she said, hearing the slight trembling in her voice. After all these years . . .

"I greet you, Jasmine Moreau," Daulo replied, his own voice dark and steady and without a single trace of genuine welcome that Jin could hear. His eyes shifted briefly to Merrick, measuring the younger man with a single glance. Then, laying down the stylus he'd been working with, he rose to his feet. "In the name of God," he demanded, "what are you *doing* here?"

Daulo lifted his eyes from the letter and shook his head. "No," he said. "I didn't write this. Nor did anyone in my household."

"Yet your driver quickly identified us and brought us in," Merrick pointed out. "Obviously, he was expecting us."

"First of all, the *driver*, as you refer to him, is in fact my son Fadil," Daulo said acidly. He ran his eyes up and down Merrick's clothing. "As to identifying you as strangers to Qasama, anyone who came within five meters of you would have known that instantly."

"What's wrong with our clothing?" Jin asked, glancing down her front. "It looks close enough to what I saw the villagers wearing."

"The design is close enough," Daulo agreed. "But the material is wrong. We stopped using it over two years ago."

"You're saying it hasn't been *sold* for two years?" Merrick asked, frowning.

"I'm saying we *stopped using it*," Daulo growled. "By order of the Shahni. All Qasaman clothing had to be remade in this new material, with older garments destroyed."

"But that's crazy," Merrick protested.

"Hardly," Jin said, wincing as she suddenly understood. "In fact, it worked exactly they way they intended."

"What—oh," Merrick broke off, his face changing as he got it. "Right."

"Indeed," Daulo said. "The real question is whether anyone else saw you."

"The gate guards were watching us," Jin said. "I don't know whether they could spot something as subtle as clothing material from a moving car, though."

"Well, we can't afford to take chances," Daulo said heavily, standing up and coming around the corner of his desk. "I'll take you to rooms and have fresh clothing brought to you."

"Thank you," Jin said. "I'm sorry, Daulo. I really did think the message was from you. The last thing I want is to bring more trouble down on your household."

"May God grant that we can avoid that," Daulo said. His voice was still grim, but Jin caught a hint of a smile at the corners of his mouth. "I'm no longer as young and reckless as I once was, after all. I'm a respectable member of the community, who would very much prefer to avoid scrutiny from the Shahni or their agents."

"That goes double for us," Jin assured him. "Don't worry—as soon as we have that new clothing, we'll be gone."

"Gone where?" Daulo asked as he gestured them toward the door. "You said you had no way to contact the alien ship."

"No, but it'll be back in two weeks to pick us up," Jin said. "We'll just find somewhere safe to hide until then."

Daulo was opening his mouth, undoubtedly to argue that there *was* no such place on Qasama, when the door was thrown open and Daulo's son Fadil hurried in. "Father, they're coming," he panted, his expression tight. "The Shahni agents. They're coming.

"They're coming *here.*"

CHAPTER FIVE

Jin shot a look at Merrick. His eyes went briefly wide, then calmed down again as he recovered his balance. "From the front?" she asked Fadil.

Fadil gave her a half-astonished, half-scandalized look. "I wasn't speaking to you," he bit out.

"Answer her anyway," Daulo ordered.

Fadil looked at his father with the same look he'd just given Jin. "Yes, from the front," he managed.

"Go and stall them," Jin said. "Daulo, we'll need those fresh clothes, *now.*"

"I'll get them," Daulo said grimly. "Meanwhile—"

"What do you mean, *stall them*?" Fadil cut in. "These are agents of the *Shahni!*"

"Which is why we need to stall them," Jin explained, fighting hard for patience.

"And how exactly do I do that?" Fadil persisted. "Tell them you've gone?"

"Don't tell them anything," Merrick said. "Welcome them in, ask about their families, get them some refreshments—you *do* still do those things, don't you?"

"Yes, of course," Daulo said. "But that will only gain us a few minutes."

"That's all we'll need." Merrick visibly braced himself. "Get me some new clothes, and I'll go down and talk to them."

"Out of the question," Daulo said firmly.

"He's right, Merrick," Jin agreed. "If anyone's going to talk to them, it'll be me."

"What, a woman?" Merrick countered. "You don't think that'll raise their suspicions?"

Jin squeezed her hand into a fist. Unfortunately, he was right. "Merrick—"

"I need those clothes, Master Sammon," Merrick said. "And you, Master Fadil, need to get downstairs and entertain our guests."

"Father?" Fadil asked in a strained voice.

Daulo grimaced. "Do it," he confirmed.

Fadil hesitated, then gave a jerky nod and headed back down the hallway. "But I don't think either of you should face them," Daulo continued. "Let me first go see what I can do."

"With all due respect, I think running interference for us will only add to any suspicions they already have," Merrick said. "No, the faster one of us comes out and spins them a soothing story, the better." He looked at Jin. "It also occurs to me that if the Shahni have been updating their facial-recognition software, they may have a fairly good idea what my mother looks like."

Jin looked at Daulo, found him looking at her. "Jin?" he asked.

"I don't like it, either," Jin admitted reluctantly. "Unfortunately, it really is probably our best shot. At worst, all he'll do is confirm suspicions they already have. Merrick, do you know yet what you're going to say to them?"

"I've got a couple of ideas," he assured her. "While I'm changing, perhaps Master Sammon can give me a quick update on the new mark of respect and anything else they've changed since you were here."

"I'll do what I can," Daulo said grimly. "Come with me. Jin, can you find your way to the women's section? If they ask where you are, it might be useful to be able to say you're in a bath."

"I can do that," Jin said, acknowledging the advice without in any way stating she would follow it. In actual fact, she had no intention of getting out of earshot of her son right now.

She squeezed Merrick's shoulder, her fingers lingering perhaps a bit longer than really necessary. "Good luck."

From the way Fadil had been talking, Merrick had expected all four of the men from the village gate to be in the house, accompanied by the two official gate guards and possibly a few other armed friends. It was therefore something of a surprise when he descended the staircase to find that only one of the four men was actually present.

The youngest of the four, in fact, if Merrick was judging the other's face properly behind his closely trimmed beard. The young man's tunic was mostly brown, with dark red and blue highlights, tied with a tan sash. His trousers were a darker brown, with low, age-scuffed boots completing the ensemble. He would have looked perfectly at home beside any of a dozen other young men Merrick had noticed on the way into Milika.

He and Fadil were in the greeting room just off the foyer, Fadil watching stiffly as his visitor studied the refreshment trays being held for him by a pair of servant girls. The young man looked calm and perfectly at home, considerably more so than Fadil himself.

Merrick took a deep breath. *Showtime.* "Master Sammon, your father said I'm to—oh; excuse me," he said, bringing himself to a slightly jerky halt a couple of steps into the others' sight. "My apologies. I didn't realize you had a guest."

"Greetings to you, friend," the stranger said, waving away the trays with a double flick of his fingertips and lifting his right hand to touch bunched fingertips to his forehead.

Merrick suppressed a smile. That one had to be the oldest trick in the book. "Greetings to you," he replied, responding with the more proper two fingers to forehead and lips that Daulo had just taught him. "I am Haiku Sinn."

"Ah! My apologies—I keep forgetting," the other man said, lifting his hand again and giving the proper mark of respect. As he did so, his sleeve fell back, and Merrick caught a glimpse of a scaled gray undersleeve beneath the tunic. "I am Carsh Zoshak. Please; join us."

"Thank you," Merrick said, starting forward again. As he walked, he keyed in his optical enhancers' infrared, and a patterned red haze appeared superimposed over everyone in the room. One of the servant girls offered her tray to him, and he selected the minced *poofoo* strip that Daulo had recommended. "Are you a friend, or a business acquaintance of Master Sammon's?" he asked Zoshak as he took a bite. It tasted a little like spiced shrimp, he decided.

"Neither, actually," Zoshak said. "I'm an inspector for the Shahni."

"Really," Merrick said, letting his eyes go a little wider. "May I ask what such an illustrious personage seeks in such a modest village as Milika?"

"I am hardly an illustrious personage," Zoshak said wryly. "My job is simply to travel around Qasama monitoring compliance with current social norms. You may have noticed me at the gate when you came through?"

"I'm afraid I wasn't paying much attention to individuals," Merrick admitted, peering closely at him. "It was my first visit to Milika, and I was eager to see what the village was like."

"Really?" Zoshak asked in a tone of polite disbelief. "A cousin to Fadil Sammon, and this is your first visit?"

"A *cousin*?" Merrick echoed, frowning. "No, not at all. What gave you that impression?"

"One of the other gate guards heard him call you his cousin," Zoshak said, his eyes steady on Merrick's face.

Merrick held his puzzled frown another second. Then, letting his face clear, he gave a short laugh. "Oh, how funny," he said. "No, he didn't call me cousin. He simply called my name: *Haiku Sinn.*"

For a moment Zoshak looked blank. Then, slowly, he smiled as well. "Haiku Sinn," he repeated. "Yes, I can see how that could have been misheard. How funny, indeed."

"I only wish I were related to the Sammon family," Merrick went on, giving Fadil a rueful smile. The other didn't smile back, but merely continued looking tense.

"If I were, perhaps it would be easier to persuade them to combine our two mining operations."

"You deal in metals?" Zoshak asked.

"Mining and refining, yes," Merrick said. "We're particularly interested in the new deposits of iridium and platinum they've uncovered." He grimaced. "Unfortunately, so are many others."

"Indeed," Zoshak agreed. "Tell me, who is the older woman who was in Master Sammon's car with you?"

"My mother, Lariqa Sinn," Merrick said. He'd thought about trying to come up with another identity for her, but there was too much risk that someone might have noticed a family resemblance. "She knows a great deal more about my father's business than I do."

"But is perhaps not an expert on fashion?" Zoshak asked pointedly.

"Oh. Yes." Merrick winced. "Yes, I know—those old clothes we were wearing."

"Clothing which should have been destroyed two years ago," Zoshak said, his voice dropping to the tone Merrick often heard from Aventinian bureaucrats quoting rules and regulations.

"I know," Merrick said again. "We usually just wear them when we're inspecting mines—we don't mind if they get damaged, you see. Unfortunately, in our haste to get to Milika after we received Daulo Sammon's invitation, we didn't bother to change."

"Or to check your fuel gauge?" Zoshak suggested, his tone lightening a couple of shades.

Merrick winced again. "Indeed," he confessed. "If we're trying to impress Daulo Sammon with our efficiency, we're not doing a very good job of it."

"Perhaps you may yet redeem yourselves in his eyes," Zoshak said. "You will, of course, destroy that clothing immediately."

"Of course," Merrick hastened to assure him. "And all the rest, too, as soon as we return home."

"Yes," Zoshak said, his tone making it clear it wasn't a suggestion. "Where *is* your home, by the way?"

"Patrolo," Merrick said. He knew nothing about the town other than that it was midway down the Eastern Arm of the Great Arc, that it had a decent mining and refining industry, and that Daulo had suggested it as Merrick's supposed home town. "You've probably never even heard of it."

"Actually, I have," Zoshak said. "I understand it has decent mining facilities and several small refineries."

"Yes, that's it," Merrick confirmed. "Also several fine restaurants, if I may be so boastful. We would be honored to have you visit us someday." He dared a small smile. "And I promise you'll find nothing illegal when you do."

"I'll hold you to that, Master Sinn," Zoshak said, smiling back. "Thank you for your hospitality, Master Sammon. With your leave, I'll be on my way."

"Of course," Fadil said. He and Zoshak made the sign of respect, Zoshak and Merrick did likewise, and then the young Shahni agent headed out again into the midmorning sunlight.

Fadil exhaled a shuddering breath. "Leave us," he said tartly to the two servant girls. "You—upstairs," he added to Merrick as the girls bowed and headed silently toward the kitchen.

Daulo and Jin were waiting at the top of the stairway. "What do you think?" Merrick asked.

"You sounded convincing enough," Daulo said. "Whether or not he *was* convinced, of course, is another question entirely."

"He wasn't," Fadil bit out, glaring at Merrick. "How could he have been?"

"Merrick?" Jin invited.

Merrick shrugged. "If he recognized me for who I was, it had to have been right at the beginning," he said. "I saw no indication of sudden surprise or excitement."

"A man could hardly become an agent of the Shahni without control of his face," Fadil said contemptuously.

"True, but I doubt even Shahni agents can control their heartbeat and the subsequent changes in their heat output," Merrick told him. "I was monitoring his infrared signature the whole time, and I saw no change."

"You can read body temperature that subtly?" Daulo asked, frowning. "I never knew that."

"It's something that was added to Merrick's generation of Cobras," Jin explained, her voice oddly distant. "My own enhancers aren't nearly so sophisticated."

"Still, it's certainly possible that I misread him," Merrick continued. "Qasaman reactions may be different from those I'm familiar with."

"Especially given the range of enhancement drugs available to us," Daulo agreed grimly. "And as you say, he may have been convinced of your true identity from the very beginning."

"He was also wearing something odd under his tunic," Merrick said. "Something gray and scaly that I've never seen before."

"Probably a krisjaw-hide armband," Daulo said. "It either means he's a good hunter, or that he likes to pretend he is."

"Never mind that," Fadil asked impatiently. "What do we do?" He jerked a thumb at Merrick and Jin. "They've been seen in our house."

"I think all we can do now is minimize any potential damage," Merrick said, "which means us getting out of here as soon as possible. If Zoshak tries to make trouble, you'll just have to claim that our story fooled you—"

"There's one other possibility," Jin said.

Merrick eyed his mother. There was an odd look on her face, even odder than the tone she'd used a moment ago. "What's that?" he asked.

"We assumed that Daulo Sammon sent me that note," she said slowly. "Only we know now that he didn't." She seemed to brace herself. "What if it was actually sent by Miron Akim?"

Merrick felt his mouth drop open. "The Shahni agent?"

"I know it sounds crazy," Jin admitted. "But I can't think of anyone else on Qasama aside from the Sammon family who ever heard my full name."

"Obolo Nardin did," Daulo said, his face darkening with memory. "I distinctly remember you telling him who you were. Rather proudly, in fact."

"Not that it made any impression on him," Jin said. "But no, I only gave him the name Jasmine. The note refers to me as both Jasmine *and* Jin." She looked at Merrick. "In which case, it's possible Carsh Zoshak showed no reaction because he wasn't here to capture us, but merely to report on our arrival."

"Ridiculous," Fadil said with a snort.

"Fadil," Daulo said warningly.

"I apologize for any disrespect, my father," Fadil gritted out. "But it *is* ridiculous. What in the name of God would the Shahni want with enemies of Qasama?"

"We aren't your—" Merrick broke off at a gesture from his mother.

"I don't know what he would want with us," Jin said calmly. "I'm simply following the logic trail."

"To a completely erroneous conclusion," Fadil insisted.

"Possibly," Jin said calmly. "I'm open to other suggestions."

For a moment no one spoke. "I have to say, I agree with my son," Daulo said. "Such a suggestion is so unlikely as to border on the completely impossible." He made a face. "Unfortunately, I have nothing more probable to offer."

"Well, then, I guess it's time Merrick and I finally paid a visit to the Shahni," Jin said. She was trying to keep her tone light, Merrick knew, but he could sense the quiet concern beneath it. The Shahni, after all, were the ones who had declared Qasama's national hatred for the Cobra Worlds in the first place. "Where do they make their headquarters these days?"

"Where they always have: the city of Sollas," Daulo said. "You understand now why your arrival on their very doorstep fifty-five years ago was such a shock and concern to us all."

"If it makes you feel any better, the choice of the team's landing zone was purely coincidental," Jin assured him. "All the official records—as well the stories I heard from my father and uncle—agree that they picked Sollas only because it was more or less in the center of the string of Great Arc settlements."

"Which is precisely why it was made the capital to begin with," Daulo said. "Which makes you capable of predicting and anticipating our actions, which offers us no comfort at all."

Merrick felt his throat tighten. *Qasaman paranoia.* He'd heard his mother and grandfather talk about it, but until now he'd never truly understood the full implications of the phrase. "So Sollas it is," he put in, hoping to turn the conversation away from supposed Cobra Worlds omniscience. "We can get a bus to there, right?"

"Buses are hardly the transport of choice for fugitives," Daulo said heavily. "No, I'd better drive you."

"We can't let you do that," Jin said firmly. "Just let us have a vehicle and a map and we'll manage it ourselves."

"Have either of you a proper license?" Daulo asked. "I didn't think so. We may be a bit casual on the point of personal identity papers—a long and very deep part of our heritage—but we are *very* firm on allowing only those so authorized to drive our roads. Among other matters, you can't purchase fuel without one."

Jin threw Merrick a helpless look, then reluctantly nodded. "I have no right to ask such risks of you, Daulo Sammon," she said. "But I see no other way. Thank you for your offer, and we accept with humble thanks. How long a drive will it be?"

"If we leave within the next hour, we should be there around dawn," Daulo said.

"Can we do that?" Jin asked. "I mean, travel at night?"

"Of course." Daulo smiled humorlessly. "Interestingly enough, the number of predator attacks has been dropping steadily over the past half century. I suppose we have your people to thank for that."

"I have a question," Merrick said, trying to visualize the Qasaman maps he'd looked through. "I can't see how we can make a trip that long without driving straight through."

"Were you wanting to stop and sightsee along the way?" Daulo asked.

"I was thinking more about driver fatigue," Merrick said. "Unless you're planning to let Mom or me drive for a while."

"Weren't you listening?" Fadil snapped. "You can't drive here."

"It'll be all right," Daulo said. "If I get tired, we can stop for a brief rest."

"Which will look highly suspicious to anyone passing by," Fadil argued.

"We'll just have to risk that." Daulo eyed his son. "Unless you have an alternative to offer."

For a long moment Fadil glared at his father. Merrick flicked on his infrared again, watching with interest as parts of the young man's image shifted between red and orange with his fluctuating emotional state. "You know what the only alternative is," Fadil said at last. "We drive them together."

Daulo inclined his head; acknowledgment or thanks, Merrick couldn't tell which. "Do you have any other equipment, Jasmine Moreau?"

"We have some packs buried off the road about half a kilometer south of the village," Jin said. "But we can hardly pick them up in broad daylight with the gate guards already suspicious."

"I'd rather not wait until nightfall to leave Milika," Daulo said. "Can you make do without them?"

"Easily," Jin said with a nod. "There's nothing in there we can't do without."

Merrick grimaced. Nothing except their camo night-fighting suits, their compact medical kits, their rope and climbing gear, and a few small smoke-and-shock diversionary devices. But she was right. If Zoshak was still suspicious, parking alongside the road while someone went for a short walk would be a suicidally stupid thing to do.

"Then as soon as we've collected some spare clothing for you, we'll be under way," Daulo decided. "Fadil, we'll take the green truck. Go make sure it's fueled—" he smiled tightly "—and add a few small boxes of recent ore samples from the mine."

Fadil frowned. "*Ore* samples?"

"If we're going to go to Patrolo to discuss joint operations with the Sinn family refining facilities, we'll need to show them samples of our output," Daulo said. "Go."

"Yes, Father." Fadil gave Daulo the sign of respect and then, grudgingly, Merrick thought, repeated the gesture to him and his mother. Turning, he went back downstairs and disappeared down a corridor leading toward the rear of the house.

"Come," Daulo said, gesturing to Jin and Merrick as he headed the opposite direction down the corridor. "We'll see about food for you while we pack a few essentials."

Merrick and Jin fell into step beside him. Behind Daulo's back, Merrick caught his mother's eye. *I hope you know what you're doing,* he mouthed silently to her.

Her lip twitched. *So do I,* she mouthed back.

CHAPTER SIX

The truck Fadil brought up was a relatively small one, about the size of an Aventinian personal transport vehicle, with a cab in front and an enclosed cargo area attached behind it equipped with front, rear, and side windows. The cab only had two main seats, but the slightly enlarged space behind it included two inward-facing fold-down jump seats.

From the gate guards' point of view, of course, the vehicle made perfect sense. With the visitors' own car supposedly waiting a couple of kilometers down the road, there was no reason for Daulo to bring a larger vehicle. He would theoretically simply drop his guests at their own car, refill its fuel tank, and then the four of them would continue on to Patrolo in a two-vehicle convoy.

But of course there was no such car conveniently waiting for them. As the four of them settled into the truck, and Merrick tried to find a comfortable position for his feet that wouldn't involve kicking his mother's, he reluctantly concluded that this was going to be a very long trip.

But at least their exit from Milika was satisfyingly anticlimactic. None of the gate guards gave them so much as a second glance as they headed out of town. Carsh Zoshak himself, in fact, wasn't even present, and Merrick dared to hope that the Shahni agent really *was* in Milika merely to check on social detail compliance.

The first major population center along the southward road was the city of Azras. There they stopped for fuel and a meal before turning northeast onto the main road that linked Qasama's five major Western Arm cities. By the time the sunlight faded away behind the forest and the stars began to appear, they were alone on the road.

Merrick spent most of the night staring out the cab window past his mother's head at the stretches of forest and plain rolling past them, or out the windshield at the winding road ahead. Occasionally, just for a change of pace, he took in the view out the rear window, looking through the mostly empty cargo area and out the cargo area's own rear window, watching the red-lit landscape disappear behind them.

He caught occasional snatches of sleep, too. But the seat and his position were uncomfortable enough that those interludes of oblivion didn't last very long. Seated across from him, his mother seemed to be having a much easier time of it, as did Fadil at Merrick's right in the front passenger seat.

A little after midnight Daulo found a long, open, and deserted stretch of highway and pulled off to switch drivers. Merrick and Jin got out as well, glad of the opportunity to stretch their legs for a minute. The forest had been cleared well back of the road at this point, and as Merrick paced back and forth he used his optical enhancers to check the tree line on both sides for predators. He spotted a single spine leopard lurking among some thorn bushes, but if the creature even noticed the humans it made no sign. A few minutes later they were all back in the truck and, with Fadil now at the wheel, they continued on their way.

The glow of approaching dawn was reddening the sky ahead when Merrick first noticed they were being followed.

"Mom?" he murmured, just loud enough to be heard over the road noise.

"I know," she murmured back. "He's been there for at least the last half hour."

Merrick stared at her. "Half an *hour*? And you didn't say anything?"

"Who's been where for half an hour?" Fadil asked, frowning at them in the mirror. "What are we talking about?"

"We're talking about the person or persons following us," Jin told him.

"We're being followed?" Daulo asked, straightening up in the passenger seat and throwing a quick look over his shoulder.

"Yes, but so far that's all he seems interested in doing," Jin said.

Fadil muttered something under his breath. "More Shahni agents?"

"Unlikely," Daulo said. "Half an hour would have been more than enough time for an agent to call for a roadblock or an air strike."

"Unless they merely want to watch us," Fadil growled.

"Again, unlikely," Daulo said. "Instead of following us, it would be much more effective for them to put a SkyJo combat helicopter directly overhead at an altitude where we would never notice it."

"Maybe it's just another traveler heading to Sollas," Merrick suggested.

"I don't think so," his mother said. "There was that half-kilometer of bad road about fifteen minutes ago where Fadil had to slow way down. A normal car would have maintained his speed on the good road until he hit the patch himself, which would have meant temporarily closing the gap between us. Instead, he slowed to match our speed, staying as far back as he could while still maintaining visual contact. *And* he also didn't slow down through the rough patch, again maintaining visual in case we turned off on one of these side roads."

"So then who *is* he?" Merrick asked.

"Probably part of a local gang of thieves," Daulo said contemptuously. "We're probably heading for their roadblock right now."

"Well, we can't have that, can we?" Merrick said. "I'll take care of it."

"How?" Jin asked suspiciously.

"I'm going to give him some car trouble," Merrick said. "Master Sammon, do we have any left-hand curves coming up? Preferably something with forest or other cover close at hand."

There was a soft glow from the front seat as Daulo consulted his map. "There's a fairly sharp left curve about five kilometers ahead," he reported. "But the nearest trees to that spot are almost twenty meters back from the road."

"Any depressions or pits anywhere along the curve?" Merrick asked.

"There's a drainage channel running along both shoulders the whole length of the curve," Daulo said. "But they're not likely to be more than half a meter deep."

"Good enough," Merrick assured him. "Can you keep the overhead light from going on when the door is opened?"

"What exactly are you planning?" Daulo asked as he reached up to the dome light switch.

"As I said, I'm going to give him some car trouble," Merrick said, swiveling his legs around the front side of his jump seat. "Lean forward, please, and crack the door open a few centimeters."

"Wait a minute," Daulo said, his tone suddenly ominous. "You're not planning to *jump*, are you?"

"Don't worry, I'll be fine," Merrick assured him. "Low-altitude aircar quick-exits are something we do all the time."

He looked at his mother, waiting for her to raise the point that, although the quick-exit was certainly taught at the academy, Merrick himself hadn't done one since graduation. But she remained silent. "As soon as I'm out, close the door and keep going at the same speed," Merrick continued. "Mom will tell you when you should slow down so that I can catch up with you."

"Understood," Daulo said. "Be careful."

He hitched his seat forward and opened his door a crack. Merrick got one hand on the seat back and the other on the doorjamb and waited.

They reached the curve, and as they turned into it Merrick eased himself alongside Daulo's seat and pushed the door open half a meter, balancing himself partway out the door. The wind buffeted hard against his face, and he closed his eyes against the onslaught as he keyed in his optical enhancers to give him some vision. For a few seconds he crouched beside Daulo, waiting for just the right moment . . . and as they approached the midpoint of the curve, he shifted his weight and dropped out the door.

He barely had time to get his legs pumping before his feet hit the pavement. For a second he thought he wasn't going to make it, that his feet would be swept out from under him and he would end up being dragged along the road.

Then his nanocomputer got his servo-driven legs into the rhythm, and he had his balance back. He released his grip on the door, angled toward the edge of the shoulder, and started to slow down. For another couple of seconds he fought the same fight against speed that he'd just won, only this time in reverse.

And as the truck continued past him down the curve, Merrick threw himself headfirst into the drainage channel beside the road, tucking his forearms against his face to protect it as he slid off the remainder of his momentum.

He'd half expected his Qasaman outfit to disintegrate under the stress, leaving him with a few bad scrapes at the very least. But the clothing was tougher than he'd realized, and it came through the ordeal with only some minor rips. Even more fortunately, the channel was dry, which meant no huge spray of water to warn the trailing car that one of their quarries had flown the coop. Ignoring the handful of bumps and bruises his landing had beaten into his arms and chest, Merrick rolled up onto his back and waited.

From his new vantage point, he heard the tailing car well before he saw it. He focused on the edge of the road, his right hand curling into firing position. The car flashed past, and in a single motion Merrick sat up, glanced a target lock onto the nearer rear wheel, and fired his fingertip laser. There was a muffled *pop* as the tire blew.

And suddenly the car was all over the road, its tires screeching as the driver fought to bring it back under control. Merrick swung himself around and rose up into a low crouch, watching the car swerving back and forth. As soon as it came to a halt, he would slip away, cut across the landscape, and catch up with his mother and the Sammons.

He was still watching when the driver abruptly lost his battle with momentum. The car shot across the center line, angled across the shoulder, and slammed down into the drainage channel on the far side.

"Damn!" Merrick bit out as he leaped up and sprinted toward the car. The idea had been to quietly and peaceably stop the vehicle, not wreck it and injure or kill everyone inside. He reached the car and bent down to look inside.

The driver was draped over the steering wheel, his head and arms limp, his face turned away. Swearing again, Merrick hurried around to the driver's side and pulled at the door. It resisted, probably knocked out of shape by the crash. He tried again, this time putting his servos into the effort, and with a horrible grinding noise the door came open.

The driver didn't move. Gingerly, Merrick reached in and touched his fingertips to the other's neck. To his relief, he found a slow but steady pulse. At least the man wasn't dead. Merrick focused on the other's face, notching up his light-amps.

And a sudden chill ran down his back. This wasn't just some random member of some random gang.

It was Carsh Zoshak.

There was the sound of tires on pavement, and he looked up to see the Sammon truck back up to a jerky halt in front of the wrecked car. "What happened?" Jin called as she jumped out of the truck.

"He lost control when I popped his tire," Merrick said grimly. "And it's not a thief. It's Carsh Zoshak."

"What?" Daulo demanded as he got out of his side of the truck and hurried to join them. "But—"

"I guess he wasn't senior enough to call in a SkyJo," Merrick said. "Mom, can you help me get him out of the car?"

"You think that's wise?" Jin asked as she leaned into the car and checked Zoshak's pulse for herself.

"Well, we can't exactly leave him here," Merrick said tersely. "I don't see any blood, but there could be a concussion or internal injuries."

Daulo came up beside them, his expression tense. "God in heaven," he breathed, looking at the unconscious Shahni agent. "What did you *do*?"

"I just popped one of his rear tires, that's all," Merrick told him. "It should have brought him to a stop and kept him there. Instead, he lost control."

Daulo snarled a word Merrick's Qasaman classes had somehow never covered. "What do we do?"

"We get him to a hospital," Jin said. "Merrick, I'll take his head. You lean him out and get his torso and legs. Daulo, is there a medical kit in the truck?"

"Yes, but only a simple one."

"We'll take whatever you've got," Jin said as she and Merrick eased the unconscious man out of the car. "I'll ride in back and see what I can do for him."

Merrick grimaced. "No, I'll do it," he said. "My training is more up-to-date than yours."

"You sure?" Jin asked, peering closely at him. "I thought you hated the sight of blood."

"So what?" Merrick growled. "Besides, I'm the one who wrecked him."

His mother hesitated, then nodded. "All right. Daulo, can you get the back of the cargo area open?"

The cargo area had a very low ceiling, and getting Zoshak inside without jostling him proved to be a delicate operation. But between them, Merrick and Jin managed it. Merrick climbed in beside the wounded man, accepted the first-aid kit Fadil handed him, and settled himself into a cross-legged position as Daulo closed the rear door.

Zoshak's teeth were chattering quietly as Merrick pried open the kit and took a quick inventory. Bandages, cleaning cloths, painkillers, a few patches of unknown purpose, and a handful of small color-coded hypos whose contents consisted of medical-looking words that Merrick had never learned. As the truck headed off again, Merrick set the kit aside and carefully eased open Zoshak's outer robe and tunic.

Back at the Sammon house, Daulo had suggested that the gray scaly material Merrick had spotted under Zoshak's sleeve was a krisjaw armband. To Merrick's surprise, it wasn't.

Beside him, the connecting window to the truck's cab slid open. "How's he doing?" Jin asked, looking through the opening.

"His teeth are chattering," Merrick said, shifting his eyes to Zoshak's face as he took off his own robe. "Well, they were a minute ago, anyway. His skin doesn't feel cold, so I'm guessing it's shock."

"You need to keep him warm."

"Already on it," Merrick assured her, laying his robe across Zoshak's legs and abdomen. "Where's Lorne and his magic health-o-meter ears when we need him?"

"You're the one who insisted on inviting yourself along on this trip," his mother said.

"Don't remind me," Merrick said. "By the way, you can tell Daulo that this krisjaw armband of his goes all the way up. *And* down."

"What do you mean?" Jin asked, frowning.

"I mean he's got a whole suit of the stuff," Merrick said. "Shirt, trousers—the works. Might have socks, too, for all I know. Either he's one heck of a hunter, or else he has serious compensation issues."

"Never mind his issues," Jin said. "What can you tell about his injuries?"

"Not much," Merrick admitted, gently kneading the usual places on Zoshak's torso. "I don't feel any swelling in his major organs. No broken ribs, either." He shifted his hands to Zoshak's arms. "Arms seem okay, too. That just leaves his head."

From the front seat, Daulo said something Merrick didn't catch. "Daulo says you can use the green hypo to wake him up," Jin repeated. "It's a mild stimulant."

"I'd rather not pump any chemicals into him if we don't have to," Merrick said, eyeing the hypos dubiously as he sealed Zoshak's tunic and robe again. "As long as he seems stable, I vote we just watch him and let a real doctor handle the treatment."

"That's probably best," Jin agreed reluctantly. "I just hate to sit here and do nothing."

" 'The patient heals; the doctor collects the bill,' " Merrick quoted. "How much farther?"

Jin glanced over her shoulder. "We're here."

Merrick ducked his head and looked between Daulo and Fadil. There, rising up from the plain ahead, framed against the red fire of the rising sun behind it, was Sollas.

The first mission to Qasama had spent the bulk of their time in and around Sollas, and Merrick had studied all the pictures they'd brought back of the city. The skyline had changed a little since then, he noted, with a few new buildings and some extra height on some of the others. But the most striking change— "Is that a *wall* around the city?"

Jin turned around again. "Certainly looks like one," she confirmed, her voice sounding odd. "Daulo, when did they put *that* up?"

"Quite a few years ago, actually," Daulo said. "A few years after your visit. You didn't know?"

"Not even a hint," Jin said. "Our observation satellites all started dying shortly after I left, and with the . . . new political climate the Council decided not to replace them."

"Probably because they would have showed that the Moreau plan had worked," Merrick put in sourly.

Fadil shot a glance over his shoulder. "The *Moreau* plan? The razorarms were *your* idea?"

"Partly," Jin told him. "Well, mostly, I suppose. But the people who opposed it wanted to smear our family, so they dubbed it the Moreau plan and worked hard to make the name stick." She turned back to Merrick. "Any change?"

Merrick looked down at Zoshak. "Nothing obvious," he reported, checking the young Qasaman's neck again. "Pulse and breathing are still steady."

"Keep an eye on him."

"I will." Merrick shifted to a side-sitting position, easing the strain on his leg muscles, and glanced out the cargo area's rear window. Thoughts of Zoshak had suddenly sparked the thought that the Shahni agent might not have been alone. But the road behind them was empty of vehicles. With a sigh of relief and fatigue, Merrick started to look away.

And paused. The road itself was clear, but there was something in the distance above it: a black spot, moving rapidly toward them out of the darker part of the sky. One of the SkyJo attack helicopters that Daulo had mentioned? Hoping fervently that it was something else —*anything* else—he keyed in his telescopic enhancers.

The next instant his vision exploded into a violent back-and-forth sway, the unavoidable price for using telescopics inside a moving vehicle. Merrick clamped down on his sudden vertigo and let his head and neck float, compensating as best he could for the bounces. An image flashed into view and then back out again before he could identify it. He set his teeth, fighting to bring it back.

And as he did, he felt his breath catch in his throat. The vehicle back there wasn't a SkyJo. It was a Troft spaceship. "Are we expecting company from the Trofts?" he called toward the cab.

"What do you mean?" Daulo asked, turning in his seat.

"There's a ship coming in from the west," Merrick told him, working furiously to maintain his hold on the image. "It's definitely a Troft, but it isn't a type I've ever seen before."

"Can you describe it?" Jin asked, bobbing her head up and down as she tried to look out the back. "It's too high for my angle."

"Looks sort of like a wrigglefish," Merrick said. "Tall but thin, at least from the front. It's—well, it's longer than it is tall, but it's too far away for me to get a definitive scale. There are two sets of short wings on each side . . . wait a minute."

"What?" Jin asked.

"He's not coming in on gravity lifts," Merrick said, frowning as the strangeness of that suddenly struck him. Troft spacecraft *always* came down on gravity lifts. "He must be using airfoils." Blinking, Merrick shut off the telescopics, trying to give his brain a brief rest.

And stiffened as his field of view expanded back to normal again. The strange Troft ship wasn't alone. There were at least fifty of them, coming out of the darkness in a wedge formation, none of them running grav lifts.

Running without the telltale red glow of grav lifts.

Merrick keyed in the telescopics again, focusing on the lead ship . . . and this time he spotted the cluster of objects nestled up beside the hulls beneath the stubby bow and stern wings. "Oh, hell," he murmured.

"What is it?" Jin asked tautly.

With an effort, Merrick found his voice. "Tell Fadil to punch it," he said, marveling at how calm his voice sounded. "Those are Troft warships. Fifty to a hundred of them."

He turned to face his mother's suddenly widened eyes. "Qasama's under attack."

CHAPTER SEVEN

"God in heaven," Daulo breathed. "Are you sure?"

"Trust me," Merrick said, looking back and forth between the various incoming ships. "There are at least twenty more of the wrigglefish ones, but also a few that look like flying sharks. I see a couple of wider ones in back too—whoops; there go their grav lifts," he said as red glows appeared in unison beneath each of the incoming ships.

"Coming in for a landing," Jin said tightly. "Looks like Sollas is the target."

"Like there was any doubt," Merrick said. "What do we do?"

"We have to warn the Shahni," Daulo insisted.

"Right," Jin said. "You have any kind of comm or radio? Ours are still in our packs back at Milika."

Daulo hissed viciously between his teeth. "Unfortunately, the only radio equipment simple villagers like ourselves may use are the short-range sets we use to communicate into the mines," he said. "Everything else is reserved for the Shahni and military."

"Maybe Carsh Zoshak has something with him," Jin suggested. "Merrick?"

"I'm on it," Merrick said, running his hands quickly over Zoshak's tunic and robe. But there was nothing. "No good," he said. "If he had something, we must have left it in the car."

"Any idea where any of the Shahni live?" Jin asked. "If we can't call them, maybe we can go pound on someone's door."

"They and their families all live together in the Palace in the center of Sollas," Daulo said. "Unfortunately, I doubt we can reach it before the invaders do."

"Depends on how smart the Trofts are," Jin said. "If they decide to secure the airfield area first—which is what *I'd* do—we might have time to get to the Shahni and at least help them get to cover."

There was a soft noise from Zoshak, and Merrick looked down to see that the other's teeth were chattering again. "We may have to postpone any door-knocking," he warned. "I think Carsh Zoshak's going into shock again."

"Daulo, check and see where the nearest hospital is," Jin said. "Someplace that can handle—"

She broke off as the forward edge of the invasion force shot past overhead, filling the air with a deep, throaty roar. For a long minute the sound continued, the truck rattling as Fadil fought the buffeting slipstream of the ships' passage.

And then the wave was past, and the sound faded away into the tense stillness of the predawn landscape.

"Someplace that can handle possible head trauma," Jin finished her sentence. "Doesn't look like they're all headed for the airfield, does it?"

"It would appear they mean to take the entire city at once," Daulo agreed tightly. "But we won't be destroyed without a fight."

"Fortunately, mass destruction doesn't seem to be part of the Trofts' playbook," Jin said. "At least, not the Trofts the Dominion of Man ran into a century ago. They prefer to conquer planets and peoples in more or less working condition. Did you find us a hospital?"

"The closest is just inside the southwestern gate," Daulo said, holding up the map for her to see. "Once he's there—"

A hand brushed Merrick's knee. "Hold it a sec," Merrick interrupted, looking down.

Zoshak's eyes were open, though just barely. "Where . . . ?" the young man whispered. "What . . . ?"

"You were in an accident," Merrick told him, feeling a fresh flash of guilt at having been the one who'd caused the wreck. "We're taking you to—where are we going?"

"The Everhope Hospital," Daulo said.

"The Everhope Hospital in Sollas," Merrick repeated. "We'll be there in just a few minutes."

Zoshak closed his eyes. "Lodestar," he murmured. "It must be Lodestar."

"What's Lodestar?" Merrick asked.

"It's another hospital," Daulo said, studying his map. "But it's near the city center. Even at this time of morning it would take an additional quarter of an hour or more for us to reach it."

Merrick nodded. "The Everhope's closer," he told Zoshak. "We'll take you there."

Zoshak shook his head weakly. "Lodestar," he insisted, his voice almost too weak to hear. "Specialist. Kambuzia."

"He says there's a specialist there named Kambuzia," Merrick repeated.

"Not smart," Daulo objected, looking over the back seat at the cargo area. "The first rule of emergency care is to obtain it as quickly as possible."

"Kambuzia," Zoshak whispered. "Kambuzia."

"Yes, but he clearly wants this Dr. Kambuzia," Merrick said, touching his fingers to Zoshak's throat. "Pulse is still good," he said, gazing down into the other's face. Zoshak's eyes had opened a little again, and behind the drooping lids Merrick could sense an unbending insistence. "I don't think he's going to be happy with anyone else."

Daulo muttered something under his breath. "Probably some relative," he muttered. "Fine. Fadil, at the ring road swing north toward the western gate instead of continuing on to the southwest entrance."

They reached the ring road and turned north. Merrick tried to see what might be happening in the city, but the wall blocked everything but the tops of the nearest buildings.

But at least there was no sound of gunfire or lasers. Yet.

The western gate was standing wide open when they arrived. It was also deserted, with no guards or other travelers anywhere in sight. "This isn't right," Fadil muttered as he drove through. "Where is everyo—?"

The rest of his question was cut off by the abrupt screech of tires on pavement as he slammed on the brakes. Merrick grabbed for a handhold and ducked down to look past his mother's head out the windshield.

And found himself gazing at the tall side of one of the Troft ships.

It was squatting on wide landing skids in the center of the intersection just beyond the gate, positioned with its longitudinal axis along the wider southeast-to-northwest avenue and its flank toward the narrower street the Sammon truck had entered by. "Regular air field not good enough for them?" Merrick muttered.

"First rule of urban occupation is to control or block major intersections," Jin said tightly. "Looks like they've decided to do both. Look at the firepower they've got under those wings."

Merrick craned his neck and grimaced. Now that the ship was close by and standing still, he was able to get some detail on the weapons mounted on pylons beneath the stubby wings. "Looks like lasers *and* missile launchers," he said.

"All mounted on individual swivels on those pylons, you'll notice," his mother said. "Makes it easy to fire in any direction."

Merrick nodded. And with Qasaman city avenues nice and straight and wide, a single gunship's weapons would command a lot of territory.

"God in heaven," Daulo murmured.

Merrick tore his gaze from the ship. Striding toward them with hand-and-a-half lasers held at the ready were four Trofts.

He felt his muscles stiffen, a sudden flood of claustrophobia gripping his heart. Each of the aliens was wearing a thick armored leotard with heavy knee-high boots and a belt that sported a small sidearm, a long knife, and half a dozen gadgets that Merrick didn't recognize. Their helmets were of an odd, almost flowing design that curved down behind them to protect the backs of their necks, with a thick plastic or glass faceplate covering their faces.

And here Merrick sat, trapped in the back of a truck, with his mother and her friends blocking most of his field of fire. If the Trofts decided to mow them all down, there was nothing he could do to stop them—

"Merrick, do you recognize the demesne pattern?" Jin asked quietly.

With an effort, Merrick forced down his fear. His mother was right—this was the time for thought and planning, not panic. Anyway, if the Trofts wanted them dead, they would have already opened fire. "I think I can see some elements of the Pua demesne," he said. "But taken as a whole it isn't any combination I've seen before."

"That's what I was thinking," his mother agreed. "Which may imply the attack isn't coming from any of Qasama's immediate neighbors, or at least not the ones who first told us about their presence here."

"What does it matter where they came from?" Fadil snarled as the Trofts continued toward them.

"I don't know yet," Jin said calmly. "But all information is eventually useful."

"*If* you live through it," Fadil bit back. "You're the brave demon warriors. *Do* something."

"Patience, my son," Daulo said. His voice, Merrick noted with a flicker of resentment, was as calm as Jin's, and far calmer than Merrick himself was feeling. "Jin Moreau, how do you wish to play this?"

"As low-key and truthful as possible," Jin told him. "We were coming to Sollas to shop around some ore samples, found an accident victim on the road, and are trying to get him to the hospital."

"We'll try it," Daulo said. "Remember to let me do all the talking."

Five meters from the truck the Trofts shifted formation, one of them approaching the driver's side while the other three fanned out sideways with their lasers covering the occupants. At a murmured word from Daulo, Fadil rolled down his window. "What's the meaning of this?" Daulo demanded, his voice stiff and even a bit haughty. "We are citizens of Qasama—"

Behind the faceplate, Merrick saw the Troft's beak moving as he said something in cattertalk. "You will remain silent," a round pin on the alien's left shoulder boomed out the Qasaman translation. "State your business in Sollas."

"We bring ore samples to the refineries." Daulo nodded back toward Merrick and Zoshak. "More importantly, we also have an injured man we found on the road. He needs to be taken to a hospital."

The Troft looked past Fadil's head into the cargo area. Merrick crouched low over Zoshak, putting as much concern into his face and his body language as he could. He had no idea whether the Troft could even read humans that closely, but there was no harm in trying. "Where was this accident?" the alien asked.

"About twenty kilometers back along the Azras road," Daulo said. "Go look for yourselves if you don't believe me."

Merrick felt his stomach tighten. If the Trofts examined the wreck closely enough to find the laser damage to the car's tires . . . but that was pretty unlikely. If they did anything, it would be a quick flyover to see that an abandoned car was, in fact, where Daulo said it was.

"Where is this hospital?" the Troft asked.

"Four blocks down that street," Daulo said, pointing toward the Troft ship blocking the road.

The alien seemed to consider. "You may take him," he said. "But on foot. No vehicles are currently permitted on the streets."

"He's *injured,*" Daulo repeated, in the tone someone might use when trying to explain something to a small child. "The extra time that would take could be fatal."

"No vehicles are currently permitted on the streets," the Troft said again. "Take him, or leave him here."

"Fine," Daulo shot back scornfully. "Fadil, pull over there."

"Do not move the vehicle," the Troft said, gesturing sharply toward Fadil with his laser as the younger Sammon started to put the truck into gear. "Shut off the engine and give me the starting mechanism."

"Why?" Daulo demanded. "This is *my* truck. You go find your own."

Fadil shot his father a nervous look. "Father—"

"Quiet," Daulo cut him off, his glare focused on the Troft. "You want me to beg? Is that it? Fine, then—I'll beg. May I *please* drive the injured man to the hospital?"

The Troft gestured again. "Get out of the vehicle," he ordered. "Give me the starting mechanism."

Daulo snorted, an angry, contemptuous sound. "Give him the keys, Fadil. Everyone else, out."

A minute later they had Zoshak out of the truck, Jin supporting the unconscious man's head while the other three carried his body horizontally on their forearms like a living stretcher. "You take terrible chances, my father," Fadil murmured tautly as they headed down the street.

"I'm a Qasaman, my son," Daulo countered, his voice still simmering with anger. "These invaders might as well know from the very start who we are whom they have challenged. Jin Moreau, do we go around the front of the alien ship, or around the rear?"

"The front," Jin said. Merrick could see from her expression that she didn't agree with Daulo's in-your-face attitude, but it was also clear she wasn't about to call him on it. Certainly not in front of the man's own son. "I want to see what the forward weapons and sensor clusters look like."

Another pair of Trofts stepped into view around the ship's bow as the stretcher party approached, their lasers not quite pointing at the humans. But they made no effort to stop or even challenge. Apparently, the word had been passed from the checkpoint that this group was to be allowed past. Jin led the way around the ship, glancing casually up at the gleaming metal as they walked. Merrick looked up, too, but he could make little of the orderly array of bumps, nozzles, pits, and intakes.

And then they were past the ship and the watchful Trofts and were heading down the deserted street. "Another three blocks, you said?" Jin asked.

"Yes," Daulo confirmed. "It should be that eight-story white building just ahead, the one with the half-circle drive for emergency vehicles."

Jin half turned, taking care not to jostle Zoshak's head as she did so. "I see it," she said, turning back. "I don't suppose the Palace would happen to be somewhere along the way?"

"Not on the path, but not far off it," Daulo said. "Two streets down and half a block to the left."

"About a block away from the hospital?"

"Correct," Daulo said. "It might be possible for me to make a short side trip while you continue on with Carsh Zoshak."

Merrick looked behind them. The two Trofts they'd passed were standing together beside the ship, their attention clearly on the four humans carrying their burden down the street. "How well is the place marked?" he asked.

"There's no large illuminated sign, if that's what you mean," Daulo said. "Why, you think the invaders may not have found it yet?"

"It's possible," Merrick said.

"But unlikely," Jin warned. "If they've done their homework, they know where all the centers of government and industry are."

Daulo muttered something under his breath. "We'll know soon enough," he said.

They reached the cross street Daulo had identified, to discover that the Trofts had indeed done their homework. Midway down the block, a large but unpretentious four-story gray-stone building had been completely encircled by armed aliens, with support from a handful of tripod-mounted heavy lasers and a pair of panel-truck-sized armored vehicles. Two of the soldiers were crouched by a tall front door, fiddling with something Merrick guessed was probably some kind of explosive. "So much for our lending assistance to the Shahni," Daulo muttered.

"Don't give up yet," Jin said. "If they haven't gotten the door open by the time we've turned Carsh Zoshak over to Dr. Kambuzia, there may still be something we can do."

They were at the hospital's main door when the flat crack of an explosive charge came from around the corner they'd just passed. "So ends your hoped-for options," Daulo growled. "And so ends freedom for the Shahni."

"Don't count them out yet," Jin warned. "If there's one thing I've learned about your people, it's that they always have a trick or two up their sleeves."

They reached the hospital and went inside. To Merrick's uneasy surprise, the reception lobby was as deserted as the street outside. "Hello?" Jin called. "Anyone here? We need a doctor. Where *is* everyone?"

"I don't know," Daulo said, nodding toward a group of gurneys lined up along the side wall. "Let's put him down over there."

They got Zoshak onto one of the gurneys. His teeth were chattering again, and Merrick took an extra few seconds to wrap the other's robe more snugly. "One of us could try to get into the hospital computer while the others search for the staff," he suggested as he checked Zoshak's pulse. "Maybe we can at least find out where Dr. Kambuzia is supposed to be."

"Good idea," Daulo said. "It should be—*God in heaven.*"

Merrick jerked his head up. Five armed Trofts had appeared around the corner from of one of the two hallways leading off the lobby and were forming themselves into a wide V-shaped wedge. "Humans, stop," the Qasaman words came from the leader's translator pin.

"We have an injured man—" Daulo began.

"You carry a radio transmitter," the Troft interrupted him. "You will submit to an immediate search."

Out of the corner of his eye Merrick saw his mother turn a sharp look on him. He gave her a microscopic shake of his head in response—as she'd already said, both their comms were still back at Milika. And Daulo had already said he and Fadil weren't allowed such devices.

Which meant that Merrick must have missed something when he'd searched Zoshak's clothing. Now the Trofts were going to give it a go, and they were likely to be a lot more thorough than Merrick had been. Wherever Zoshak's transmitter was hidden, they would find it.

Merrick didn't know what would happen after that. But he was pretty sure it wouldn't be pleasant. "You don't have to search," he spoke up impulsively, digging beneath his tunic. "I have it."

He held his breath as Daulo and Fadil turned astonished faces toward him. But Jin, at least, was instantly on her son's wavelength. "Yes, give it to them," she put in before any of the aliens could respond. "While he does, we need to get our friend to the doctor." Without waiting for permission, she started pushing Zoshak's gurney toward the hallway leading off the other end of the lobby.

She'd gotten three steps before the Troft leader apparently recovered from his surprise at such chutzpah from a mere human. "Stop!" he snapped.

Jin frowned at the alien, managing to get two more steps before coming to a confused halt. "What's the problem?" she asked, glancing back at Merrick. Her hands came casually together, her left forefinger tapping the little finger of her right hand. "I said he would give it—*God in heaven*—" She broke off, her eyes going wide as she focused on the empty corridor behind the Trofts.

And as the two Trofts in the rear of the V started to turn around, she activated her sonic disruptor.

The disruptor wasn't really an antipersonnel weapon, having been designed mainly for shattering glass and brick and crystalline-based electronic equipment. But at close range, its effect on living beings was also nothing to sneer at. The two Trofts closest to the center of the blast jerked as if they'd been punched in the face, while the ones at the edges staggered like drunkards, all of them clearly fighting to hold on to their balance long enough to deal with this unexpected attack that had apparently sneaked up from behind them.

They were still trying to make their uncooperative bodies turn the necessary hundred eighty degrees to look behind them when Merrick lifted his right hand and activated his stunner.

A short, low-power laser blast shot out of his little finger, its frequency carefully tuned to expend most of its energy on the air instead of on the Troft at the other end. An instant later, a high-voltage, low-amperage lightning bolt shot out of the electrode beside the laser emitter, the current riding the partially ionized pathway that the laser flash had just created.

A full-power arcthrower blast from that same electrode would have fried the Troft where he stood, even through battle armor. The much less energetic stunner, or so the theory went, would merely knock him out.

The theory turned out to be correct. Without even a gasp, the Troft collapsed to the floor and lay still.

He was still falling when Merrick shifted his aim to the next alien in line and again fired his stunner. Four more shots, and it was over.

"Backup," Jin murmured, nodding toward the corner where the Trofts had appeared.

Merrick nodded and headed across the lobby, his hands curled into fingertip-laser firing position, his heart thudding painfully with reaction. He'd never used his stunner outside the Sun Center practice range, certainly never against another living being.

And suddenly the old family stories and histories had come boiling off their nice, neat pages. This was real. This was combat.

This was war.

"God in heaven," Daulo's shaking voice came from behind Merrick. "What *was* that?"

"Stunner," Jin told him. "Something else Merrick has that I don't. Merrick?"

Merrick reached the corner and paused, his audio enhancers reaching out ahead of him. *A spine leopard hunt,* he told himself firmly. *Just think of it as another spine leopard hunt. With really weird-looking spine leopards.*

There were no sounds of footsteps coming from the hallway. Cautiously, he eased an eye around the corner.

"Clear," he called back softly. There *were* faint noises of a sort coming from down there, though. Not Trofts, but soft, tense Qasaman voices. "I may have found the doctors and staff," he added, turning his enhancers off again." He turned back to look at his mother. "Do you want me to check—?"

He broke off, his eyes refocusing on the gurney behind his mother and the two Sammons, the gurney where they'd laid Zoshak.

The *empty* gurney where they'd laid Zoshak. "Mom!" he snapped, jabbing a finger.

The others turned to look. "What in—? Where did he *go*?" Daulo demanded.

"No idea," Jin said grimly as she hurried to the far corridor where she'd been heading when the Troft stopped her. "He's not down here," she reported, peering around the corner. "But there's a stairway just off the lobby. Just a minute."

She paused, and Merrick spotted the twitch of cheek muscles as she keyed in her audio enhancers. "He's on the stairs," she said. "Moving fast." She threw an unreadable look at Merrick. "I guess he wasn't as injured as he looked."

"That's impossible," Merrick protested. "He had a slow heartbeat. How do you fake a slow heartbeat?"

"Forget the *how* and concentrate on the *why*," Jin said, waving him forward. "Daulo, Fadil; go check on the hospital staff. See if they need any help. Merrick and I will go find Carsh Zoshak."

The stairway was quiet as Jin and Merrick went in. "You sure the footsteps were in here?" Merrick asked as he looked upward through the gap between the switchback flights of stairs.

"Yes, I could hear the echo," Jin said. "Sounded like he was taking the steps three at a time, which means he could have made it all the way to the top floor by now."

Merrick frowned. *Three* at a time? Not only had Zoshak not been injured, he'd been in a lot better shape than Merrick had guessed. "What do we do?"

"He seemed to be going for speed, not stealth," Jin said. "That implies distance, which implies a high floor. Let's start at the eighth and work downward."

They headed up, their servos allowing them to also take the steps three at a time. At the top, Jin listened briefly at the door, then opened it and slipped through. Merrick followed, and found himself in a long, light-blue corridor lined with numbered doors.

He keyed in his audio enhancers. Above the general background murmur that seemed to pervade any center of human activity, he could hear what sounded like two different nearby voices. They were too quiet for him to distinguish individual words, but there was no mistaking the underlying urgency. "Left side," Jin murmured. "Four or five doors down."

She headed off. Merrick keyed off his enhancers and followed.

They were within a few meters of the door when Merrick began to make out actual words. "—easy, Your Excellency," Zoshak was saying. He did not, Merrick noted a bit resentfully, sound even dazed, let alone seriously injured. "Lean on me—I can take your weight."

Jin glanced back at Merrick, crossed the last two steps to the doorway, and strode into the room. Merrick followed.

And came to a sharp halt beside his equally motionless mother. Across the room, standing beside an elaborate recovery bed, Zoshak had a supporting arm around an old, frail-looking man dressed in a hospital gown, a robe, and a pair of soft boots. Between the two of them and the door, facing the two Cobras, was another young man, his tunic partially open to reveal the same scaled gray outfit Merrick had seen on Zoshak.

Only this man was also wearing a matching set of gloves, and both hands were raised to point at the intruders, his little fingers extended, the other fingers curled back over his palms with his thumbs resting tautly against the ring-finger nails.

The same position a Cobra would use to fire his fingertip lasers.

Merrick felt his stomach tighten. What in the Worlds had he and his mother gotten themselves into?

"Step away, enemies of Qasama," the young man bit out, his eyes blazing defiance and anger and a complete absence of fear. "Step away, or die."

CHAPTER EIGHT

"Take it easy," Jin said, lifting her hands to show their emptiness, her heart and bad knee throbbing in unison as she stared at the positioning of the young man's hands. No—it wasn't possible. The Qasamans *couldn't* have created their own Cobras. Not from scratch, not even with the bodies of her former teammates to examine. This had to be some kind of bluff. "Just take it easy," she said again. "We're not your enemies."

"You are the demon warrior Jin Moreau," the other ground out. "You are here, and we have been invaded. What conclusion *should* we draw?"

"Those are *Troft* ships out there, not ours," Jin pointed out.

"From which we conclude that you and the Trofts are in league," the Qasaman countered.

"We're not in any sort of league," Jin said. "We trade with some of them, but that's all."

"And we don't even trade with this bunch," Merrick put in. "Their demesne markings aren't like any we've ever run into before."

The Qasaman spared a quick glare at Merrick, then turned his eyes back to Jin. "Then why are you here?"

Jin winced. This was going to sound incredibly lame. "I was invited."

"By whom?"

"I don't know," she had to admit. "I received a written but unsigned message urgently requesting my presence on Qasama."

"Most likely from Daulo Sammon," Zoshak spoke up, an edge of urgency in his voice. "Ifrit, we need to leave this place. If His Excellency is taken, this will all have been for nothing."

"There's no profit in escaping enemies who stand before us if other enemies stand at our back," the other Qasaman countered, his face hardening even further. "And liars are ever enemies."

"I'm not lying," Jin insisted as calmly as she could. There was a narrow tube running along the outer edge of the little finger of each of the Qasaman's gloves, she noted, the tubes extending all the way back to his wrists. Dart throwers with compressed-air propulsion, most likely, possibly modeled after the palm-mate gun Decker York had used during the Cobra Worlds' first Qasaman mission. That was probably what she and Merrick were facing, not Cobra-style fingertip lasers.

But why then was the Qasaman holding his hands that way? Had they deliberately adopted Cobra-style triggering for their dart guns? "And it wasn't Daulo Sammon who asked us here," she added.

"Someone else, then?" the Qasaman suggested, his voice carrying the subtle undertones of a hidden trap. "Someone else you might have met during your last intrusion onto Qasaman soil?"

Jin hesitated. It was a trap, all right. Only which way did it point? Would invoking Miron Akim's name help her or damn her? She had no idea what had happened to Akim in the past three decades, whether he had worked his way up the ladder or whether his brief and reluctant association with her had completely ruined his career.

But she had no choice. The Qasaman was angling for a name, and she had only one to offer him. "It's possible the invitation came from a former Shahni agent named Miron Akim," she said.

The Qasaman smiled tightly, and Jin could practically hear the sound of the trap snapping shut. "No, Jin Moreau, it didn't," he said. "Miron Akim did *not* invite you here."

"How do you know?" Merrick demanded. "*We* don't even know who sent the message. How could you?"

"Because, demon warrior," the Qasaman bit out, "I am Siraj Akim, *son* of Miron Akim."

Merrick felt his mouth drop open. "You're his—?"

And then, abruptly, something flashed past the room's window. "Watch it!" Jin snapped, dropping into a crouch.

"What was it?" Zoshak demanded. He, too, had dropped lower, bringing the old man down into a crouch alongside him. "I saw something go by the window."

"Some kind of aircraft," Jin said. "Looks like the Trofts have started a serious search of the hospital."

"And so now your mission is plain," Siraj accused coldly. "You led them here against us."

"It wasn't them, Ifrit," Zoshak said, his voice respectful but firm. "The attackers detected my communications with you and the Nest."

"That is claimed to be impossible," Siraj insisted.

"Let's figure out later how they did it," Jin said. "Right now, it's obvious you're trying to get this gentleman out of here before the Trofts find him. Merrick and I can get out of your way, or we can help you. Your choice."

Siraj snorted. "And why would you wish to help us?"

"In the name of God, Ifrit," Zoshak snapped. "We have no time for this. You have two options: kill them, or trust them." He looked at Merrick. "For myself, I trust them."

For perhaps five of Jin's accelerated heartbeats Siraj continued to stare at her. Then, to her relief, he slowly moved his thumbs away from the curled fingers and lowered his hands. "Very well," he said. "But we travel under *my* command."

"Absolutely," Jin assured him, feeling some of the tension drain out of her. The reprieve was only temporary—that much was obvious from his expression and tone. But at least they weren't going to have a firefight here and now. "What do you want us to do?"

Siraj gestured to Merrick. "You: help Djinni Zoshak."

Jin felt her eyebrows creeping up her forehead. *Djinni*, *Ifrit*—both names were echoes of ancient Earth Middle Eastern spirit mythos . . . and the Qasamans had always called Cobras *demon warriors*. Another coincidence, like the dart gun triggering?

"We might do better to lay him flat," Merrick suggested as he crossed to Zoshak's side.

"We can't," Zoshak said. "There's still residual healing fluid in his lungs, and his torso must be kept upright.

You and I will form a cross-seat, our hands interlocking with each other's wrists to form a square."

"Yes, I know that one," Merrick said. "But we really don't need both of us. I can carry him by myself, which would free you up in case there was trouble."

"You will both carry him," Siraj ordered before Zoshak could answer. "We travel toward the rear stairway, at the end of the hall most distant from the lobby. You—Jin Moreau—see if the corridor is clear."

Jin nodded and turned back to the room's doorway, the skin between her shoulder blades crawling with unpleasant anticipation. If Siraj meant to kill her, now was his best chance to try it.

But nothing came poking or stabbing or burning into her back, and she reached the hallway to find it still deserted. "Clear," she called softly, looking both ways and then stepping out into the center of the passageway.

The others stepped out of the room to join her, Siraj first, then Merrick and Zoshak with the old man sitting on their intermeshed forearms, his arms draped loosely over the younger men's shoulders. The soft plastic water bottle that had been sitting on the table beside the bed, Jin saw, was now resting in the old man's lap. "Rear door, you said?" she murmured.

"Yes," Siraj said. "You have spearhead."

Spearhead? Probably their term for *point*, Jin decided. With a nod, she set off down the corridor, her audio enhancers searching for sounds of movement ahead.

"Where *is* everyone?" Merrick asked softly from behind her. "The Trofts didn't put the whole staff downstairs, did they?"

"The doctors and attendants on this floor have taken shelter in the various patient rooms," Siraj said as he came up beside her. "I ordered them there when I first arrived." He gave a short, low hiss. "If I'd known how quickly the invaders would focus on this place and the Palace, I would have risked bringing him out alone."

"So His Excellency is one of the Shahni?" Jin asked.

Siraj darted her a dark sideways look. "His identity is none of your concern," he said stiffly.

"No, of course not," Jin agreed. "My apologies."

For another two steps they traveled in silence. "I am told the other demon warrior is your son," Siraj said.

"Yes," Jin told him, wondering how he'd known that. "My eldest."

Siraj grunted and again fell silent.

They were halfway to the brightly-lit EXIT sign at the far end of the hallway when Jin's enhancers picked up the faint sound of hurrying footsteps ahead of them. "Someone's on the stairs," she warned, stepping sideways to the nearest door and trying the knob. It was locked; with a boost of strength from her wrist servos, she snapped it open. "In here," she said, swinging the door wide.

"No," Siraj said, motioning her back to the center of the corridor. "We meet them here."

"I meant that Merrick and Carsh Zoshak can go in there while you and I—"

"We meet them here," Siraj repeated tartly. "All of us together."

With a supreme effort, Jin kept her mouth shut. Didn't Siraj see that facing an enemy with half his force burdened with an invalid was a stupid thing to do? Even worse, with one of his two available *Cobras* burdened that way?

But she couldn't say anything. Not a woman. Not in this society.

But Zoshak could. Jin opened her mouth to suggest he do just that—

The door ahead slammed open, and five armed Trofts boiled into the corridor. They'd been closer than Jin had realized. "Stop!" the leader's translator pin barked.

Siraj motioned, and the group of humans came to a halt. "Is that all they can say?" Merrick muttered.

"What now?" Jin asked quietly as the Trofts strode toward them, sorting themselves into the by-now-familiar wedge formation.

"Follow my action," Siraj murmured back. "And do not reveal your true nature."

Jin shot him a frown. Beneath the other's cold eyes, a hint of a grim smile was tugging at the corners of his mouth.

And suddenly she understood. The old man being carried by two of their number, the whole group being caught in the middle of an open hallway—it wasn't simply stupidity or carelessness. Siraj had deliberately staged the scene in order to lower the Trofts' expectations and therefore their guard.

It was a good and subtle plan, and now that she knew about it Jin could appreciate the tactic. Nevertheless, as the Trofts approached, she took a moment to put targeting locks onto each of the aliens' foreheads behind their transparent faceplates. Whenever she next fired her fingertip lasers, her servos would move her arms and hands to make sure those targets would be the first ones hit.

There wasn't much point in looking harmless, after all, if it ended up getting you killed.

The lead Troft put a finger over his translator pin as he walked, and Jin notched up her audio enhancers. [Five humans, we have them on the eighth floor west,] she heard the murmured cattertalk over the relative thunder of the aliens' footsteps. [Weapons, none are visible.]

"Take his weight," Zoshak murmured to Merrick.

The lead Troft acknowledged something Jin couldn't hear and lowered his hand from his translator. Taking the cue, Jin also lowered her audio enhancement. "Where do you take the old human?" the Troft asked as he and his squad stopped two meters in front of Siraj.

"To a treatment room," Siraj said, pointing toward one of the doors the Trofts had just passed. "That one, right there."

The two Trofts in the rear turned to look where he was pointing. As they did so, Siraj abruptly leaped forward, grabbed the lead Troft's laser, and twisted it effortlessly out of the alien's grip. [Soldiers—!] the Troft yelped, his outburst cut off as Siraj slammed the laser's butt hard against the side of his helmet.

Jin sprinted toward her side of the wedge as the stunned Troft collapsed to the floor. The other soldiers were already in motion, two of them swinging their lasers toward Siraj, the other two lining up their weapons on Jin. Jin dodged sideways out of their line of fire, hoping to draw the muzzles far enough away from the old man that when she fired her fingertip lasers there would be no chance that any of the aliens would get off a dying shot in that direction.

Something caught the corner of her eye as it shot past over her shoulder from behind her. It was the old man's water bottle, arrowing toward the two Trofts on her side of the wedge and sending the aliens reflexively jerking back from the incoming missile.

And as they did, Siraj fired a casual-looking sideways burst from his captured laser that sliced the bottle open and flash-heated the water just as it splashed across the Trofts' faces.

Their faceplates protected them from any actual injury, of course. But the simple fact of having liquid splashed violently and unexpectedly in front of their eyes distracted them for a fatal half second. One of them managed to get off a shot, the burst going wild.

And then Jin was there, ripping open the first Troft's faceplate and throwing a servo-powered punch into his throat bladder. Snatching the laser from his suddenly limp grasp, she hurled it sideways it at the farther of the two Trofts on Siraj's side, hoping to take him out or at least distract him as Siraj waded into his own battle. Another pulled faceplate and punch finished off her second opponent, and she turned to help Siraj, her hands curling into laser-firing position.

Her help wasn't necessary. Jin's two Trofts had barely thudded to the floor when Siraj's pair joined them.

"My father was right, Jin Moreau," Siraj commented as he tossed his captured laser disdainfully onto the body of the nearest Troft. "You are indeed a capable fighter." Half turning, he motioned to Zoshak. "Quickly, now."

The group resumed its journey down the hallway. "I trust you're not expecting to push the innocent routine any farther," Jin warned. "You can bet there are already backup troops on the way."

"They are welcome to the exercise," Siraj said coolly as he came to a halt well short of the stairway door. "Djinni Zoshak?"

Jin blinked as Zoshak brushed past her and pulled open a half-meter-wide panel set into the wall, a panel labeled *Laundry*. "You're kidding," she said.

Neither Qasaman bothered to answer. Zoshak climbed feet-first into the shaft, maneuvering himself all the way to the rear and turning to face the others, sliding down until only his head and upper chest were visible. "Ready," he said, holding out his arms.

"Mom?" Merrick asked uncertainly.

Jin peered at the shaft. It was considerably deeper, front to back, than it was wide, which left plenty of room in front of Zoshak for a second person to join him. But that didn't make the idea any less lunatic.

But by now, all other exits from the floor were undoubtedly blocked. "Go ahead," she told Merrick. "They seem to know what they're doing."

Still looking doubtful, Merrick eased the old man's legs through the opening. Siraj moved in to assist, and together they worked their burden into Zoshak's waiting arms. Gripping the old man firmly around his chest and waist, Zoshak began a rapid but clearly controlled slide downwards. "You next, Jin Moreau," Siraj said, nodding toward the shaft. "Use the pressure of your feet against the sides to control your descent." His eyes narrowed. "Do *not* lose control and fall."

"I won't," Jin promised as she climbed into the shaft. It felt narrower than it looked, and she sent up a quick note of thanks that she wasn't claustrophobic.

Unfortunately, she quickly discovered that her servos hadn't been designed with this sort of maneuver in mind, and that her own leg muscles weren't nearly strong enough on their own to apply the pressure needed to control her descent. Fortunately, some of her upper-body servos *did* work in the proper direction, and pressing her elbows and upper arms against the sides of the shaft did the trick.

She'd made it a couple of meters down when the shaft darkened as Merrick came in above her. There was a moment of soft scraping as he figured out the necessary technique, and then silence as he joined her and Zoshak in their mass slide. Another few meters, and the shaft went completely dark as Siraj brought up the rear, closing the flap behind him.

A minute later, they reached the bottom of the shaft and a bin half full of white sheets. Jin held position until Zoshak had extricated himself and the old man from the bin, then followed.

She found herself in an institutional laundry facility of the sort she'd seen a hundred times in thrillers and comedies. This was the first time she'd ever actually been in one, though, and she found her nose crinkling at the crisply intense smells pervading the place. "What now?" she asked when Merrick and Siraj had joined them.

"That is your decision," Siraj said, eyeing her coolly. "You may leave now, and we shall most likely not meet again. Or you may come with us and ensure that His Excellency arrives safely at his destination."

Jin snorted. Her and Merrick, alone in hostile territory, with an even more hostile enemy having just invaded? "Not much of a choice there, Siraj Akim," she said. "We're with you. How exactly do we get His Excellency out?"

"There is a secret exit from this level that we can use." A ghost of a smile flickered across Siraj's face. "We have been preparing for war for many years, Jin Moreau."

"Only you've been expecting the wrong opponents," Jin pointed out.

"Perhaps," Siraj said, his voice neutral. "You will again take spearhead—" he looked at Merrick "—and you will carry His Excellency." He started toward the laundry room door.

"Wait a minute," Jin said with a surge of sudden guilt. In the excitement of the past few minutes, she'd completely forgotten about Daulo and Fadil. "We first have to go get our friends."

"No," Siraj said flatly. "We must go now."

Jin braced herself. "I understand," she said. "Merrick, you go with them."

Merrick's jaw dropped. "*What*? Mom—"

"Help them get him to safety," she cut him off, working hard to filter her apprehension out of her voice. "I'll catch up with you later."

"Mom, this is *crazy*," he growled.

"You want me to just leave Daulo and Fadil to the Trofts?" Jin countered.

Merrick clamped his mouth shut. "Of course not. Fine—I'll come with you."

Jin looked at Siraj. There was a watchful look in his eye, the same look she'd seen there earlier when he'd asked who else she knew on Qasama. "No," she said. "I can get Daulo and Fadil out myself. You help Siraj Akim and Carsh Zoshak."

"But—"

"They're our allies now," Jin said firmly. "This is war, Merrick. Follow your orders."

He took a deep breath. "Where do we meet?"

"Two blocks south of the gate where we came in," she said. "Show yourself for two minutes at fifteen and forty after each hour until we make contact."

He nodded, still clearly unhappy with the arrangement but knowing it was useless to argue further. "Good luck," he said.

"God be with you," Zoshak added.

"Thank you." Jin nodded to Siraj. "And with you." She turned toward the door.

"Wait," Siraj said; and to Jin's surprise he stepped to her side. "I will accompany you."

"I appreciate your offer, Siraj Akim," Jin said, frowning at him. "But I thought we just decided it would be safer if His Excellency had a three-man escort."

"Djinni Zoshak knows the route," Siraj said. "He and your son can follow it without significant danger." He smiled humorlessly. "Allow me to put it more bluntly: I trust them with His Excellency more than I trust you alone in Sollas."

Jin suppressed a grimace. So much for being allies. "As you wish," she said. "Merrick, I'll see you later."

The hallway outside the laundry room was deserted. Zoshak turned to the right; with a final nod at his mother, Merrick followed, the old man balanced across his forearms. "Stairs are this way," Siraj said, pointing to the left.

"Just a second," Jin said as a rack of freshly washed white medical coats caught her eye. "A little camouflage might not be a bad idea."

They each took a coat and slipped it on. "You might want to take off those gloves, too," Jin added. "They don't exactly look hospital-issue."

"This will do," Siraj said, taking three more coats and folding them into a bundle that would hide his hands. "Take spearhead."

Jin's enhanced hearing was picking up sounds of hurrying feet and rapid cattertalk well before she and Siraj reached the top of the stairs. It was thus no surprise when she stepped out into the corridor to find it full of Trofts. Two of them stopped abruptly at the sight of the humans, leveling their lasers as one of them moved his beak in inaudible cattertalk. "What are you doing here?" the Qasaman translation came.

"Don't shoot," Siraj gasped, his eyes wide, his face taut with astonishment and fear. Whatever else the man might be, he was a competent actor. "My name is Rajeem Tommarno. Lanara Summel and I are laboratory technicians. We were asked to bring some spare coats to the doctor's station on this floor."

"Why?" the Troft asked.

"I don't know," Siraj said. "Three coats—that was all they said."

For a moment the Troft eyed him. Then, taking one hand from his laser, he gestured Siraj over. Siraj hesitated, then stepped gingerly up to him and held out his bundle for inspection. The Troft pawed systematically through the coats, clearly searching for anything that might be hidden inside the folds of cloth. Finding nothing, he stepped back, shifting his laser back into a two-handed grip "This soldier will take you," he said. "You will stay there until other notice is given."

"Yes, of course," Siraj assured him, backing hastily away. The other Troft took a step down the corridor and paused expectantly. "Yes, of course," Siraj said again, and started off. Jin joined him, the Troft soldier falling into step a cautious couple of paces behind them.

"They seem upset," Siraj murmured to Jin.

Jin grimaced. Twenty Trofts in this corridor alone, plus who knew how many dozens more elsewhere in the hospital. "Having their soldiers beaten into the sand does that to military types," she murmured back. "I guess I should have insisted you get out with the others while you could. This isn't going to be easy."

"It may turn out to be not quite the challenge you believe," Siraj said calmly. "In here."

He led the way under an archway into what appeared to be a patient receiving and processing area. The alcove was deserted except for a pair of Trofts flanking a door at the rear of the area. Jin eyed the various desks and computer stations as they maneuvered their way through, noting that the chairs were all facing different directions, without a single one being tucked neatly beneath its desk. When everyone had left, they'd left in a hurry.

"Go to the door in the rear," the Troft behind them ordered.

The two guards eyed the group as they approached. One of them started to speak, and Jin notched up her audio enhancers. [These humans, why are they here?] the guard demanded.

[The two civilians inside, to them they bring disguises,] the Troft behind Jin said. [The enemy combatants we seek, perhaps these are the ones.]

The door guards' expressions went a little harder. [Yet these disguises, they bring *three* of them,] the spokesman pointed out.

[An additional and unknown enemy, such may lurk nearby,] the escort agreed. [Watchfulness, we will maintain it.]

[The humans, we will watch them closely,] the guard assured the escort grimly.

The Troft behind Siraj nudged the Qasaman with the muzzle of his laser. [The door, go through it.] "Go inside."

"Yes, of course," Siraj said. He reached the door, pushed it open with his forearm, and went through. Jin followed, once again lowering her enhancers.

The room beyond the door was a lounge of sorts, with computer monitors scattered among the couches and cushions to allow the doctors and staffers to keep an eye on what was happening with their patients. There were about a dozen men and women in the room, some pacing nervously, the rest sitting alone or in quietly conversing pairs. Flanking the inside of the door were another pair of watchful Troft soldiers.

And seated on a couch at the rear of the room, painfully conspicuous in their non-medical garb, were Daulo and Fadil.

Siraj nudged Jin to their right, away from the door. "I will take Daulo Sammon the coats," he said. "As the soldiers watch me, you will move behind you to the fire alarm."

"*If* they watch you," Jin warned, glancing casually over her shoulder at the Trofts. Out of the corner of her eye she spotted the alarm Siraj had mentioned: a small red plate set into the wall with a thumb-sized lever set into it.

"They will," Siraj assured her. "There are two civilians, yet I have *three* coats. They will watch closely to see what I do with the third."

"If you say so," Jin said frowning. Either Siraj was making a monumental leap of logic, or else he'd eavesdropped on the conversation outside and understood enough cattertalk to know the Trofts were already thinking in that direction. "When do you want me to set off the alarm?"

"You do not set off the alarm," Siraj said. "The alarm is activated by pushing the lever downward. You will, instead, push the lever in—it will resist, so push firmly—and once it is in you will pull it *upward*."

"Which will do what?"

"It will help us," Siraj said. "Go now."

Jin looked around the room, pretended to notice someone she recognized and started over toward him.

Halfway there, she pretended she'd changed her mind and drifted instead to the side, coming to a halt a pace away from the wall and the fire alarm. Siraj had meanwhile crossed to Daulo and Fadil and was whispering urgently to them. From the two villagers' expressions, it was clear they had no idea who this man was and weren't particularly happy at having extra attention being drawn their way. *So far, so good,* Jin thought, and looked over at the two Trofts by the door.

To find that Siraj's plan had worked exactly halfway. One of the Trofts was indeed thoroughly engrossed in Siraj's inaudible conversation. Unfortunately, the other was gazing just as intently at Jin.

She shifted her attention back to Siraj. He was gazing sideways at her, his eyebrows cocked in silent question. She gave him a tiny shrug, followed by an equally microscopic tilt of her head toward the Trofts. Siraj inclined his head slightly in reply and turned back to Daulo. There was another short conversation, and this time it was Daulo who looked a question at Jin. She gave him a small nod, wondering uneasily what Siraj's new plan was and what the Trofts were thinking about all this. She was hardly an expert on alien body language, but she'd seen enough annoyed Trofts to have the unpleasant feeling that the one focused on her was looking for an excuse to shoot something.

Across the room, the quiet conversation ceased and Daulo and Fadil stood up. Siraj handed a lab coat to each of them, and the two villagers headed toward opposite rear corners of the room.

And with that, the two Trofts now had *four* humans they needed to keep a close eye on. Jin held her breath, waiting for her personal watchdog to shift some of his attention to one of the others. Half a second's worth of inattention, maybe less, and she would be able to get to the fire alarm without being shot.

She was still waiting for that half-second window when the door opened and the two Trofts who'd been standing guard outside strode in.

Jin grimaced. So much for that approach.

So much, too, she decided suddenly, for letting Siraj call the shots here. The Trofts were probably still a little off-balance after the brief battle upstairs, but that confusion wouldn't last long. She and the others had to get out of here before the invaders got their balance back. Focusing on each of the Trofts in turn, she set up targeting locks on their heads, starting with the one watching her. It was risky—if her watchdog decided she was making suspicious movements he could probably get off a shot before she could take him down. But if she didn't do something—

And then, Siraj raised his hands and pointed both of them at Jin. "Now!" he shouted.

Jin froze in disbelief as all four of the Trofts spun around, their lasers tracking toward her. With that single barked word, Siraj had just quadrupled the odds she was already facing. Was he *trying* to get her killed?

Maybe he was. Maybe that was why he'd insisted on accompanying her up here in the first place.

And then, to Jin's astonishment, all four lasers changed direction in midtrack as the Trofts turned their attention back to Siraj.

All of the Trofts, including Jin's own guard.

Jin didn't waste time wondering why they would do something so foolish. Stepping to the wall, she pushed in the lever and pulled it up.

Nothing happened.

For a fraction of a second she just stood there, staring at the alarm. She'd expected something instantly lethal or at least instantly dramatic: targeted lasers or machine guns, flash-bang grenades, or at least stun-strobe lights. But nothing.

Nothing, that is, except that her sudden movement hadn't gone unnoticed. The four Troft lasers changed direction again in midturn, this time tracking back toward Jin. She turned toward them, bringing up her own hands, consciously relaxing her muscles to let her nanocomputer and its programmed evasion reflexes take over the instant it became necessary.

Her hands were halfway to firing position, and the first Troft's laser was nearly lined up on her torso, when a pair of brilliant blue flashes lanced out from Siraj's hands and blew off the side of one of the other Trofts' helmets.

Jin fired her own lasers even as she turned to look more closely at Siraj's hands. So those slender tubes, which she'd earlier pegged as dart guns, were in fact real Cobra-style lasers.

But there was no time to consider the ramifications of that now. She turned back to her own target.

To find to her dismay that his laser was now pointed directly at her chest.

Unlike Siraj's lasers, hers hadn't even penetrated the Troft's helmet.

Reflexively, she fired again, cursing under her breath as her arms swung of their own accord to send another ineffective shot at the second Troft she'd targeted instead of the Troft she really wanted to shoot at. She threw herself to the side, canceling the rest of the targeting locks as she did so.

The Troft in front of her fired, the shot burning past her shoulder. Desperately, she flashed a new targeting lock on him, slamming to the floor just as Siraj took out another of the aliens with a second pair of shots. Wincing as the jolt of her landing drove spikes of pain through her arthritic joints, she fired her antiarmor laser, her nanocomputer wrenching her joints still further as it twisted her body around to bring her left leg to bear on the designated target. She half closed her eyes, watching the Troft swinging his own weapon toward her, wondering who would win the race.

She did, but just barely. This time, her more powerful antiarmor laser blasted with gratifying speed though the armor her fingertip lasers had failed to penetrate. She targeted the last remaining Troft as the first collapsed to the floor, firing again as her swinging leg continued its arc.

Her shot and Siraj's got there at the same time. The alien went down, his head effectively vaporized.

Jin rolled back to her feet, her joints still throbbing from her barely controlled fall. Siraj's hands, she noted uneasily as she straightened up, were still curled in firing positions, his face unreadable as he gazed across the room at her. "Nice job," she said as conversationally as she could into the room's sudden deathly silence. "What now?"

For a moment Siraj didn't move or speak, his hands still ready, his little fingers not quite pointed at Jin. Perhaps wondering if this was the chance he'd been waiting for to deal with this other enemy of his world. Jin stood equally motionless, her heart pounding, keeping her own thumbs away from her fingernails . . .

And then, to her relief, Siraj lowered his hands to his sides. "Check the corridor," he said, his voice brisk and businesslike as he started across the room, gesturing to Daulo and Fadil to join them. "Confirm that it's safe."

Safe? Frowning, Jin stepped to the door and cautiously pushed it open.

And felt her jaw drop. Three humans and five Trofts were visible out in the corridor, lying in crumpled heaps. "What in the—?" She broke off, throwing a stunned look at Siraj. "Did I just—?"

"They are merely asleep," Siraj assured her as he and the two Sammons joined her. "A quick-acting gas, released into every part of the hospital except the room where the system is activated."

"Nice," Jin managed, feeling a whisper of relief. Relief, and a little embarrassment that she'd automatically assumed the worst. Surely even the Qasamans wouldn't indiscriminately slaughter this many of their own people without absolute need.

"But the reprieve is only temporary," Siraj warned, sweeping his gaze around the rest of the room. "You—return to your homes, or seek shelter in those of friends. Go now. In the name of the Shahni."

The staffers glanced at one another. Then, without question or protest, they made their way calmly to the door. Siraj stepped aside, motioning Jin and the Sammons to do likewise, as the staffers filed though the doorway and disappeared in both directions down the corridor. "You realize, of course, that the Trofts outside will see them," Jin said quietly.

"And may stop them for questioning," Siraj agreed as he started across the receiving area. "They will say nothing."

"What if the Trofts insist?"

"That will take time," Siraj said. "At this point, time works to our advantage."

Even at the possible cost of their lives? With an effort, Jin kept her mouth shut. Maybe her earlier assumption about the lengths the Qasamans would go to hadn't been all that far off the mark. "Where are we going?" she asked instead.

"We follow Carsh Zoshak," Siraj said. "Daulo Sammon, you and your son stay close behind me." He hesitated, just noticeably. "You, Jin Moreau, will guard our back path."

He headed off at a brisk stride toward the stairway. Daulo threw Jin an unreadable look, then turned back and concentrated on keeping up with Siraj. Fadil, for his part, seemed intent on pretending Jin didn't exist.

The exit from the laundry room level was hidden behind a tool rack near the end of the hallway. The small landing behind the door was only dimly lit, but with her optical enhancers Jin could see there were three or four floors' worth of narrow switchback stairways leading down into the gloom. What was at the bottom of the stairs she never found out; midway down the second flight, Siraj opened a hidden door in the side wall and led the group into another dimly lit tunnel heading off at right angles to the first.

The road didn't end there, either. There was a whole warren of tunnels beneath the city, with a bewildering array of cross-tunnels, stairways, descending ramps, and occasional booby traps that Siraj carefully deactivated and then reactivated once they were past. Several times Jin considered asking where exactly they were going, but each time decided there was no point. Even if Siraj was willing to tell her, the name or location would probably be meaningless to her anyway.

The trip seemed to take forever, but according to Jin's nanocomputer clock they were in the tunnels for only seventeen minutes before Siraj opened a final door and led the way into a well-lit room whose only furnishings were a pair of Qasamans seated behind transparent body shields and armed with nasty-looking machine guns. Siraj exchanged a set of countersigns with them, then led the way past to one of three doors leading off the room.

"What is this place?" Daulo asked as they walked down another corridor.

"A refuge prepared against the onslaught of war," Siraj told him. "There are many such as this beneath the cities and larger villages. In here."

He opened one of the doors and gestured the others inside. Jin stepped through the doorway.

And came to an abrupt halt. Five other Qasamans were standing silently along the walls of the room, all of them wearing identical grim expressions above their scaled gray bodysuits.

Seated in a wooden chair in the center of the room, his hands manacled behind him, his ankles similarly fastened to the chair legs, was Merrick.

"What in the *Worlds*?" Jin bit out, her eyes flicking around the room. "Siraj Akim, what is the meaning of this?"

Siraj remained silent. So did the other Qasamans. "Merrick?" Jin asked, looking at her son.

"You know that old gag, Mom?" Merrick asked, his voice taut. "The one that goes, 'I could tell you, but then I'd have to kill you'?" His lip twitched. "I think our hosts may be taking that seriously."

CHAPTER NINE

Jin looked around the room, her pulse once again pounding. The five gray-suited Qasamans were standing casually enough, with their arms hanging loosely at their sides. But all five were wearing the same laser-equipped gloves as Siraj, and all five had their fingers curled almost into firing position. All they needed to do was twist at their wrists and squeeze their fingernails, and she and Merrick would be in the center of a kill zone. "All right," she said as calmly as she could. "You've made your point."

"What point would that be, Jin Moreau?" Siraj asked.

"You didn't bring us all the way here just to kill us," Jin said. "You could have done that anywhere along the way."

"What, with you standing behind me?" Siraj countered. "That would have been difficult."

"The marching order was your choice," Jin reminded him. "You could have put me in front of you at any point. Certainly long enough to dispose of me."

Siraj's lip twitched. "We may yet do that."

"Why?" Jin asked. "What have we done against you or the Qasaman people?"

"You are a demon warrior," a new voice said from behind her.

Jin turned to see a gray-haired man enter the room through another door. His face was lined, his walk the careful gait of someone with sensitive bones. Probably somewhere between eighty and eighty-five years old, she estimated. "Yes, my identity's been established," she said. "And you are . . . ?"

He smiled tightly. "Come now, Jin Moreau," he admonished. "Have the years been so unkind to me?"

Jin blinked. The years had, actually—the man looked to be a good thirty years older than she was, and she still couldn't reconcile his face with her memories. But his *voice*—"Miron *Akim*?" she asked.

"Of course," he said. His smile faded away. "Why else do you think you and your son are not already dead?"

Jin took a careful breath. "I received a note," she said. "I assumed—"

"Yes, I've heard of your story." The elder Akim held out his hand. "Show me."

Jin reached inside her tunic, noting the extra wariness of the gray-suited guards as she did so. "It was delivered to my home on Aventine," she said, pulling out the paper and handing it over.

Akim took the note and studied it briefly. "Convenient," he said, handing it back. "Also conveniently unsigned." His gaze hardened a little more. "Why are you here?"

"I've already told you," Jin said. "The answer isn't going to change just because you keep asking."

"No, I suppose it won't." Akim eyed her thoughtfully. "My people don't trust you, Jin Moreau. My own son doesn't trust you. Why should I let you live? You *or* your son?"

Jin took a careful breath. His people and his son didn't trust them . . . but Akim had rather conspicuously left his own name off that list. Maybe there was still enough doubt in his mind for her to talk their way out of this. "Because you've just been invaded," she told him, "and because you need all the assets you can get. Merrick and I can be two of those assets."

"Or you could be two more of our invaders," Siraj put in.

"We just helped you rescue someone out from under the Trofts' noses," Jin reminded him. "Why would we do that if we were allied with them?"

"Perhaps in order to infiltrate this facility," Akim said, gesturing at the room around him.

"Oh, please," Jin said scornfully. "You would hardly have brought four strangers to a place you genuinely wanted kept secret. This can't be anything more important than a minor staging area."

"Perhaps you hoped we would take you deeper," Siraj said.

"Knowing how you feel about us?" Jin asked. "Now you accuse us of being not only enemies, but *stupid* enemies."

"Or very clever enemies," Akim said. "What would *you* do in our place?"

Jin studied his face. But it was giving nothing away. "I'd try to find a way to split the difference," she said.

"You don't trust us, and I can't think of any way we can prove we're genuinely on your side."

She looked at Siraj. "And to be honest, I can't blame you for that attitude," she conceded. "Not after the mistakes our people have made with yours."

" 'Mistakes'?" Siraj bit out. "Is that what you call them?"

"Call them whatever you want," Jin said, turning back to Akim. "So as I say, let's split the difference. You take Merrick and me back up to street level, and you'll never have to see us again."

"Where would you go?" Akim asked. "Back to Milika with Daulo Sammon and his son?"

Jin looked at Daulo. His face was just as wooden as Akim's. "No," she said. "Not even if Milika was willing to accept us. A Cobra's greatest strength is subterfuge, and for that we need a population base large enough for us to blend in. No, our war against the Trofts will be much more effective here in Sollas."

"*Your* war?" Akim asked.

"You are our people, Miron Akim," Jin said. "Whatever our differences in the past, you're part of humanity. We aren't going to sit by and let some group of Trofts think they can pull off a stunt like this."

"And so you propose to challenge the invaders to single combat?" Akim asked. "How long do you think you would survive against a force this size?"

"I don't know," Jin admitted. "But I think we might all be surprised."

"Perhaps," Akim said. "But the question is moot. We cannot allow you to rampage through Sollas under no authority but your own."

"Then let us fight with you," Jin offered.

"Not without proof of your loyalty," Siraj interjected.

Akim inclined his head. "Unfortunately, my son is right. We seem thus to have arrived at an impasse."

"What if we could prove you can trust us?" Merrick spoke up.

"How do you propose to do that?" Akim asked.

"You've had me in this chair for over half an hour," Merrick said. "My mother's also been here for several minutes now, and you've spent most of those minutes threatening our lives. If we're on the Trofts' side, why haven't we taken out the whole bunch of you and escaped?"

Siraj snorted. "Against six Djinn? You boast overmuch of your strength, demon warrior."

"It's not boasting if you can do it," Merrick countered. "And you've never seen a Cobra in action before."

"*I* have," Akim said. "And you *are* boasting, Merrick Moreau. I know all of your weaponry, and where those weapons lie hidden within your body. With your ankles manacled to the chair, and your hands fastened behind you with your thumbs blocked from your fingers, you are indeed helpless."

"You boast in turn of your own cleverness, Miron Akim," Merrick said calmly. "Do you really think it's this easy to restrain a Cobra?"

Jin winced. This was not a good direction to be taking this conversation. "Merrick—"

"Quiet, Mother," Merrick cut her off, his gaze steady on Akim. "How about it, Miron Akim? My mother spoke of us being an asset to you. Shouldn't you at least see what Cobras are capable of before you decide whether or not to throw us away?"

Akim folded his arms across his chest, one thumb stroking thoughtfully across his lip. "An interesting challenge, demon warrior," he said. "What exactly do you propose?"

"Before your men can get their hands into firing position, I'll be out of this chair," Merrick told him. "I'll have my own hands pointed at the ceiling, as proof I intend no harm against any of you."

"You court serious danger," Akim warned. "What if my Djinn are faster than you realize?"

"I'm willing to take that risk," Merrick said. "At the very least, we'll find out what kind of soldiers they are. Do we have a deal?"

Akim cocked an eyebrow. "Very well," he said. "Djinn, arms at your sides. Let us make this a fair competi—"

Right in the middle of the word, Jin was rocked backward as a terrific blast from Merrick's sonic disruptor hammered through the room.

Even knowing that would be Merrick's first move, she was still nearly knocked off her feet. The Qasamans, taken completely by surprise, had it far worse. They staggered backward, grabbing for sections of wall or each other as they tried to keep their feet under them.

The blast was still reverberating when, in the center of the chaos, Merrick straightened convulsively in his chair, his back arching, his legs snapping upward against the shackles binding his ankles to the chair legs. For maybe half a second nothing happened; and then, with a multiple snap of breaking wood, the chair shattered beneath him, dropping him onto his back on the floor.

He rolled over the wreckage onto his stomach, and Jin got her first clear look at his shackles. They were like regular wrist cuffs, except that the chain connecting the loops had been replaced with a thick metal bar. There was also some kind of flange stretching up from each cuff across his palm, blocking his fingers and preventing him from bringing his hands into firing position.

But Merrick didn't even bother trying to bring his fingertip lasers into play. Stretching his arms as far away from his back as he could, he bent his left leg tightly at the knee and fired a blast from his antiarmor laser that vaporized the center of the bar. Pushing off the floor with his now freed hands, he leaped to his feet.

Someone across the room spat something, and Jin saw that one of the Djinn had gotten his balance back and was swinging his arms up into firing position. Merrick glanced over his shoulder at a spot on the ceiling behind him, bent his knees, and jumped. There was a blur of motion punctuated by two rapid-fire thumps as his nanocomputer executed a standard Cobra ceiling flip, first turning him halfway over to hit the ceiling feet first, then turning him another hundred eighty degrees to land upright on the floor.

And an instant later Merrick was standing behind Akim, his arms raised in the air. "Done," he called.

The Djinni ignored him. Still weaving with the aftereffects of the sonic, he brought his hands up in front of his chest. Squinting furiously, he cocked his thumbs against his ring finger nails.

"Hold!" Akim snapped. He looked a little unsteady himself, but his voice was rock-hard. "Djinni Ghushtre, stand down."

For a long moment Jin thought the younger man was going to ignore the order. He held his posture, his expression thunderous as he glared at Merrick. Merrick himself didn't move, his hands still pointed harmlessly upward, his body half shielded behind Akim.

"You heard Miron Akim," Siraj said into the brittle silence. "Stand down."

Slowly, reluctantly, Ghushtre lowered his hands. "That was not fair," he growled. "He cheated."

"Do you expect an enemy to play by rules of your choosing?" Akim countered. "Do you count on him to inform you of his plans before launching them?"

"This was not to be combat, but a test," Ghushtre insisted. "Tests *do* have rules, and you had not finished stating them."

"Then *I* am the offended one, not you," Akim said, his voice hardening. "And I choose to take a larger view than my own honor and pride."

Ghushtre snorted. "What can be higher than honor?"

Akim looked him squarely in the eye. "What is higher than honor," he said quietly, "is victory."

He turned to Jin. "Come, Jin Moreau," he said, gesturing toward the door he'd come in through. "You and your son. We need to speak."

The room Akim took them to was the size of a mid-rank Aventinian politician's office, only with a much smaller desk and six chairs facing it rather than the standard two that Jin was used to. There were no pictures or framics on the walls, either, the only decoration being two rows of video monitors, all currently blank. Possibly some kind of ready room, Jin decided as she followed Akim toward the desk. Maybe they were deeper into the Qasamans' secret labyrinth than she'd thought.

"Please; sit down," Akim said, gesturing to the row of chairs. He circled the desk and sat down behind it. "May I call for some refreshment?"

"No, thank you," Jin said, frowning at him. The cold, distrustful Qasaman from the other room had suddenly become calmer, even marginally friendly. *Who are you,* the old half joke ran fleetingly through her mind, *and what have you done with the real Miron Akim?* "You said we needed to speak?"

"If you truly wish to assist us, yes." Akim hesitated. "I should first apologize for our behavior out there." His lip twitched. "For *my* behavior out there."

"Not a problem," Merrick assured him. "We understand you had to play to your audience."

"Who, the other Djinn?" Jin asked, frowning. "I thought you were in charge of them."

"I was referring to the private audience," Merrick told her. "The ones watching on the hidden cameras."

Jin blinked. "There were *cameras* in the room?"

"Of course," Merrick said, as if it was too obvious even to mention. "Middle of the wall to my left and somewhere behind you. Probably the doorjamb."

"So the cameras weren't as undetectable as I was promised," Akim commented thoughtfully. "Interesting."

"Oh, I didn't actually see them," Merrick said. "But when one's host glances at a couple of blank sections of wall two or three times in the same conversation, it's obvious what's going on." He raised his eyebrows. "From which I gather escaping from my cuffs really *was* a test?"

"Very good," Akim said with a wry smile. "You are indeed your mother's son."

Jin felt her cheeks warming. No, Merrick was his *father's* son on this one—quiet, calm, and with Paul's eye for detail. Jin herself, in contrast, seemed to have lost whatever limited combat sense she'd once had. She'd better get with the program, and fast.

"Yes, it was indeed a test," Akim continued. "Not for my benefit, as you've already surmised—I know perfectly well what you demon warriors are capable of."

"Cobras," Merrick corrected him mildly.

Akim inclined his head. "What you Cobras are capable of," he said. "But the Shahni had to be convinced of your abilities." He grimaced. "Convincing them that you're worthy of trust is another matter."

"Wait a minute," Jin said, fighting to get her brain back on line. Why was it so hard to think tactically anymore? "It was the *Shahni* who were watching? I thought the Trofts had them trapped in the Palace."

"What, with this whole rabbit warren underneath the city?" Merrick countered. "I doubt they set it up just so people could sneak out of hospital laundry rooms."

"In theory, you're correct," Akim said. "In practice . . . your mother has always thought of us as being paranoid, Merrick Moreau. Unfortunately, when the test came, we weren't paranoid enough."

Merrick threw Jin a sharp look. "You mean they're still *in* there?"

"Seven of the nine escaped," Akim said. "But all were slow to move, and those seven barely made it to the secret exit in time. The two who remained behind hoped to send out an alert to the rest of the planet and then sabotage the communications system. They were still performing that task when the invaders entered the Palace and cut off their escape."

"Do the Trofts know who they have?" Jin asked.

"The invaders don't actually *have* anyone," Akim corrected. "The Shahni were able to reach a hidden safe room, which the invaders haven't yet located."

"But it can only be a matter of time," Merrick said.

"True." Akim's lips compressed into a thin line. "Which is why I'm asking you to go into the Palace and bring them out."

For a moment, even Merrick's calm cracked. "You *what?*" he asked. "*Us?*"

"You're the only ones who can do it," Akim said heavily. "The only ones who can take the invaders by surprise."

"What about your own Djinn?" Jin asked. "If your son Siraj is any indication, a few of them should be more than capable of taking on a group of armed Trofts."

"If a commando raid was feasible, we would certainly mount it," Akim told her. "Unfortunately, such is not the case. We were forced to shut down the Palace escape route after the Shahni left, lest the invaders discover the entrance and find their way into the subcity. The only routes into or out of the Palace are now through the main doors."

"And your Djinn can't go in that way," Merrick said slowly, "because the Trofts would spot their power suits."

Jin frowned. "Their *power* suits?"

"Of course," Merrick said, looking puzzled. "How else did you think Carsh Zoshak and Siraj Akim made it down the laundry chute that way?"

"I just assumed—" Jin broke off in embarrassment. Her brain just wasn't working today. She must be more tired than she realized. "They're not Cobras?" she asked, turning back to Akim.

"That's indeed what we hoped to create," Akim said ruefully. "But even with—" He broke off.

Jin felt her throat tighten with memories. "With the bodies of my companions available to study?"

"As you say," Akim conceded. At least, Jin noted distantly, he had the grace to look pained. "Even so, we haven't been able to master the technique of adding ceramic to the bones and laying down the necessary array of optical control fibers. The creation and programming of the small subbrain computer also remains a mystery to us."

"So since you couldn't go inward, you went outward," Merrick said, nodding. "Hence, exoskeleton fighting suits."

"Exactly," Akim said. "The suits are made of treated krisjaw hide—extremely strong and resilient, with a fiber stiffening meshwork added throughout the longer sections to provide additional support. Servo motors similar to yours are situated at the major joints, which react instantly to the Djinni's movement in order to enhance his strength."

"And, of course, they've got metalwork lasers in the gloves," Jin said. "How are those aimed?"

"Each Djinni has small sensors implanted in his eye lenses," Akim said. "Wherever he looks, that's where the servo motors will aim and fire the lasers."

"Nice," Merrick said approvingly. "Not quite as versatile as our targeting locks, but a lot better than simple dead reckoning. Where's the computer that does all this?"

"In the collar and extending downward along the spine." His lip twitched. "It was thought that an attack strong enough to destroy the computer would probably also destroy whatever was beneath it."

Jin grimaced. And since a computerless Djinni was probably a soon-to-be-dead Djinni anyway, the two events might as well be simultaneous. "Do they have any other weapons?" she asked.

"They have a short-range sonic weapon designed to induce nausea and loss of balance," Akim said. "Dangerous to use in an enclosed space, as it may backfire on the Djinni himself." Akim inclined his head toward Merrick. "Unlike, apparently, the weapon you used. If I may ask, how did you successfully aim and fire your large laser at your restraints?"

"Actually, I cheated a little," Merrick admitted. "When the Djinn first brought the restraints into the room, it was obvious where they were going to go. So I simply put a target lock on the center of the bar."

"And your laser was able to fire without you being able to see it?"

"The servos give kinesthetic feedback positioning data to the nanocomputer," Merrick explained. "Once the target lock is on, I could hit the target with my eyes closed."

Akim shook his head. "Remarkable."

"We like it," Merrick said. "Anything else in the Djinn bag of tricks?"

"Their visual tracking method also permits them to accurately fire other weapons besides their glove lasers," Akim said. "They also carry small gas canisters for use in enclosed spaces, with filters already surgically implanted in their nostrils."

"What about their radios?" Merrick asked. "I assume that's what the Trofts zeroed in on back at the hospital."

"They have a transmission system copied from those used by the first visitors from your worlds." Akim grimaced. "We'd hoped they would prove as undetectable for our use as they'd been for yours."

"That would have been nice," Merrick said. "Unfortunately, you had no way of knowing that those particular gadgets came from our local Trofts."

"And so the invaders can detect them with ease," Akim said grimly. "That'll pose a serious problem."

"You still have that rock-layer waveguide system under the Great Arc, don't you?" Jin asked.

"Yes, but it only works for hard-wired communications between cities and villages," Akim said. "Mobile signaling between combat units cannot use it. Unless you have something newer we might be able to use?"

Merrick shook his head. "Most of our combat these days is against spine leopards, the things you call razorarms. Not much need for private communications with that."

"No matter," Akim said, his dark eyes flashing sudden fire. "If necessary, we'll fight the invaders without communications. If necessary, the Djinn can and will launch a massive frontal assault against the Palace."

"Of course they will," Merrick said hastily. "We understand that."

"We ask for your help only to prevent unnecessary and useless deaths," Akim insisted, almost as if he was trying to convince himself as much as he was Jin and Merrick.

"We understand," Merrick repeated. "Do you have a plan for getting me inside?"

"Wait a minute," Jin protested, feeling her chest tighten. "Shouldn't we at least think about this a little longer?"

"There's no time," Merrick told her. "The Trofts aren't just sitting around congratulating each other on a job well done. They'll be going through the place with a fine-mesh strainer, hunting up official papers and military data and anything else they can find. Sooner or later, they're going to find the safe room."

"I know that," Jin said, struggling to find the words that would express what she was feeling. This wasn't some carefully planned, carefully coordinated operation like those her grandfather had run during his own war against the Trofts. It wasn't a quick hit-and-hit against a group of inexperienced Troft merchants, either, like the little adventure she herself had survived three decades ago. This was a full-blown invasion force, with real soldiers and real military weapons. Couldn't Merrick *see* that?

"Mom, we have to do this," Merrick said quietly. "Remember what Carsh Zoshak said back in the hospital, that the Qasamans had to either trust us or kill us? Well, that works both ways. Either we prove we're trustworthy, or we can't ask them to risk giving us their protection."

Jin stared at him. At the grimness in his face, but also the underlying excitement behind his eyes.

And slowly, she understood. Of course he could see the terrible danger he was facing. But he didn't care. The people of Aventine had all but rejected the Cobras, with many in the government trying to marginalize them, phase them out, or shunt them off to Caelian where they could be ignored. Merrick had watched in frustration as his chosen profession—indeed, his entire family history—had been increasingly brushed aside by people who hadn't the faintest idea what Cobra commitment and sacrifice had meant to their own safety and security.

But that wasn't how the Qasamans saw it. Right here, right now, Merrick was both appreciated and needed. After years of suffering beneath the contempt of people like Governor Treakness, that had to feel good.

And on top of all that, this was the first chance her eldest son had ever had to show what the Cobras were capable of. Down deep, Jin knew that he wasn't going to let that chance pass him by. No matter what stood in his way.

Not even if it was his own mother.

"I just meant we can't go off half-cocked," she said, trying hard to keep the sudden surge of emotion out of her voice. "We'll need schematics of the building, the location of the safe room, pictures of the two Shahni so that we can identify them—" she looked at Akim "—and anything else Miron Akim has undoubtedly already thought of that I haven't."

"Upper-class clothing, for one thing," Akim said. His expression was controlled, but Jin could hear a new hint of hope in his voice. "I also have the schematics if you wish to look at them. But that won't be critically important, since I'll be accompanying you the entire way."

"Very kind of you," Jin said. "But hardly necessary."

"On the contrary," Akim said. "The Shahni won't trust two strangers who come in asking them to leave their sanctuary. Besides, our best chance of entering is to announce ourselves as diplomats intent on negotiation with the invaders. Neither you nor your son can carry off such a charade, but I can."

He gestured. "Come. I'll take you to a place where you can change your clothing and have a bit of refreshment while you study the schematics."

There was food and drink waiting for them when they reached the preparation room. Merrick's stomach was growling, but he was too exhausted from his mostly sleepless night to do more than sample each selection.

Fortunately, the room had also come equipped with a cot, and after obtaining his mother's promise that she would wake him in half an hour he lay down and fell deeply asleep.

He awoke to that dazed, sluggish sensation that always accompanied a short nap on top of a serious sleep deficit. The sluggishness vanished when he discovered that, instead of the half hour he'd requested, he'd been allowed to sleep for nearly two hours.

"You needed the rest," Jin told him, not even looking up from the schematics Akim had spread out over the table. "And there wasn't really anything you needed to do."

"Except maybe learn a little about where we're going?" Merrick growled, trying to put some righteous indignation into his words. But it was a waste of effort. She was right—he'd been way too tired to even tackle spine leopards, let alone armed Trofts. All the preparation and strategy sessions in the Worlds wouldn't do him any good if he was too fuzzy to shoot straight.

"Miron Akim and I both know the layout," his mother assured him. "It's highly unlikely all three of us will end up getting separated."

"And if we are, it will likely be because we're in the midst of combat," Akim added. "At which point your job will be to clear out as many of the invaders as possible while I attempt to reach the Shahni."

"Your new clothes are in the bathroom," Jin said, nodding toward a half-open door. "Get dressed and we'll give you a quick summary of the plan."

The plan turned out to be considerably more wide-ranging than Merrick had expected. "Teams of Qasaman soldiers will be attacking five different locations throughout the city once the two Shahni have been moved to safety," Akim said, pointing to circled locations on a map of Sollas. "The Palace itself, the airfield control tower, the Southfield underground manufacturing facility, the western gate where you entered Sollas, and one of the city's eastern market areas."

"What's in the market area?" Merrick asked, eyeing the map over Akim's shoulder.

"Nothing," Akim said, a grim amusement in his voice. "But if we attack the invaders there, they may assume there's something of military value in the area and waste effort and resources trying to locate it."

Merrick grimaced. A neat little red herring, that. He wondered if the locals would be equally amused when hoards of Trofts descended on their neighborhood. "The troops will be assembling in the underground tunnels, I assume?" he asked.

"No, the main assaults will come from nearby buildings," Akim said. "But there will be small squads of Djinn waiting in the subcity to attack from within once the invaders' eyes are turned outward."

"And after the Shahni are out?" Merrick asked.

"None of the forces move until then," Akim confirmed. "Have you any further questions?"

Merrick slid the Palace floor plans out from beneath the city map and gave it a quick scan. There were actually two safe rooms, he saw, one on the second floor amid the administrative offices and one on the fourth in the living areas. Both rooms were well hidden, each nestled into a few square meters of floor space that had been subtly carved out from the rooms around them. "No, I think that's it," he said. "I assume we won't be using our real names."

"I will, though my title will be that of Senior Administrator to the Shahni," Akim said. "You are Haiku Sinn, my driver and assistant. Your mother is Niora Kutal, a specialist in law and procedure. We're requesting a meeting with the invasion leadership in order to open communications regarding their occupation of Qasaman territory."

Merrick looked at his mother. "You spent my nap time getting a law degree?"

"Hardly," Jin said. "But I think I can guarantee I know more about Qasaman law than any of the Trofts will."

"You're ready, then?" Akim asked.

Merrick nodded. "Let's do it."

"One final thing," Akim said, looking suddenly uncomfortable. "Understand that I say this not of myself, but at the direction of the Shahni." Visibly, he braced himself. "Daulo Sammon and his son Fadil will be held as hostages to your good behavior. Should you betray us, they'll be immediately put to death."

Merrick felt his jaw drop. Of all the underhanded—

"Of course they will," Jin said calmly.

Merrick stared at his mother. "You *knew* about this?"

"No, but once he said it, it was obvious," she said. "Probably why Siraj Akim offered to help me rescue them in the first place."

"Of course," Merrick said, trying to sound as calm as his mother despite the hard knots in his stomach. *Paranoid culture* . . . "Anything else?" he asked Akim.

"No," Akim said, clearly relieved that that particular task was now behind him. Or maybe he was simply relieved that the Cobras had taken it so calmly. "Follow me."

Akim led the way through another maze of tunnels that eventually led back to the surface in a part of Sollas

Merrick didn't recognize. They emerged from a set of row houses to find a black limousine waiting for them at the curb. Merrick got behind the wheel, giving the controls a quick scan while his mother and Akim got into the back seat. The limo was considerably fancier than the Sammons' truck, but the important controls and gauges seemed to be in roughly the same places. Akim gave him a minute of instruction on the specific protocols of Qasaman city driving, then another half minute's worth of directions back to the Palace, and they were off.

There were no other cars on the city's streets to hinder travel, but the Troft barriers and checkpoints more than made up for it. Every third intersection or so was blocked by a handful of armed Trofts, many of them supported by an armored vehicle with a mounted swivel gun fastened to its roof. At each stop Akim lowered his window, gave his name and new title, and demanded he be permitted passage to the Palace to speak with the Troft commanders. Each time, the Trofts conferred by radio with someone higher in authority, and the car was passed through.

They also encountered two more of the tall, slender gunships along the way. Merrick, who'd never particularly liked city driving, found himself sweating as he carefully maneuvered the car through the narrow gap between gunship and curb under the Trofts' watchful eyes. Whether by luck or unexpected skill, he made it both times without even scratching the limo's paint.

And then, sooner somehow than he'd expected, they were back at the Palace. "Looks like they're setting up camp," he commented as he eyed the wide canopy the Trofts had erected beside the Palace entrance. Beneath the canopy, a handful of the aliens were setting up long tables and portable computer equipment.

"Most likely preparing to interview and register the citizens," Akim said. "An invader's first task is to control the movements of the people he's invaded."

One of the Trofts standing guard by the curb stepped into the street and held up a hand toward the approaching car. Merrick eased the car to the curb, and once again Akim rolled down his window. "I am Senior Administrator Miron Akim—" he began.

"You are known and expected," the Troft's translator pin boomed. "The commanders have agreed to meet with you."

"Excellent," Akim said briskly, popping open his door. "My assistants—"

He broke off as the Troft pushed the door closed again. "You will follow that vehicle to their location," he said, gesturing with his laser at an armored vehicle that had pulled out into the street in front of them.

"Follow it where?" Akim demanded, a sudden edge beneath the official arrogance in his voice. "I told you I wish to speak to your leaders."

"You will follow that vehicle to their location," the Troft repeated, his own tone hardening as he gestured again. As he did so, Merrick noticed the alien's hand dip into a pouch at his waist. "Go now, or their invitation will be rescinded."

Akim glared at the Troft. "Very well," he said icily. "Haiku Sinn, follow the vehicle as instructed."

He rolled up his window as Merrick shifted the car back into gear. As he did so, out of the corner of his eye he saw the Troft reach his hand up past the window, and there was a soft thud as he slapped the roof.

Ahead, the armored car pulled away and headed down the street. Grimacing, Merrick followed. They were going to see the Troft commanders, all right.

Only they were going to see them in the wrong place.

CHAPTER TEN

"Great," Merrick muttered as he drove. "Now what—?"

"Quiet," his mother said. "Miron Akim, change places with me."

Merrick frowned, watching in the mirror as the two of them exchanged seats. His mother partially rolled down the window Akim had been sitting beside and slipped her hand up through the opening. For a moment she seemed to feel around; then, with a brief grimace of effort, she pulled against something, and Merrick caught a glimpse of a small object falling past the window onto the pavement. "All right, it's off," she said, pulling her hand back inside and closing the window again.

"What was it?" Akim asked. "A bomb?"

"I doubt it," Jin said. "Not much point in subtlety when they've got all those guns. My guess is that it was a bug so they could listen in on us, maybe get a preview of who we were and what we want."

"So what *do* we want, now that Plan A is blown?" Merrick asked.

"There may still be opportunities," Akim assured him. "Let's first see were we're taken."

"Looks like we're heading toward the airfield," Merrick suggested as the Trofts at the next checkpoint waved the two vehicles though. "Maybe the commanders are still aboard one of their ships."

"Perhaps," Akim agreed. "Though they'd be foolish indeed to allow three potentially dangerous persons into one of their vessels."

"The airfield control tower, then?" Jin offered. "It gives a good defensive view of that end of the city, not to mention the airfield itself."

"I agree," Akim said. "The control tower is definitely the most likely destination. If we're taken inside . . . " He trailed off, and in the mirror Merrick saw him grimace. "We'll have only one real option," he continued reluctantly. "One of us will have to escape from the invaders' custody and confirm to the Shahni that the rescue plan is no longer viable." His eyes locked on to Merrick's in the mirror. "That will be your task, Merrick Moreau."

"Shouldn't it be you?" Merrick asked. "I mean, you're the one they'll listen to."

"Unfortunately, the route you'll need to take will be dangerous for a man of my age," Akim said. "We'll have to trust that they'll accept your word and instructions."

Merrick looked at his mother in the mirror. But if she had objections she was keeping them to herself. "You're the boss," he said with a sigh. "What do I do?"

"There's a trapdoor in the rear corner of each elevator in the tower," Akim told him. "It will drop you into a net, which will then drop you through the false floor of the shaft to a landing below. The trip will be stressful, but not lethal."

"That's good to hear," Merrick said dryly. "What happens once I'm at the bottom?"

"From the landing a door leads into the subcity," Akim said. "There should be a squad of Djinn waiting there, and you'll instruct them that Plan Saikah must be initiated."

"What's Plan Saikah?" Merrick asked.

"Our best hope for throwing off the invaders," Akim said. "There's no need for you to know the details."

Merrick felt a chill run through him. An all-out assault on the Trofts? "All right," he said. "What do I do after I deliver the message?"

"That will be your choice," Akim said. "You may assist the Djinn, if they're willing to accept your aid, or you may step aside."

"I have a question," Jin said. "What happens to the Shahni in the Palace during Plan Saikah?"

"They'll serve Qasama in their own way," Akim said. "There—our destination."

Merrick shifted his full attention back to the view through the windshield. Sure enough, the airfield tower loomed ahead, with one of the wrigglefish-like sentry ships flanking it on either side. "How do I trigger the trapdoor?" he asked.

"I'll do that," Akim said. "Just make sure you stand in the right rear corner of the elevator as you face the doors."

Their pilot car led the way to a set of large doors and came to a halt. Four of the six Trofts guarding the entrance detached themselves from the others and strode toward the limo, their lasers covering the vehicle. "Prepare yourselves," Akim said. "And allow me to do the talking."

For the immediate moment, though, there wasn't any call for talking. With a handful of curt orders from one of the Trofts, the aliens herded the three humans into the tower and down a hallway to what had probably originally been a conference room. Over the past few hours, the Trofts had transformed it into a clearing station, complete with bolted-down interrogation chairs and a full staff of techs and armed guards.

They started with Akim, two of the guards firing questions at him about his family and background as one of the techs ran a handheld scanner over his clothing. After that it was Merrick's turn, and he could feel sweat collecting beneath his collar and in his armpits as he answered the questions and watched the tech's face for signs of surprise or confusion. Cobra gear was supposed to be undetectable unless someone was specifically looking for it, but as far as Merrick knew that theory had never been tested. Certainly not under conditions like these.

It was thus with a huge sense of relief that he watched the tech finish his sweep and step back without shouting a panicked warning. Whatever trouble they were expecting to find, Cobras apparently weren't on the list.

"What is your purpose here?" one of the Trofts asked after Jin had also been cleared.

"To speak to your commanders," Akim said, his voice the controlled stiffness of someone carrying out an errand he hadn't particularly wanted. "The Shahni wish to know why you have invaded Qasaman territory, and to open discussions leading to your departure."

The Troft covered his translator pin and started murmuring in cattertalk. Merrick ran his auditory enhancers up—[The humans, our presence they wish to discuss,] he said. [The leader, the garb of a senior Shahni official he wears.]

He received a reply and lowered his hand from his pin. "Follow," he said, and strode out of the room. Akim followed, with Jin behind him and Merrick behind her. Behind Merrick, two more Trofts brought up the rear.

Twenty meters later, they arrived at an alcove and a pair of elevators guarded by four more Trofts. One of the latter punched the call button as the party approached, and both sets of elevator doors slid open. The Troft leading the way turned and backed into the leftmost car, his eyes and laser trained on the humans. "Come," he said.

Akim nodded, but instead of following the other inside he stopped at the door and gestured Merrick to enter ahead of him. Merrick nodded and continued forward, hoping he could get inside before the Trofts started wondering about the sudden change in marching order.

But the Trofts merely stood impassively by as Merrick walked into the elevator. The lead Troft, to Merrick's relief, hadn't taken the corner above the trapdoor, and he casually crossed the car and took up position there. One of the other Trofts stepped into the elevator behind him and touched the lowest button on the control panel.

And to Merrick's stunned disbelief, the doors slid closed and the car started down.

"Wait!" he yelped, lunging toward the doors. Or trying to lunge, anyway; he managed only a single step before the first Troft swung the muzzle of his laser around and jabbed it warningly into Merrick's ribs. "We can't leave—Senior Administrator Akim is still outside."

[Fools, you think we are they?] the Troft at the door spat. [Spies, we do not understand that you are?]

The Qasaman translation had barely begun when Merrick grabbed hold of the laser barrel poking into his ribs and twisted it hard, shifting the muzzle out of line with his side and trying to pull it out of the Troft's grip.

But the Troft didn't let go, not even as the unexpected tug pulled him off his feet. He hung on grimly, his beak clacking unintelligibly as he fought for possession of the weapon. Merrick tried twisting the laser in the opposite direction, but the alien still kept hold of the weapon. The other Troft leaped forward, shoving at Merrick's arm with one hand and jabbing the muzzle of his own weapon into Merrick's face with the other.

And in that frozen fraction of a second, Merrick's body moved.

He let go of the laser he and the first Troft were fighting over, shrugging off the second Troft's grip on his arm and following through with a blindingly fast sweep of his hand across the weapon to knock it out of line. The momentum of the sweep twisted Merrick's shoulders around; and as his whole body did a quick corkscrew to the right his left hand swung up, little finger extended, the other fingers curled tightly toward his palm, and fired a burst of laser fire at each of the two Trofts' foreheads.

Only neither alien dropped over dead. Instead, the transparent faceplates blackened at the points of impact, blocking off the main brunt of the blasts.

But enough had gotten through to send a shock of pain through both aliens. Merrick grabbed again at the first Troft's laser, and this time he was able to wrench it from the alien's grip. Spinning it around, he jammed it upward beneath the lower edge of the alien's faceplate and fired.

There was a brilliant flash, and the soldier dropped to the floor. Merrick spun the weapon around, elbowing the remaining Troft's laser aside, and fired a second shot under that one's faceplate, sending him crumpling to the floor beside the first.

Merrick stared down at the bodies, his heart thudding in his ears, his breath coming in short gasps. *My God,* the thought flashed across his numbed mind. *Was that me?*

Of course it had been him. It had been his body, his combat reflexes, his Cobra weaponry.

He closed his eyes, fighting the sudden urge to vomit. Never before had he used his power against another person. Never before had he even been tempted by anger or frustration to do so.

He'd killed two people. Not spine leopards, mindless predators who would cut a murderous swath through someone's ranchland if they weren't eliminated. He'd killed two living, sentient beings.

He clamped his teeth tightly as a second wave of nausea swept through him. Up until now he'd thought only about the fear-edged respect Miron Akim had shown for him and his mother, a respect in stark contrast to the disdain that radiated from so many of Aventine's people. Thoughts of combat had been little more than a hazy backdrop to that warm glow of vindication, a vague and sanitized mural consisting of images of fire and triumph and glory. This blood and stillness and stench of burned flesh wasn't what he'd expected. Wasn't at all what he'd signed up for.

He took a shuddering breath. Only it was, he knew. He'd signed up willingly, even eagerly, and it was too late to back out. Not when there were people out there who were counting on him.

People like Miron Akim . . . and Merrick's mother.

Merrick winced. Jasmine Moreau, daughter of Justin Moreau, granddaughter of the legendary Jonny Moreau. She wouldn't panic in this situation. *Hadn't* panicked, in fact, when she'd found herself facing similar danger all those years ago.

You boast overmuch of your strength, demon warrior, Miron Akim's son Siraj had scoffed. Maybe he'd been right.

It was time to find out.

Merrick gave his head a sharp shake, and as the haze in front of his eyes vanished he realized that the elevator was still heading downward. Apparently, the fight and his brief surge of horrified introspection and self-pity had lasted only a few seconds.

He checked the elevator indicator, noting that they were passing the second subbasement, and tried to think. With Jin and Merrick stuck here at the airfield, it was clear that Akim assumed the two Shahni trapped in the Palace would have to be abandoned.

Probably he was right. But maybe he was wrong.

Reaching down, Merrick picked up one of the Trofts' lasers. So far, the invaders had no idea that there were Cobras on Qasama. The longer that ignorance could be maintained, the better. Steeling himself, he pointed the laser at the black spot he'd made in the first alien's faceplate and squeezed the trigger.

The Troft weapon was considerably more powerful than Merrick's fingertip lasers, and the blast had no trouble getting through even the darkened faceplate and through the mass of skin and bone behind it. A reminder, Merrick thought grimly, that he'd better make damn sure he didn't end up at the receiving end of any future blasts.

Shifting aim, he repeated the camouflage on the second Troft, then lifted the weapon toward the side of the car. He had no idea how to trigger the secret trapdoor Akim had told him about, or whether the net would deploy properly if he simply blasted the floor open. He certainly wasn't ready yet to just throw himself blindly down a Qasaman elevator shaft. Aiming at a spot about chest height, he shifted the laser to continuous mode and squeezed the trigger.

The beam lanced out, sizzling like cooking breakfast meat as it sliced through the relatively thin metal of the car wall. Merrick carved out a human-sized opening, then dropped the weapon back onto the floor and peered through the hole he'd created.

A meter away, the wall of the shaft was sliding past, its surface covered with cables and protrusions. Bracing himself, Merrick picked out a suitable spot and jumped, grabbing on to a convenient set of handholds. He locked his fingers around the cold metal and looked down in search of similar purchase for his feet.

Just as the elevator car settled to a stop a meter below him.

Merrick blinked, embarrassment and chagrin sweeping across him as he saw the elevator shaft floor no more than half a meter below the car. The Trofts had been taking him to the tower's lowest level, and he'd now arrived.

But the chagrin at his unnecessary derring-do vanished as a far more urgent thought belatedly gripped him. When the car doors opened, and the reception committee saw the two dead bodies in there . . .

There was a faint creak as the doors started to open. Merrick looked frantically around, but there was nowhere he could see where he could hide. From the corridor beyond the elevators came a sudden explosion of startled cattertalk—

And even knowing how stupid and predictable it was, but unable to think of anything better, Merrick stepped onto the car's roof and dropped silently onto his stomach.

Just in time. Against the shaft wall he saw a multiple flicker of shadows, and with the scraping of leathery armor against metal a pair of Trofts climbed out of the car through Merrick's newly blasted hole. Merrick pressed himself as flat onto the roof as he could, wondering tensely if the Trofts would be able to jump high enough to catch a glimpse of him up here.

Fortunately, they didn't seem interested in trying. From the sounds of their footsteps, they were instead working their way around the car, easing cautiously around the rear toward the larger open area on the far side. Possibly hoping to get a better view of the car roof from over there?

Abruptly, Merrick tensed. No, of course the searchers weren't going to bother with the top of the car. Not when the Trofts one floor up could simply open their own elevator doors and look directly down on him.

He looked up. Those doors were still closed, but they wouldn't stay that way for long. No exit for him that direction. Meanwhile, the two roving Trofts were still poking around the shaft on the far side of the car.

Which left Merrick only one option. Getting a grip on the edge of the car, he rolled his legs over the side, making sure not to come anywhere near the hole and any more Trofts prowling around in there. He took half a second to let his swing dampen out, then dropped as quietly as he could onto the shaft floor. Dropping flat onto his stomach, he slid underneath the car.

The gap between car and floor was smaller than it had looked when he'd been hanging on to the wall a few moments ago, and he found the space an ominously snug fit. But at least he was finally out of sight.

But again, probably not for long. He could see the roving Trofts' feet as they continued to move around, the sizes and angles of their shadows now indicating that they were shining lights up along the inside of the shaft. Unless one of them had already looked beneath the car, they would surely eventually get around to doing so. And if there was one guaranteed fact in the universe right now, it was that Merrick wasn't going to be doing any serious fighting from under here.

But if he was lucky, he might not have to.

The trapdoor will drop you into a net, Akim had said, *which will then drop you through the false floor of the shaft to a landing below.* The floor beneath him certainly didn't *feel* false, Merrick observed as he wriggled his way over to the car's rear corner. It felt as solid as any other floor he'd ever been on.

But Merrick had studied all the records from Grandpa Justin's mission half a century ago, and he knew that the airfield tower elevators went a lot deeper than just a couple of subbasements. This had to be the false floor Akim had talked about, which meant there had to be a way through it somewhere.

But if the rabbit hole was directly under the trapdoor, Merrick couldn't find it. He ran his hands over the grimy concrete, keying in his light-amplification and infrared enhancements to help in his search. But he couldn't find a single trace of anything that seemed out of the ordinary.

The muffled footsteps across the shaft changed tempo. Merrick looked in that direction, to see that the two

Trofts were retracing their path around the rear of the car, heading back toward the hole.

And if they decided to check under the car one more time before they gave up their search . . .

Cursing silently, Merrick frantically renewed his search. But there was still nothing. He rolled up onto his side facing the Troft feet, raising his hands into firing position. A futile gesture, he knew—the minute he fired, everyone in the shaft, the car, and the corridor would know instantly where he was. If they decided they still wanted him alive, they could recapture him with ease. If they didn't, all they had to do was open fire through the floor of the elevator car.

The Trofts were at the rear of the car and starting around the last corner when Merrick heard a soft snick.

And without a whisper of warning, the floor beneath his elbow suddenly gave way.

He grabbed for support as his upper body started to fall into the large, irregularly shaped hole that had magically opened up in the thick concrete. He looked for the missing section of flooring, saw it swinging gently from hinges at the far end. Getting a grip on the edge of the hole, he pulled himself forward and down into the opening.

For a moment he hung there, studying the underside of the floor in the dim backwash of light from the elevator shaft. The false floor was constructed on long metal I-beams, one of which ran right along one edge of the trapdoor. Shifting his grip to it, he held on one-handed as he reached over and pulled the trapdoor back up into place. It closed with another soft snick.

And then all was silence.

For a long minute Merrick just hung there, listening to the indistinct sounds of activity overhead. It was hard to tell through the thick floor, but he couldn't hear any of the extra urgency that might mean his escape had been spotted. Within half a minute, all of the sounds had faded away. The hunt, apparently, had moved elsewhere.

Merrick took a deep breath, painfully aware of how close he'd just come to his own death. Something else that hadn't entered into his calculations when he'd volunteered to join this war. He took a few more deep breaths, sternly ordering his heart to calm down, then keyed his light-amps to full strength.

It was a waste of effort. The shaft extension stretching down around him was completely and utterly dark, without a single bit of light coming in from anywhere that even his optical enhancers could detect. He shifted to infrared, hoping his own body might be radiating enough in that wavelength that he could at least see *something*. But aside from giving him a view of the two or three square meters of false floor directly above him, that didn't work either.

Switching back to his light-amps, he let go with one hand and aimed his little finger into a random section of the darkness. He touched his thumb to his forefinger nail—the laser's lowest setting—sent up a silent prayer that he wasn't aiming at anything important, and fired.

The shaft below him stretched deep enough that even the laser flash wasn't bright enough to show where it ultimately ended. But it was more than adequate to show the semicircular platform five meters below the spot where he was hanging. Bracing himself, he let go.

He hit the platform with a solid, metallic thud, bending his knees as he landed to absorb some of the impact. The shaft was still pitch black, but his glimpse of the platform had also shown a door in the shaft wall across from where he now stood. Moving carefully forward, one hand extended in front of him, he made it to the wall.

He pressed his ear against the metal and held his breath, his auditory enhancers keyed to full power. The wall was alive with the hums, thumps, and rumblings of distant machinery, but there were no sounds of human activity that he could detect.

Still, Akim had said there would be Djinn down here somewhere. Turning his enhancers back down again, he tried the knob and found it unlocked. Pushing the door open, he stepped through into a space filled with the soft mustiness of dust and age and long neglect. Unlike the shaft, this place had a little light, a faint glow coming from somewhere to Merrick's left. Closing the door behind him, he started to activate his light-amps.

And suddenly, a blazing white light exploded in his face.

He jerked back, squeezing his eyes tightly against the blaze as he reflexively threw one arm up to protect his face. "Well, well, well," a voice growled from somewhere behind the light. "What have we *here*?"

The Troft stepped into the elevator behind Merrick . . . and to Jin's stunned horror, the doors closed behind him, leaving her, Akim, and the other five Trofts still outside.

Wait! Ruthlessly, she stifled the word before it could make it past her lips. She was a woman in a patriarchal society, and it would look suspicious if she spoke up instead of Akim.

Only Akim wasn't speaking up. He was just standing there, not even looking at Jin, apparently without a single shred of concern that their little group of infiltrators had just been split up. One of the Trofts gestured toward the right-hand elevator, and Akim merely nodded and stepped inside, leaving Merrick to whatever fate the Trofts had planned for him.

But whatever those plans were, they were about to be canceled. Glancing casually around, Jin set a targeting lock on each of the five Trofts' foreheads. Her fingertip lasers were useless against their faceplates, but a drop onto her back and a sweep of her antiarmor laser would leave her free to pry open the elevator doors and either drop onto the top of Merrick's car if they'd taken him down or else to jump up to the underside if they'd taken him up. Either way, another blast from her antiarmor laser would get her inside—

"Niora Kutal."

Jin jerked out of her frantic train of thought. Akim was standing in the elevator, gazing at her with the mix of authority and aloofness she'd seen on so many Qasamans as they dealt with female subordinates. "Yes, Miron Akim?" she managed.

"Attend," he said, making a small gesture toward his side.

But what about my son? "Of course," she said instead. Lowering her eyes like a good Qasaman woman, her jaw tight as she fought to control her pounding rage and fear, she stepped into the elevator. Akim was right. Whatever the Trofts had planned for Merrick, blowing their cover now wouldn't do him any good.

And he wasn't seven years old anymore, either, she reminded herself firmly. He was a competent, capable adult.

And a Cobra.

She stepped to Akim's side. The five Trofts piled in behind her, lasers leveled and ready, their sheer numbers and bulk forcing the two humans all the way to the rear of the car. The doors slid shut, one of the Trofts punched a button, and they headed up.

"To whom do you take us?" Akim asked into the silence.

No one bothered to answer. In the close confines, Jin heard a faint voice coming from somewhere, and keyed up her auditory enhancements. [—of his presence,] the cattertalk whispered. [A full search of the elevator shaft, it is being made.]

Jin felt her muscles tense. Were they talking about Merrick? Had he escaped?

[The other humans, under close guard hold them,] the voice continued.

None of the five Trofts stiffened, gasped, or showed any other visible reaction to the report. But it seemed to Jin that the ring of lasers moved perhaps a centimeter or two closer to her and Akim.

She took a careful breath, feeling her heartbeat slow a little. But only a little. Merrick had apparently escaped, and escaped alive. But had he taken that action on purpose, as Akim had ordered, so that he could go warn the Djinn of the change in plan? Or had he panicked, as his grandfather Justin had when facing an eerily similar situation?

There was no way for her to know. She could only hope that, either way, he would make it safely to the subcity.

She raised her eyes to one of the Troft faces gazing at her above his leveled laser. The double sets of eyes gazed back through the faceplate, the main eyes a dark blue, the three tiny compound eyes grouped around each of the main ones largely colorless in the elevator's artificial light. She lowered her gaze, taking in the vaguely chicken-like beak, the double throat bladders, and the flexible radiator membranes on his arms. The Troft's outfit was similar to the usual leotard-like garment the traders on Aventine wore, except that his was festooned with various equipment pockets and hooks and was clearly armored.

Why were they here? The Qasamans had had contact with the local Troft demesnes—that much had been obvious fifty years ago, when the Trofts had provided the Worlds with a Qasaman translation program prior to their first mission here. Had the Qasamans annoyed someone enough to invite this kind of response? Had some Troft demesne decided it was running out of room, and Qasama offered the most convenient and attractive expansion?

The elevator came to a stop at the topmost floor, and the doors opened to reveal another group of five Trofts with weapons at the ready. Apparently, the aliens weren't taking any chances that their other two human visitors might make a break for it. The Trofts in the elevator filed out, the two groups of aliens forming themselves into a sort of double receiving line out in the corridor. It was, Jin thought as she and Akim passed between the lines, very much like the honor guard she'd sometimes seen at official Aventinian receptions.

Except for the drawn weapons, of course. And the way the lines re-formed into a guard behind them.

"To whom do you take us?" Akim asked again.

Again, the Trofts ignored him. The two humans were escorted through a couple of turns and arrived at last at an open door. At a gesture from one of the aliens, they went inside.

The room was clearly an executive office, complete with a large expanse of carpeted floor and a panoramic window that opened out onto the city of Sollas stretching out to the south. But unlike most offices, the only furniture here was a pair of metal armchairs sitting back to back across the room by the window.

Armchairs with wrist and ankle shackles attached and ready.

"Sit down in the chairs," one of the Trofts ordered.

"What is this?" Akim demanded, not moving from the doorway.

The muzzle of a laser prodded against the small of his back. "Sit down in the chairs."

"I was sent to speak with your commanders," Akim insisted as he moved with clear reluctance into the room.

"You were sent to spy," the Troft countered. "Sit down in the chairs."

"This is a breach of all proper diplomatic protocol," Akim continued stiffly as he seated himself with strained dignity, nodding to Jin to do likewise. "Do you now propose to interrogate us like common criminals?"

"No," the Troft said to him as four of the aliens moved in and fastened the shackles around their wrists and ankles. "If you are high enough in your leaders' counsels to negotiate, you are high enough to be sorely missed by those same leaders."

His arm membranes fluttered. "You are no longer negotiators. You are now hostages."

CHAPTER ELEVEN

"Get that light out of my eyes," Merrick snapped. "You trying to ruin what little night vision I have left?"

The light didn't waver. "Who are you?" the voice demanded. "What are you doing here?"

"My name is Merrick Moreau," Merrick told him. "I was sent with Miron Akim—"

"Merrick *Moreau*?" a new voice cut in, the source moving as someone apparently came forward from the rear of the group. "What are *you* doing here?"

This voice Merrick recognized. "Greetings, Carsh Zoshak," he said. "As it happens, I'm on a mission for Miron Akim. Come on—vouch for me and get them to turn off this light."

"Not so fast," the first voice said darkly. "If you're Merrick Moreau, you're supposed to be at the Palace."

"Unfortunately, the Trofts didn't get that memo," Merrick said. "They intercepted us outside the Palace and sent us here to the airfield."

" 'Us'?" Zoshak asked. "Is Miron Akim also here?"

"Yes, somewhere up in the tower," Merrick said. "At least, I think he's still there. The Trofts separated us."

"Where did they do this?" Zoshak asked. "At the elevators?"

"Yes, but I don't know if Miron Akim and my mother were put in the other one or just taken somewhere on the ground floor."

"The other elevator is currently on the top floor," a third voice reported. "That's probably where they were taken."

"Is that where the Troft commanders have set up their headquarters?" Merrick asked.

"The supreme commanders are not here," the first voice said. "Only local commanders."

Merrick grimaced. So much for the Trofts taking them anywhere within close reach of any of the invasion's chief organizers. Still, he shouldn't have expected the aliens to be that naïve. "Miron Akim sent me with a message," he said. "He said that since we hadn't been able to get to the trapped Shahni you were to initiate Plan Saikah instead."

There was a moment of silence. Then, to Merrick's relief, the blinding light went out. "Plan Saikah?" the first voice asked carefully. "Are you certain?"

"Very certain," Merrick assured him. "Why? What is it?"

There was a soft sigh. "It is a sentence of death."

A shiver ran up Merrick's back. "For you?"

"We are not concerned with our own deaths," the other said stiffly. "Facing danger for Qasama is our duty and our honor. I was speaking of the Shahni who will soon be lost to us."

"We cannot simply condemn them to such a death, Jol Najit," Zoshak said urgently. "Not without at least making an attempt to rescue them."

"And how would you do that, Carsh Zoshak?" the first voice—Najit—countered. "Would you have us chew through the barriers like demented rodents?"

"What kind of barriers are we talking about?" Merrick asked. His eyes were recovering now, enough for him to see that the glow he'd noticed when he'd first arrived was coming from the display and controls of a small monitor built into the elevator shaft wall. In the dim light, he could see that besides Zoshak and Najit there were three other Djinn in the room. "Because maybe if we—"

"We are talking about barriers that cannot be breached with the necessary speed and silence," Najit cut him off. "Now be quiet—we have work to do."

"I'm just trying to help," Merrick said doggedly, trying to visualize the Palace floor plans he'd glanced at earlier. Given the location of the safe room, even if Plan Saikah was a brute-force assault the Shahni should still have a pretty good chance of surviving long enough to be rescued. "If we could open up a pathway—"

"I said be *silent*, demon warrior," Najit bit out. "You are not part of this."

"I understand that," Merrick said, trying to keep his voice calm. What part of *I'm trying to help* didn't Najit get? "Since I'm not part of your group, there's no particular place I have to be."

"An excellent point," Najit growled. "Go somewhere else, and be out of our way." He turned his back on Merrick and headed toward the monitor station.

"So I guess I'll just pop over to the Palace and get the Shahni out," Merrick called after him.

Slowly, Najit turned around, and even in the dim light Merrick could see the rigid set to the other's face. "Let me make this clear, demon warrior," he said. "You are to stay out of our way. *Completely* out of our way. You will not go to the Palace, you will not return to the airfield tower, you will not stand or sit or lie in the path of any Qasaman forces. Do you understand?"

"Yes, I understand," Merrick said quietly. "You've been given a mission. Well, so have I. And though you may find this hard to believe, I feel as strongly about mine as you do about yours."

For a long moment the two men locked eyes. The other four Djinn were listening silently, their hands not quite curved into laser firing positions. "The only remaining way into the Palace is through the outer doors," Najit said at last. "Attempting to enter that way will prematurely alert the invaders to our intentions."

"It might also draw more of them inside the Palace," one of the other Djinni murmured.

Najit's expression changed subtly. "True," he said thoughtfully. "That might be useful."

"I wasn't really thinking about running the gauntlet they've got set up outside the Palace," Merrick said. "I was hoping for something a little more subtle and less exposed."

Najit shook his head impatiently. "I've already told you. There is no other way in."

"There has to be," Merrick insisted. "Come on, think. The building has plumbing outlets, air system intakes—there must be *something* that a human body can squeeze through."

"What about the communications conduit?" Zoshak suggested, pointing toward a large metal cylinder about two-thirds of a meter in diameter running vertically from floor to ceiling beside the monitor console.

"Too small," Najit said. "And the plumbing and air systems were specifically designed to keep intruders out."

"Wait a second, not so fast," Merrick said, eyeing the cylinder. "Is this the same sort of conduit that runs down from the Palace?"

"Yes, but it is filled with bundles of shielded communications cables," Najit said.

"Cables can be dealt with," Merrick said, crossing to the cylinder and running a fingertip thoughtfully along the metal. If the cylinder's wall wasn't too thick, there ought to be plenty of room for him to climb up the inside. He'd have to come up with something to use for hand- and footholds, but it could be done. "I assume these are the cables that carry signals down to that basalt waveguide you use for intercity communications?"

Abruptly, the room behind him went deathly quiet. Carefully, he turned his head around.

None of the Djinn had moved. But all five of them were now wearing Najit's same stiff expression. "What?" Merrick asked.

"How do you know about the waveguide?" Najit demanded, his voice low and dangerous.

"Oh, come on—we've known about it since our first visit," Merrick said, keeping his own voice calm. Busy facing down Qasaman stubbornness, he'd almost forgotten about Qasaman paranoia. "I'm sure my mother mentioned that to Miron Akim when she was here last."

"We cannot let the invaders learn about that," Najit said.

"Are you suggesting I might run off and tell them?" Merrick asked.

"Perhaps," Najit said. "Or you might be captured, and offer a trade for your life."

Merrick's thoughts flashed to Daulo and Fadil Sammon, locked up somewhere by the Shahni as hostages to the Cobras' good behavior. "I'm not offering them any deals," he told Najit icily. "I'm not taking any, either. Get this through your skull, Jol Najit: I'm on your side. As far as I'm concerned, until the Trofts are off this world, I *am* a Qasaman."

There was another short silence. Then, beside Najit, Zoshak stirred. "He won't find his way through the subcity to the Palace without assistance," he murmured. "I request permission to accompany him."

Najit's lip twisted, but there was no surprise in his face that Merrick could see. Clearly, he wasn't happy with any of this. Just as clearly, he'd already figured out which way it was going and had bowed to the inevitable. "Plan Saikah will take one hour to prepare," he said. "It will *not* wait upon you."

"Understood." Zoshak turned to Merrick. "You still wish to take this risk upon yourself, Merrick Moreau?"

The doubts and fears from the elevator flickered like dry lightning through Merrick's mind. No, he *wasn't* sure. But someone had to do it, and it might as well be him. "We're wasting time," he said.

Zoshak nodded. "Follow me."

He slipped past Merrick, breaking into a jog as he passed the door leading into the elevator shaft, and headed down an increasingly darkened corridor. With a controlled burst of speed, Merrick caught up and fell into step behind him, keying in his light-amps to make as much use as he could of the monitor glow receding in the distance behind them.

A few meters later they rounded a corner into almost complete darkness. Merrick thought about pointing that out, decided that if Zoshak could stay on his feet and not run into a wall, so could he.

Fortunately, Zoshak wasn't interested in playing that kind of game. "Are you all right?" he called softly as he flicked on a small light attached to his collar. "Is this light bright enough?"

"It's fine," Merrick assured him, keying back his enhancers a couple of notches. "How far is the Palace? I got a little turned around on the drive."

"At this pace, perhaps fifteen minutes," Zoshak said. "But we should try to go faster if possible."

"I can if you can," Merrick said. "Are we in that much of a rush? I assumed that if the Shahni had stayed hidden this long, they would probably be good for another hour or two. And I'm thinking that Plan Saikah might kick up a nice diversion for us."

Zoshak threw an odd look over his shoulder. "Didn't Miron Akim tell you?"

"Tell me what?" Merrick asked.

"About Plan Saikah," Zoshak said. "The first step is the detonation of the explosives built into the Palace walls."

Merrick felt his mouth drop open. "No, he damn well did *not* tell me that," he ground out. "Are you saying you're going to blow the Palace with two of the Shahni still inside?"

"The Shahni, and many of the invaders," Zoshak reminded him. "Perhaps some of their highest leaders. It's a fair gamble."

"Only if you're the one standing outside pushing the button," Merrick said. "Who came up with this crazy plan, anyway?"

Zoshak looked him straight in the eye. "The Shahni."

Briefly, Merrick tried to envision a situation where Aventinian governors like Tomo Treakness would deliberately sacrifice their lives in order to inflict unknown levels of damage against an invader. But his imagination wasn't up to it. "In that case, you're right, we might want to step it up a little."

"Agreed," Zoshak said, picking up his pace. "Let me know if I go too fast for you."

"Don't worry about me," Merrick said, matching the Qasaman's speed as he turned the bulk of the work over to his leg servos. "I'm right behind you."

The door closed behind the Trofts, and Jin heard the click of a lock.

And she and Akim were alone.

"Well, *damn,*" she muttered, looking around. The room had seemed empty enough a minute ago when the Trofts had led them in here. Now, on closer examination, it looked even emptier. There were nail holes in the walls where paintings had once hung, decorative hooks in the ceiling that had once supported planters or hanging artworks, and deep indentations in the carpet marking the former positions of desk, chairs, and other furniture. It looked rather like a student apartment, hastily and carelessly abandoned at the end of the term.

She frowned as the oddness of that belatedly struck her. Why would the Trofts have bothered to take down the paintings and planters? Had they been afraid their soon-to-be prisoners would somehow break free and find something in the room to use as a weapon? In that case, they'd missed the most obvious bet of all: the metal chairs she and Akim were shackled to, which weren't even bolted to the floor.

Or had the Trofts removed everything so that the prisoners wouldn't suspect hidden cameras or microphones lurking among the palm fronds? Smiling to herself, Jin keyed in her telescopic enhancements and took another, closer look at the nail holes.

There they were: a pair of tiny cameras nestled into two of the holes on opposite sides of the room. It was a little hard to tell, but one of them seemed to be angled slightly toward the door, while the other was angled toward the two prisoners. The Trofts hadn't skipped the audio, either: hanging in the near corner of the room, masquerading as a plant hook, was the telltale perforated plastic of a small microphone.

"All you all right, Niora Kutal?" Akim asked from behind her.

Using her assumed Qasaman name, which meant that he also knew or suspected they were being monitored. "I'm unharmed, Miron Akim, but highly offended," she replied stiffly. "We're ambassadors, and not to be treated in this way."

"Agreed," Akim said, and beneath his own tone of controlled outrage Jin could detect a hint of approval for her quick pickup of the situation. "The invaders will have a great deal to answer for when this is over."

"If they think this will frighten us or the Qasaman people, they're gravely mistaken," Jin agreed. Bracing herself, she activated her omnidirectional sonic.

A tingle ran through her, an unpleasant vibration as the speakers buried inside her body slipped through harmonics of natural body resonances. The pitch altered as the sound dug into the walls, seeking out similar resonances with the cameras and microphone . . .

"Are we under attack?" Akim asked quietly.

Jin didn't answer, focusing instead on counting down the seconds. It was supposed to take about a minute for the sonic to find all the possible resonances and vibrate the bugs into paralyzed uselessness. She let the minute tick by, then gave it another fifteen seconds just be on the safe side. "No, that was me," she said, answering Akim's question. "The hidden cameras and microphone shouldn't be picking up anything now."

"Excellent," Akim said. "But speak toward the window, please."

Jin obeyed, noting out of her peripheral vision that he'd also turned his face in that direction. "Nice view," she commented, gazing out at the city stretched out in front of them.

"I was thinking about the cameras," Akim said. "In case your attack wasn't entirely successful."

"Ah," Jin said. "Okay. We also should keep our mouth movements as small as possible. They may also have someone out there on a rooftop with a telescope and a computer that can read human lips."

"Ah," Akim said. "Yes—good point."

"As to the cameras, they're not actually destroyed, just gone way too fuzzy to see anything useful," Jin continued. "And the mike should be delivering nothing but a low-pitched hum right now. So how do we play this?"

For a moment Akim was silent. "How much do you know about Troft military doctrine?"

"The Dominion of Man had more experience with it than anyone wanted," Jin said. "But that was over a century ago. I assume their tactics and strategy have undergone a lot of change since then."

"Yet their basic psychology has likely remained essentially unaltered," Akim pointed out. "From our admittedly limited understanding of them, I wouldn't have expected them to so eagerly take hostages."

Jin gazed out the window at the Troft ships and the brilliant morning sky beyond. Now that she thought about it, she realized Akim was right. The records from the Dominion's war against the Trofts had indicated that *hostage* wasn't a term the aliens generally applied to living beings.

Still, the Troft Assemblage was made up of hundreds of demesnes. Maybe different rules applied to the particular group that had invaded Qasama. "Maybe they've learned to adapt to their particular target," she suggested.

"No," Akim said flatly. "Basic psychology is by definition basic. It doesn't change that drastically."

"You know the Trofts well, then?" Jin asked, a flash of annoyance running through her. The Cobra Worlds had been trading with Trofts for multiple decades, dealing with the aliens on a regular basis. Yet Akim presumed to tell *her* what the Trofts could or couldn't do?

"We've studied them as best we could," he said. "Trading vessels have occasionally come and gone over the past fifty years, though we've given them no encouragement to return." He snorted gently. "And of course, there was the group you and I dealt with."

Jin frowned. "I thought all of them made it off-planet before your people arrived."

"They did," Akim confirmed. "But their interactions with the Qasamans they had dealt with left detectable changes. Studying those changes gleaned for us a fair amount of useful information."

A shiver ran up Jin's back. "I don't even want to know what you had to do to get that."

"The subjects of the study were in no danger."

"I wasn't thinking about them," Jin said. Over the years the Qasamans had built up a large pharmacopoeia of mind-enhancing drugs, each one individually tailored to temporarily improve memory, perception, observation, or reason. The Qasamans had also developed a tradition—a borderline insane one, in Jin's opinion—of using those drugs.

Insane, because however effective the drugs might be they also demanded a terrible price. Habitual users could suffer anything from premature aging to brain damage to a quick and probably painful death.

In fact . . .

Jin felt her throat tighten. Miron Akim had been a young man when Jin had first visited Qasama, no more than ten years older than she was. Yet when they'd met again a few hours ago in the subcity, she'd guessed his age to top hers by at least thirty years.

She turned her neck a little farther around, taking a good, long look at his profile. His face was calm enough, but now that she was looking for it she could see a brightness and intensity in his eyes that she hadn't noticed before.

He hadn't come along on this trip just to play native guide to her and Merrick while they freed the trapped Shahni, she realized with a sinking feeling. He was here for some other purpose entirely.

"So if we're not hostages, despite their words, we must assume we're here for some other purpose," Akim went on. "We must discover or deduce that purpose."

I thought you already knew everything about Troft psychology. With an effort, Jin held back the words.

"Let's start at the beginning," she suggested instead. "We were allowed in on the pretext of meeting their leaders, but were instead chained up without any of those leaders making an appearance."

"Chained *after* our party had been split up," Akim said slowly. "And then locked in an empty room without guards but with hidden monitors."

"*And* right in front of a window," Jin said as that odd fact suddenly struck her. "Where we can see across the whole city."

"And can be seen in turn by everyone outside." Akim snorted. "We aren't hostages, Jin Moreau. We're bait. They wish to see what a Qasaman rescue operation looks like."

"I think you're right," Jin agreed, her face warming with embarrassment that she hadn't figured that one out on her own. It was exactly the same trick the Trofts had pulled on her grandfather, after all, only in reverse: they'd set him up to escape from a fortified base so that they could gather data on Cobra weapons and techniques in a more or less controlled environment. "They're going to be sorely disappointed, though." She looked sideways at Akim again. "Aren't they?"

"I don't know," Akim admitted. "Plan Saikah makes no provision for the rescuing of hostages. But in this case . . . some of the Djinn may take it upon themselves to seek us out."

"Terrific," Jin muttered. "Either we let the Trofts see Djinn in action, or we tip them off that there are Cobras on Qasama."

"Neither of which is acceptable," Akim said flatly. "We must find a third alternative."

"I'm game," Jin said. "How much time do we have?"

Akim hissed thoughtfully between his teeth. "From the time our forces are alerted as to the change in the operation . . . perhaps an hour."

Jin grimaced. That wasn't much time. "Then we'd better get busy," she said. "Let's put our heads together and see what we can come up with."

The room Daulo and Fadil were taken to was small but pleasant enough. There were three cushioned chairs, a water dispenser, a small fruit grouping, and an equally small basket of travel-style snack and meal packages. It was, for Daulo, an unexpected courtesy, given how less comfortable a cell the Djinn could have chosen to put them in.

Fadil, though, didn't seem to see it that way. For the first hour of their incarceration he paced the room like a caged krisjaw, answering his father's comments and questions with terse replies just barely within the bounds of courtesy. A few minutes into their second hour he abandoned his pacing and dropped into one of the chairs, staring at the fruit as if he expected it to explode at any moment.

Daulo's first thought was that his son was fighting between the desire to eat and the conflicting desire to avoid showing the weakness of hunger in front of the Djinn. It was only when the elder Sammon got up and picked out a pomegranate for himself that he discovered Fadil wasn't actually gazing at the fruit, but at something far more distant, something only he could see.

In someone else, such a state might have indicated meditation or focused thought. But Daulo knew better. In Fadil, at least in his younger days, such concentration had usually followed a deliberate insult by a member of a rival family, and the concentration had subsequently led to the boy's carefully planned response to that insult.

And villager that he was, he almost couldn't help but see their incarceration at the hands of city people as such an insult.

But he'll think it through, Daulo tried to assure himself. *He'll realize that behavior in time of war isn't the same as in time of peace.*

And if he didn't, it would be Daulo's job to convince him of that. Hopefully before the boy did something foolish.

He had finished his pomegranate and was dozing in his chair when a sudden pounding startled him awake. He looked up to see Fadil standing at the door, pounding on it with the heel of his hand. "Someone!" he called. "Someone come!"

"Fadil!" Daulo snapped. "What are you—?"

"Someone come!" Fadil called again.

There was the click of a lock and Fadil stepped back as the door swung inward to reveal a gray-clad Djinni. "What do you wish?" the Djinni asked.

"I wish to see someone in authority," Fadil said, his voice respectful but firm.

The Djinni shook his head. "All such are occupied."

"Then let me see the man from the hospital," Fadil countered. "The one your companion Carsh Zoshak was so eager to free."

"Just a minute," Daulo put in as he hastily gathered his robe about him and scrambled to his feet. He had no idea who the mysterious old man was, but the fact the Shahni had sent two Djinn to get him out ahead of the Trofts implied he was *not* the sort of person from whom a simple villager demanded an audience. "Fadil—"

"Quiet, Father," Fadil said calmly. "We brought two Cobras here to help with the war, Djinni. You owe us for that."

"And an audience with His Excellency is what you wish in repayment?" the Djinni asked. Despite the seriousness of the situation, Daulo could nevertheless hear a hint of amusement in the Djinni's voice. A city dweller, speaking down to a villager, and Daulo could only pray that his son wouldn't also hear the telltale tone.

If the younger man did, he made no sign. "If that's how you choose to see it, yes," he said.

The Djinni cocked his head. "Very well," he said, taking a step back out of the doorway and gesturing Fadil forward. "Do you wish to speak with him as well, Daulo Sammon?" he added as Fadil strode past and disappeared down the corridor.

Daulo absolutely did not, and he very much wanted to say so. But Fadil was already on his way, and Daulo could hardly leave his son to face the results of this strange insanity alone. "Thank you," he said, and hurried from the room.

He caught up with Fadil a few paces from a door flanked by two more Djinn, both of whom were eyeing the approaching villagers with uncomfortable intensity. "Fadil, what are you *doing*?" Daulo murmured tautly into his son's ear.

"Showing these city dwellers that villagers will not simply stand by and take what is handed to them," Fadil said.

Daulo winced. "Fadil—"

And then there was no more time for talk, because one of the Djinn pushed open the door and Fadil strode inside. Cursing under his breath, Daulo followed.

The room beyond the door was the same size as their cell, but much better furnished. Instead of chairs, the entire rear quarter of the room was piled with large cushions, on which sat a frail old man with a lined face and sunken cheeks. His piercing eyes were focused on a pair of computers sitting on a low table in front of him, and wafting through the air was the faint scent of a mild incense. "I bid you welcome, Fadil Sammon," the old man said, raising his eyes to his visitors as Fadil came to a halt a respectful three paces away from the computer desk. Like the guards outside, his gaze was intense, but he didn't seem bothered or even surprised by the intrusion. "And you, Daulo Sammon," he continued. "I am Moffren Omnathi, advisor to the Shahni. How may I be of service?"

Daulo felt his breath freeze in his throat. *God above.* This wasn't just some important old man. It wasn't even some random Shahni advisor, or even one of the Shahni himself.

This was *Moffren Omnathi.* The man assigned to escort the first Aventinian mission around Qasama, and the one who had first detected their deception. The man who had thrown together a plan for their capture on the fly, and had caught on to their second and more subtle deception, and who would have taken the entire group of them captive had it not been for the unexpected power and weaponry of the Cobras. The man whose quick military action years later had succeeded in capturing a great deal of Troft equipment after Obolo Nardin's failed bid for power.

Moffren Omnathi was more than just a hero. He was a legend.

And Daulo and his son had just barged in on him.

Daulo looked sideways at Fadil. The other recognized Omnathi's name, all right, and for a second his resolve seemed to falter. But then he took a deep breath and squared his shoulders. "Forgive the intrusion, Your Excellency," he said, making the highest sign of respect. "But a grave injustice has been done to us, which I pray you will see fit to rectify."

"And what injustice is this, Fadil Sammon?" Omnathi asked.

"Our home has been invaded, Your Excellency," Fadil said. "Yet my father and I have been forced to sit idly doing nothing."

He drew himself up. "I request your permission to be given a weapon, assigned to a unit, and allowed to fight."

Daulo stared at his son, feeling the universe tilt around him. Of all the things he had imagined Fadil might say, this was one possibility that had never even crossed his mind. "Fadil, what—?" He broke off, looking back at Omnathi. "I beg your pardon, Your Excellency—"

"Peace, Daulo Sammon," Omnathi said calmly, his bright eyes boring into Fadil's face. "Yet you already provide an important service to Qasama, Fadil Sammon."

"Only that of hostage, Your Excellency," Fadil said. "A guarantee for the behavior of Jin Moreau and Merrick Moreau."

Daulo felt his throat tighten. He'd hoped Fadil wouldn't figure that out.

"But two such hostages are hardly necessary," Fadil continued. "Especially since my father is the only one Jin Moreau truly knows and truly cares about. Let him stay here and be guarantee of her loyalty. Give me a weapon and let me fight for my world."

Omnathi studied him a moment in silence, then shifted his gaze to Daulo. "You disapprove of your son's offer, Daulo Sammon?" he asked.

"Not at all, Your Excellency," Daulo hastened to assure him.

"You are surprised, then?"

Daulo looked at his son. "Yes," he admitted. "But also proud."

"Indeed." Omnathi looked back at Fadil. "You are willing, then, to give your life for your people?"

"If need be, yes." Fadil drew himself up. "But hopefully not before I've given the Trofts ample opportunity to do the same."

Omnathi smiled. "So be it. Can you handle a weapon?"

"We of the villages still mount razorarm and krisjaw hunts," Fadil said with an edge of pride. "I've killed one of each within the past six months. I doubt the Trofts are nearly as quick on their feet."

"We shall soon find out." Omnathi looked over Fadil's shoulder to the Djinni who had taken up silent guard in the doorway. "Take Fadil Sammon to the simulation range," he ordered. "Assess his ability with a weapon, and assign him accordingly."

"Yes, Your Excellency." The Djinni stepped out of the doorway and gestured. "Master Sammon?"

Fadil gave Daulo a brief nod. "Father," he said, and strode from the room.

"And you, Daulo Sammon?" Omnathi asked.

With a start, Daulo realized he was still staring at the doorway where his son had disappeared. "Your Excellency?" he asked, turning back to Omnathi.

"Do you wish to follow your son into combat and danger?"

Daulo frowned. "I stand where the Shahni so order," he said formally. "But I understood I was to remain as hostage to the Moreaus' behavior."

Again, Omnathi smiled. But this time, there was no humor there. "The Moreaus' behavior is based on their belief that you and your son are under threat of death," he said. "Whether such a threat actually exists is irrelevant."

Daulo stared at the old man, his blood running suddenly cold as he focused on the other's shining eyes and the other marks of enhancement drug use. Omnathi was pushing his intellect to the fullest as he prepared Sollas for war.

And if he was willing to give even a pair of untried villagers guns . . . "We don't have enough men, do we?" Daulo asked quietly. "This attack isn't going to succeed."

Omnathi lowered his gaze to the computers in front of him. "Every hour we delay a response is an hour the invaders will use to settle themselves ever more firmly into their defensive positions," he said. "We have no choice but to attack as quickly as we can, with all the strength we have, and to trust to God for victory."

"I understand," Daulo murmured. It wasn't, he noted, exactly an answer to his question. Or perhaps it was. "I haven't been on a hunt in several years," he continued. "But I still remember how to use a rifle."

"Then the Djinni outside will take you to the range," Omnathi said gravely, his shining eyes still on the computers.

Clearly, he was dismissed. "Your Excellency," Daulo said, making the sign of respect. Turning, he left the room.

CHAPTER TWELVE

Merrick's first journey through the subcity earlier had left him with the impression that it had been designed by cross-eyed moles. Now, as he headed toward the Palace with Zoshak, he concluded that those same moles had also had one set of legs shorter than the other.

Still, even as he privately cursed the unexpected jags in the passageway and the uneven footing, he could understand the military logic that had gone into the system. With all the curves, drops, and angles in the corridors, any enemy who got in here could be held off for days by a relative handful of defenders. The attackers would have to use explosives or smart missiles to break free, which Merrick guessed would merely collapse the local tunnel area, blocking further access to the system and possibly burying attackers and defenders alike.

Twice along the way he heard Zoshak making the same odd teeth-clicking sound he'd heard while the group in the Sammons' truck was coming toward Sollas. Then, he'd assumed Zoshak was going into shock; now, he knew it was part of the Djinni's radio comm system.

It was definitely a good thing to let any defenders in the subcity know that he and Zoshak were coming. It wouldn't be so good if the Trofts on the surface were able to pick up the transmissions, as well.

But if the aliens heard the signals, they were too slow on the uptake to do anything about it. Eight minutes after leaving the airfield tower, the Cobra and the Djinni arrived beneath the Palace.

The monitor room, a duplicate of the one beneath the tower, was deserted. "Where is everyone?" Merrick asked, looking around as Zoshak busied himself with the monitor.

"Why would anyone be here?" Zoshak countered as he ran quickly through a set of images. "The Palace situation appears as we expected."

"Trofts?" Merrick asked.

"Didn't you see them?"

"You went through the images pretty quickly," Merrick pointed out.

"Yes, there are Trofts." Zoshak stepped over to the vertical cylinder. "Can you get this open?"

"Sure," Merrick said, going over to join him. Curving his fingers over into firing position, he aimed at a spot about knee height and gave the cylinder a blast with his fingertip lasers. To his surprise, the metal merely sputtered and sizzled without breaking open. "Uh-oh," he murmured.

"What do you mean, *uh-oh*?" Zoshak demanded. "Can't you cut through it?"

"Not like this." Merrick backed up, target-locking a horizontal line across the tube at about waist height. "You don't care about the cables inside, do you? Never mind—the whole place is going to blow anyway. Move away and watch your eyes." Putting a forearm over his own face, he lifted his left leg and fired his antiarmor laser.

A brilliant beam of blue light lit up the room, accompanied by a much louder sizzling from the cylinder. Merrick finished his sweep and shut off the laser, then lowered both his leg and his arm.

The metal that had successfully resisted his smaller lasers had succumbed without fuss to the larger one. The cylinder now sported a neat two-centimeter-wide gap, the cut edges glowing a dull red. "That's better," Merrick said as the stink of vaporized metal tingled his nostrils. "I'll make another cut, and we'll be good to go."

"One moment." Stepping forward, Zoshak wrapped his arms tightly around the cylinder above the gap. "Sound carries well in confined places," he added. "We don't want something this heavy crashing to the floor."

"Good point," Merrick agreed, targeting another cutting line half a meter above Zoshak's head. "I hope that suit of yours is good against hot metal sparks."

"It is," Zoshak said dryly. "Do be careful not to miss."

"Don't worry." Again protecting his eyes, Merrick lifted his leg and fired.

Again, the room lit up with blue light, and with a muted clunk of breaking metal the section came free. "You need a hand?" Merrick asked.

"No," Zoshak said. Sliding the section out of line with the rest of the cylinder, he set it down on the floor. Merrick stepped up beside him and peered into the opening.

To his surprise, it was completely empty. "Aren't there supposed to be cables in here?" he asked quietly.

"You mean the ones you just cut through?" Zoshak suggested as he straightened up.

"I don't think so," Merrick said, stepping aside. "See for yourself."

Zoshak ducked his head into the gap, shining his collar light upward. "You're right," he said. "The Shahni must have cut all of them."

"Of course they did," Merrick said as one of Miron Akim's earlier comments suddenly came back to him. "The Shahni who were left behind were trying to sabotage the equipment. Cutting all the cables and letting them fall a hundred meters would pretty well cover that." He reached up into the cylinder, running his fingers along the slightly rough metal surface. "Should be able to get decent traction," he decided, looking over at Zoshak's gloved hands. "I don't suppose you have a spare set of gloves I could borrow?"

"I'm sorry," Zoshak said. "Will your hands be all right?"

"Hopefully, I can do most of it with my elbows and knees," Merrick said. "Let's go." He stepped up onto the lip of the cylinder and pressed his elbows against the sides.

And stopped as a horrible thought suddenly occurred to him. "Oh, hell," he said softly.

"What?" Zoshak asked sharply.

Merrick looked up into the darkness. "Do you know if there's a cap on the tube somewhere inside the Palace? Or does the cylinder go all the way up into the roof?"

"There's a cap at the fourth-floor communications room," Zoshak said. "Why?"

"How sturdy is it?"

Zoshak stared at Merrick, his expression hardening as he got it, too. "It's quite substantial," he said. "Certainly as substantial as the cylinder itself."

"Then we're in trouble," Merrick said, a tightness settling into the pit of his stomach. If the top was capped, and his fingertip lasers weren't powerful enough to cut through the metal . . .

"No, it just means you'll have to travel upside down," Zoshak said briskly. "Sit down and slide your feet upward into the cylinder."

Merrick made a face. But the other was right. Sitting down beside the cylinder, he lifted his legs up into the opening, straightened his hips and back, and pushed himself up into a handstand with his legs as far up the cylinder as he could get them. He got his balance, then walked backwards on his hands and got his palms up onto the cylinder lip. "This is as far as I can go on my own," he told Zoshak, blinking against the dizziness as the blood rushed to his head.

"Hold still." Zoshak squatted down facing Merrick and got his hands underneath Merrick's shoulders, squeezing his palms into the narrow spaces between neck and arms.

And to Merrick's astonishment he lifted the Cobra the rest of the way out of the gap up into the cylinder. "Can you hold there a moment?" Zoshak murmured.

"I'll try," Merrick said, pressing his forearms and shins as tightly against the cylinder walls as he could. "How's this?"

"Perfect." Quickly, Zoshak let go of Merrick's shoulders and climbed into the shaft beneath him. With his feet straddling the lip, he reestablished his grip. "All right. Hmm. This will be difficult."

"Hang on—let me try something," Merrick said. Shifting around so that his back was pressed against the tube, he tried pushing against the wall with his forearms. To his mild surprise, he slid upward a few centimeters. "Looks like you won't have to push me the whole way," he said, sliding himself up another few centimeters.

"Try using your feet, too," Zoshak suggested. "Press with the edges or soles and then bend your knees inward."

Merrick tried it. This time he moved nearly twice the distance of his first two tries. "Probably as good as it's going to get," he said, resettling his elbows and knees and repeating the operation. "Okay. Let's go."

The trip was agonizing. Merrick was able to turn most of the work over to his servos, which at least relieved the strain on his muscles. But there was no such protection for his hands, and the rough metal slowly but steadily rubbed them raw. Combined with the constant thudding of blood in his head, it made for a more miserable experience than anything he'd gone through since graduating from the Academy. Closing his eyes, trying to focus on his forearms instead of his slowly disintegrating hands, he kept going.

It was therefore something of a shock when he stretched out his legs that last time and bumped his feet into something solid. "We're here," Zoshak whispered.

"Right," Merrick said, settling himself against the wall and trying to clear his head. First step, the thought seeped through his pounding skull, was to see if any Trofts were nearby. Pressing his ear against the metal, he keyed in his auditory enhancers.

And found himself in the center of a soft but bewildering tangle of sounds and voices. "Well?" Zoshak prompted.

"Quiet," Merrick said, fighting to untangle the cacophony. From the sheer number of conflicting noises it almost sounded like the Qasamans and Trofts were having a dinner-dance party. Yet everything was oddly muted, as if the partygoers were afraid the neighbors would hear.

And then the obvious answer penetrated his numbed brain. The metal cylinder was funneling sounds to him from all four levels of the building. More importantly, the fact that everything sounded quiet even with Merrick's enhancements going implied that the fourth-floor area around him and Zoshak was in fact deserted.

Or it just meant that the Trofts babysitting that particular communications room were being very quiet.

There was only one way to find out. Keying down his audio enhancements again, Merrick tucked his right leg down as far as he could out of the way and aimed his left heel at the edge of the cylinder's cap. "Watch your eyes," he warned Zoshak, and fired.

The familiar blue light blazed, and a second later a rain of metal sparks began to burn into Merrick's legs and hips, joining the pressure in his head and the throbbing in his palms. Squeezing his eyes shut, ignoring this fresh source of pain, he swept his leg around the edge of the lid, slicing it free of the cylinder. The blue light vanished as he shut down his laser.

And without warning Zoshak put his hands on Merrick's shoulders and shoved, and Merrick found himself flying straight up out of the cylinder like a cork from a champagne bottle, his feet knocking aside the severed lid on the way. He had just enough presence of mind to grab the upper edge of the cylinder with one hand as he passed, checking his upward motion before he could slam feet-first into the ceiling and swiveling himself into a circle that landed him more or less upright on the floor.

Fortunately, his nanocomputer was more alert than he was, and bent his knees to absorb the impact. Snapping his hands up into firing position, blinking to clear his vision, he looked around.

He was in a small room with an electronics-laden wraparound desk pressed up against two of the walls. Above the desk were rows of monitors like the ones he'd seen down in Akim's subcity command center, all of them currently dark. The cylinder lid he'd knocked off had landed on the desk, hopefully with a minimum of noise.

Still, even if the Trofts had finished checking these upper floors, it was unlikely that they'd simply abandoned them. "Where's the entrance to the safe room?" he asked Zoshak as the latter pulled himself out of the cylinder.

"Two rooms to the left, behind a blue and white tile mosaic," Zoshak said, pointing. "I just hope the Shahni are up here, and not in the second-floor safe room."

"Well, this is where they cut the cables, anyway," Merrick pointed out as he crossed to the door. "Otherwise we'd have run into dangling cable ends two floors down. Be quiet a second."

He pressed his ear to the door and keyed his enhancers. Nothing. "Sounds clear," he said. "I'll go check it out."

"Be careful," Zoshak warned. "There may be a roving patrol."

"Probably," Merrick said grimly. "You find the Shahni and get them ready to travel."

The Shahni apartment levels, as Merrick had noted earlier from Akim's floor plans, had been designed with an open layout: wide hallways opening smoothly into lounges, dining areas, and media rooms, with only the various sleeping rooms closed off from the general space. What the floor plans hadn't shown was the fact that the wide corridors were liberally sprinkled with sculptures on carved or molded pedestals, many of them partially recessed in half-cylindrical or semispherical wall niches. Other sections of wall were covered with colorful, intricate tapestries or more of the tile mosaics that Zoshak had mentioned. Quietly, Merrick moved along the colorful displays of the main corridor, his senses alert for trouble.

He was halfway to the elevators when he heard the soft sounds of rhythmic footsteps coming his way.

He looked around. To his left was one of the hanging tapestries, to his right a large vase on a pedestal within a half-cylindrical floor-to-ceiling niche. Getting a grip on the pedestal, he pulled.

The combination was heavier than it looked, and he had to brace one foot on the wall and use his servos to get the thing to move. He pulled it about fifteen centimeters out into the hallway and then slipped around behind it. Set into the ceiling directly in front of the vase was a directed light, which a quick fingertip laser shot blasted into darkness, putting Merrick's hiding place into partial shadow. Another quick slash with the lasers cut a vertical line in the tapestry across from him and then added enough of a horizontal cut at the top to suggest a hidden doorway had been opened and then hastily and imperfectly shut. Crouching down, he set one palm against the vase and the other against the midpoint of the pedestal and prepared himself.

Ten seconds later, the footsteps grew louder as the Trofts came around one of the corners, then faltered as the aliens spotted the dead light and the damaged tapestry. For a moment the footsteps stopped completely, and there was a moment of indistinct muttering as one of the soldiers called it in. *Be overanxious,* Merrick urged them silently. *Be overanxious, and just a little bit careless.*

The soldier finished his report. Merrick held his breath; and then they were there: two Trofts, dressed in the same helmets and armored leotard outfits Merrick had seen on the aliens at the airfield control tower. Both had their lasers pointed at the tapestry, ready for something to come jumping out at them from behind it. One of them turned his head to check out the niche across the hall.

And as he jerked with surprise, Merrick shoved with all his servos' strength against the pedestal and vase, hurling them across the hall.

The impacts knocked both soldiers off their feet, slamming them into the tapestry and the solid wall behind it. One of them managed to get off a wild shot before he hit that burned harmlessly into the floor.

And then Merrick was beside them, ripping open their faceplates and punching hard into their throat bladders. Hefting the heavy pedestal up into his arms, he hurried down the hallway toward the elevator. If the backup hadn't been coming before, it was definitely on its way now.

The stairwell door beside the twin elevators was alive with the sounds of racing Troft feet when Merrick reached it. He set the pedestal against the door, using another nearby pedestal to help wedge it in place. The elevators showed no sign of activity, but he gave each of the doors a quick spot-weld just in case, then headed back toward the safe room.

The camouflaged door was standing partially open as he came around the final corner. He was nearly there when Zoshak slipped out of the safe room, a compact but deadly-looking submachine gun gripped in his hands. "What was that noise?" he asked, peering past Merrick's shoulder.

"That was the roving patrol," Merrick said. "It's not roving anymore." Stepping past Zoshak, he pulled the door all the way open. "Are our guests about ready to—?"

He broke off. Akim had said that two of the Shahni were trapped in here. Only it wasn't just a pair of old men standing silently in the hidden room. The two old men were accompanied by an old woman, a young man and a young woman, and two boys of perhaps six and eight.

"What the—?" Merrick grabbed Zoshak's arm as the other came up beside him. "I was told we were rescuing two Shahni."

"We are," Zoshak said grimly. "And yes, they're ready."

"What about the others?"

"There's no time," Zoshak said stiffly. "They must remain behind."

Merrick stared at him, his mouth dropping open in astonishment. "They're *what?*"

"There's no time," Zoshak repeated. "Quickly, now, before more aliens arrive. Your Excellencies?"

One of the Shahni stepped forward. The second paused to squeeze the old woman's shoulder and then followed. "Wait a minute," Merrick protested. "We can't just leave these people here to die."

"We have no choice," the second Shahni said firmly. "There is insufficient time to bring everyone through the escape route Djinni Zoshak has prepared."

"Then we'd better find some other way out for them," Merrick said harshly. "Plan Saikah starts with blowing up the Palace, remember?"

"And so we will serve our people," the young man said. His hand, Merrick noted, was tightly gripping the young woman's.

"Are the children to serve the same way?" Merrick demanded.

"They are sons of Qasama," the young man said, letting go of the woman's hand and resting one hand on each of the two boys' shoulders. "They will do what is necessary."

"There *is* no other way out," the first Shahni said impatiently. "And we waste time."

Merrick focused on the boys' faces. Both were trying very hard to be as brave and determined as their parents, but the younger one was clearly teetering on the point of tears.

The only route now into or out of the Palace is through the main doors, Miron Akim had said, and the first Shahni had now confirmed it. Unfortunately, it was an exit currently blocked by multiple layers of armed Trofts.

Merrick's old spine leopard hunting squad might have been able to cut through them all. But the squad wasn't here, and Merrick didn't have a hope of defeating that many enemies, especially not once the element of surprise was gone.

Which meant he had to somehow get the Trofts to leave on their own.

"Can you get the two Shahni out by yourself?" he asked, turning back to Zoshak. "Piggyback them down on your shoulders or something?"

"What nonsense is this?" the first Shahni growled. "You have been ordered to bring us out. You will obey that order. *Now.*"

Merrick kept his eyes on Zoshak. "Carsh Zoshak?"

Zoshak looked at the two children. "It would be difficult for the one directly above me," he said hesitantly. "He would carry much of the weight of the second upon his own shoulders."

"We waste time—" the first Shahni said.

"What are you proposing?" the second Shahni interrupted.

"I'm proposing that Djinni Zoshak bring you both out," Merrick told him, "while I attempt to do the same with the others."

"You think you can carry all five of them upon *your* shoulders?" the first Shahni scoffed. "This is foolishness. I insist you carry out your orders."

Merrick turned to face him. "Technically, Your Excellency, I'm not—"

"It can be done," the second Shahni again interrupted. "I will take center position, above Djinni Zoshak's shoulders, with Shahni Melcha's weight upon me."

"Thank you, Your Excellency," Merrick said, turning back to Zoshak. "Can you do it?"

Zoshak's lips were pressed tightly together, but he gave a short nod. "I believe so," he said.

"Then get them to the cylinder and get in," Merrick said. "I'll be there in a minute to help them in behind you. Any idea how long before Plan Saikah starts?"

"Approximately ten minutes," Zoshak said, motioning the two Shahni toward the door.

"Can you find out more exactly?" Merrick asked.

"It would require me to transmit the request," Zoshak warned. "The invaders have already shown they can detect those signals."

"That's okay," Merrick assured him. "In fact, at this point, the more transmissions out of here, the better." He gestured to the young man. "I'll need some kind of timer," he continued. "It doesn't have to connect to anything, but it has to have a visible countdown display. Is there anything in here you can rig up to do that?"

The young man glanced at the two Shahni, as if for confirmation that he was allowed to talk to this upstart stranger. "There's an assembly timer in the lounge," he said. "It calls the Shahni to meetings, marking the time remaining until the opening prayer."

"But the display has repeaters throughout the building, including the lower floors," the young woman put in. "The invaders may see it."

"Perfect," Merrick told her. "Carsh Zoshak?"

"Twelve minutes and thirty seconds," Zoshak reported.

"Set the timer to hit zero twelve minutes and thirty seconds from now," Merrick instructed the young man. "Then return here, and leave the door open so I can get back in. Come on, Djinni Zoshak—let's get you and the Shahni out of here."

They headed back toward the communications room. "I hope you have a plan," Zoshak warned quietly. "I don't know how you see things on your world, but here we're expected to obey orders precisely. We were told to rescue the Shahni. That's all that matters."

"And you *are* rescuing them," Merrick reminded him. "As for how we do things on the Cobra Worlds, we absolutely do *not* abandon anyone if there's a chance of saving them."

"Even at the risk of your own life?"

An echo of the brief battle in the control tower elevator flashed through Merrick's mind. Before that, he'd never fully appreciated the ramifications of the fact that war meant he would have to kill.

Just as he had never before appreciated on a gut level that he might also have to die.

But he certainly couldn't confess such fears and doubts in front of a dedicated soldier like Zoshak. Personal and national pride both demanded Merrick maintain some shred of dignity here. "Yes, even then," he said, trying to sound strong and fearless. "What other purpose does a soldier have?"

For a moment Zoshak was silent. Merrick winced, wondering if the other had penetrated his deception and was wondering what kind of coward he was traveling with. "We've been told you demon warriors come from a soft people," the Qasaman said at last. "It appears we were wrong."

Merrick snorted quietly, Governor Treakness's contempt for the Cobras flashing to mind. "Don't fool yourself—my people have plenty of softness," he said grimly. "But we still have a few pockets of strength left."

The two Shahni were waiting in the communications room when Merrick and Zoshak arrived. The first was gazing down into the open cylinder, an incredulous look on his face. "You expect us to travel through *this?*" he demanded.

"It is passable," Zoshak assured him as he hopped up onto the desk and slipped his legs into the cylinder. Pressing his feet firmly against the sides, he stood upright and slid smoothly downward until only his head was visible. "Shahni Haafiz, you'll need to climb up onto the desk and place your feet on my shoulders," he said. "Mind your hands—the cylinder edge is sharp in places."

Haafiz looked at Merrick. "Your assistance," he ordered.

"Certainly." Merrick stepped forward and held out a hand. "Lean on me, Your Excellency."

Haafiz took hold of Merrick's forearm and hoisted one foot up onto the desk.

And suddenly a small knife flashed in his other hand, driving straight at Merrick's heart.

CHAPTER THIRTEEN

It was so unexpected that for that crucial fraction of a second Merrick's eyes and brain refused to grasp the fact that he was under attack by a man he was risking his own life to save. But his nanocomputer had no such emotional limitations. Even as the knife tip drove through Merrick's clothing and into his skin his servos were twisting his torso away from the blade while at the same time shoving him backward.

But even Cobra reflexes could move a man only so fast from a dead stop. As Merrick twisted and fell onto his back he could feel the throbbing pain in his chest and the warm spreading wetness of his own blood. "What are you *doing?*" he gasped, pushing himself desperately backward along the floor on his torn palms.

"You think I do not know who and what you are, enemy of Qasama?" Haafiz bit out, jabbing his knife toward Merrick, an edge of bright red now coating the gleaming metal. "Better for my family to die together in honor than to allow them to fall into your hands and those of your allies."

"I'm not working with the Trofts," Merrick protested, clutching at his wound. The sudden pressure sent a dazzling stab of new pain through the torn skin. "I came here to help you."

"And here is where you will die," Haafiz said. Shifting the grip on his knife, he started toward Merrick. Merrick braced himself, flicking a target lock on to the knife.

And then, through the open doorway behind him, he heard a dull thunderclap and the crackle of scattered debris hitting tiled floor. "You hear that?" he demanded as the Shahni came to a sudden halt. "That's the Trofts getting through the barricade I set up to slow them down."

"That *you* set up?" Haafiz scoffed.

"There is no time for foolishness," Zoshak snapped. His face was rigid, his eyes staring in horror and disbelief at the spreading stain on Merrick's tunic. "Shahni Haafiz, you must come to me now, or die."

The Shahni hesitated another moment. Then, contemptuously tossing the knife to the side, he turned and climbed up onto the desk. Zoshak slid farther down the cylinder and Haafiz put his legs in. As he slid downward, the other Shahni climbed in on top of him, this one not even bothering to glance in Merrick's direction. Another moment, and he, too, was out of sight.

Leaving Merrick, bleeding and alone, to face the Trofts.

"Damn," Merrick muttered, pressing his hand to his chest as he carefully got to his feet, the throbbing agony in his chest momentarily eclipsed by an equally throbbing rage. What the *hell* did Haafiz think he was doing? And who the hell did he think he was doing it to? Staggering on suddenly wobbly knees, Merrick made his way across to the cylinder. He would like nothing better than to jump up onto the desk, aim his antiarmor laser down the cylinder, and give His Exalted Excellency Shahni Haafiz one last second of wisdom-enhancing pain before he died.

He couldn't do that, of course. Not even if he could guarantee that such a blast wouldn't kill two innocents in the process.

But he would remember Shahni Haafiz. He would remember him well.

The metal lid he'd burned off earlier was still lying on the desk. Setting it back on top of the cylinder, Merrick fired three quick shots with his fingertip lasers, spot-welding it into place. Then, pressing one hand against his chest wound, wondering how deep the Shahni's blade had gotten and how fast he was losing blood, he headed back toward the safe room.

He was nearly there when five Trofts suddenly appeared, their lasers pointed at him. "Human, stop!" the translator pin boomed.

"We have to get out of here," Merrick gasped, putting a weaving stagger into his walk as he continued toward them, trying to look like a man on his last legs. "They wouldn't listen—they wouldn't stop it. He stabbed me—"

"Human, *stop!*" the Troft repeated, more emphatically this time.

"He tried to kill me," Merrick said, finally coming to a shambling halt. "He stabbed me, and then they left."

"Who left?" the Troft demanded.

"The Shahni who were hiding here," Merrick said. There was a sudden commotion behind the Trofts and another group of aliens appeared, pulling and dragging the five Qasamans who Merrick had left in the safe room. "They were hiding with them in that secret room," Merrick added, pointing at the newcomers. "They're going to blow up the building and kill us."

One of the Trofts stepped to the side, covering his translator and muttering urgent-sounding cattertalk into his radio. "Didn't you hear me?" Merrick pleaded, putting some desperation in his voice. "They're going to blow up the building. You have to get us out of here."

"How do they plan to do that?" the lead Troft asked. "With artillery?"

"The bombs are already built into the walls," Merrick said, wondering dimly whether the aliens were serious or just humoring him.

But the tone of the soldier still talking with upper command was anything but light-hearted. Even more telling, all the aliens were exhibiting the telltale fluttering of radiator membranes that was the mark of serious emotion. They believed him, all right.

And only then did it occur to him that Shahni Haafiz's sneak attack might have something to do with that. A human in the Shahni's palace would almost certainly be lying to Qasama's invaders. A human who those same Shahni had tried to kill might not be.

"Which walls?" the Troft demanded.

That was, Merrick realized with a sinking sensation, a damn good question. He'd hoped to sell this story to the Trofts, but had never really expected to get even this far with it. Apparently his bloody tunic, plus the ticking countdown timer the young Qasaman man had set up, had convinced someone to take the whole thing seriously.

Only now he was expected to point out some actual explosives as confirmation. Without any such proof, the Trofts would probably put his story down to an elaborate hoax and go about their business. At least until the building turned to fiery dust eight and a half minutes from now. "I don't—" Merrick began.

"Traitor!" the Qasaman man shouted suddenly. "Don't tell them!"

Merrick jerked, the movement sending a fresh wave of pain through his chest, the words themselves digging deep into his soul. Couldn't these people understand that he was trying to help them? Were they all so full of unthinking rage at what his parents and grandparents had done that they couldn't see anything beyond that?

And then he took another look into the young man's eyes. Eyes that were holding steady on Merrick even as the rest of his face twisted with rage and contempt. Eyes that waited until Merrick was looking straight at them, and then flicked to his right.

And with that, some of the frustrated weariness lifted from Merrick's shoulders. The young man was onto Merrick's plan . . . and despite Qasama's corporate institutional rage at the Cobra Worlds, he was willing to cooperate. "You want to die?" Merrick demanded, throwing every bit of acting ability he'd ever had into selling it.

"I will die with honor," the young man snarled, again twitching his eyes to his right. "Let them die, too, like the dung worms that they are."

"You die however you want to," Merrick bit out. "I'd rather live." He pointed at the wall the Qasaman had indicated. "You want to see some of the explosives? You can start with that wall right there."

The lead Troft snapped an order, and one of the soldiers grouped around the Qasamans stepped across the hallway, sprung a long knife, and stabbing into the wall between a pair of standing sculptures. He twisted the knife hard over and pulled, and a half-meter chunk of some plaster-like substance came free.

And behind it, nestled into the space between the a pair of thick wooden supports, was a square meter's worth of a plastic-wrapped gray clay.

The lead Troft didn't waste even a second gawking. [The prisoners, take them below,] he snapped, loud enough for Merrick to hear even without using his enhancements. [Their bindings, fasten them along the way. The commanders, warn them immediately.]

"And that's just one of them," Merrick said as the Trofts grabbed the Qasamans' arms or jabbed lasers into their ribs, getting the group moving down the hallway toward the elevators. A second later Merrick bit back a gasp of pain as his own arm was grabbed and he was hustled off after the others.

And as they hurried along, one of the Trofts wove in and out of the Qasamans, fastening their arms behind them with chain-link wrist shackles. Merrick watched the operation closely, studying the restraints and trying to figure out where best they could be broken. Unlike the solid-bar shackles the Qasamans had used on him earlier, chains were harder for his nanocomputer to pinpoint when it didn't have any optics available for positioning data. The place where the chain was fastened to the right wrist cuff, he decided, would be his best bet.

The Troft finished with the Qasamans and headed toward Merrick with one final set of shackles in hand.

Merrick glanced a target lock onto the spot he'd chosen, and silently let the alien pin his arms behind him.

The elevators were both waiting when the group arrived. The five Qasamans and their escort were guided into one, while Merrick and his own five-Troft guard took the other.

Merrick took a careful breath as the elevator started down, his nose tingling with the subtle scents of Troft and metal and armored leotard, his mind's eye flashing with unpleasant images from his last time in an elevator with Qasama's invaders. But this wouldn't be a replay of that other deadly ride. This time, he was going to cooperate fully with the Trofts. Right up to the moment when he stopped.

"Three minutes," the sergeant called softly from the hallway. "All gunners, stand ready."

Lying flat on his belly on one of the Lodestar Hospital's beds, Daulo took a moment to reflect on the irony of the whole situation. Earlier, Jin Moreau and Siraj Akim had gone to tremendous lengths to get him and Fadil out of this very place. And yet, now here they were again, joining a dozen other Qasaman soldiers preparing to throw this invasion down the enemy's throat.

On the face of it, moving troops into a building that the Trofts had already sequestered could be considered the height of foolishness. But on the other hand, bypassing the guards the Trofts had set up at the hospital's entrances had been simplicity itself, thanks to the subcity passages. And Daulo had to admit that after Jin and Siraj Akim had put the Lodestar into the center of Troft attention it was probably the last place the invaders would expect the Qasamans to come back to.

It was also unarguable that this particular line of eighth-floor rooms gave a perfect view of the rear of the Palace and the enemy soldiers guarding that section of the perimeter.

"Uh-oh," Fadil murmured from the bed beside Daulo's. "Look there, Father, at the group heading toward the street."

Daulo shifted his gaze to the street running along the front of the Palace. There were two different groups there, one consisting of five Qasamans and a half-dozen Troft guards, the other composed of a single human and five more of the aliens. "What about them?" he asked.

"Look closely at the singleton," Fadil said. "I believe we know him."

Frowning, Daulo swung his rifle around, centering the scope on the man Fadil had indicated.

It was Merrick Moreau.

"You suppose this is part of his plan?" Fadil suggested, his tone making it clear that he thought exactly the opposite.

"Enough chatter," the sergeant crouched beside the window growled. "If you villagers can't keep your minds and eyes where they're supposed to be, I'll find something else for you to do."

"Our apologies," Daulo said, his face warming with embarrassment and annoyance. *Villagers.* Not fellow soldiers, or fellow snipers, or even fellow Qasamans. Just *villagers.*

He stole a final look at the street as Merrick Moreau and his guards filed through the massive rear doors of the first of the two armored trucks the aliens had pulled to the curb, while the group of Qasamans were ushered into the one behind it.

He could only hope that being taken prisoner *was,* in fact, part of Merrick Moreau's plan.

"It's time," Miron Akim murmured from behind Jin.

With a start, Jin jolted out of a light doze and checked her nanocomputer's clock. Fifty-eight minutes of Akim's estimated hour to Plan Saikah had passed. "Right," she confirmed. "Let me get turned around."

Looking casually over at one of the room's two hidden cameras, she put a targeting lock on it. Then, gripping her chair's armrests, she started rocking her body back and forth, steadily walking her chair around toward the window.

"You still wish to destroy the window first?" Akim murmured.

"It's our best chance of hiding who I am," Jin reminded him. "At least for a little longer."

"And every minute that truth is concealed is valuable," Akim agreed with a sigh. "Very well. Proceed."

Jin continued to walk the chair around until she was facing the window. As she settled herself into place, she glanced behind her across the room and put a targeting lock on the second hidden camera. Then, turning back to the window, she lifted her arms off the armrests as high as the shackles permitted and began curving her hands into a series of sign-language configurations.

Not genuine ones, of course. Or at least, nothing that would make any sense to anyone watching her. She'd learned some of the gestures when she was a girl, mostly so that she and her sister Fay could talk together at family gatherings without the adults eavesdropping on their conversation. Once Fay had married and moved off Aventine, though, Jin's abilities had waned to the point where she could now barely even remember the finger-spelling letters.

But the Trofts had no way of knowing that. For all they knew, the random set of gestures she was making might be an esoteric Qasaman battle code. If they were good little soldiers, they would be recording her every move and trying to figure out what she was trying to say.

And with their attention now hopefully pointed in the wrong direction, she activated her sonic disruptor.

She started the weapon at low power, giving its sensors time to search for the window's resonance. In principle, this was no different than the trick she'd pulled back at the Sun Center when she'd shattered the glass surrounding the observation catwalk. In practice, though, the size of this window made the whole thing considerably less certain. Not only would the resonances be harder to hit, but it would take a lot more power to actually shatter the glass.

And if she couldn't make that happen, her hoped-for diversion wasn't going to happen.

Deep within her, she felt a subtle change in vibration as the sonic locked onto the window's resonance. Still making her nonsense hand signals, she fed more power to the weapon. Ten seconds, she decided. If she couldn't break the glass in ten seconds she wasn't going to break it at all. Out of the corner of her eye, she saw Akim join in the fun with hand signals of his own.

Her mental countdown had reached nine seconds when, without even a warning crack, the window blew up in their faces.

The explosion was so unexpected and so violent that Jin nearly missed out on the opportunity she'd been trying to create. But then her brain unfroze, and as the flying glass swirled past her and Akim she twisted her hands into cross-fire positions and fired her fingertip lasers.

Her nanocomputer responded with its usual deadly efficiency, gouging a pair of black-edged holes in the walls where the hidden cameras had been, hopefully fast enough that the Trofts would assume they'd been taken out by shards from the exploded window. Shifting aim, Jin cross-fired at her own wrist shackles, blasting apart the metal and freeing her hands. Another pair of shots freed her legs, and then she was out of her chair, turning toward the door. If the Trofts had left guards out there, they would be charging in any second now.

But the door remained closed. Keeping one eye on the panel, Jin cut Akim free of his chair, and together they headed across the room.

They were nearly to the door when it finally slammed open and a pair of Trofts charged through.

A blast from her antiarmor laser could have taken them out instantly. But Jin had something a bit more subtle in mind. Putting a targeting lock on the lead Troft, she bent her knees and shoved herself off the floor straight toward him.

The combination of targeting lock and leap kicked Jin's nanocomputer into the programmed ceiling flip that Merrick had performed earlier for Akim and the other Djinn. Only this time, it wasn't a sturdy ceiling that took the impact of her feet, but the Troft, who gave an agonized cough of expelled air as he went flying back into his companion. Jin herself bounced back from the impact, again turning halfway around as her nanocomputer tried to finish the ceiling flip, and landed on her side on the floor. She scrambled up into a crouch as

Akim grabbed one of the Trofts' lasers and did a quick one-two slam to their helmeted heads. "Come," he snapped to Jin. Flipping the laser around into firing position, he stepped over the unconscious aliens and out into the hallway.

And threw himself to the floor as a pair of laser shots blazed through the air from down the hallway to the left.

Biting out a curse, Jin again bent her knees and leaped forward. Her arcing path shot her just through the doorway, her momentum breaking as she grabbed the door jamb with her left hand and brought herself to a sudden halt. She caught a glimpse of four Trofts at the far corner, two of them in kneeling positions in front of the other two as another pair of shots cut through the space where she would have been if she'd let her leap carry her all the way into the hallway.

The Trofts were busily correcting their aim as Jin fell flat onto her back on the hallway floor beside Akim and slashed her antiarmor laser across them, collapsing them into crumpled heaps.

"Quickly," Akim murmured from her side as he scrambled to his feet.

"Shall I clear us a path?" Jin asked, eyeing the corner beyond the dead Trofts. There were bound to be more of the aliens gathering somewhere on the far side.

"No need." Akim crossed to the wall across from the office they'd just broken out of and rested his hand against a decorative wall-mounted plaque.

And two meters to the right, a section of the inner wall popped open. "Quickly," he said again, nodding Jin toward the opening.

Jin threw a final look at the dead Trofts. So much for not revealing who she really was. But maybe the Troft commanders would assume someone had simply used one of their own lasers on the victims. Stepping behind Akim, she slipped into the narrow entryway.

From the way Akim had described the elevator escape route earlier, Jin had expected to find herself in some kind of emergency drop shaft. To her surprise, the hidden door led instead into a narrow corridor that stretched away to her left, its far end hidden by a gentle inward curve. She took a couple of steps into the passageway, pausing there until Akim had joined her and closed the secret door, plunging them into total darkness.

Or rather, nearly total darkness. Activating her optical enhancers, Jin discovered there was a faint light coming from around the curve ahead. "Where are we?" she whispered.

"On the outer rim of the central monitoring room," Akim whispered. "Follow the corridor, but make no noise."

Jin looked past Akim's shoulder at the hidden door behind him, wondering what they would do if and when the Trofts found the way in. With Akim between her and any intruders, she would be severely limited in her ability to fight off any such attack.

"Don't concern yourself with pursuit," Akim said. He did something, and a section of the wall rotated silently to seal off the passageway behind him. "Should the invaders find the door, the passage will now lead them in the opposite direction. Now go."

They were nearly to the curved section when the whole building gave a gentle shake around her. Jin looked back at Akim, her stomach suddenly tightening. "The Palace?" she whispered.

His expression in her amplified eyesight was tight and grim. "Yes," he confirmed. "Hurry—the attack here will begin very soon."

Jin nodded and continued on. The adrenaline rush of the earlier activity had worn off, and she could feel a dozen points of stinging pain and the warmth of trickling blood where shards from the exploded window had dug a new set of wounds into her face and arms and chest. Ignoring the injuries, she reached the curve and walked around it.

And came to a sudden halt. She'd expected to find some kind of secret exit that would get them out of this place. Instead, clearly visible behind a layer of tinted plastic on the corridor's inner wall, was the central monitoring room Akim had mentioned.

A monitoring room currently filled to the rafters with Trofts.

Jin twitched back from the dark plastic, feeling horribly exposed. "Go further in," Akim whispered, pressing a hand impatiently into her shoulder. "Don't be concerned—we aren't visible."

Jin wasn't nearly so sure about that. Still, from the Trofts' frantic hand and head movements, not to mention their vibrating radiator membranes, it did appear that they had other matters occupying their attention at the moment. Keeping her movements slow and smooth, she sidled farther down the corridor, studying the room and its occupants as she went.

Not all of the Trofts appeared to be line soldiers. Not even most of them, she realized as she focused on the unarmored leotards most of the aliens were wearing. The only actual combat troops were a pair of armed Trofts standing guard by each of the room's two doors, plus another four standing at the sides of a large curved glass window that opened out onto the airfield and the rows of Troft ships parked across the open space. "What now?" she whispered as Akim moved into view of the room.

"We wait," he said. "And we watch."

Jin frowned. Watch? For what?

And then, through the window, she caught the flicker of gunfire.

The Qasamans were attacking the airfield.

She took a deep breath, methodically target-locking the eight armed Trofts in the control room and preparing herself mentally for combat. "I'm ready," she murmured. "Just tell me when."

There was no answer. "Miron Akim?" she prompted, turning to look at him.

And felt a shiver run up her back. Akim wasn't looking at her. He was instead gazing into the room, his eyes bright and unblinking, his lips making small movements as if he was talking silently to himself.

Earlier, Jin had wondered if he'd had come on this mission with some other purpose in mind than the ostensible one of freeing the two Shahni trapped in the Palace. Now, she finally understood what that purpose was.

Akim wasn't here to fight. He was here to observe. To see how exactly the Trofts would react to Plan Saikah.

Jin looked away from him back into the monitor room, fighting back a reflexive flicker of anger at having been lied to this way. She should have known there would be layers of other motivations lurking behind the obscuring veil of the Qasamans' distrust of her and Merrick.

Still, if Akim's goal had been observation, he'd certainly found a good place to do it. As the gunfire picked up outside, the monitor room burst into quiet but frenetic activity. The unarmored Trofts hunched over their consoles, their radiator membranes fluttering like crazy, their beaks snapping in rapid-fire cattertalk. The soldiers were equally tense, the ones at the window gazing tautly out at the battle that had been joined, the ones at the doors taking up full defensive positions, their lasers leveled against possible intrusion.

And unless Akim had lied to her about the extent of the Qasaman attack, there could be Djinn coming through those doors at any minute. "Do you want me to take them out?" she murmured. "Miron Akim? Shall I eliminate the soldiers?"

She counted ten seconds before Akim finally stirred. "We're finished here," he murmured. "The wall behind you. Give it a gentle push."

Jin turned around, studying the smooth wall. "Where?" she asked, looking in vain for the subtle clues as to where the wall ended and the hidden door began.

"There," Akim said, tapping his fingertips on an otherwise unremarkable section of the wall, his eyes still on the activity in the monitor room. "Push there."

Bracing her feet against the floor, Jin placed her palms against the wall and pushed. Nothing happened. She reset her feet and hunched her shoulders in preparation for another try, wondering if the whole wall was supposed to move, and wondering too why such an escape route was even here when obviously only someone with Cobra or Djinni strength could operate it.

"Enough," Akim said. He took a step backward, squatted down, and pulled up a thick section of floor, revealing a narrow shaft leading downward into darkness. Attached to one side of the shaft were a set of metal rungs. "Follow," he told Jin as he took hold of the top rung and lowered himself into the shaft. "Pull the door closed behind you—it will seal automatically."

A moment later they were heading downward, the faint sounds of voices and running feet drifting in through the shaft's walls. Jin tried her audio enhancers, but there was too much distortion and echo for her to tell whether the voices were Troft or human. Occasionally she also heard what sounded like volleys of laser fire.

They had gone perhaps three floors when a sudden surge of dizziness swept over her.

Reflexively, she looped her right arm through the nearest rung, crooking her elbow around the cold metal as she gripped her forearm with her left hand to make sure she didn't fall. The blackness of the shaft seemed to spin around her, twisting her brain into a hard knot and threatening to empty her stomach right where she stood.

"Jin Moreau?" Akim called softly from beneath her. "Are you all right?"

"I don't know," Jin said, clenching her teeth against the waves of vertigo.

"Do you need me to carry you?"

Jin took a careful breath. The dizziness was fading, as inexplicably as it had begun. "I'm all right," she said. "Just let me catch my breath a minute. Keep going—I'll catch up."

"We go together," Akim said firmly. "What happened?"

"I don't know," Jin said. "It felt like I'd been hit with a sonic weapon—dizziness and nausea and all that. You felt nothing?"

"No," Akim said. "And we certainly wouldn't have installed any such traps in these exits. Those most likely to use them would be poorly equipped to find and disable such barriers."

Jin nodded. That was pretty much the same conclusion she'd already come to.

Of more immediate importance, the simple act of nodding hadn't threatened to take off the top of her head. "I think I'm all right now," she said, cautiously readjusting her grip on the rung. "Go ahead—I'm right behind you."

They continued downward. Jin took each rung carefully, making sure she had a solid grip with one hand before releasing the other. The voices and running feet and gunfire still echoed through the shaft, and she wondered vaguely if the Qasamans were winning.

And tried not to wonder what was happening to her.

CHAPTER FOURTEEN

Merrick's first indication of how seriously the Trofts were taking their new prisoners was the sheer thickness of the rear double doors on the truck they marched him up to. The doors were dauntingly thick, heavy with the sort of armor that would have worn well on a frontline urban assault tank.

It was only as he stepped into the vehicle and got a look at the interior that he understood why it had such security overkill. Instead of the plain benches and equipment racks or attachment rings he would have expected to find in a troop carrier, the vehicle was instead equipped with padded walls, monitor and communications screens, and a half dozen luxuriously upholstered and padded couches.

This wasn't a simple troop carrier. It was a senior officers' transport.

"Sit," one of the Trofts piling in behind him ordered, punctuating the order with a poke from his laser.

"Watch it," Merrick growled, striding past the rear couches and sitting down on the rightmost of the two front ones. And suppressing a grim smile.

Because the Trofts had made a mistake. A big one. A normal troop carrier would probably have had a personnel section that was sealed away from the driver's cab. A prisoner transport certainly would have.

But not this vehicle. This vehicle was for VIPs, who would want to see what was going on as they drove along, studying terrain and troop positions through the thick glass windshield.

Which meant there wasn't even a partial barrier between where Merrick was sitting and the driver sitting on the left side of the cab.

He'd barely gotten himself settled when the rear doors thudded shut. The driver apparently already had his orders, and immediately shifted into drive and pulled away from the curb. A moment later, they were lumbering down the street.

"Where are we going?" Merrick asked, turning back toward the Trofts behind him.

None of them bothered to answer. None of them had made any move to settle onto the fancy couches, either, Merrick noted, instead propping themselves against the walls or bracing themselves into the rear corners. Despite the vehicle's slight roll and occasional bounce, though, all five lasers were holding remarkably steadily on Merrick.

"Well?" Merrick tried again, shifting his gaze to each of the Trofts in turn as he put a targeting lock onto each faceplate. His fingertip lasers hadn't done much good earlier against those faceplates, but his more powerful antiarmor laser shouldn't have that problem. "Come on—how about a little consideration?" he continued. "I just saved all your skins from the self-destruct, you know."

"That remains to be seen," one of the Trofts finally said. "If you lied, it will go badly for you."

The words were barely out of his mouth when a thunderous blast slammed into the truck from behind, lifting its rear end momentarily off the street and sending the whole vehicle into a violent swerve.

And as the Trofts grabbed at the walls for balance, Merrick opened fire.

It would have been better if he could have tackled the soldiers first, while the element of surprise was still with him. But the first targeting lock he'd set up, back inside the Palace, had been on his shackles, and that was where his first shot had to go. He triggered his left fingertip laser, hoping the Trofts bouncing around the transport would be too preoccupied to notice what was happening.

His hand twitched and curled as the nanocomputer shifted it into position, and with a flash of heat across his wrist the cuff broke in half and Merrick was free. Rolling over onto his side on the couch, he lifted his left leg and triggered his antiarmor laser.

But the Trofts had indeed noticed that first blast. Even as Merrick's laser began to blaze its precision shots across the open space, all five aliens opened fire.

Merrick's nanocomputer took over, swinging his shoulder violently backward, twisting his torso to send him rolling off the couch onto the floor. But in the cramped space even programmed reflexes could only do so much. As Merrick fired his final shot, a brilliant flash stabbed across his vision and a burning stab of pain lanced across his right cheek.

Clenching his teeth against the agony, he pushed himself shakily back up onto the couch. His cheek felt like it was on fire, and his right eye could see nothing but a giant purple blob. Switching to his optical enhancers, he peered forward into the cab.

The driver was still fighting the wheel as the aftershocks from the Palace explosion continued to shake both the vehicle and the ground beneath it. Whether the Troft was aware of what had just happened behind him Merrick couldn't tell, but he had no intention of giving the alien time to react to it. Shoving himself off the couch, he staggered across the weaving vehicle into the cab, grabbed the driver's arm and pulled him out of his seat, then threw him across the cab to smash headfirst into the window on the opposite side.

To Merrick's surprise, the soldier didn't simply bounce back off of the obviously strengthened glass, but instead went straight through as the impact popped the window neatly out of its frame and onto the street. The Troft himself ended up half in and half out of the cab, hanging limply through the window with his legs dangling inside. Dropping into the seat behind the wheel, Merrick pressed his foot on the accelerator to get back up to speed and gave the controls a quick once-over. Everything seemed simple and straightforward enough.

He peered into his side-view mirrors. The other transport was still following closely, apparently with no idea that anything was wrong. For a moment Merrick wondered why the driver was ignoring the Troft hanging out though the window, then realized that part of the transport's exterior wouldn't be visible from the other driver's position.

But the soldier would be extremely visible to any other Trofts they might happen to pass. Whatever Merrick was going to do, he had to do it before they ran across a patrol or vehicle and the alarm was raised. Taking a deep breath, he pressed the accelerator to the floor.

With a muted roar from the engine, the transport leaped ahead. The sudden change in speed seemed to take the other driver by surprise, but a second later he also began to speed up. Merrick continued to accelerate, watching as the transport behind him slowly closed the gap.

And as it settled into place a few meters behind him, Merrick braced himself against the wheel and jammed on the brakes.

Once again, the other driver was caught completely by surprise. This time, though, the results were immediate and cataclysmic. Even as Merrick fought the sudden yawing from his own transport, the other vehicle plowed full-tilt into the rear of Merrick's.

There was a horrendous grinding of metal and both transports jumped forward, the impact jamming Merrick's back and head into the thin seat cushion and the unyielding metal behind it. He wrestled the vehicle to a halt, jammed the gearing into park, and wrenched open the door beside him. Jumping out, he headed back.

The Trofts had built their transports well, he found as he reached the other vehicle. Despite the force of the collision, neither was badly damaged, with the hood of the rear vehicle merely showing some external crumpling and the doors of Merrick's bent inward slightly at the point of impact. Jumping up onto the top of the rear vehicle's hood, Merrick peered in through the windshield.

The collision might not have affected the vehicle itself much, but the same couldn't be said of its passengers. The driver was draped over the steering wheel, his torso twitching with some kind of reaction Merrick couldn't identify. Behind him, both the prisoners and their guards were sprawled on the rear compartment floor, some of them motionless, the rest making the slow movements of dazed people fighting their way back toward full consciousness.

Jumping back down onto the street, Merrick tried the door handle. It was locked, of course, but he already knew the way in. Aiming his little fingers at the lower edge of the window, he fired his lasers, methodically vaporizing a line through the metal lip protecting the thick glass.

And then, without even a hint of warning, his peripheral vision caught a flicker of movement from the transport's rear.

Once again, his nanocomputer took over, shoving him back from the door and toward the ground as it swung his hands up to aim at the unexpected threat.

But it wasn't the Trofts from inside the transport, as he'd assumed. Sprinting silently toward him were two Qasamans in gray Djinn outfits with matching gloves and soft helmets. "Moreau?" one of them called.

"Yes," Merrick confirmed, scrambling to his feet again. "There are prisoners in the back—"

"We know," the Qasaman cut him off as they stopped beside him. "Carsh Zoshak sent us. I am Narayan—how can we assist?"

"We need to unseal this window," Merrick said, turning his fingertip lasers on the frame again. "It pops right out—their idea of an emergency exit, I suppose."

"Understood," Narayan said, stepping up beside Merrick and adding his more powerful glove-mounted lasers to the operation. "Baaree: see to the rear."

The second Qasaman nodded and headed back along the transport's side. "Wait—come back!" Merrick called after him. "Waste of time—you can't get in that way."

"He knows that," Narayan said calmly. "His purpose is to provide a diversion."

Merrick swallowed, a flush of embarrassment warming his face. "Oh."

Sure enough, a moment later the transport began to vibrate as Baaree began pounding with loud uselessness against the rear doors. Merrick kept his eyes on his work, trying to ignore the throbbing pain in his cheek and chest.

Ten seconds later, he and Narayan had finished. "Now we need to pop it out," Merrick said, wincing as he eyed the narrow gap beneath the window. It was barely wide enough for his fingertips, with burning hot metal all around it. But without anything handy that he could use as a pry bar, his fingers would have to do.

He was steeling himself for the task when Narayan deftly shouldered him out of the way, brandishing a thick-bladed knife he'd produced from somewhere. "I'll do it," he said. "Take a moment and assess the enemy threat."

"Right," Merrick said, his knees suddenly starting to tremble with fatigue, shock, and probably loss of blood. Stepping back to give Narayan room to work, he looked around.

Earlier, when he and his mother and Miron Akim had driven to the control tower, it had seemed like the area was crawling with Trofts. Now, in contrast, the aliens were conspicuous by their absence, at least in and around the couple of blocks within Merrick's view. Whatever else Plan Saikah had or hadn't accomplished, it had certainly cleared the enemy troops off the streets.

But the lack of ground troops didn't mean the Trofts didn't still control the city. As Merrick stepped out of the transport's shadow, he found himself gazing at one of the Trofts' big wrigglefish sentry ships as it squatted on guard two blocks away.

A shiver ran up his back. The weapons clusters beneath the stubby forward wings were tracking back and forth, a constant reminder of the death and destruction ready to be unleashed at the touch of a button. So far the operators of those weapons didn't seem to be reacting to this particular drama, but Merrick doubted that would last much longer. Once the aliens realized what was happening, they would certainly try to do something about it.

There was a sudden crackling thud, and Merrick turned back to see the transport's window pop neatly out of its frame. "Come," Narayan called, reaching in through the gap and opening the door. As Merrick hurried back to join him, the Djinni grabbed the twitching Troft driver, pulled him out onto the street, and bounded inside. Merrick grabbed the edge of the door and started to follow.

And nearly lost his grip as a blast of reflected sound slammed over him from inside the transport. "Djinni Moreau!" Narayan called, his voice suddenly slurred. "Assist!"

Shaking his head to clear it, Merrick pulled himself up into the cab and around the seat into the transport's main compartment.

When he'd looked through the windshield right after the two vehicles had crashed, he'd seen the passengers and their Troft guards sprawled on the floor where the impact had thrown them. But in the minute since then, the situation had changed dramatically. Four of the six aliens were back on their feet, one of them battling for his laser with the young Qasaman man who had tangled the chain of his wrist shackles around the weapon's muzzle and was trying desperately to keep the aim away from himself and the other prisoners. One of the other Trofts was pounding at the young man with the butt of his laser, trying to knock him away from the first soldier. In the far corner the young woman was standing with defiant helplessness between her children and the lasers of the other two conscious aliens. To Merrick's left, the old woman had thrown herself on top of one of the Trofts who hadn't yet made it back to his feet, trying to hold him down with the sheer weight of her body.

It was a scene that should have been vibrant with violent activity, but at the moment no one was doing much of anything at all. Everyone in the vehicle, human and Troft alike, was staggering with the effects of Narayan's sonic blast.

Everyone except Merrick.

He took out the two Trofts facing down the woman and children first, wrenching the laser from the nearest alien's grip and slamming it hard into his faceplate, then repeating the action with the second. He turned next to the aliens grappling with the young man, only to find that one of them had recovered enough from the sonic blast to try to bring his weapon to bear. Merrick responded by locking on to the alien's faceplate and blazing an antiarmor laser shot that dropped the Troft to the floor.

And then suddenly there was a movement to Merrick's left, and he spun around as Baaree, the Djinni who'd been providing the diversion at the transport's rear, bounded in through the driver's door, his glove-mounted lasers blazing away at the remaining Trofts. Merrick shifted his attention to the alien still trying to shove the old woman off him, targeted his helmet, and silenced him with another antiarmor blast.

Seconds later, it was over. "Nicely done," Merrick said, stepping over to the still shaky young man and blasting off his wrist shackles as Narayan helped the old woman to her feet. "We have a plan for getting out of here?"

"There's an escape tunnel three houses behind us," Narayan said, his voice still a little slurred as he gestured Baaree toward the transport's cab. Baaree nodded and stepped into the cab, sitting down behind the wheel. "We'll back the transport there and escape into the subcity."

"Sounds good," Merrick said, going over to the young woman and children and getting to work on their shackles. "Let's hope the engine still works."

His answer was a sudden jerk as the transport wrenched itself free of the other vehicle and began rolling backward. "No problem," Baaree called.

"Excellent," Narayan said, crouching down to peer out the side windows as the transport began to pick up speed. "As quickly as possible," he added. "We don't know when the invaders will—"

And without warning, the interior of the transport suddenly lit up with brilliant flash of blue light and a thunderclap and wave of superheated air that slammed Merrick up against the rear doors. Once again his nanocomputer took over, throwing him sideways toward the floor in an attempt to get him out of the line of fire. Both eyes were dazzled into uselessness, and he keyed in his enhancers to try to see what was going on.

He almost wished he hadn't. The entire windshield had been shattered by the sheer intensity of the blast, and everything in the cab that was flammable was ablaze with roiling flames and a thick, foul-smelling black smoke.

Baaree himself was no longer burning. There was nothing left of him to burn.

The Trofts in the sentry ship two blocks away had found their shot.

"Djinni Moreau!" a voice gasped through the crackle of flames. "Djinni Moreau!"

"Here," Merrick called back, closing his eyes tightly against the smoke and turning in the direction of the voice. Narayan was crouched at the side of the transport, the old woman coughing violently at his side, the Djinni's body curled half over hers to protect her as best he could.

"Can you see the others?" Narayan called back. "My eyes are blocked."

Merrick looked around, keying in his enhancers' infrared to try to penetrate the thickening smoke. The young couple and their children were huddled together in the rear of the transport, their bodies wracked with silent coughs. "They're okay," he reported. "We're going to need a new plan."

"Did they shoot through the windshield or the transport roof?" Narayan asked.

Merrick looked back at the front of the vehicle. The windshield, as he'd already noted, was completely gone. But the metal roof of the cab, though blistered, was still quite solid. "The windshield," he reported. "But we can't stay in here forever."

"We won't," Narayan said. "The rear doors are the same—" He broke off into a fit of coughing.

"Are the same material," Merrick finished for him, turning and targeting the three hinges on the left-hand door. Making sure the Qasamans were all out of splatter range, he lifted his leg and fired three quick shots.

With a screech, the door broke free, its outer edge sagging outward against the lock that still held it to the pillar between the doors. "One away," Merrick called. "Come on."

A handful of seconds later Narayan was at his side, feeling his way with one hand as he led the old woman with the other. "I still can't see to shoot," he said.

"I got it," Merrick said. He crossed to the young family, led them away from the door on that side, and blew that set of hinges. "Can you get one of them?" he asked.

In answer, Narayan moved to one of the doors, fumbling a bit as he got his hands through the crack beneath it. "Ready."

Targeting the door's lock, Merrick blasted it free, severing the last connection with the rest of the transport.

The door sagged suddenly in Narayan's grip, but the Djinni's power suit was up to the task and the heavy panel didn't fall. Grunting with the strain, Narayan manhandled the door back up to his level, leaning back to balance it against his chest and cheek. Then, stepping carefully out onto the street, he half turned to put the door between himself and the distant Troft ship's lasers. Merrick winced as the sudden cross breeze sent an extra wave of heat washing over them from the fire still blazing in the transport's cab. "Beside me," Narayan ordered.

The young man helped the old woman down from the transport's rear and positioned the two of them behind

Narayan and his new shield. "You will bring the others?" the Djinni added.

"Of course," Merrick said. "Go."

"Stay close," Narayan said. With the two Qasamans close behind him, he began backing rapidly down the street.

Merrick looked at the young woman, her two children clutched close to her sides in the choking smoke. "You ready?" he asked.

"We are in your hands," she said simply.

Turning back, trying to ignore the flashes of laser light sizzling over his head as the Troft sentry ship fired shot after shot at Narayan's shield, Merrick blew the lock, sending the remaining door slamming to the ground with a dull thud. Jumping out beside it, he got a grip on one edge, angled it to the side, and got his other hand underneath it. He locked his finger servos solidly in place and levered the door upward. "Now," he called to the woman.

She was already out of the transport, still holding the boys tightly to her sides, and at Merrick's order she moved them all behind the shield, coming close enough to Merrick for him to feel her breath on his neck. "Crouch down," Merrick warned her, taking a moment to look over his shoulder. Narayan and his two charges were just disappearing into a narrow walkway between two of the houses, their shield battered and warped by the Trofts' attacks but apparently still solid. Turning back, Merrick hunched over, lowering the door to provide as much protection as he could to their legs and feet. "Now," he ordered.

The door had been rocked with four blasts of laser fire by the time they reached the walkway. Merrick held the shield in place against the side of the nearest house, letting the woman and children slip away and hurry down the passage. Then he followed, dropping the half-vaporized door behind him.

Narayan was waiting by an opening in the side of one of the buildings along the walkway. "Hurry," he called, gesturing to Merrick as the woman and boys disappeared through the door.

Merrick nodded, clenching his teeth as the scene in front of him began to waver. The adrenaline of the battle and mad-dash escape was starting to fade, and the shock and blood loss were starting to make themselves felt again. *Just get to the door,* he told himself. *That's all you have to do. Just make it to the door.*

He had made it through the door, and Narayan had closed it behind them, when the blackness finally took him.

"*Fire!*" the sergeant at the hospital window snapped.

Pressing his cheek against his rifle stock, Fadil held his breath and gently squeezed the trigger. The rifle bucked against his shoulder, and as he brought the weapon back to position he had the satisfaction of seeing the Troft he'd targeted sprawled on the ground. All around him, his father and the others were also firing, dropping the invaders like the vermin they were. Grinning tightly, Fadil lined up his sights on the next Troft in line.

And with a sudden buzzing sound, something came flying in through the window. It hit the sergeant full in the chest, the breaking-stick crack of its explosive not quite loud enough to cover the man's agonized scream. Clenching his teeth against the sound, Fadil checked his aim and fired his second shot, dropping another enemy soldier.

He was lining up the muzzle on his third target when he heard the sound of multiple buzzings coming toward them.

And then, with a multiple blast of a hundred carefully placed explosives, the entire Palace disintegrated in a cloud of fire and smoke and debris. Fadil flinched back, reflexively lifting his rifle in front of his face to shield his eyes.

The roar of the Palace blast was still hammering his ears when the rifle shattered in his grip.

Fadil heard himself cry out as shards of metal and wood sliced into his arms and shoulders and the side of his face. Dimly, he felt a hand grab his arm and yank him sideways, pulling him off the bed he was lying on and tumbling him onto the floor.

And then the entire room seemed to explode, and as the flame and agony and noise rose all around him, he fell into darkness.

CHAPTER FIFTEEN

The room around Merrick was ablaze with light as he dragged himself back toward consciousness. He winced away from the glare, trying to turn his head, trying even harder to close his eyes. But nothing seemed to do any good.

It was only as he untangled his arm from some kind of obstruction and brought his hand up in front of his face that he came awake enough to realize that his eyes *were* shut, and that the light was coming in via his optical enhancers. Apparently, he'd never gotten around to shutting them off after the battle.

He shut them off now and carefully opened his eyes. He was lying on a bed in what seemed to be a long, wide corridor with rows of beds on both sides. Some of the beds were empty, but most were occupied by figures wrapped in the same kind of hospital gowns the old man they'd broken out of the Lodestar Hospital had been wearing.

And the obstruction Merrick had had to free his arm from turned out to be a small group of thin tubes and wires that were connected to various places on his arm and torso. He frowned down at them, trying to trace them out and hoping he hadn't pulled out anything important.

"Welcome back," a familiar voice said from his left.

Merrick twisted his head around. Carsh Zoshak was sitting on a chair behind him and beside a rolling equipment table. "Thanks," Merrick said. "How long was I out?"

Zoshak shrugged. "A couple of days," he said. "You were in pretty bad shape."

"I was, wasn't I?" Merrick agreed, the memory of all his injuries flooding back to him. He'd been so busy checking out his surroundings over the past minute or so that he hadn't even thought about checking out himself. Carefully, he touched his cheek where the Troft laser had burned it.

To find that it was completely healed.

He frowned, pressing a little harder against the skin, and then gently sliding the finger up and down. The skin felt a little leathery beneath the growth of beard stubble, but it wasn't the hard leather of scar tissue. More importantly, there was no pain.

Nor was there any pain in his chest where Shahni Haafiz had tried his best to knife him open. He slipped a hand beneath his gown and touched the skin, to find the same slightly leathery consistency and no sign of torn flesh.

He looked back to find an amused smile on Zoshak's face. "I gather you're impressed?" the Djinni suggested.

"Very much so," Merrick assured him, a sudden coolness dampening his initial excitement at his remarkable healing. For all this to have happened so quickly . . . "I assume this means you used some of your drugs on me?"

Zoshak's smile faded. "Of course we did," he said. "Would you have preferred to spend weeks in a recovery room?"

"No, of course not," Merrick said. He touched his cheek again, thinking about the stories he'd heard about the Qasamans' drugs and their sometimes dangerous side effects.

Still, the Shahni were surely taking care not to damage their soldiers. *Any* of their soldiers, even interlopers like himself and his mother.

Speaking of whom—"Have you heard anything about my mother and Miron Akim?" he asked.

A shadow seemed to cross Zoshak's face. "I have," he said. "They were both able to escape their captors and return safely to the subcity."

"How safely?" Merrick asked, something ominous stirring inside him as he tried to read the other's expression. "Were they injured? Lightly? Seriously? Dangerously?"

"Neither was injured in their escape."

"After their escape?" Merrick persisted. "Before their escape? Come on, Carsh Zoshak—I need to know."

Zoshak's lips compressed briefly. "Your mother may have some other medical problems," he said reluctantly. "Problems unrelated to their mission."

Merrick grimaced. She had medical problems, all right. All Cobras her age did. "Are they going to check her out?"

"I believe they've already done the tests and are studying the results," Zoshak said.

"Can I see her?"

"Certainly, after the doctors discharge you," Zoshak said. "That should be later today, or tomorrow at the latest."

"Can't we sneak over there right now?" Merrick asked. "I promise to be good and keep the meeting short."

"Not until you're discharged," Zoshak said firmly. "Until then, you must remain in the ward."

Merrick peered down the line of beds, hoping to spot a doctor or nurse with whom he could argue the point. But he couldn't see anyone who seemed to be in charge.

But he'd had enough experience with doctors on Aventine to know that he'd probably be wasting his breath anyway. "Fine," he said with a sigh. "Can you at least tell me how the battle went?"

A muscle in Zoshak's cheek twitched. "The part you and I played was very successful," he said. "Those we rescued are safely in the subcity, where they've joined in the fight against the invaders. Mali Haafiz, in particular, asked me to extend her gratitude for your service to her and her family. She was the older woman," he added. "The wife of Shahni Haafiz."

"Who was the one who tried to kill me."

Zoshak grimaced. "Yes."

"I take it he has no more doubts about me?"

Zoshak's eyes slipped away. "Shahni Haafiz is very busy with the city's defense," he said obliquely.

Merrick felt a stirring of anger. "Meaning he still thinks I'm your enemy?"

"Keep your voice down," Zoshak warned, glancing almost furtively at the nearby beds. "Keep your words and your identity to yourself."

Merrick's budding anger vanished. The look in Zoshak's eyes . . . "Did something go wrong?" he asked quietly.

For a moment Zoshak didn't answer. Then, his shoulders seemed to droop. "Everything went wrong, Merrick Moreau," he said quietly. "We thought we were prepared for anything. We weren't. We thought we could take on any enemy who dared attack us. We couldn't."

Merrick felt his throat tighten. "How bad?"

Zoshak seemed to brace himself. "Thirty percent casualties, killed and wounded, among the Djinn who were deployed." He hesitated. "Among the regular soldiers, sixty percent."

Merrick stared at the Djinni in disbelief. Even in his great-grandfather's war against the Trofts the casualties hadn't been *that* bad. "But some of the wounded are going to recover, aren't they?"

"If their lives on the other side can be considered recovery," Zoshak said, an edge of bitterness in his voice. "Many will be crippled, or at the very least severely limited in what they can do. But that's not the point. The point is that what should have been a staggering blow against the invaders failed."

"I'm sorry" was all Merrick could think of to say.

"As are we all," Zoshak said with a sigh. "Ironic, isn't it, that the only clear successes all day were those that you and your mother were involved in." His gaze flicked to Merrick's left leg. "Those long lasers give you a strong advantage over even the Djinn."

"They're definitely handy," Merrick agreed. "But your glove-mounted lasers are no slouches, either. They're certainly stronger than our fingertip versions."

Zoshak hissed. "For all the good that did us."

"It did a lot of good," Merrick insisted. "For starters, I can't shoot through the Trofts' faceplates, with that instant black-block system of theirs. You can."

"The faceplates, perhaps," Zoshak conceded. "But our glove lasers aren't nearly powerful enough to penetrate their main armor." He snorted again. "I'm told the designers of our combat suits considered putting such a laser along the left calf, but ultimately rejected it as being too difficult to aim."

"It *is* a little tricky," Merrick agreed. "But you already have implants on your eye lenses for targeting, right? Couldn't they have tied an antiarmor laser into that system?"

"I don't know," Zoshak said. "Perhaps it wouldn't work because our system requires both eyes to be on target. The positioning of a calf-mounted laser would normally require us to fire it with only one eye on the target."

So either the Qasamans' computers couldn't handle the kind of targeting system Cobras routinely used, or else their power suits' servos weren't up to the necessary fine tuning. "So we got nothing out of the attack except a couple of the Shahni and their families?"

"The invaders took casualties," Zoshak said. "But we didn't permanently recover any buildings, nor did we inflict any serious damage on their weaponry or ships before we were pushed back. Particularly the ships."

"Yes, I saw what those sentry ships could do," Merrick said, grimacing at the memory of Djinn Baaree's fiery death.

"Yet the shipboard and vehicle weaponry was only a small part of our defeat," Zoshak said. "Many of our casualties were caused by small, self-homing missiles that seemed to seek out the sound of the soldiers' gunfire."

"I remember stories about things like that from my great-grandfather's war," Merrick said ruefully. "Not much you can do about them except try not to let the Trofts get close enough to use them."

"What do you mean, close enough?" Zoshak asked, frowning. "Some of the missiles were launched from over two blocks away."

"Two *blocks?*" Merrick asked, frowning. "They were able to lock on to gunfire noise from that far away? Accurately?"

"Accurately enough to kill and wound our soldiers," Zoshak said grimly.

Merrick scratched at his cheek stubble, trying to remember everything he'd ever learned about what little the Cobra Worlds' trading partners had let slip about Troft weaponry. Gunshots *did* have a fairly unique sound pattern, he knew. But for a missile to make that identification, then have enough sensor scope and memory to figure out the proper vector and guide the weapon there was starting to sound awfully complex. Especially for something small enough for antipersonnel use.

Unless the gunfire had come as a barrage, which would give the missile current-time data and allow it to take its electronic time locking in on the sounds. "Were the soldiers using machine guns or single-shot weapons?" he asked Zoshak. "And do we know how big the missiles were?"

"I don't," Zoshak said, standing up. "But if you feel up to a short walk, we could go speak to one of the field officers."

"I thought I wasn't supposed to leave the ward."

"You won't," Zoshak assured him. "Several of the wounded officers are in this facility. Perhaps one of them will be awake and willing to speak to you."

"It's worth a try," Merrick said, eyeing the tubes still poking into his arm. "Though come to think of it, I'm not sure how portable I am at the moment."

"Very portable," Zoshak assured him as he walked around the end of the bed. "Give me a moment, and I'll extend the medical stand's wheels."

A minute later they were walking down the corridor between the twin lines of beds. Merrick found himself feeling a little light-headed, and made sure to keep a firm grip on the rolling stand to help maintain his balance. At the end of the corridor they turned in to a much longer corridor that had likewise been equipped with beds and patients. As in Merrick's ward, most of the beds were occupied, and Merrick found his stomach churning as he noted how many head and chest wounds seemed to be in evidence.

He was passing yet another bed when the occupant's half-bandaged face suddenly leaped out at him. "Hold it," he said, grabbing Zoshak's arm and peering at the sleeping man. "Is that—?"

"Merrick Moreau?" a strained but familiar voice spoke up from the next bed over.

Merrick tore his eyes away from Daulo Sammon's closed eyes. Sure enough, Daulo's son Fadil was peering up at him from the next bed. He didn't look much better than his father, but at least his face seemed mostly undamaged. "What in the Worlds are you doing here?" he demanded as he stepped to the young man's side.

"What does it look like we're doing?" Fadil countered. "We're two of the casualties of the great Plan Saikah."

"Yes, but—" Merrick shot a look at Zoshak, who was standing a couple of paces away with a stony expression on his face. "I meant, why were you wounded in the first place," he said, turning back to Fadil. "Miron Akim told us the Shahni were keeping you and your father as hostages for our good behavior."

"And so they were, until I asked permission to join in the battle." Fadil smiled weakly. "They graciously allowed us to do so."

Merrick winced. "I'm sorry."

"You need not apologize, Merrick Moreau," Fadil said. "It was my decision, and that of my father, that put us here." He looked over at Zoshak. "And I would make the same decision again," he added, an edge of pride or challenge slipping into his voice.

"You may yet have that opportunity," Zoshak said. "You and every other villager on Qasama."

"We stand ready," Fadil assured him.

For another moment the city dweller and villager continued to stare at each other. Then, Zoshak stirred. "Merrick Moreau wishes information about the invaders' antipersonnel missiles," he said.

"They were fast, and they were deadly," Fadil growled. "What more do you need to know?"

"I want to figure out how they were aimed," Merrick said, trying to keep his voice calm. "Djinni Zoshak suggested they might have homed in on the sounds of your gunfire. Were you actually shooting when the missiles arrived?"

"We opened fire on the sergeant's command," Fadil said with the air of someone who's told the same story way too many times already. "The first missile struck him—I don't know how soon afterwards. Not long. The rest of the missiles came in a group. One of them hit my rifle, and then my father pulled me down on the floor as all the rest began exploding. Everyone was killed except us. Does that tell you anything?"

"Maybe," Merrick said. "You say the sergeant was hit first. Was he firing like everyone else?"

"I already said he was."

"And how far away were the Trofts you were shooting at?"

"We were in the hospital from which you and I escaped earlier," Fadil said. "Top floor. Our targets were the Trofts on the Palace grounds. Do a calculation, or ask someone to loan you a measuring tape."

Merrick scratched his cheek thoughtfully. At least a block's worth of distance, then. "And the main group of missiles arrived together?"

"I already said that, too," Fadil said impatiently.

"And you all had projectile rifles?" Merrick persisted. There was something here, something he could sense but couldn't quite get a handle on. "No lasers?"

"No," Fadil said.

"But teams using lasers against the invaders suffered the same fate," Zoshak put in.

"Really?" Merrick asked, frowning. "But lasers don't sound anything like projectile guns. How did the missiles home in on them?"

Zoshak shrugged. "Possibly through their heat signatures."

"Maybe," Merrick said, thinking back to the rescue of Mali Haafiz and the others of her family. "But in that case, why didn't the Trofts use them against Djinni Narayan and me? We were using our lasers like crazy out there."

"There may have been no one nearby who carried the launchers," Zoshak pointed out. "The Palace explosion and the multiple attacks drove most of the ground troops to cover." He grimaced. "At least briefly."

"I suppose," Merrick said, getting a firmer grip on his med stand as his head started to swim a little. "I still don't think that's the whole answer."

"Are you all right?" Zoshak asked.

"Just feeling a little dizzy," Merrick assured him. "Two days of no food, probably."

"Or two days on healing medication without time to purge the drugs from your system," Zoshak said, stepping forward and taking his arm. "Time you were returned to your bed."

"Wouldn't argue the point even if I could," Merrick agreed. "Thank you for your time, Fadil Sammon. And thank you, too, for your willingness to risk your lives."

Fadil snorted gently. "As if risking our lives for Qasama means anything to you."

"It does," Merrick told him. "Whether you believe it or not."

He turned away, paused a moment to wait for the spots in front of his eyes to fade out, then headed back the way they'd come. "I'm okay," he assured Zoshak as the other continued to hold his upper arm. "You don't have to hang around if you don't want to."

"It's not a problem," Zoshak assured him. "I'm happy to assist you."

"And I'm happy to have your company," Merrick said. "But you surely must have better things to do than visit the troops in the recovery ward."

Zoshak was silent for another two steps. "You misunderstand, Merrick Moreau," he said. "I'm not your visitor. I'm your guard."

Merrick swallowed. "Oh," he said.

They made the rest of the trip in silence.

Jin looked up from the report, her throat tight. "Thirty percent," she murmured.

"Yes," Miron Akim confirmed, his back unnaturally stiff as he sat in a chair beside Jin's hospital bed. He looked tired, Jin thought, his facial skin sagging, his eyelids clearly being held open by sheer force of will.

Jin herself had spent the past two days resting up after being healed from the glass cuts she'd received when she blew out the tower office window. Distantly, she wondered how Akim had spent those two days. "I don't know what to say, Miron Akim," she went on, laying the report on the bed beside her. "Is that the end, then? Do you have any fighting force left at all?"

"Of course we do," he assured her. "Less than a quarter of our soldiers and Djinn were committed to this first battle, and many of the wounded will recover enough to fight again." He grimaced. "The true horror of this loss was that we brought to it both the coordination of a preplanned attack and the element of surprise. That combination should have been sufficient to at least stagger the invaders, if not defeat them outright. To have instead paid so high a cost for so little a gain is a disaster."

His eyes bored suddenly into hers. "A disaster which we have no intention of revealing to the general populace."

"Understood," Jin said with a shiver. It was a given that secrecy and censorship were a necessary part of any wartime effort . . . but whether even a government as strict and powerful as the Shahni could keep something like this quiet remained to be seen. "Which leads directly to the question of why you're telling *me* about it."

"Because I come with two questions I must ask," Akim said. "The first . . . we have never trained for this sort of war, Jasmine Moreau. What we *have* trained for has clearly been ineffective. Your people, on the other hand, have fought against the Trofts. More importantly, *you* have fought against the Trofts. My first question, then, is whether you can offer advice and insight that will enable us to mount a more successful resistance."

Jin let out her breath in a huff. "That's a tall order, Miron Akim," she warned. "And understand that I'm not as well trained in combat as I wish I was. I'll have to think on the matter, but a couple of thoughts do come immediately to mind. First off, Cobras weren't designed for use as regular frontline troops. Our mission has always been one of harassment and sabotage, using small groups and infiltration tactics. I think that's also the direction your Djinn need to go."

"And the tactics themselves?" Akim asked. "You're familiar with them?"

"I had the standard Cobra course in military theory," Jin said. "But it was brief and largely theoretical. You and your military planners are undoubtedly far more knowledgeable than I am."

"Still, you have the advantage of having worked with such groups," Akim said. "But I understand that you need time to contemplate. Take what time you need, but no more than necessary."

"I'll be as quick as I can," Jin promised. "And the second question?"

Akim cocked his head slightly. "This may sound strange, but is there a value to razorarms that we're unaware of?"

Jin blinked. A value to *razorarms?* "What sort of value?"

"That is precisely the question." Abruptly, Akim stood up. "Come. I'll show you."

He waited until Jin had pulled on a robe and slippers, then led the way out of the private room into the subcity's maze of seemingly identical hallways. Jin walked carefully, favoring her bad left knee, trying to read the mood of the soldiers and civilians moving briskly back and forth down the hallway on their various errands. If any of them was worried about the failures of Plan Saikah, they weren't showing it.

Or perhaps they simply didn't know just how bad a failure it had been.

A few minutes later they reached a door flanked by a pair of armed soldiers. Akim gave them a hand signal as he and Jin approached, then stepped between them and pushed the door open. Pausing on the threshold, he gestured Jin inside.

Jin had expected an ordinary conference room. Instead, she found herself in a duplicate of the airfield tower control room. An exact duplicate, in fact, or at least exact within the limits of her memory.

"Over here," Akim said, brushing past her and heading across the room, circling the Qasamans who were gathered in twos and threes around the monitor stations.

Jin followed, glancing at the various monitors as she passed. Each display seemed to be active, with either a single image or else a short loop of words or images or track lines. It was, she realized with an eerie feeling, a complete reconstruction of the handful of seconds she and Akim had been standing in the hidden corridor.

Earlier, she'd wondered what Akim had been doing for the past two days. Now she knew.

"Here," Akim said as he stopped by a monitor no one else seemed to be interested in at the moment. "Sit down, and tell me what you see."

Jin slid into the chair in front of the monitor, wincing a bit as her bad knee gave a last twinge, and skimmed the display. It appeared to be a status report on—"Spine leopard captures," she murmured, frowning.

"In the forested areas to the north and west of Sollas," Akim said, tapping a list of latitude/longitude pairs. "Reports from the villages in those regions confirm the presence of large invader transports moving back and forth."

"Yes, but *spine leopards*?" Jin objected, frowning at the display. If she was reading the numbers correctly, the Trofts had already captured twenty of the predators by the time Akim took his mental snapshot of their activities, only a few hours into the aliens' occupation. If they were still at it, she could only guess how many they might have picked up since then. "What do they want with them all?"

"That was my question to you," Akim reminded her. "You've stated that your worlds have trade dealings with the Trofts. You've also been studying the creatures far longer than we have. So again I ask: are razorarm pelts in demand? Or is there something in their nature or biochemistry that would make them valuable to the invaders?"

"Nothing I've ever heard of," Jin said, staring at the display with a mixture of horror and revulsion. Could this whole invasion—all the death and destruction the Trofts had rained down on Qasama—be nothing more than a bizarre resource grab?

No—that made no sense. Qasama was as big as any other inhabitable world, with the Qasamans themselves occupying only a relatively small fraction of its land area. In the sixty years since the Cobra Worlds had brought the first spine leopards here, the animals had surely spread out far enough into uninhabited regions that anyone wanting to harvest them could simply travel out into the wilderness and do so.

But if the Trofts didn't want the predators as trophies, what *did* they want them for?

Unfortunately, there was only one reason Jin could think of, and it wasn't a pleasant one. "I think the people of Sollas are about to get some unexpected company," she told Akim grimly. "Best guess is that the Trofts are planning to release them into the cities and villages in the hope of keeping your soldiers and Djinn busy shooting something besides them."

"Yes, that was our thought as well," Akim said. "But it's been nearly three days since the invasion began. If the invaders intend to flood our streets with predators, why haven't they done so? What are they waiting for?"

"You're right, that doesn't make any sense," Jin said, grabbing for the edge of the desk. Suddenly, without warning, the dizziness she'd felt on the airfield tower escape ladder was hitting her again. "Maybe they're . . . waiting until they have . . . enough to—"

"Are you all right?" Akim asked sharply. "Jasmine Moreau?"

The last thing Jin remembered before the darkness took her was Akim's hand closing around her arm.

CHAPTER SIXTEEN

The dishes from the evening meal had been cleared away, the ward lights had been dimmed for the night, and Merrick was starting to drift off to sleep when he heard the sound of measured footsteps coming his direction.

He rolled over, grunting like a sleeping person might, and activated his optical enhancers. Six Djinn in full combat suits were marching quietly down the corridor toward him.

Merrick turned his head slightly to give his enhancers an angle behind him. The chair Carsh Zoshak had been occupying for most of the day was vacant. Time for the changing of the guard?

He looked back at the approaching Djinn, this time concentrating on their faces. The enhancers had limited detail sensitivity, but as near as Merrick could tell every man in the group was wearing the same grim and wary expression. And all eyes were definitely focused on him.

He continued to play asleep as the Djinn arrived at his bed. One of them stepped to Merrick's side, waited until the other five had fanned out into a semicircle at the foot of the bed, then carefully touched Merrick's shoulder. "Merrick Moreau?" he murmured. "Djinni Moreau?"

Merrick inhaled sharply, the way his brother Lorne always did when woken out of a deep sleep, and opened his eyes. "What is it?" he asked, blinking in feigned surprise at the group gathered around him. "Is something wrong?"

"You are summoned," the Djinni beside him said. "Your clothing is in a drawer beneath the bed. Dress quickly."

"Where are we going?" Merrick asked as he pulled the blanket aside and sat up, bracing himself for a fresh bout of the dizziness he'd experienced earlier in the day. But this time there was nothing. Maybe the healing drugs were finally out of his system. "Has something happened?"

"Dress quickly" was the only reply.

Two minutes later, they were all heading back between the rows of sleeping patients in the direction the Djinn had come from. His escort, Merrick noted uneasily, had fallen into step around him in a two-in-front, four-in-back formation, the same setup Cobra units typically used with civilian VIPs in spine-leopard-infested areas. It allowed the Cobras to focus maximum firepower to the front and sides, while protecting the group's rear with their own bodies.

Only there weren't any spine leopards in the subcity. And Merrick was hardly a helpless civilian.

Maybe that was the point.

The corridors were quiet and mostly deserted, with only the pairs of guards at each corridor intersection as evidence that the citizenry hadn't simply picked up and left. Occasionally someone else would come by, either walking with the briskness of someone on an errand or else plodding along with the weariness of someone long overdue for sleep.

The trip ended at a door guarded by two pairs of armed guards and another pair of Djinn. One of the guards opened the door as Merrick and his escort approached, revealing a darkened room beyond. Merrick keyed in his infrared enhancers as he walked inside and spotted three figures seated behind a long, curved table about ten meters away at the far end of the room. His rear guard filed in behind him, the door was closed, and a set of low-level lights came on.

The figures Merrick had seen turned out to be three old men, dressed in what were obviously some kind of ceremonial robes. The two on the ends were men Merrick had never seen before, but the one in the middle was someone he recognized all too well.

"Step forward, Merrick Moreau," Shahni Haafiz ordered, his voice stiff and unfriendly.

Merrick glanced at the Djinn standing on either side of him. Their full attention was on Merrick, their expressions unreadable. Turning back to the Shahni, Merrick walked forward until he was a meter from the table. "If you wanted to apologize to me, Shahni Haafiz," he said, "a nice note would have been sufficient."

"Hardly, enemy of Qasama," Haafiz growled. "You were summoned here for judgment."

Merrick felt a chill run through him. "For which of my actions is judgment called?" he asked, flicking a look at each of the other two men. Their eyes were hard, their expressions as studiously neutral as those of the Djinn guard.

"Disobeying the direct order of a Shahni of Qasama in time of war is by itself punishable by death," Haafiz said. "Other charges include—"

"And the fact that I brought your family out alive instead of leaving them to die counts for nothing?" Merrick interrupted.

"It does indeed count for something," Haafiz said darkly. "If you had let them be as you were ordered, dozens of the invaders would have died inside the Palace. Instead, your warning allowed most of them to escape."

"And that would have been a fair trade for you?" Merrick countered. "A few enemy soldiers for your wife and family?"

Haafiz didn't even flinch. "Yes," he said flatly.

Again, Merrick looked at the other two Shahni. Again, there was nothing there but cold detachment. They meant it, he realized with a shiver. All three of them.

What kind of soulless people *were* these, anyway?

"In that case, I must offer my apologies," Merrick said, not quite managing to filter all the contempt out of his tone. "I obviously misunderstood the relationship of Qasama's rulers to Qasama's people."

"I have not finished," Haafiz said, ignoring both the comment and the underlying sarcasm. "Other charges include putting Qasaman citizens unnecessarily at risk, forcing us to permanently seal away at least two entrances to the subcity, and forcing us to demonstrate the window booby-trap system to the enemy."

Merrick frowned. "What booby-trap system? I didn't break any windows."

One of the other Shahni leaned toward Haafiz and murmured something, and Merrick activated his audio enhancements. "—against the other one, the female," the other was saying.

"No matter," Haafiz murmured back. "They act in concert. Their crimes are thus shared."

The other Shahni nodded and straightened up again, and Merrick notched down his enhancements, feeling a frown creasing his forehead. Clearly, they'd been talking about his mother and something she must have done during her own escape from the airfield tower.

Which led immediately to a question that hadn't occurred to Merrick until just now: namely, why wasn't she here? Did Haafiz have a separate kangaroo court planned for her? Or was this just his ham-handed way of getting back at Merrick for the unforgivable sin of making him look foolish by getting his family out alive after Haafiz had declared that to be impossible?

"For these actions, and the secondary effects stemming from them, you are hereby ordered into custody," Haafiz intoned. "Such custody will continue until the invaders are thrown off our world, or until you prove yourself trustworthy and of no further danger to the Qasaman people."

"How do you suggest I do that?" Merrick asked, fighting back a sudden surge of anger. Even under the truncated rules of wartime courts-martial, this whole thing was a joke. "Or would I be wasting my time to even try? I get the feeling there's no proof of any sort that would satisfy you."

"Of course there is," Haafiz said. "But what that proof will consist of, you must discover for yourself." He picked up a gavel from in front of him and lightly double-tapped it against the tabletop. "Sentence is passed. Guard: escort the prisoner to his cell."

Merrick turned around as the six Djinn started toward him. He could take them, the thought flitted through his mind. He'd already proved that in front of Miron Akim and that first group of Djinn. A burst from his sonic, a quick ceiling flip to get behind Haafiz and the other Shahni, and he would have the leverage he needed to get out of this whole insane mess.

He took a careful breath. *Steady,* he warned himself. Because Akim and the Djinn *had* seen that trick, and if there was one thing his mother had impressed on him it was that Qasamans learned fast. The Djinn would be ready for it this time. And if Haafiz's plan was to goad him into proving that he *wasn't* trustworthy, that would be the fastest way for Merrick to hand himself over on a silver platter.

The group of Djinn stopped in front of Merrick, again positioned for a two/four arrangement. "Merrick Moreau?" the leader prompted, gesturing back to the door.

Merrick looked back at Haafiz. "My mother and I are trustworthy, Shahni Haafiz," he said, keeping his voice calm and measured. "We're also the best weapon you have against the Trofts. Until you understand those two things, more of your people are going to die. Consider that when you start placing guilt."

It was as good an exit line as any. Turning his back on the three old men, Merrick stalked toward the door.

The cell block was several corridors away from the midnight court room, roughly the same distance as the recovery ward but in the opposite direction. The cell they ushered him into was about as bare-bones as possible: a windowless concrete-walled room, three meters square, equipped with a bolted-down bed, a sink/toilet combination, and an overhead light which was currently giving off the same low, nighttime glow as he'd seen back in the recovery ward. The door was three-centimeter-thick metal, with a peephole at eye level and a narrow flap at the bottom, the latter presumably for delivering meals.

"Nice décor," Merrick commented, glancing around the cell as he stepped inside. "I don't suppose you'd let me give my mother or Miron Akim a call and let them know where I am?"

None of the Djinn bothered to answer. One of them swung the door closed, and there was a muted thunk as the lock engaged. Pressing his ear to the door, Merrick heard the footsteps fade away into the silence of the night.

He held that pose for the next few minutes, his audio enhancements at full strength, trying to determine if he was all alone in the cell block or if there were other prisoners. But he heard nothing. He repeated the experiment at the room's walls and back, and then at the sink/toilet's plumbing. He was able to pick up a few sounds from the latter, but the noises were soft and unidentifiable.

Finally, with nothing better to do, he went to the bed and lay down. The cell door, which would be an imposing barrier to the average prisoner, would probably collapse within minutes against a Cobra antiarmor laser. He could think of at least two other scenarios that would similarly leave him on the outside of the cell and his jailer or jailers on the inside.

But he knew better than to try any of them. Chances were good that Haafiz had put him in here precisely in the hope of goading him into breaking out, thereby vindicating his own belief that the Cobras were a danger to the Qasamans.

Of course, there was also the possibility that breaking out was the way to prove he *wasn't* a threat. If he broke out, then deliberately didn't harm anyone . . .

But he'd already done that for Akim, and it obviously hadn't impressed Haafiz in the slightest. No, the grouchy Shahni had to be angling for something else.

But what that something was, Merrick hadn't a clue.

With a sigh, he closed his eyes. His dizziness hadn't returned, but that didn't mean he was completely recovered from the quick-healing regimen the Qasamans had put him through. A good night's sleep to flush the rest of the drugs out of his system, and maybe he would be better able to figure out what the hell the Qasamans wanted from him.

Resting his forearm across his eyes to block out the last of the overhead light, he settled down to sleep.

The attendant had just brought Fadil's breakfast when he spotted the Djinni Carsh Zoshak striding toward him along the ward corridor.

Quickly, Fadil grabbed his spoon and dug into his breakfast stew, pretending to be engrossed in his meal. The last thing he wanted right now was to have to speak or even nod a greeting to a city dweller who didn't even try to hide his contempt for villagers like Fadil and his father. If he was lucky, the Djinni would be busy on some errand and would likewise pretend not to notice Fadil. Spooning up a mouthful of the thick stew, he shoved it into his mouth.

"Fadil Sammon?"

Fadil sighed. On the other hand, if he was lucky he wouldn't have ended up in the middle of an alien invasion in the first place. Lifting his gaze from his bowl, arranging a neutral expression across his face, he gave Zoshak the sign of respect. "Good morning, Djinni—"

"Have you seen Merrick Moreau this morning?" Zoshak interrupted.

Fadil suppressed a grimace. Apparently, Zoshak wasn't even going to bother with common courtesy. "Why would I have seen him?" he countered. "He and I are barely acquaintances."

"He's missing," Zoshak said. "The nurse said he was transferred out of his ward in the middle of the night, but there was no destination point listed."

"Again, why should this have anything to do with me?" Fadil countered.

Zoshak grimaced. "My mistake," he said. "Forgive the interruption." He lowered his gaze briefly to Fadil's bowl. "Return to your meal," he added, and strode off.

Fadil watched him go, a sourness tightening his stomach. But at least the other had made it short.

"Fadil."

Fadil turned his head. His father was lying motionless in bed, clearly still weak after his own medical ordeal. But behind the drooping lids his eyes were alert and accusing. "You bring dishonor upon our house," he said.

"How?" Fadil demanded. He wasn't in the mood for this. "The man asked a question. I answered him."

"And you don't care what might have happened to Merrick Moreau?"

Beside him, out of his father's sight, Fadil curled his hand into a fist. He *really* wasn't in the mood for this. "Why should I be concerned?" he asked. "Merrick

Moreau is about as non-helpless a person as I've ever met."

"And you owe him nothing?"

Fadil forced himself to meet his father's gaze. "No, I don't," he said flatly. "Neither do you."

The elder Sammon made a sound that seemed half cough and half grunt. "His mother saved my life," he reminded Fadil.

"And you in turn saved hers," Fadil said. "It seems to me that you and she are even."

For another moment Daulo gazed at his son in silence. Then, with a twitch of his lip that might have been a grimace, he closed his eyes. A minute later, his chest had settled into the slow rhythm of sleep.

With a sigh, Fadil turned back to his interrupted breakfast. But the stew no longer tasted as good as it had a minute ago.

Blast Merrick Moreau, anyway. And blast Jasmine Moreau, and the Shahni, and the city dwellers, and the Trofts. And while he was at it, blast his father, too.

His father was still sleeping when Fadil finished his breakfast. He set the tray aside, then carefully got to his feet. The attendants and nurses at his ward's main station should have records from all the other wards, as well as this one. Maybe the right questions, asked in the proper way, would give him some idea of what the city dwellers had done with Merrick Moreau.

The other eleven Djinn in Zoshak's squad were already in their chairs when Zoshak arrived at the briefing room. So were the members of two other squads. So were the men of a full unit of regular Qasaman soldiers. Whatever was in the works, it was big.

Miron Akim, standing on the low platform in the front, gave Zoshak a somewhat cool look as he slipped into his chair, but didn't say anything. Zoshak's squad leader, Akim's son Siraj, wasn't so restrained. "You're late," he muttered as Zoshak slipped into the empty seat beside him.

"My apologies, Ifrit Akim," Zoshak said, bowing his head to the other. "I had an errand, and misjudged my time."

"Misjudging time in the midst of war can be fatal," Siraj countered. "And not only to yourself. You need to—"

"Enough," a voice said quietly from behind Zoshak.

Zoshak turned, and felt his breath catch in his throat. Seated alone in the far back corner was Senior Advisor Moffren Omnathi. "The point has been made," Omnathi said in the same measured voice. "Marid Akim, you may begin."

"Thank you, Advisor Omnathi," Akim said, bowing his head to Omnathi and shifting his attention back to the gathered Djinn. "The Shahni have selected a mission for you," he announced. "You will be attacking the invader sentry ship currently standing guard at the intersection of Barch and Romand Streets, with the goal of neutralizing its external weaponry and thus permitting an attack force to overwhelm its forces and capture or destroy it."

Zoshak nodded to himself as a map came up on the display behind Akim. The intersection was on the city's western side, a block north of the Freegate market area and far removed from the airfield tower or any other critical area. If the invaders suspected an attack on one of their ships, that particular one would be low on their list of possibilities.

"In the aftermath of Plan Saikah, the invaders are undoubtedly feeling very safe," Akim continued, his dark eyes drifting across the assembled warriors. "We intend to shake that feeling of security."

"Understood," Siraj said briskly. "Have you and the Shahni a plan?"

"We do," Akim said. He touched a button, and a position/movement overlay appeared on top of the street map. "It will be a sundown attack, just as the market is closing and the customers are returning to their homes."

Zoshak felt his stomach tighten. "So there will be civilians in the fire zone?" he asked.

"There will be as few as possible," Akim assured him. "But some will necessarily have to be there. The Djinn will need to dress as civilians and mix with them in order to get within attack range of the ship and the ground troops guarding its base."

"We'll do whatever we have to," Siraj said, throwing a warning look at Zoshak. "When is the attack to take place?"

Akim seemed to brace himself. "Tonight."

A murmur rippled across the room. "*Tonight?*" Siraj echoed carefully. "With less than a day to learn the plan and practice it?"

"I regret that you weren't given earlier notice," Akim said. "But the Shahni deem it necessary to send this message as soon as possible."

Though it won't be much of a message if we all end up slaughtered, Zoshak thought darkly. But he kept his mouth shut. His commander was annoyed enough with him as it was.

And surely the Shahni had considered that possibility when they'd set the attack's timetable.

"I will begin by detailing the plan," Akim went on. "After you've asked any questions, we'll adjourn to the arena for practice."

As Djinn plans went, this one was fairly straightforward, certainly more so than the complexities and cross-city timing of Plan Saikah. It was actually feasible, Zoshak decided, that they could pull it off with only a day's worth of practice.

"Very well, then," Akim said after he'd finished and a few questions had been asked and answered. "The arena should be set up. We'll assemble there in ten minutes for practice. Djinni Zoshak, remain behind a moment."

Zoshak stayed seated, wondering uneasily what Akim wanted, as the rest of the Djinn and soldiers filed briskly from the room. Akim waited until they were all gone, then left the platform and came to stand directly in front of Zoshak. "I understand you were looking for Merrick Moreau this morning," the older man said. "Why?"

"I was concerned for his well-being," Zoshak said. "He fought bravely for Qasama, and I wanted to make sure he was being properly cared for."

"No other reason?" Akim persisted.

Briefly, Zoshak wondered if Moffren Omnathi was still sitting behind him. But he didn't dare turn to look. "I also wondered when he would be able to fight again," he said. "He's a powerful and capable warrior, a great asset to our effort against the invaders." He paused. "In fact, if I may speak freely, I would suggest he could be a great asset in the mission you have set before us."

Akim cocked his head. "Are you suggesting that Qasaman warriors and Djinn are not capable of dealing the necessary blow to our enemies' confidence?"

"I suggest only that the blow will be stronger and more memorable were he to assist us," Zoshak said, picking his words carefully. Usually, he had no trouble reading the thoughts and intentions behind people's words. But Akim's thoughts were hidden behind a mask he couldn't penetrate. "I also suggest that he is able and willing to serve Qasama."

"Merrick Moreau will indeed serve Qasama," Moffren Omnathi's voice came quietly from behind him. "But not in the way you suggest."

Zoshak swallowed. Senior Shahni advisors had better things to do with their time than sit in on the briefing of a single military mission. They *certainly* had better things to do than stay on after that briefing to watch a very minor warrior being lectured by the Djinn's supreme commander. "In what way *will* he serve, may I ask?" he said.

"That is none of your concern," Akim said stiffly. "The fate of Merrick Moreau and his mother rest now in the hands of the Shahni."

"And you will make no further inquiries as to their whereabouts or condition," Omnathi added. "Nor will you mention either of them again. Do you understand?"

A cold lump settled in Zoshak's chest. "Yes, Advisor Omnathi," he said.

"Good," Akim said. "Dismissed."

Making the sign of respect, Zoshak stood up and turned back toward the door. Omnathi was looking down at some notes, ignoring the Djinni, but Zoshak gave him the sign of respect anyway.

No, he wouldn't inquire about Merrick Moreau, Zoshak thought grimly as he hurried down the corridor. Nor would he mention either of the Cobras again. He was a good Qasaman, and obedient to his leaders.

But no one could stop him from thinking about the Moreaus. Or prevent him from wondering what exactly the Shahni were up to.

CHAPTER SEVENTEEN

The sun had disappeared behind the western line of buildings, and the sky overhead was starting to take on a hint of darkness, when the loudspeaker in the center of the Freegate market area boomed the five-minute tone. "Five minutes," Zoshak said quietly to the young woman beside him as they pretended to search through the nearly empty bins of vegetables.

"I'm ready," the woman replied.

Zoshak studied her profile. She wasn't ready, of course. There was no way she could be. There were no female soldiers on Qasama, which meant Iuni hadn't had any training in combat technique or contingency thinking or any of the other skills that prepared a warrior for the sort of situation that was about to happen. Iuni was simply an average citizen who'd volunteered to risk her life today in defense of her city and her world.

Beyond that single fact, Zoshak knew nothing about her except her first name, and he wasn't even sure about that. The Shahni insisted that any soldier who might be captured was to carry as little potentially useful information within him as possible. Iuni might be just an ordinary citizen, but she could also be the daughter or wife of someone in authority. Either way, it wasn't something anyone wanted the invaders to learn.

Three minutes to go. Zoshak looked over at the baked goods booth next to the vegetable stand, to find the vendor looking back at him. Zoshak gave the other a microscopic nod, got one in return, and touched Iuni's arm. "Hurry and make your selection," he told her. "I'll go get the bread."

He headed toward the booth, throwing a brief glower at the pair of armored Trofts standing ten meters away as he walked. A dozen of the aliens had been wandering around the edges of the market area for most of the hour Zoshak had been here, not quite intruding on the shoppers' space, but nevertheless keeping a watchful eye on the proceedings.

From the snatches of conversation Zoshak had overheard from his fellow citizens, he gathered the prevailing theory was that the Trofts were playing mind games: trying to make their presence felt, or else emphasizing that the Qasamans no longer owned their city or their world. Zoshak's own theory was that the diversionary attack three days ago on the invaders in the Sunrise market area across town had led the aliens to believe there was something of military value hidden in *all* of Sollas's market areas.

In theory, that was all to the good. Forcing the Trofts to waste time and energy looking for soldiers among the vegetables was time and energy that couldn't be used elsewhere on Qasama. In practice, though, he wished that the Trofts had picked a different market area to concentrate on today.

The man at the baker's booth gave the sign of respect as Zoshak came up to his counter. "Good afternoon," he said as Zoshak returned the gesture. "How may I help you?"

"A loaf of bread, please," Zoshak said, making sure to pitch his voice at a normal conversational level. The idea was to keep all of this looking perfectly normal to any of the invaders who happened to be watching or listening.

"I'm afraid this is all I have left," the man said, stooping down behind the counter and bringing out a long, spindly, splotchy loaf of French bread. "Not one of our best, as you can see," he added, cradling the loaf almost tenderly in both hands. "It's four and a half, if you want it."

Zoshak hissed out a sigh. But after three days of alien occupation, that was indeed the current inflated price for a loaf that size, and any Trofts who'd been paying attention to the day's transactions would know that. "Very well," he said.

Pulling a handful of coins from his pocket, he sorted out the proper ones and laid them on the counter. "Careful, now," the baker warned, leaning the loaf over the counter to him.

Not careful because the loaf looked on the verge of shattering into a dozen pieces, Zoshak knew, but careful because the thing was far heavier than any actual bread could possibly be. Zoshak took the loaf, wincing a little as his wrists momentarily tried to bend the wrong way. He got the joints back under control, pulling his hands up and in where the servos in his combat suit could take more of the weight. "Thank you," he nodded to the baker, and retraced his steps to the booth where Iuni was waiting.

She looked up as he approached, only a slight tightness around her eyes betraying her tension. "You bought *that?*" she asked with obvious disapproval.

"And we were lucky to get it," Zoshak told her, wishing briefly he knew whether or not the Trofts were even paying attention to them. It would be a shame to go through this whole prearranged scene if they weren't.

The loudspeaker gave its final double boom, signaling the end of the shopping day. "Fine," Iuni said. "Better carry it like that—it's not going to fit in any of the bags. And *don't* let it break."

"I won't," Zoshak promised, pulling the loaf close in to his chest. "Come on, let's get home."

Iuni nodded and turned their collapsible shopping cart around, pushing it away from the market plaza and toward the Troft sentry ship looming over the street to the northwest. Several of the other patrons, Zoshak noted peripherally, were heading in that same direction, some singly, others in couples. On the far side of the street, half a block ahead, two of the couples were chatting together as they pushed side-by-side baby carriers. Behind them, Zoshak could hear the sounds of moving boxes and closing doorways as the merchants closed up shop for the night.

Zoshak gave the sentry ship a casual once-over. It was a good six meters taller than the buildings immediately around it, dominating the entire area. Grouped around its base at both ends were squads of Troft soldiers, their laser rifles held ready across their armored chests. The ones nearest Zoshak and Iuni were giving a close look to each Qasaman who passed their positions. A few of the pedestrians returned the aliens' gazes, but most of the others just ignored them.

The apartment building Zoshak and Iuni had come out of earlier was across from the sentry squad and almost directly beneath the ship's stubby starboard wing and its assortment of mounted weapons. Iuni pushed the cart to the building's outer doorway and stopped, digging through her handbag for the key. Zoshak, still clutching the loaf to his chest, turned a haughty look on the aliens.

The look didn't go unnoticed. Two of the Trofts shifted position slightly, turning their bodies so that they had merely to drop their muzzles from their cross-chest positions to target him. Zoshak responded by adjusting his own stance and hefting the loaf exactly the same way the Trofts were holding their lasers.

That earned him the attention of a third alien, this one not only turning in his direction but actually lowering his laser into firing position. Zoshak ignored the silent warning, his eyes still on the Trofts, his loaf of bread still held rifle-style across his chest. The more aliens who were watching him when the timer ran down, the fewer there would be to shoot at the Djinn working their way along the other side of the street.

From the receiver buried in the bone behind his right ear came the quick double-click of a fifteen-second warning. "You have that door open yet?" Zoshak called behind him, pitching his voice loudly enough for the Trofts to hear. "Hurry up—the air's starting to stink out here."

"I've got it," Iuni said, her voice suddenly taut as she caught the cue and knew the attack was about to begin. "Can you help me with the cart?"

Zoshak continued to stare at the Trofts for another few seconds, then turned his back on the aliens. Iuni was standing in the open doorway, tugging on the front of the cart as she tried to pull it over the threshold. Zoshak stepped up to the rear of the cart and began nudging it with his forearms as if attempting to help without breaking the loaf of bread.

With his body blocking the Trofts' view, he set the loaf upright in the cart. Keeping his movements small, he reached into his tunic and retrieved the combat suit gloves that had been hidden there. He slipped them on, feeling a brief tingle as the gloves' servos connected to the power and control surfaces in the sleeves, and this time he was able to pick up the loaf without any strain at all.

There was a final double-click from his implanted receiver. Turning back to face the Trofts, he stretched out his arms, holding the loaf vertically as if offering the bread to the aliens, and squeezed the center.

And as the street around him suddenly erupted in gunfire from the buildings and laser fire from the other Djinn surrounding the sentry ship, the missile burst from its bread coating and blasted upward toward the underwing weapons cluster.

Zoshak leaped to the side as the brief jolt of exhaust fire washed across his face. Lifting his hands, he fired a pair of bolts at the nearest Troft sentry's laser. The weapon blistered and then shattered, blowing out a cloud of metal splinters and sending its owner staggering backward. Simultaneously, one of the other sentries jerked and fell to the pavement as a combination of projectile and laser fire took him down.

There was a brilliant flash from above him. Zoshak looked up to see the missile he'd just launched disintegrate five meters from its target, blown apart by one of the weapon cluster's point-defense lasers.

Unfortunately for the Trofts, Miron Akim and the other tacticians had anticipated that. Instead of the muffled pop of vaporized explosives and electronics, the missile erupted with a spray of evil-looking green liquid. Even as the lasers continued to fire uselessly at it, the liquid continued upward on the missile's original trajectory and splattered against the cluster.

Zoshak didn't wait, but leaped away to the side, pushing his leg servos to their limit. The liquid was reasonably viscous, but he had no intention of being anywhere nearby when it started dripping back to the ground. He landed five meters away just as the first few drops began to rain onto the street, sizzling violently as the concentrated acid burned through the paving material.

A laser bolt burned past Zoshak's side. Dropping into a crouch, he snapped off a couple of shots of his own, catching the Troft soldier across his faceplate. At this range the bolts probably wouldn't penetrate the self-shielding, but at least the plastic's protective blackening would interfere with the alien's vision. Before the Troft could do more than fire off a couple more wild shots in Zoshak's general direction a heavy machine gun somewhere above him sent a short burst across the alien's helmet and torso, sending him flying backward to slam up against the sentry ship's bow. Another alien raised his laser toward the Qasaman gunner, and Zoshak stitched another pair of black lines across his faceplate.

And then, as Zoshak grabbed for one of the throwing weights at his belt, a brilliant beam of light slashed through the air above him, and the Qasaman machine gun went abruptly silent.

Reflexively, Zoshak threw himself sideways, looking up in disbelief and dismay as a second blast of laser light shattered the pavement where he'd just been standing. The acid wash *had* hit the cluster—he'd seen the impact himself. Every one of the weapons up there ought to be out of commission.

But they weren't. None of them. All six of the lasers were firing, targeting the Djinn still engaging the ground troops, as well as those running toward the ship's fore and aft hatches. The heavier missile launchers hadn't yet fired, but the tubes were tracking back and forth as if looking for a worthy target. One of the machine guns farther down the street shifted aim toward the weapons cluster, and once again the Trofts' lasers lashed out. For a long moment the machine gun continued to fire, and Zoshak held a brief hope that the gunner would survive. But the lasers continued to fire, and a few seconds later the machine gun finally went silent.

And then, Zoshak's receiver implant gave the triple-click order for retreat.

God in heaven, he thought viciously. But there was no other choice. With the weapons clusters still operational there was no hope of success, and to continue would simply cost more lives without any gain. He clicked back an acknowledgment and straightened up, looking around for any of his fellow Djinn who might need assistance—

His only warning was a slight flicker of motion from the corner of his eye. He threw himself to the ground beside the slabs of broken pavement the Troft laser had gouged into the street as a wave of tiny antipersonnel missiles shot past, exploding like a volley of firecrackers against the wall behind him. Another wave was right behind the first; grabbing the biggest piece of shattered pavement he could reach, he rolled half over, holding the slab up as a shield. A half-dozen of the missiles exploded against it, blasting off splinters and chunks. He rolled back to his feet, still holding the slab for protection, and began backing through the chaos toward the alley where the closest emergency exit was located.

He was the first of the Djinn to make it through the hidden door and into the safety of the subcity. A Djinni from one of the other squads was the second. Siraj Akim was the third.

There wasn't any fourth.

Jin was gazing up at the hospital room ceiling, listening to her rumbling stomach and wondering when the evening meal was going to be delivered, when she heard the sound of running feet outside her door.

She frowned, activating her audio enhancers. There appeared to be two different groups of footsteps out there: one group running to her left, the other, heavier group heading to her right.

And the group heading right was accompanied by occasional metallic clinks. The kind of clinking that weapons and military equipment made as they bounced against belts and chests.

Reaching to her left arm, she carefully disengaged the two IV tubes that still remained after the battery of tests the doctors had put her through. Then, slipping into the soft boots and robe beside her bed, she padded to the door and opened it a crack.

A line of civilians was running to her left, some of them carrying small equipment consoles or record boxes.

Others, mostly hospital staff, were pushing wheelchairs or assisting the more ambulatory patients. Down the hall, she could see other doors opening in sequence as the staffers systematically cleared out the rest of the patients.

On the opposite side of the hall, heading to Jin's right, was a line of grim-faced soldiers.

She pulled the door open all the way. One of the passing soldiers caught her eye and jerked his thumb silently in the direction the civilians were going. "Wait," Jin said quietly. "I can—"

He didn't even pause, but just kept going. "I can help," Jin muttered under her breath. She lifted a hand to the next soldier back, but he merely gave her the same thumbs-back gesture.

Jin grimaced. But there was clearly no time to argue the point, even if she could find someone to argue it with. Spotting a gap in the traffic flow, she left her room and joined the civilians heading to the left.

She'd gone only about fifty meters when she spotted a familiar face: Fadil Sammon, hurrying toward her behind two burly soldiers. "Fadil!" she called, holding out a hand toward him. "Fadil Sammon!"

He jerked at the sound of his name, then finally noticed her. "There you are," he said, stepping out of the soldiers' line and falling into step beside her. "I was on my way to see you. I can't—"

"What's going on?" Jin interrupted. "Are the Trofts coming in?"

"Sounds that way, yes," Fadil said grimly. "There's been some kind of breach, anyway. The Shahni have ordered this area evacuated."

Jin half turned to look at the departing soldiers. She should be back there, she knew. She should be on her way to the breach, helping to defend the people of Qasama—

"No," Fadil said firmly, grabbing her arm and turning her back around front. "They can do it themselves."

"Who can?" Jin asked. "The Qasamans? Or the city people?"

Fadil muttered something under his breath. "Come on—the seal is just ahead."

Jin had noticed several seals during her travels around the subcity. They would have been hard to miss, actually: red-rimmed slabs of stone or reinforced concrete set into the sides of strategically placed corridors or doorways, ready to be slid into position to block off any further access. Some of them had gunports or firing niches nearby that guards could use, others had red-striped ceilings just behind the slabs marking something ominously labeled as avalanche zones.

This particular seal had no such backups, just a pair of Qasaman soldiers waiting tensely by the slab as the refugees streamed past. One of them, a few years older than the other and wearing sergeant's insignia, frowned hard at Jin as she and Fadil slipped through with the others—

"Jasmine Moreau?" he called suddenly.

Jin stopped, stepping to the side out of the way of the hurrying civilians. "Yes," she confirmed.

"A message from Miron Akim," the sergeant said. "He asks if you will remain here until all have passed."

"Why?" Fadil demanded. "She's not a soldier."

"It's all right," Jin said, touching his shoulder. "Go on."

Fadil hesitated, then gave a snort and rejoined the line of civilians. "Did Miron Akim say what he wanted me to do?" Jin asked the sergeant.

"The seal will need to be closed when everyone's past," he told her, his voice tight. "That duty usually goes to a Djinni, but we've received word that none are available in this sector."

A cold knot settled into Jin's stomach. "Did they say why not?"

"No," the sergeant said. "Just that none was available." He looked back over his shoulder at her. "Miron Akim said that you were here, and that we were to stop you when you came through and ask for your assistance."

"No problem," Jin assured him.

The flow of refugees had faded to a trickle of hospital workers when the faint sound of gunfire began to echo down the hallway.

The other soldier snarled something under his breath. He was young, Jin noted as she studied his profile. Actually, neither of the two was all that old. Certainly neither could have had any experience in the sort of warfare their world had suddenly been plunged into.

Or had they? The city/village rivalry that Jin had seen and heard of on her first visit to Qasama was clearly still going strong three decades later. Could that rivalry have occasionally boiled up into actual shooting combat?

Daulo hadn't even hinted at any such violence on his world during their conversations. But then, he wouldn't have. Not to her and Merrick.

"It's time," the sergeant said quietly.

Jin frowned. The gunfire was still going strong. "What about the soldiers?" she asked.

"They will return to the subcity by a different route." The sergeant hesitated. "Or not at all."

Jin clenched her teeth. *Let me go to them,* the words and plea flashed through her mind. *I can help.*

She took a deep breath. "What do I do?" she asked instead.

"Pull up on this," the sergeant said, indicating a long lever set into the wall just inside the slab. "More than once, I think."

With Jin's first tug on the lever it became clear why Djinn were generally tasked with this job. Even with the gearing that was obviously built into the system the lever took a lot of effort to pull. The first hundred-eighty-degree rotation moved the slab perhaps a centimeter into the corridor; ratcheting the lever back down, she hauled up on it again, and again, and again, until the slab completely blocked the corridor.

"What now?" Jin asked as she released the lever and stepped away from it.

Both soldiers were staring at her with a mixture of awe and uneasiness. But the sergeant merely nodded back down the hallway. "This way," he said. "Miron Akim wishes to speak with you."

Given all the civilians and medical personnel that had just come through the area, Jin had expected it to be crowded with masses of displaced people. To her surprise, though, the corridors didn't seem much busier than she'd usually seen them. Wherever the refugees had gone, they'd gone there quickly and efficiently.

The soldiers led her through the usual maze of corridors to a door guarded by a single soldier. "Jasmine Moreau?" the guard asked formally as Jin and her escort came up to him. "Miron Akim offers his regrets, and states that he was called away on urgent business," he continued, reaching over and opening the door. "He asks that you wait for him inside, and that you examine a file he has left for you."

"Thank you," Jin said. "And thank you," she added to her escort, giving them the sign of respect.

Neither of the soldiers returned the gesture. Either she'd done it wrong, or else word had spread that the visitors from the Cobra Worlds weren't worthy of the sign.

The room was typical of what she'd seen in the subcity: small and sparsely furnished, with a desk and computer terminal and two wooden chairs. Lying beside the terminal was a single dusky-red file folder. Circling around behind the desk, wondering briefly if the door would be locked from the outside, she sat down and opened the folder.

The sheet of paper on top was a report of some sort, a listing of Troft activities from one of the villages, complete with alien troop numbers, types of air- and spacecraft observed, and a timeline that indicated it was a single day's report. She leafed briefly through the rest of the papers, noting the differing times and village names but that all of them followed essentially the same format. Leave it to the Qasamans, she thought with a touch of grim amusement, to be organized even down to their paperwork.

She was skimming the fourth page when a particular entry belatedly caught her attention: *razorarms captured.*

Frowning, she settled down to read.

It was an axiom of war, she'd heard once, that numbers quoted in the heat of battle or delivered by civilians should never be taken entirely at face value. But if the numbers in the various villager reports were even halfway accurate, the Trofts had been incredibly busy. In the three days since their invasion they'd already hauled nearly four hundred razorarms out of the forest and loaded them aboard cargo carriers. The reports were a bit vague on the techniques involved—apparently none of the observers had managed to get very close to the scene of the action—but it seemed to include multiple small aircraft as spotters and some kind of tranquilizer gas bombs.

Of even more interest was the fact that the Trofts were apparently leaving the razorarms' mojos behind.

She was midway through the papers when Akim arrived. "My apologies," he said as he closed the door behind him. He had a folder of his own, Jin noted, a light green one. "No—please," he added, waving Jin back to her seat as she started to rise and seating himself in one of the other chairs facing her. "Did you finish reading the file?"

"I only made it through about half the reports, but I was able to skim the rest," she said, studying his face. His expression was under rigid control, but there was a dark tightness around his eyes, a darkness she hadn't seen even on the day of the invasion itself. "They've been busy, haven't they?"

"That they have," Akim said. "The question remains: why?"

"I see two possibilities," Jin said. "One, they mostly want the razorarms. Two, they mostly want to leave mojos in the forests *without* symbiotic companions."

"An interesting possibility, that last," Akim said. "Yet if they wanted the mojos to be alone, why not simply kill the razorarms out from beneath them? Why bother taking the animals away alive?"

"A good point," Jin conceded. "Are we sure the razorarms haven't shown up in any of Qasama's cities or villages?"

"Not that we know of," Akim said. "Of course, there are many smaller villages and settlements outside our communication range. Still, if sending razorarms into those villages was the goal, why not do their hunting in those same areas? Why choose animals from near Sollas and transport them the entire distance?"

"No reason I can see," Jin agreed. "So it would seem they're simply taking the most convenient animals, the ones that are near where all their heavy transports are already located."

"Here at Sollas," Akim said, nodding.

"Right," Jin said, frowning as something else occurred to her. "The transports *do* leave those areas once they have their razorarms, don't they?" she asked. "I didn't see that in the reports."

"Yes, they invariably leave," Akim confirmed. "But where they go, we have no idea." He cocked his head, and Jin thought she saw a subtle change in the man's expression. "Could it be that the invaders want them for the same reason you brought them to Qasama in the first place? That they wish to seed an enemy's land with quick-breeding predators?"

Jin stared at him, a horrible sensation rippling through her. There it was, staring her suddenly in the face.

And it was so terribly obvious. How in the *Worlds* had she missed it? "That's it," she said, her throat tightening against the words. "You're right, Miron Akim. That's exactly what they're doing.

"Only the enemy you mention isn't Qasama. The enemy is us."

Akim nodded, his expression going even darker. "So indeed I have suspected from the first," he said, an edge of accusation in his tone. "All the more so since you never suggested the possibility."

"Because I didn't think of it," Jin said, embarrassment and chagrin flowing in around the sudden heartache. Her worlds—her people—her family, under Troft attack. "I don't know why not. It's so obvious."

"Perhaps," Akim said, his voice a shade less angry. "But even if true, it cannot be the entire truth. If your world is their target, why invade Qasama at all? There are many unoccupied territories where they could hunt razorarms with little effort and less resistance."

Jin sighed. "They invaded you because you're here," she said quietly. "And because you're humans."

Akim's eyes bored into hers. "Explain."

Jin took a deep breath. "A century ago there was a war between the Dominion of Man and an alliance of demesnes at that end of the Troft Assemblage. The reasons for it are muddled, but they don't really matter. What matters is that the first the Dominion knew about Troft animosity was when the alliance's troops landed and occupied two of our worlds." She lifted her arms slightly. "We were the Dominion's response."

"Forces who could move easily among the occupied peoples," Akim said, nodding. "And could fight back from that concealment."

"Keeping them distracted and softening them up until they could be ultimately driven off," Jin said. "The problem was that once the war was over, there was nowhere for the surviving Cobras to go. They didn't really fit in with their old homes anymore, a good percentage of the general populace was terrified of them, and the political leaders simply wanted them to go away." She smiled tightly. "It was my grandfather's brother, actually, who came up with the answer: send the remaining Cobras past the Assemblage as guardians and police for a new group of human colonies."

Akim frowned. "And the Trofts actually agreed to this?"

Jin shrugged. "The demesnes who'd lost the war didn't have a lot of say in the matter," she reminded him. "The rest of them didn't seem to particularly care one way or the other whether humans went zooming back and forth through their space." She grimaced. "Or maybe they all just recognized the opportunity buried inside the apparent humiliation."

Akim straightened suddenly, as if a missing piece of the puzzle had just fallen into place. "Because you were now hostages to the Dominion's good behavior."

"Exactly," Jin said. "The Dominion's idea, I think, was that having a group of Cobras out here would be a nice two-front threat against the Trofts to keep them from further mischief. But if it was, it backfired. Badly. Barely twenty years after we got here the corridor we'd been using was closed, cutting us off from the Dominion."

"You must have been perturbed, to say the least," Akim murmured.

"Actually, it was our idea," Jin told him. "My grandfather's, to be specific, worked out along with his brother. They forced the closure of the corridor, ending the Dominion's threat of a two-front war."

"So the Dominion lost the lever it had hoped for," Akim murmured. "But the Trofts didn't."

"The Trofts didn't," Jin agreed, her stomach tightening. "And apparently someone's decided it's time to cash in."

"Apparently," Akim said grimly. "I wonder what the Trofts have done to your Dominion this time."

"Or what the Dominion has done to them," Jin said. "But from this end of the universe, it doesn't much matter who started it or why. What matters is that someone has decided we're a potential threat that needs to be neutralized."

"And they believe Qasama to be your allies?"

"They probably don't care whether you are or not," Jin said. "Remember, these are most likely Trofts from the Dominion side of the Assemblage who don't care a damn about our political relationships. They've come here to punish the Dominion by suppressing human colonization, period."

"I see," Akim said. "It would have been nice to have known this sooner."

Jin winced. "I know," she said. "I'm sorry, Miron Akim. I don't know why I didn't think of it before. I just can't seem to think like I used to. Old age catching up with me, I guess."

"No apologies needed," Akim said, an odd tone in his voice. "And I wish it was merely old age." Reaching to his lap, he picked up the green folder. "I have the results of your last group of tests."

"And?" Jin asked carefully.

Akim visibly braced himself. "You have a brain tumor, Jasmine Moreau," he said quietly. "A highly virulent one.

"In two months, perhaps three, you will die."

CHAPTER EIGHTEEN

Jin stared at him, feeling the blood draining from her face. Her strange inability to think straight, her unexplained blackouts . . . "Are you sure?" she heard herself ask.

"Very sure," Akim said. "I'm sorry. I wish it were otherwise."

"Is there anything that can be done?"

Akim pursed his lips. "The doctors will study the data and see if there are any options." He hesitated. "But you have to understand that they have other matters occupying their attention at the moment."

"Of course." Jin took a deep breath. Two months. "All right," she said. "What can I do until then?"

"There are dietary techniques that may slow the process," Akim said. "Bed rest may also be of some use."

Jin shook her head. "You misunderstand. What I meant was, until the doctors have time to study my case—and probably haul me in for more tests—what can I do to help in the war?"

A muscle in Akim's cheek twitched. "I appreciate your offer," he said. "But I'm afraid your service to Qasama is at an end. Aside from anything else, we can hardly risk you having a blackout during a combat operation."

"I suppose," Jin conceded, marveling at how calm she was. Or perhaps how numb she was would be a more accurate description. Even on Aventine, doctors had little chance against a brain tumor. On Qasama, in the middle of a war, the odds were undoubtedly far worse. "I'll need to tell Merrick. Can I see him? Or hasn't he recovered yet from his injuries?"

"No, he should be recovered by now," Akim said, the odd note back in his voice. "I'll see if I can locate him. Wait here, please, and continue reading through the file."

Like she would really be able to concentrate on Troft troop movements now. *Two months to live* . . . "All right," she said.

She'd been trying to focus on the papers for nearly an hour when a knock finally came on the door and a tall young man in a gray Djinni combat suit and shocking —for a Qasaman—red hair stepped into the doorway. "You are Jasmine Moreau?" he asked formally.

"Yes," Jin said.

"Marid Miron Akim sent me to bring you to him," the Djinni said shortly. "Follow me."

"May I know your name?" Jin asked, making no move to stand up.

The other glared. Perhaps he didn't like being in the presence of an enemy of Qasama. "I am Ghofl Khatir, Djinn Ifrit of Qasama," he said shortly.

"Honored to meet you, Ifrit Khatir," Jin said, nodding to him as she got to her feet. "Please; lead the way."

She crossed the room, but to her mild surprise, Khatir remained in the doorway blocking her exit. "We will be meeting with your son on a matter of intense importance," he said. "Miron Akim requests that you do not speak of personal matters at this time."

"Will there be a time provided for such a conversation?" Jin asked, resisting the impulse to simply pick him up by the arms and move him out of her way.

"You must ask Miron Akim about that," Khatir said, finally stepping back out into the corridor. "Follow me."

The room he took her to was larger than the one she'd just left but only slightly better furnished. Three men were waiting: Miron Akim, Carsh Zoshak, and Merrick.

Merrick was on his feet even before she was all the way into the room. "Mom!" he said, hurrying toward her and gripping her arm. "Are you all right?"

Jin glanced at Akim, noting the stiffness in his face. "I'm fine," she said, giving her son a quick once-over. "*You're* the one who got all shot up."

"I'm fine," Merrick assured her, dismissing his condition with a quick wave of his hand. "They did a good job of patching me up."

"Save your personal conversation for another time," Khatir said brusquely as he stalked past them. "We have work to do."

"Courtesy, Ifrit Khatir," Akim admonished him mildly. "But he's correct. The hour is late, and we have much to discuss. Please; be seated."

Gripping Merrick's hand, Jin stepped to the row of chairs in front of Akim and sat down in one of them. Merrick sat beside her; to her mild surprise, Zoshak took the seat on Merrick's other side. Khatir, in contrast, pointedly moved one over from Jin's other side, leaving an empty chair between them.

"We suffered a serious setback today," Akim began, his eyes touching each of their faces in turn. "More importantly, many Qasaman lives were lost." He gestured toward Zoshak. "Djinni Zoshak was the only survivor not currently undergoing medical treatment. He'll describe what he saw and experienced from the ground."

Jin listened silently as Zoshak related the attack on the Troft sentry ship and its aftermath. "Have any of you any questions?" Akim asked when he had finished.

Jin looked at Merrick. He looked back and gave her a small shake of his head. "I have one, then," Akim continued. "The acid Djinni Zoshak and the others used should have quickly destroyed or at least seriously damaged any alloy of the sort the invaders are known to use in their ships. Do you, Jasmine Moreau or Merrick Moreau, have any idea why it didn't do so?"

With an effort, Jin dragged her mind back from images of carnage. "Your statement implies you've examined Troft ship construction," she said. "May I ask when and where you did this?"

"That information is classified," Khatir put in.

"Over the years we've had the opportunity to take spectroscopic samplings from four Troft trading ships," Akim said, ignoring Khatir's comment. "The alloys were all very much of a kind, with only slight variations in the percentages of the admixed metals."

Jin looked at Merrick. "Any ideas?" she invited.

He shrugged. "Those were probably local Troft traders," he pointed out. "This bunch seem to be from some other demesnes. I suppose they could use entirely different hull materials."

"Maybe," Jin said doubtfully. "But unless my high-school physics has been completely outdated, hullmetal is pretty much basically hullmetal. You need certain characteristics for the hyperdrive to haul the whole ship along with it instead of just blasting its way through the bulkheads and taking off on its own."

"Unless the Trofts have come up with a new alloy that also works," Merrick said. "Neither of us is exactly an authority on these things." He turned to Zoshak. "Did the acid do *anything* to the weapons? Slow them down, set the barrels drooping—anything?"

"Not that I could see from the ground," Zoshak said grimly. "They were certainly functional enough to kill our soldiers and Djinn."

"With lasers," Akim said suddenly.

Jin looked at him. "What?"

"The invaders fired at our soldiers with lasers," Akim said slowly, his eyes on Zoshak but his gaze focused somewhere more distant. "But I don't believe they ever fired their missiles. The small antipersonnel missiles, yes, but not the larger ones from the clusters. *Any* of the clusters."

"Perhaps they saw no need to spend them," Khatir suggested.

"No," Zoshak said, a sudden new edge to his voice. "I remember a specific instance, when a machine gunner was firing at the weapons cluster. A missile would have made quick work of the gunner, possibly bringing down the entire building and reducing all resistance from that direction. But instead the invaders fired a barrage of laser shots until he was silenced."

He looked at Merrick. "And yet the launchers *were* tracking. I remember seeing them swinging back and forth as if looking for targets."

"Maybe they wanted to limit the amount of destruction they were causing," Jin suggested, a bit hesitantly.

"That's not one of their concerns," Akim said firmly.

"He's right," Merrick seconded. "I saw some of what they did during Plan Saikah. They might not be ready to nuke Qasama back to the stone age, but you attack them and they'll fight just back as hard as anyone else." He frowned. "Though come to think of it, they didn't use missiles against Narayan and me, either, when we were rescuing Shahni Haafiz's family."

"Because the missile launchers on that sentry ship were occupied elsewhere," Akim said. "You were perhaps unaware that other forces were attempting to distract the invaders so that your rescue could succeed."

Merrick winced. "Oh," he said. "You're right. I didn't see that."

"The question remains as to why the missiles weren't used this evening," Zoshak said. "Could the acid have done some damage, but not enough for us to notice?"

"But if the lasers worked—" Merrick broke off. "Do those weapons clusters retract?"

"You mean into the ship?" Akim shook his head. "No, I don't believe so. There's no place for them to retract into, and the pylons seem permanently attached."

Merrick grunted thoughtfully. "Did you pick up the Troft ships on radar as they were coming in toward Sollas?"

"We don't normally use active sensor equipment," Akim said, studying Merrick closely. "Such techniques run the risk of betraying the observer's location."

"That they do," Merrick agreed. He turned a tight smile on his mother. "But the Trofts wouldn't have known that. Especially not Trofts from this far out of town."

And suddenly Jin saw where he was going. "The ships are sensor-coated," she breathed.

"Bingo." Merrick turned back to Akim. "She means there must be some kind of coating on the hullmetal that deflects or absorbs radar signals," he explained. "Something thin that wouldn't interfere with hyperspace travel, but would help protect them from unfriendly eyes while they were here."

"Is this a technology your own warships use?" Khatir asked.

"We don't *have* warships," Merrick told him. "And our handful of transports *want* to be visible to radar when they're coming in for a landing. The point is, the coating is what the acid attacked, not the alloy you were expecting."

"And how is it that this material is impervious to acid?" Zoshak asked, sounding confused.

"Oh, I'm sure it's not," Merrick said. "But Miron Akim implied the acid you used was specially tailored for hullmetal. Regardless, whatever punishment the acid did was absorbed by the coating, leaving the hullmetal itself mostly undamaged."

" 'Mostly'?" Khatir asked.

"Yes," Akim said, his voice suddenly thoughtful. "Because the interior of the missile tubes wouldn't have been treated with that coating. Enough acid must have penetrated into those areas to render them unsafe to use."

"Then we have our solution," Zoshak said, a growing excitement in his voice. "We mix a two-stage acid, the first to eliminate the coating, the second to destroy the metal itself."

"And how exactly do you propose we create this new acid?" Khatir asked with exaggerated patience. "Shall we ask the invaders for the chemical parameters of their radar-absorption material?"

Zoshak seemed to deflate. "Oh," he said in a more subdued voice. He looked at Merrick. "Unless *you* know something about this material?" he asked hopefully.

"Sorry," Merrick said. "But we may not have to be that clever. Whatever the stuff is, it's not likely to be able to absorb radar *and* also hold up to intense laser fire." He looked at Akim. "In fact, I'd bet that a Cobra antiarmor laser could easily take it out."

One of Akim's eyebrows twitched. "Are you volunteering to participate in the next attack?"

"A moment," Khatir spoke up. "As designated Djinn commander of the next assault, I wish to state that I do not *want* Merrick Moreau along. We have lasers of our own, which we're quite capable of using."

"It would be a foolish warrior indeed who would turn down expert assistance out of pride," Merrick countered.

"I do not turn down assistance out of pride," Khatir snapped, glaring at Merrick. "Take offense as you choose, but the fact is that I do not trust you."

"Yet I've proven my willingness to work for your freedom against the invaders," Merrick reminded him. "And I've proved my capability, as well." He looked at Akim.

"Shahni Haafiz suggested I need to find a way to prove my trustworthiness. I submit that helping Ifrit Khatir and his men take out a Troft sentry ship is as good a way of doing that as any."

Jin frowned at him. She hadn't heard anything about any Shahni demands. "When did you speak to the Shahni?" she asked Merrick.

"It was an informal little meeting," Merrick said, a flick of his eyes warning her to drop it. "Miron Akim?"

"It may be possible," Akim said, his eyes shifting back and forth between Jin and Merrick. "I'll submit your proposal to the Shahni." He paused, shot a look at Khatir, then turned back to Merrick. "In the meantime, we now have a direction for our new attack plan," he continued. "Thank you all for your time and insights."

"Do you have a planned timing yet for the attack?" Merrick asked.

"Certainly not before tomorrow night," Akim said. "Possibly not until a day after that. I want Djinni Zoshak and the other survivors from his squad to join with Ifrit Khatir's squads, and their medical treatment and recovery is not yet complete."

"What do you want us to do until then?" Merrick asked.

A faint smile twitched at the corners of Akim's mouth. "For the next few hours, at least, you should probably sleep. You've been assigned a bed in Djinni Zoshak's barracks. He'll show you there."

Jin braced herself. "Before he goes," she spoke up, "I wonder if I might have a little time alone with him."

For a moment, it looked to her like Akim was going to say no. But then he bowed his head. "Of course," he said. "You may use this room if you'd like. I'll leave a soldier outside to show him to his quarters." He smiled faintly. "And another to guide you to your new hospital room, as well," he added. "Ifrit Khatir, you'll come with me."

"As you wish, Marid Akim," Khatir said. Sending one last glower at Merrick, he rose and followed Akim out of the room.

"It's good to see you again, Jasmine Moreau," Zoshak said, smiling uncertainly at Jin as he also stood up. "Merrick Moreau, I'll see you later." With a nod at each of them, he headed out.

Merrick turned to Jin. "You have a *hospital* room?" he asked.

Jin took a deep breath. This was not going to be easy. "I've had some tests done, Merrick . . . "

It was nearly two hours later when Merrick finally arrived at the bunk the soldier pointed out to him.

It felt more like it had been two years.

He was too weary to bother undressing farther than just fumbling off his shoes before curling up on the hard mattress, his mind a swirl of anger, fear, and a horrible, horrible grief. A parent, he'd heard someone say long ago, shouldn't have to bury his or her children.

Neither should a twenty-seven-year-old son have to bury his mother.

And it would be his responsibility to do that, he knew. His responsibility alone. They were trapped on Qasama, with no hope of getting back to Aventine before the end.

Which meant his mother wouldn't have a chance to say a proper good-bye to Lorne or Jody. Or even to her husband.

Merrick closed his eyes against the tears welling up and spilling out onto the pillow. *It's not fair!* he screamed silently at the universe. *Not her. Not now.*

But the universe didn't care. Or rather, the universe had its own unbending laws to adhere to. Thirty-two years ago Jasmine Moreau had made the choice to follow in her family's footsteps, knowing full well what the cost would be. Now, the price had come due.

Merrick pressed his face against the pillow, feeling his tears soaking the case and spreading out to chill his cheeks and forehead. Had she really, truly understood the full consequences of that decision? For that matter, did any of those who chose to become Cobras really understand? Could any normal, healthy teenager or twenty-something genuinely comprehend their own death?

But ultimately, willingness or ignorance didn't matter. All that mattered was that Merrick was going to lose his mother. And farther down the road, he himself would lose half of his own life's potential span.

Or even more. He was, after all, in the middle of a war.

And the most hateful and painful irony of it all was that the people for whom they were making this sacrifice didn't even appreciate it. The people of the Cobra Worlds watched the Cobras' deaths with indifference or resentment. The Qasamans would watch with distrust and hatred.

"Are you all right?" a whisper came from Merrick's side.

With an effort, Merrick forced back the tears. This wasn't Zoshak's concern. "Sorry," he whispered back, striving to keep the emotion out of his voice. "Sinus trouble. I didn't mean to wake you."

Zoshak was silent long enough that Merrick thought he'd fallen asleep again. "I've cried myself, you know," he said quietly. "There's no shame in being afraid."

A flash of anger shot through Merrick. "Is that what you think?" he bit back. "You think I'm a coward?"

"I didn't say you were a coward," Zoshak said. "Do you wish to talk? We can go to one of the briefing rooms if you want privacy."

Merrick sighed, ashamed of his burst of anger. Zoshak was only trying to help. "There's nothing to talk about," he said. "Maybe later when . . . never mind."

"Never mind what?" Zoshak persisted. "We're comrades in war, Merrick Moreau. I'd like to think that we're also on the path to becoming friends. Whatever it is you need or want, please tell me."

Merrick shook his head. This was going to sound so stupid. "I was just going to say that I don't know anything about Qasaman burial customs," he said. "Maybe you'd be willing to help me when the time comes."

There was a sound of shifting sheets, and in the darkness Merrick saw Zoshak sit up. "What's happened?" the Djinni asked, his voice suddenly tight.

Merrick closed his eyes. It wasn't fair to share this burden with Zoshak, he knew. But Zoshak had asked.

And to be honest, Merrick didn't want to have to face this alone. With the rest of the Moreaus light-years away, Zoshak was the closest thing to family or friend that Merrick was likely to find. "My mother's dying," he said quietly. "Miron Akim says she has no more than two or three months to live."

"God in heaven," Zoshak breathed. "What is it? What's wrong with her?"

"Cancer," Merrick said. "A brain tumor. Maybe some side-effect of our Cobra implants—God knows there are enough of them."

"A brain tumor," Zoshak repeated. Even in a whisper his voice suddenly sounded odd. "And it's inoperable?"

Merrick swallowed hard. "Miron Akim said the doctors would be studying the possibilities. But I know the doctors on Aventine have a lousy success rate with tumors like that. I can't imagine your doctors just casually go in and cut them out, either."

"Why not?" Zoshak asked, still in that same odd tone. "They do."

Merrick stared across the darkness at the vague shape that was Zoshak. "What?" he asked carefully.

"Qasaman doctors routinely remove brain tumors from cancer victims," Zoshak said. "Did Miron Akim say anything about this one that would make it inoperable?"

Merrick blinked at the last tears still leaking from his eyes, reflexively fighting against this sudden new hope. No—it was too easy. Zoshak had to be mistaken. Surely Akim wouldn't have left such a sense of doom hanging over his mother's head otherwise. Surely he would have given her hope . . .

"Merrick Moreau?" Zoshak asked, his voice suddenly a little uncertain. "Did Miron Akim say anything about your mother's tumor?"

"No," Merrick said, once again struggling to keep the emotion out of his voice. Only this time the emotion wasn't grief. This time, it was pure, white-hot rage.

Because now he knew what was going on.

The bastards. The stinking, rotten, ice-hearted *bastards.*

"I need to speak to Miron Akim right away," he said as calmly as he could. "Do you have any idea where he might be?"

"At this hour? I would assume he's asleep in his quarters."

"I don't think that guy ever sleeps," Merrick said, trying to think. If he were a ice-hearted, stinking bastard, where would *he* go? "Are there any tactical or strategy-planning rooms nearby?"

"Not that I know of," Zoshak said.

"What about a high-level conference room?" Merrick asked, his mind flashing back to yesterday's confrontation with Shahni Haafiz and his two cohorts. "The one they took me to wasn't too far from the recovery ward I was in."

"Yes, I think I know the one," Zoshak said. "What's going on?"

"Miron Akim's betrayed me," Merrick said bluntly. "Or at least, I see it as a betrayal. Maybe you wouldn't."

For a long minute Zoshak was silent. "Let's find out," he said at last. "Give me a moment to get dressed."

There were more people moving about the subcity than had been in evidence the previous night, Merrick noted as Zoshak led the way through the maze. But fewer of them were civilians, and more of them were grim-faced soldiers.

Briefly, he wondered if the Trofts had managed another breakthrough like the one he'd heard about from earlier that evening. But even with his audio enhancers at full strength he could hear no sounds of gunfire. The soldiers were probably there to make sure the Trofts didn't make it deeper into the Qasamans' refuge.

Ten minutes later, they arrived at a door flanked by two soldiers standing at parade-ground attention. "Looks promising," Merrick said. "But then, all these doors look alike."

"By deliberate design, of course," Zoshak murmured back. "It doesn't look like they want company, though."

"We don't always get what we want," Merrick said. "Thank you for your assistance, Carsh Zoshak. You'd better head back to the barracks. After tonight you won't want to be too closely associated with me."

"Yet if I leave now, how will I ever know whether I consider Miron Akim's actions to be betrayal?" Zoshak asked calmly. "Besides, without me you won't be able to get in." Out of the corner of his eye, Merrick saw the other flash him a wry look. "Without harming someone, I mean. Follow me."

He picked up his pace, moving a couple of steps out in front of Merrick. "Greetings, warriors of Qasama," he said formally as they approached the guarded door. "We have urgent business with those within. Step aside, and allow us to pass."

Merrick saw the soldiers' eyes flick down to Zoshak's gray Djinn combat suit, then to Merrick as he trailed behind, then back to Zoshak. "I'm sorry, Djinni," one of them said in the same formal tone. "Shahni Haafiz gave word they were not to be disturbed."

Merrick felt his throat tighten. Haafiz. Why was he not surprised?

"We have important business," Zoshak insisted, not slowing as he continued toward them. "Stand aside."

"We have orders," the soldier repeated, his hand getting a grip on his shoulder-slung rifle.

And suddenly, Merrick had had enough. "Let me talk to them," he said, lengthening his stride and stepping past Zoshak.

The soldiers' faces had gone stone-like, and both were starting to swing their rifles up into firing positions, when Merrick lifted his hand and fired his stunner.

The first soldier jerked as the high-voltage current slammed into him, scrambling nerve pathways and collapsing him into an unconscious heap on the floor. The second soldier had just enough time to widen his eyes when Merrick sent him to join his friend. Without even breaking stride Merrick grabbed the doorknob, twisted it and shoved the door open.

Once again there were three men seated at the curved table at the end of the room, with Shahni Haafiz again at the center.

But this time the rest of the cast had changed. Instead of two more Shahni, Haafiz had Moffren Omnathi at his right and Miron Akim at his left.

And standing in front of them, in the place where Merrick himself had been standing only hours earlier, wide eyes turned toward the unexpected intruders—

"Merrick," Jin gasped. "What are you doing here?"

"Step aside, Mother," Merrick told her shortly, his eyes steady on Akim. "Miron Akim and I have some business to conduct."

CHAPTER NINETEEN

Jin felt her heart catch in her chest as Merrick strode across the room toward her. *No,* she pleaded silently. *Not now.* "Merrick, go back," she said with as much firmness as she could pull together on the spur of the moment. "You don't understand."

"Oh, I understand," Merrick told her, his voice dark and simmering with rage, the natural calmness he'd inherited from his father gone like leaves in a gale. "I understand just fine."

"Stay where you are," Shahni Haafiz snapped, his voice betraying no hint of Jin's own fear. "There are Djinn to both sides of you."

"Really?" Merrick said, still moving forward. Jin saw her son's eyes twitch—"Then I suggest you warn them to be very careful," he continued. "I've locked up on the three of you, and Moffren Omnathi there will tell you that we Cobras are very hard to kill. One of the Djinn opens fire, and all three of you die." He pointed at Haafiz. "You first, of course."

"You didn't come here to kill," Omnathi said quietly. His face, unlike Haafiz's, showed no sign of emotion. "Else we would be dead already."

"True enough," Merrick agreed as he came to a halt beside his mother. Zoshak, Jin noted peripherally, had stopped a few paces back from them, silently watchful but making no attempt to interfere. "Two points. First, I came to let you know that I'm on to what you did to me, and what you tried to do to my mother."

"Merrick—" Jin tried again, laying a warning hand on his arm.

"And second," Merrick said, shaking off her hand, "I came to make a deal."

For a long moment the room was silent. The three Qasamans gazed hard at Merrick, and Jin held her breath. Then, to her relief, Haafiz stirred and made a small hand gesture. "Very well, Cobra Moreau," he said. "Speak."

"It didn't make sense," Merrick said, his eyes shifting back and forth among the three men behind the table. "Why spin me this big prove-yourself-trustworthy line and lock me up to think about it, and then just open the door and let me out a few hours later?"

"Perhaps it was an act of mercy," Omnathi suggested. "A chance to spend some time alone with your mother to hear of her medical condition."

"Yes, and we'll get to that in a minute," Merrick said, the sudden darkness in his tone sending a shiver up Jin's back. "But if that was the case, why not lock me up again afterward instead of sending me to a regular barracks? No, the only way it made sense was if you no longer needed whatever it was you'd originally wanted from me."

He looked at Jin. "And then, lo and behold, I find out that this whole terminal brain tumor thing is nothing but a scam. That you could go in there tomorrow and pull it out if you wanted to." He looked back at the three Qasamans. "And you *do* want to . . . because while you're in there, you can pull out something else. The thing you were hoping I would think to offer you while I was rotting away in solitary.

"You want a Cobra nanocomputer."

Once again, the room fell silent. "Very good, Cobra Moreau," Omnathi said at last. "Did I not warn you, Shahni Haafiz, that they were not to be underestimated?"

"Perhaps," Haafiz said calmly. "But their cleverness is irrelevant."

"I don't think so," Merrick said. "You see, I happen to know that you had access to Cobra nanocomputers once before." He looked at his mother, and to her relief Jin saw that his uncharacteristic anger was fading away. "You had the bodies of my mother's team, which is where you got the Djinn glove lasers and trigger mechanisms." He looked at the men again. "So if you have all of those, why do you still need one of ours?"

"Why waste our time asking questions to which you already know the answers?" Haafiz growled. "The nanocomputers you speak of had degraded by the time we were able to study them."

"Yes, they had," Merrick said. "By deliberate design, of course. Which brings me to the deal." He drew himself up. "You operate on my mother, remove the tumor and heal her completely. In return, I'll let you take out my nanocomputer and tell you how to keep it from degrading."

"An interesting offer," Haafiz said, smiling thinly. "Unfortunately, you're too late."

Merrick's eyes narrowed. "What's that supposed to mean?"

"He means," Jin said gently, "that I've already made them the same offer. Only they'll be getting *my* nanocomputer, not yours."

Merrick turned startled eyes on her, and in his face she could see his sudden chagrin as he belatedly realized he'd been so preoccupied with his confrontation that it hadn't even occurred to him to wonder what she was doing here in the first place. "No," he said flatly. "They get mine, or they don't get either of them."

"Perhaps we should simply take both," Haafiz said.

"*Or* you don't get either of them," Merrick repeated, glaring at him. "I can play games, too."

"This isn't a game, Merrick Moreau," Akim spoke up quietly. "This is survival."

"That's your excuse for manipulating us this way?" Merrick bit out. "After we've both risked our lives to help you?"

"We manipulated you because we had no choice but to do so," Omnathi said. There was no pleading in his voice that Jin could detect, nor any regret or even embarrassment at having been caught out in their scheming. "The fact is that the defenses we've so carefully prepared over the years have failed. Without the new possibilities represented by your nanocomputers, we have no chance of victory against the invaders. We'll continue to throw ourselves uselessly against their might until attrition takes the last of us."

Merrick looked at Jin, then shifted his eyes to Akim. "What about your Djinn?" he asked. "They've got the capability to be nearly as good as any Cobra. In fact, in some ways, they're better than we are."

Akim shook his head. "Their training and tactics are based on real-time squad coordination," he said. "But the invaders' ability to lock their antipersonnel missiles on to our radio signals renders that coordination impossible."

Merrick grimaced. "I wondered about that," he said. "I heard stories that they were tracking gunfire noise, but the ranging distances seemed way too big."

"In actual fact, they do track gunfire sounds, but only once they're within two or three meters of a target," Akim said. "The point is that your nanocomputer's programmed movements give you a far better capability of working alone than any Djinn possesses. We need that capability if we're to mount an effective defense of our world."

"Maybe," Merrick said. "But even once you have a working nanocomputer—"

"The other point is that it's not just Qasama that's in danger," Jin put in, silently pleading with her son not to say anything more. "The Trofts have been out in the forest since the invasion began, capturing spine leopards and loading them aboard transports. We think they're planning to take them back to the Cobra Worlds."

Merrick snorted. "What, we don't have enough of them there already?"

"They're not going to be dumping them in the wastelands," Jin said tartly. "They're going to turn them loose inside the cities."

Merrick stared at her. "You're jok—" He broke off, glanced at Akim, then looked back at Jin. "You can't be serious."

"Why not?" Akim said. "If you wish to neutralize the police, create a massive accident that draws them to the scene. If you wish to occupy warriors, give them something more urgent to do battle with."

"We also think they may not have launched their attack yet," Jin said. "They wouldn't want to just dribble the predators into Capitalia or Pindar and give us time to figure out what they were up to. They have to be planning to dump them all in at once so that everyone will be running around in panic while they consolidate their positions."

"Yes," Merrick murmured, his eyes narrow with thought. The last of the anger was gone, Jin saw with relief, and he was finally thinking again. "Which means we still might have a chance to warn them," he said. "Get hold of a ship somehow and get back to Aventine. *If* we can move fast enough."

"Which is the bargain Jasmine Moreau has just made with us," Omnathi said. "She'll give us her nanocomputer. In return, we'll provide you with transport back to your world."

"Really," Merrick said. "Did Qasama develop spaceflight capability when we weren't looking?"

"Who is to say we have not done exactly that?" Haafiz asked loftily.

"Please, Your Excellency," Omnathi rumbled. "No, Merrick Moreau, we obviously haven't. But there are always ways." He eyed Merrick closely. "Provided, of course, that both parties to an agreement truly intend to honor their commitments."

Merrick looked at Jin. "Mom—"

"We have no choice, Merrick," Jin cut him off firmly. If she couldn't convince him that this was the only way, the questions and doubts would haunt the rest of his life. Just as her own questions and doubts had haunted hers. "I can't do any more here. Even after the tumor is removed it'll take me weeks to recover to the point where I could do any fighting. You, on the other hand, *can* still fight. If you give them yours, they won't have either of us to help them."

Merrick swallowed. "And if I decide the cost is too high?"

"You're talking about the price of freedom," Jin reminded him. "Both of us proclaimed ourselves willing to pay that price when we put on the uniform."

Merrick closed his eyes. "Have I ever told you how much I hate your sense of logic?"

"Everyone always has," Jin said, wincing as an unwanted memory from thirty-two years ago flashed across her mind's eye: her arguments to her father and Uncle Corwin that, despite years of precedent and custom, she was the best possible person to become a Cobra and go on the Qasama mission. "But only because I'm usually right."

"Mom—"

Jin stopped him with a hand to his cheek. "My husband, daughter, and other son are back there," she said quietly. "They'll have no warning of what's about to happen unless we make this deal. Please let me serve them in this one last way."

For a long minute he just gazed at her, and Jin could see the swirling emotions fighting themselves across his face. "When?" he asked at last.

Jin felt some of the tension fade from her throat. "As soon as possible," she said.

"But not until after you've assisted with the attack on the invader sentry ship," Omnathi put in.

Merrick gave him a look that was half disbelief and half disgust. "What, sacrificing the rest of my mother's life isn't enough for you?" he demanded. "You want me to fight, too?"

"Have you not sworn to protect Qasama from its enemies?" Haafiz countered. "Have you not stated that until the invaders are off this world that you *are* a Qasaman?"

"At any rate, it'll take time to prepare for your return to your worlds," Omnathi added. "As short a time as possible, of course."

"Of course," Merrick said stiffly. "Fine. Miron Akim, have you chosen your attack plan yet?"

"It'll be ready by nine tomorrow morning," Akim promised. "At that time you'll join Ifrit Khatir and his team for a briefing." His eyes flicked over Jin's shoulder. "As will you, Djinni Zoshak," he said, raising his voice. "I suggest you both return now to your barracks for sleep. One way or another, tomorrow is destined to be a busy day."

"Understood." Merrick looked at Jin. "You want me to walk you back to your quarters?"

"I'll do that," Akim said, standing up. "I have a few other matters to discuss with her."

"I could walk with you," Merrick persisted.

"You have been ordered to your barracks, *Qasaman,*" Haafiz cut in. "You have already spoken of the price of freedom. Do not force me to demonstrate the price of disobedience."

For a bad moment Jin thought Merrick was going to argue the point. But he'd apparently had enough conflict for one night. "As you wish, Shahni Haafiz," he said with all the formality anyone could want. "Until tomorrow, Miron Akim."

"Tomorrow, Cobra Moreau," Akim said with a nod.

Squeezing Jin's hand once, Merrick forced a strained half smile and headed back toward the door. Zoshak, still without saying a word, also turned as he passed, falling into step beside him.

"Jasmine Moreau?"

She turned to see that Akim had circled the table and come up beside her. "We'll use this door," he said, gesturing toward an unobtrusive exit tucked away behind a display board. "It'll bring us more quickly to your room."

Jin didn't speak until they were walking down yet another of the subcity's corridors. Unlike all the others she'd been in, though, this one seemed completely deserted. A special parallel corridor system reserved for the Shahni and other high-ranking officials? "We *could* have let Merrick come along, you know," she commented as they walked. "I doubt we're going to talk about anything he shouldn't hear."

Akim made an odd sound in the back of his throat. "Actually," he said reluctantly, "we are."

They were halfway back to the barracks when Merrick finally couldn't stand the silence anymore. "Well, come on," he growled at Zoshak. "*Say* something. Even if it's just to lecture me on how I shouldn't be rude to one of the Shahni."

"What do you want me to say?" Zoshak asked calmly. "You *shouldn't* be rude to the Shahni."

Merrick grimaced. "Yeah, I know."

"But the ultimate fault lies with Shahni Haafiz and Advisor Omnathi, not with you," Zoshak continued. "They shouldn't have tried to manipulate you that way. Not when you'd already proven your willingness to serve our people."

Merrick grimaced again. Perversely, Zoshak's support only made him feel worse about the whole confrontation. "I suppose you can't really blame them," he said. "They've grown up hating us. A person doesn't toss all that aside just because someone lets the bad guys take a few shots at him."

Zoshak was silent for another few paces. "One thing I don't understand. I thought your equipment enhanced your normal abilities without being a substitute for them. Yet you state that your mother will die without her nanocomputer?"

Merrick sighed, the whole situation once again wrenching at him. "She won't literally die," he said. "But the condition she's going to end up in might as well be death. Our nanocomputers control our servos, not just their extra-strength capabilities but also the normal everyday movements. Without that control, the servos won't function. Every movement she makes will be against little motors that don't want to move and will have to be forced. Throw in the inherent extra weight of our ceramic laminae, and it'll be like she's wearing exercise wraps all over her body. Add in the arthritis and anemia that are already starting to affect her, and you have a prescription for a living hell."

"Is there nothing that can be done to help?" Zoshak asked. "Perhaps implant a new computer?"

"In theory, I suppose that could be done," Merrick said. "But the equipment to do that is forty-five light-years and a long visit to a Qasaman brain surgeon away.

The point is that she'll have to go through her surgery and recovery in that state." He shook his head. "I'm just worried about what it'll do to her."

"And so you volunteered to take her place," Zoshak said, his voice thoughtful. "Willing to sacrifice yourself for your family."

Merrick shrugged. "Probably sounds a little selfish," he admitted. "After all, without my nanocomputer, I'd be pretty much out of the war. That's a lot safer than going out in the streets and getting shot at."

"I hardly consider such a sacrifice to fall under the heading of selfishness," Zoshak said. "I was merely noting that you're perhaps more like us than you realize."

An hour later, as Merrick finally began to drift off to sleep, he was still wondering whether being like the Qasamans was a good thing or a bad thing.

Jin sighed. "Merrick won't like this," she said. "Neither will Shahni Haafiz."

"Nor will probably anyone else on Qasama," Akim agreed soberly. "But my concern right now is for you, Jasmine Moreau. What do *you* think?"

Jin looked away from him. What *did* she think of Akim's plan?

Perhaps more importantly, what *could* she think with a tumor grinding inexorably away at her brain and mind? Merrick had commented earlier on her sense of logic, but she wasn't at all certain she could even trust her thought processes anymore. Especially not when it concerned something this potentially explosive. "You're the one putting your life on the line here," she pointed out instead. "You're the one who told me thirty years ago that on Qasama treason is punishable by death."

"Oh, they can't afford to execute me," he scoffed, waving a studiously nonchalant hand. "Not in the middle of a war. I'm far too important to them."

"That's an assumption," Jin warned. "And Shahni Haafiz in particular seems to be largely driven by pride."

Akim smiled sadly. "Aren't we all driven partially by pride?" he asked. "Even you, with your desire to warn your people of the Troft attack."

"That's not pride," Jin insisted.

"Isn't it?" Akim countered. "Tell me, how were you treated when you returned home from your last time on Qasama? Were you honored for your service in helping to eliminate a threat to our world? Or were you vilified for that action?"

Jin grimaced. "The latter, I'm afraid. In fact, my uncle lost his political position because of me. Is it that obvious?"

Akim shrugged. "You came here with only your son," he reminded her. "An honored and respected warrior would have answered the summons with a full contingent of warriors."

Jin stared at him. "Then you *did* send the message."

Akim shook his head. "Not I," he said. "Perhaps it came from one of the Shahni, though who that could be I can't even begin to guess. More likely the note was from Daulo Sammon, who is now simply lying about it. My point was that I was treated much the same way you were. On the surface I was honored for my role in eliminating Obolo Nardin's threat. But beneath that layer of gratitude lay a quiet anger and suspicion for my having cooperated with you. That distrust lasted long after most of the Shahni had forgotten even my name, let alone what specific crimes I was accused of committing."

He smiled tightly. "So I'm not a stranger to charges of treason, Jasmine Moreau. And if preventing my people from beating themselves mindlessly against an enemy they can't defeat is treason, then I'm willing to wear that badge."

"I admire your courage, Miron Akim," Jin said. "You rather remind me of my uncle that way."

"I'll take that as a high compliment," Akim said gravely. "Then you'll do this?"

"Yes," Jin said, a tingle running up through her. With that word, and that promise, the deal was made. There would be no going back. "You know the real irony here? Two weeks ago, back on Aventine, I was wishing something dramatic and dangerous would happen to our worlds. Something that would remind them that the Cobras are still a vital part of our society." She shook her head. "As the saying goes, one should be careful what one wishes for."

"We have that saying here, too." Akim took a deep breath and exhaled it in a tired-sounding sigh. "I'll escort you back to your room now. Get as much rest as you can."

Jin felt her stomach tighten. "It's set for tomorrow, then?"

"Barring any last-minute problems, yes," Akim confirmed. "The Djinn can be made ready in time, and delay only favors the invaders."

"I suppose so," Jin said. "Will I be seeing you again before then?"

Akim shook his head. "I'll be occupied all day with other matters."

And even if he wasn't, he probably wouldn't want to be seen with her anyway. "Understood," Jin said. "Good luck to you, Miron Akim."

"And to you, Jasmine Moreau," he said. He hesitated, then touched his fingers to his forehead and lips in the sign of respect. "Travel with God."

Ten minutes later, the nurse bade Jin good night and closed the door to her room. Listening to her heart pounding in her ears, she closed her eyes and tried to go to sleep. And wondered if she would ever see Miron Akim again.

CHAPTER TWENTY

The rooftop beneath Merrick was cold and hard, the warmth of the day's sunlight long gone. Above him, the Qasaman stars glittered in a cloudless sky, their patterns subtly different from the ones he'd grown up with on Aventine. Beside him, Zoshak and the other three Djinn of their squad huddled together in the radar and infrared shadow of the building's heat-plant chimney.

And directly in front of him, past the edge of the building's roof, was the Troft sentry ship, the same one Zoshak's team had attacked the previous day. Theoretically, or so Akim had said, now that the Trofts were alerted to possible attacks on their ships, one that had already repulsed an attack would be thought unlikely to be the target of a second one.

Theoretically.

"Two minutes," Zoshak murmured.

Merrick checked his nanocomputer's clock circuit. One minute and fifty-eight seconds, according to his count. "Check," he murmured.

"You ready?" Zoshak added, hunching his shoulders to resettle the heavy backpack he was wearing.

Merrick grimaced. Crouching in the middle of a Qasaman rooftop, dressed in a Qasaman Djinn combat suit—which the techs assured him would alter his infrared signature to something nonhuman, should the Trofts happen to pick up on him—surrounded by Qasaman warriors, preparing to take on an alien warship. Was anyone, he wondered, ever ready for something like that? "As ready as I'll ever be," he murmured back.

"This time we'll succeed," Zoshak said firmly. "I have no doubts. We'll show them that Qasamans—" He gave Merrick a lopsided smile. "That *humans* aren't to be trifled with."

"Let's hope they get the message," Merrick said, studying the shimmery mass of alien metal in the distance and doing one final ranging check. The wing supporting the weapons cluster was six meters above the level of the rooftop, plus another three from the edge.

An impossible jump for a normal human. Also well beyond the range of a Djinni in a combat suit, though Merrick doubted the Trofts knew enough about Djinn to have positioned their sentry ship that deliberately.

No problem at all for a Cobra.

Assuming, that is, that Merrick's borrowed combat suit didn't get in the way. The techs had also assured him that the built-in computer had been disconnected and that there would be no residual resistance or sluggishness from the suit's servos. But Merrick had had only limited opportunity to experiment with his new outfit between the day's practice sessions, and he couldn't quite shake the feeling that it might suddenly turn against him at the worst possible moment.

He peered across the rooftop again, where Siraj Akim and his squad were supposed to be waiting on the rooftop on the far side of the avenue, ready to provide cover fire for Merrick's team. Siraj had insisted on being included in this second attack on the sentry ship, and his father and the other team leaders had signed off on it, but that was yet another bad feeling Merrick couldn't shake. It had been barely a day since Siraj had led his original squad in the first disastrous attack on this same target, and Merrick wasn't at all sure Siraj was up to trying it again this soon.

Oddly enough, he had no such doubts about Zoshak. The Djinni crouched beside him seemed to have come out of that experience stronger, more determined, and somehow more optimistic than he'd gone into it. Siraj Akim, though, seemed to have come out darker and grimmer.

Merrick had seen that sort of response a few times before, in Cobras whose mistakes during a spine leopard hunt had gotten someone killed. Sometimes it took months or even years for them to fully snap out of it.

Which led to the even more interesting question of why Siraj was not only aboard, but had also been put in charge of Ghofl Khatir's team.

That one bothered Merrick a lot. True, Khatir had been decidedly unenthusiastic about having to work with the offworld Cobra, and it was possible that Miron Akim had decided he wasn't right for the job after all.

But for him to then replace Khatir with his own son was even more ominous. Was this Akim's version of the old get-back-behind-the-wheel philosophy, that the best therapy for Siraj's dark mood would be to lead the charge on the return engagement?

Certainly Siraj seemed determined to do it right this time. Even after Merrick's team had been declared fully prepared, Siraj had insisted his own squad stay in the arena for more drills. The question was whether the Djinn was being driven by thoroughness, or obsession.

"One minute," Zoshak murmured.

Merrick took a deep breath and tried to put his concerns about Siraj out of his mind. It hadn't been his place to question Miron Akim's authority in these matters before, and it wasn't his place to be second-guessing him now. Long ago, Merrick's mother had trusted her life to Akim, and it had worked out all right. He would just have to hope that thirty years hadn't dulled the older man's judgment. Getting a fresh grip on the heavy rope bridge coiled up beneath his left arm, he watched his clock circuit count down to zero.

Exactly half a second later, the neighborhood exploded with the thunder of automatic gunfire.

It was an awesome display of firepower, particularly given that no one had any illusions that it would do any good against the sentry ship's thick armor. The entire point of the attack was to draw the Trofts' attention away from the small groups of men huddled here on the rooftops. The crucial question was whether or not the aliens would really let themselves be fooled this way.

And then, beneath the wing, Merrick saw the lasers and missile launchers of the weapons cluster swivel around and began spitting their deadly fire toward the impertinent humans who insisted on fighting against their new overlords.

"Five seconds," Zoshak announced tensely.

Merrick squeezed his hand into a fist. Over the years the Qasamans had slowly built up a profile of the basic Troft mind, and had concluded that it would take five seconds from the opening salvo of their counterattack until they were mentally and emotionally committed to that course of action.

But even five seconds was an eternity when you were at the business end of an enemy barrage. There were Qasamans behind each of those chattering machine guns, and the delay that would help protect Merrick's team would cost some of them their lives.

"Go!"

Merrick shoved himself out of his crouch, leaning forward into an all-out sprint toward the edge of the roof. The under-wing lasers were still firing at the other attackers, the Trofts apparently still unaware of this new threat closing in on their flank. Merrick kept going, waiting tensely for the moment when someone aboard the ship would suddenly notice him and bring one of those lasers to bear . . .

And then, sooner somehow than he'd expected, the edge of the roof loomed directly ahead. Gauging his distance, giving his stride one final tweaking, he ran to the very edge and jumped. There was a tense half second as he soared toward the sentry ship, a half second of ballistic flight where no programmed reflexes could do him a damn bit of good if the Trofts locked up on him—

And then he was there, landing neatly on the center of the wing's two-by-three-meter expanse. He braked quickly to a halt, then spun around and hurled the coiled rope bridge back toward the rooftop. Zoshak was in position; catching the coil, he snapped out the bridge's anchoring spikes and jabbed them hard into the rooftop. Getting a firm grip on his own end, Merrick dropped onto his back, bracing one foot against a small ridge at the wingtip and the other against the wing's trailing static discharge wick. He stretched the bridge tight and locked his arm servos in place.

And with a multiple thud that jarred him with each footstep, the rest of the Djinn ran single-file up the bridge and onto the wing.

Zoshak was the last one up. As he stepped past Merrick onto the wing, Merrick tossed his end of the bridge to one of the other Djinn, waiting beside him for that purpose, then bounded back to his feet and followed Zoshak toward the line where the wing joined the hull. Out of the corners of his eyes, he saw the remaining two Djinn climb up onto the crest of the hull and crouch down into guard positions.

Zoshak had his backpack off by the time Merrick arrived beside him. "Ready?" Merrick called over the noise of the gunfire.

Zoshak nodded. Lifting his left leg, Merrick aimed at the wing's inner edge and fired his antiarmor laser.

The sizzle of vaporizing metal was lost amid the cacophony still going on around them. But the shimmery flash as the laser cut into the wing was all Merrick needed to know that his guess had been correct. There was some sort of radar-absorption material coating the metal, a coating that was burning off with gratifying speed in the laser's focused heat.

The metal beneath it was another story. It was thick and strong, and as Merrick tracked his laser slowly along the edge of the wing he saw he was barely managing to carve a shallow groove. If the Qasamans' fancy acid didn't work, this whole exercise was going to be for nothing.

He was nearly finished when a flash of something caught the edge of his eye. He looked up—

To see a flicker of brilliant blue light coming from somewhere on the other side of the hull crest.

He felt his chest seize up. It was the Trofts over there. It had to be. They'd gotten up there somehow, and were coming for him and his team.

And the two Djinn up there who were supposed to be watching for that kind of flanking maneuver were just *standing* there?

"Move it!" he snapped to Zoshak. Without waiting for acknowledgment, he leaped up from the wing onto the crest. In the pulsating light from the laser he could see a handful of figures gathered on the other weapons wing. Cocking his ring fingers into laser firing position, wondering if he could get all of them before they took him down, he threw himself into a shallow dive onto the wing.

He was midway through his jump when it suddenly registered that the figure he could now see standing at the inner edge of the wing wasn't actually *holding* the laser that had caught his attention. The beam was, instead, blasting downward from the figure's left foot . . .

Even with his mind frozen with stunned disbelief, his nanocomputer was up to the task of landing him safely on the wing. But the figure had spotted him. It reacted instantly, throwing itself flat onto the metal surface and spinning around on its back to bring its laser to bear—

"Mom!" Merrick barked. "Don't shoot!"

"Merrick?" his mother's voice came from the Djinn-suited figure as she jerked her laser away from him. "What are you doing here?"

"That's *my* question," Merrick gritted out. "You're supposed to be on an operating table somewhere."

"I meant, what are you doing on this side of the ship?" Jin demanded as she scrambled back to her feet. Even in the dim light, Merrick could see that her face was pinched with pain from the quick-dodge maneuver his sudden appearance had forced her into.

"Get back over there," Siraj Akim snapped, coming up beside Merrick. "This operation depends on everyone following the plan as ordered."

"He's right," Jin seconded. "Get over there and let me finish up here."

"Right," Merrick said through clenched teeth as he stepped past her and hopped up onto the hull again. Like he could be expected to follow a plan that he didn't know half of. If he made it through this alive, he promised himself darkly, Miron Akim was going to have some *very* serious explaining to do.

Zoshak was crouching beside the groove Merrick had carved in the wing when he made it back to his side of the ship. "What's going on?" the Djinni asked.

"We've got company," Merrick growled. "Miron Akim sent my mother along with Siraj Akim's squad to take out the other wing. How's it going here?"

Zoshak gestured. "See for yourself."

Merrick peered down at the wing. Actually, there wasn't a lot to be seen through the wispy white smoke pouring up from the crack he'd cut through the metal's coating. Briefly, he ran through his optical enhancers' various settings, but none of them did much good against the smoke. "Any idea how we'll know when we're deep enough to cut through the control cables?" he asked.

"When the weapons fall silent," Zoshak said, carefully dribbling some more acid from his flask into the smoking groove. "We'll get word—"

"Incoming aft!" one of the Djinn up on the hull snapped a warning. An instant later he gurgled and collapsed as a barrage of laser bolts riddled him from somewhere to their rear.

"Watch it!" Merrick shouted, dropping flat onto the wing and pulling Zoshak down with him. At the other end of the ship a dozen armored Trofts had appeared and were moving toward them along the hull, their lasers spitting fire at the intruders.

Frantically, Merrick looked around. But there was literally no cover anywhere to be had. Nowhere to hide, and only one place to run. "Get out of here!" he snapped at Zoshak as he swiveled around to bring his antiarmor laser to bear. "Leave the acid and take the others down the bridge. I'll cover you."

"Yes, cover me," Zoshak snapped back as he set down the acid flask and headed at a quick crawl toward the end of the wing and the bridge waiting there.

Clenching his teeth, Merrick targeted the first three of the approaching Trofts with his antiarmor laser. If the aliens had been traveling single file, he might have been able to take all of them. But they were bunched together, using each other's armored bodies as partial shields.

He could hear Zoshak doing something with the bridge now, and only then did it occur to him that for the rest of the Djinn to escape someone was going to have to hold the end of the bridge for them. A laser shot grazed across his upper arm, and his nanocomputer took over, rolling him away from the shot as his own laser continued firing. From the far side of the crest he could see other flashes of blue light as his mother joined in the battle, and he sent up a quick prayer for her safety. The Djinn were firing, too, the flashes from their glove lasers fainter in comparison with either the Troft or Cobra weapons, and Merrick wondered if their efforts were doing anything more than distracting the aliens. There was a sudden movement at Merrick's side.

And he jerked reflexively as something long and dark and big went whipping across his line of sight, spinning in a flat arc toward the rear of the ship. He had just enough time to recognize it as their rope bridge before it slammed into the cluster of Trofts, sending their shots wildly in all directions as it wrapped them in a tangle of rope and wood.

"Attack!" Zoshak shouted. He leaped past Merrick onto the hull, his glove lasers blazing at the Trofts, the two remaining Djinn of his team right behind him.

Merrick leaped to his feet, hesitating as he tried to decide whether to join the mad rush or stay here and try to pick off more of the attackers. But the Trofts were pushing their way free of the bridge and starting to fire again, and there was no more time for thinking or planning. Gauging the distance, he bent his knees and jumped.

He had just left the wing when a brilliant laser flash lanced across the space he'd vacated, blasting a cloud of metal splinters from the wing's trailing edge. Merrick bit out a curse as he glanced down at the smoking metal, wondering where that shot had come from. A second later he hit the hull crest, landing two meters in front of Zoshak and the other Djinn and barely four meters away from the approaching Trofts. A half-dozen alien lasers tracked toward him—

Their shots went wild as Merrick fired a full-power burst from his sonic. He fired again, staggering them back, then thrust his right hand forward and activated his arcthrower.

The lightning bolt caught the lead Troft squarely in the torso, throwing him backward into the two directly behind him. Merrick shifted aim and fired the arcthrower again, this time catching one of the Trofts' lasers and shattering it into a burst of shrapnel.

He was lining up on one of the other Trofts when a laser shot caught him in his stomach.

For that first frozen second there was no pain, only the horrifying realization that his luck had finally run out. His knees buckled as the shock swept through him, and he felt himself falling as if in slow motion. He heard a voice shout his name as he landed hard on his knees, and from somewhere behind him he saw a sudden barrage of brilliant blue laser shots flashing across the remaining Trofts, throwing clouds of vaporized metal from their armor and twisting and throwing them into little piles of death.

And then, suddenly, the pain was there, rushing through him like a flash flood in a mountain arroyo. He gasped, gripping his stomach with both hands, feeling himself swaying as his eyes dimmed and he started to fall over.

He was headed face-first toward the hull when a hand came from behind him and grabbed him beneath his left arm in a steadying grip. A second hand took his other arm, and suddenly he was being lifted upright again, swaying a little as the two people made a mad dash along the hull. Dimly through the pain he saw an open hatchway with another Troft helmet just emerging, and then a gray-suited figure leaped over him from behind and a blue laser bolt sent the Troft tumbling out of sight. The figure stopped beside the hatchway, sending a flurry of bolts down into the opening as Merrick's handlers hustled him past. Through his wavering vision he could see the sentry ship's aft wings looming ahead . . .

With a jolt, he snapped back to consciousness and found himself sitting in the middle of one of the aft wings. Crouching in front of him was Siraj Akim, sorting quickly through a set of small hypos. Behind him, Zoshak was crouching beside the hull end of the wing, more white smoke drifting around him as he poured acid into the metal. "What—?" Merrick croaked.

"Just sit still," his mother's taut voice came from behind him, and only then did he realize that her grip on his upper arms was what was holding him upright. "Siraj Akim is trying to stabilize you."

Merrick turned his head to look toward the forward wings, wincing as he spotted the motionless bodies lying there. "Where are the others?"

"Most gave their lives for Qasama," Siraj said grimly as he carefully stuck the needle into Merrick's side. "I've already ordered the survivors away."

"The Trofts started firing at us with the weapons clusters under these aft wings," Jin explained. "Must have done some quick recalibrating—usually you can't fire on your own ship that way."

"They seem to have managed it just fine," Merrick said, knowing that she was talking mostly to distract him. Or to distract herself.

He focused on Siraj's grim expression as the Djinni selected another hypo. Yet more Djinn deaths on the young man's conscience. He wondered how Siraj was feeling, but his mind didn't seem to be working very well. But at least the pain was fading. "Did we take the ship?" he asked. "I mean the ground troops. Did they get inside?"

"I don't think so," Jin said. "And it's about to be too late. You feel that?"

With an effort, Merrick concentrated what little mind he seemed to have left. "The vibration?" he asked.

"Right," Jin said. "The Trofts are about to—there we go."

Merrick blinked as the cityscape around them suddenly shifted. The sentry ship they were huddled on was lifting off the pavement on its gravity lifts, rising above the level of the surrounding buildings and starting to turn toward the spaceport.

"So once again we've failed," Zoshak said bitterly. "More lives lost for nothing."

"At least we chased them away," Merrick said, a fresh ache flooding through him at Zoshak's words. He tried to think of what they might have done differently, how they might have pulled out the victory that Zoshak and Siraj deserved and the Qasamans so desperately needed. But his mind was drifting. "Sends them a message, anyway."

Zoshak hissed between his teeth. "You'll forgive me if I don't find that message worth the cost."

"You are forgiven, Djinni Zoshak," Siraj said.

Merrick frowned, trying to focus his increasingly bleary eyes on the other. Siraj was actually *smiling*. A grim, vicious smile, but a smile nonetheless. "You all right?" Merrick asked.

"I'm quite well, thank you," Siraj said. "You speak of a message, Merrick Moreau. And you, Djinni Zoshak, speak of cost." Dramatically, he pointed toward the street below. "Behold."

Merrick turned his head. In the center of the market place that their particular sentry ship had been overlooking, a large section of pavement had opened up to reveal a dark, deep pit. Too big a hole for individual soldiers, his sluggish mind realized, but also with no visible ramp for ground vehicles.

Which left only . . . "Mom?" he croaked.

And caught his breath as a helicopter shot out of the opening. A slender helicopter, lean and deadly-looking as an Arkon's dragonfly, black and gray in the reflected light, clusters of weapons visible beneath its own set of stubby support wings as it climbed rapidly into the sky. Hard on its tail was a second gunship, and a third, and a fourth, and a fifth.

Behind him, Merrick heard his mother gasp. "*SkyJos?*" she said.

"Indeed," Siraj confirmed, and there was no mistaking the satisfaction in his voice. "Trapped uselessly in their underground hangar until *we* drove their unsuspecting guardian away."

The words were barely out of his mouth when the SkyJos opened fire.

The earlier diversionary attack on the sentry ship had been loud. But it was nothing compared to this. Merrick gazed out across at the city, wishing he could close his ears against the hammering as the SkyJos fired lasers and heavy missiles and multiple hailstorms of armor-piercing rounds at their invaders.

The Troft sentry ships didn't have a chance. Caught on the ground, their weaponry designed for repulsing ground-based attacks, they began to disintegrate beneath the pounding. A few of the more distant ones made it off the ground, but by the time they did other hidden nests around the city, now likewise freed from their enemy guardians, were sending their own fleets of SkyJos to join in the attack.

Away to the north, Merrick could see the first signs of movement from the airfield as some of the larger Troft ships tried to beat the approaching Qasamans into the air. One of the heavy ships succeeded in its attempts, rising above the buildings and picking up speed as it turned toward the nearest group of incoming SkyJos.

An instant later it was caught in a terrifying pillar of fire as the control tower it was passing over disintegrated in a thunderous explosion. The crippled ship veered violently sideways, tried to back up, then crashed to the ground. From the multiple flashes of secondary explosions, Merrick guessed it had probably crashed on top of some of the other Troft ships.

He turned back to Siraj. "You're right," he slurred through suddenly numb lips. "That was one hell of a message."

The last thing he remembered as Siraj's face blurred and then faded into darkness was the sight of a pair of SkyJos coming up behind Siraj, their lowered grab nets fluttering in the breeze.

CHAPTER TWENTY-ONE

The deep-forest village was quiet and dark as the SkyJo settled into the center square. "Where is everyone?" Jin asked as the pilot cut the engines.

"He's waiting," the other said tersely, pointing to one of the larger houses bordering on the square. "You go alone."

Jin unstrapped from her jumpseat, keying her optical enhancers as she did so. There were two men flanking the building's front entrance, standing with the stiffness of military guards. "Understood," she said, turning for a final look at Merrick. His eyes were closed, and even in the dim light she could see that his face was unnaturally pale. But his chest was rising and falling rhythmically, and the stretcher's readouts were showing a cautious stability in his other vital signs.

"He's waiting," the pilot repeated.

"Go ahead," Zoshak said. "Ifrit Akim and I will wait with him. Go and find out what this is all about."

"All right," Jin said, wondering what exactly she was going to tell the two of them when she came back. According to the plan, she and Merrick were to have been brought out here alone, not with a pair of Qasaman hitchhikers in tow. Certainly not with Miron Akim's own son along for the ride.

But there was nothing for it now but to play it through and hope Akim was able to improvise. Opening the gunship's side door, she stepped out onto the wet grass and started toward the house.

From the air, the village had looked deserted. From ground level, it looked dead. There were no lights showing anywhere that Jin could see, and the only sound aside from the light wind rustling through the trees and bushes was the faint whooshing from the second SkyJo flying high cover above them. Even her infrareds were unable to pick up human heat sources in any of the buildings except the one she was heading for.

Had Miron Akim cleared out the entire village for this?

One of the two door guards stirred as she approached. "He's waiting," he said, leaning over and pushing open the door. "First room on the right."

"Thank you." Stepping between them, Jin walked into the house and turned into the indicated doorway.

And stopped abruptly in her tracks. "Good evening, Jasmine Moreau," Moffren Omnathi said gravely from the depths of an armchair in the center of the room. "How nice to see you again."

It took Jin two tries to find her voice. "And you as well, Advisor Omnathi," she said between frozen lips, her heartbeat thudding suddenly in her chest.

"Yet you seem surprised to see me," Omnathi said calmly. "Almost as if you were expecting someone else."

"Indeed," Jin said as calmly as she could. So it was over. Akim's plan, and her own hopes. Omnathi had found out about it, and it was all over. "Tell me, what have you done with Miron Akim?"

"I?" Omnathi asked, as if surprised she would even think such a thing. "I do nothing to anyone. Surely you know that."

"Of course," Jin said. "My mistake. You merely give the orders. Others carry them out."

"Yes," Omnathi said. It was a simple statement of fact, unencumbered by either embarrassment or pride. "But do not concern yourself," he continued. "As I'm sure Miron Akim himself told you, he is far too valuable to be disciplined."

"I'm relieved to hear that," Jin said. As if she actually believed it. "Do my son and I stand in similar positions?"

"You made an agreement with the Shahni," he reminded her, his voice going a shade darker. "Your nanocomputer for the chance to warn your people of the impending Troft attack. Despite that agreement, you and Miron Akim conspired to send both you and your son away without fulfilling your side of the bargain."

"Yes, I know what was said and done," Jin said, suddenly tired of playing games. "Whatever you're going to do to us, get on with it."

"Please; indulge me," Omnathi said gravely. "I lay out the facts solely to impress upon you the understanding that I know everything there is to know about the path you and Miron Akim have chosen." He paused. "So that you will know that I speak from full understanding when I tell you I agree with that path."

Jin's bewilderment must have shown in her face, because Omnathi actually smiled. "You doubt my sincerity?" he asked. "Or merely my sanity?"

"I'm . . . confused," Jin managed. Was this some sort of cruel joke? "If you disagreed with the original deal . . . ?"

"Why did I not speak up?" Omnathi sighed. "Because despite the firm belief of our people, the Shahni's decisions are not always wise. In this case, they completely failed to understand the realities of our situation. Even if I held your nanocomputer in my hand right now, it would take months to decipher the programming and weeks or months more to construct enough of them for our needs. After that it would be months before we learned how to create the fiber control network and the bone laminae, to say nothing of the necessary techniques for implanting the servos."

"None of which you've been able to do in thirty years of trying," Jin murmured. "Miron Akim told me."

"In fact, it has been far more than thirty years," Omnathi said. "We have been trying to reconstruct your weaponry ever since your people's first visit here six decades ago. Even with your wholehearted assistance, I fear we would still fail in our attempts."

His gaze drifted away from her, his eyes focused on infinity. "No, Jasmine Moreau," he said quietly. "The promise of your nanocomputer, even offered in good faith, is a false hope. The Trofts were handed a terrible defeat tonight, and indeed many of them have fled from our world in disarray. But if this is indeed a war against all humankind, they will not stay away for long. They will return, more cautious and more determined. And we will have no further surprises with which to shake them."

His eyes came back to her. "We can survive for a season. But barring a miracle, ultimate victory cannot and will not be ours. Not alone. Not without aid from your people. If you fail to fulfill your promise to Miron Akim, Qasama will die."

Jin swallowed hard. Never before had she seen a Qasaman leader stripped of his pride and bluster and supreme confidence in himself. It was eerie, and more than a little unnerving.

But as she looked into Omnathi's eyes, she felt her fatigue and uncertainty hardening into a brittle, ice-cold resolve. Behind the cultural arrogance were real, genuine human beings. Human beings worth saving. "I won't fail, Moffren Omnathi," she promised him quietly. "Whatever help I can find, I *will* bring back to you."

"Then I will trust you." Omnathi smiled again, but this time the smile was edged with sadness. "For indeed, I have no choice."

Placing his hands on the armrests, he pushed himself carefully to his feet. "Come. Your departure is at hand."

He walked past Jin out into the hallway and turned toward the rear of the house. "Where are the rest of the villagers?" Jin asked as she moved up beside him.

"The women and children have moved to nearby mines or ravines for safety," Omnathi said. "The rest are out in the forest, either hunting wayward Trofts or guarding the transport we have captured for your use."

Jin pursed her lips. "You *do* know, don't you, that I don't know how to fly a Troft ship?"

"That is being taken care of as we speak." Omnathi stopped at a door and gestured to it. "Please; after you."

Jin opened the door and stepped through into a large, brightly lit dining room, to find herself facing an extraordinary sight. Seated at a long dining table was a bedraggled-looking Troft, wearing a standard, unarmored leotard. Behind him stood two Qasamans, a young man and woman, the former wearing a Djinn combat suit, both of them peering unblinkingly at the alien's every move. Off to the side was a third Qasaman, this one a middle-aged man. The latter looked up as Jin and Omnathi entered, but none of the others in the room seemed to even notice them. Omnathi flicked his fingers at the older Qasaman, who nodded and turned back to the Troft. [An attack, it comes from behind,] he said in cattertalk.

The Troft's hands reached to the table in front of him, his fingers darting back and forth across the smooth wooden surface. [A radio challenge, it requires a response,] the Qasaman said.

The Troft swiveled around in his seat and again drummed his fingers, this time on a different part of the table. Like he was punching actual buttons, Jin thought, and operating an actual control board.

Which was, she realized abruptly, exactly what he thought he was doing.

She looked sharply at Omnathi. "The pilot of the transport we have obtained," the other murmured. "He believes himself to be in his control room."

Jin looked at the two young Qasamans, a shiver running up her back. And even as the middle-aged man manipulated his drugged Troft puppet, the two observers were watching his every move, their own drugged minds recording every nuance of his actions.

"You do not approve?" Omnathi asked.

With an effort, Jin pushed the shivers away. "It'll get us home," she said. "That's all that matters."

Out of the corner of her eye, she saw Omnathi nod. "Good," he murmured. "They will be finished soon. Let us go examine your vehicle."

The Troft transport was parked about a hundred meters from the village, nestled into a small clearing that fit it so well that Jin suspected the trees had been cut down specifically for the purpose. "There were nearly a dozen razorarms in the cargo bay when we took the vehicle," Omnathi said as the two of them walked through a sentry line of grim-faced villagers. "We assumed you wouldn't wish to be bothered with their care and feeding during the voyage home and therefore released them back into the woods."

Jin nodded. It might have been smarter to leave the predators aboard in case they ran into an advance ship near Aventine whose crew decided to be suspicious and examine their cargo. But it was too late to do anything about that now. "How big a crew will we have?" she asked as Omnathi led the way through the open hatchway.

"Only the two you saw back there," Omnathi said. "The woman is Rashida Vil, the man is Ghofl Khatir."

"Yes, I thought that was him," Jin murmured. "He's also a Djinni."

"Obviously," Omnathi said. "Interestingly, he was slated to lead tonight's attack on the sentry ship. The attack you weren't originally scheduled to take part in," he added offhandedly.

Jin swallowed. That had also been part of the deal she'd worked out with Miron Akim, something to give the attack better odds of success. Was there anything about her private conversations, she wondered, that Omnathi didn't know? "What happened?" she asked.

"Nothing mysterious," Omnathi assured her. "Miron Akim learned he was a qualified pilot and so pulled him off the attack so that he could be sent here to prepare for your flight to Aventine."

And put in his own son as second squad leader instead. Jin had wondered about that, especially so soon after Siraj's defeat the previous day. "And the young woman?"

"Rashida Vil is also a qualified pilot, and is furthermore fluent in the Troft language," Omnathi said. "That will be helpful if there are any sentries still in position over Qasama who will need the pilot's pass codes and clearances. As to the rest of your fellow travelers, I presume you already know them."

Jin frowned. Fellow travelers, plural? "Isn't it just my son and me?"

"Hardly," Omnathi said. "You didn't really think Miron Akim would allow you to leave Qasama without an escort, did you?"

Jin grimaced. No, actually, she shouldn't have thought that. "Let me guess," she said. "His son Siraj is coming."

"Correct," Omnathi confirmed. "And as long as Djinni Zoshak is here anyway, he might as well also accompany you."

"There's really no need for you to send them," Jin said. The thought of taking a group of Qasaman Djinn into the middle of Capitalia . . . "You know as well as I do that the treatment I received this morning only temporarily shrunk my tumor. If I don't come back to Qasama I'll still have no more than three months to live."

"I have no doubts that you'll return," Omnathi assured her calmly. "If for no other reason than to get your son."

Jin jerked her head around. "We had a deal, Moffren Omnathi," she bit out.

"A deal I was fully prepared to carry out," Omnathi said. "But the situation has changed. Merrick Moreau is far too badly injured to accompany you now. He needs treatment, and he needs it here."

A red haze of fury seemed to drop down in front of Jin's eyes. No wonder Omnathi had been so willing to honor Akim's deal and let her leave. He'd known all along that he had a hostage to her good behavior. "And if during this treatment his nanocomputer just happens to fall out into someone's hands?"

"Did I spend precious minutes of my life explaining my reasoning to you for nothing?" Omnathi countered, his voice going cold. "I have already told you I do not want his nanocomputer. Allow me to make it even clearer: I will not take his nanocomputer. Based on his performance this night, I am far more interested in seeing him healed and fighting again on our side."

Jin glared at him, the red haze slowly fading away. He could be lying, of course. But the logic held true.

And if he *was* lying, her tired brain and eyes would never pick up on it anyway. "He'll fight for you," she said, turning away. "Provided the Shahni allow him to do so."

"I will deal with the Shahni," Omnathi promised grimly. "As Miron Akim said to you once, victory is more important than honor."

He took a deep breath. "Let us return to the SkyJo. You may say your final farewells to your son, and I shall instruct Djinni Zoshak and Ifrit Akim on their new mission." His lip twitched. "Their reactions, I expect, will be most interesting."

"Father?" Fadil Sammon called gently.

For a moment the man lying on the hospital bed made no reaction. Then, to Fadil's relief, Daulo Sammon's eyes opened a bit. "Fadil?" he murmured.

Fadil breathed a quiet sigh of relief. At least his father was lucid this evening. With the array of healing drugs coursing through his veins, that wasn't always the case. "I came to say good-bye, Father," he said. "I'm going off for a while, and I don't know when I'll be back again to see you."

He waited patiently while his father's sluggish mind processed the words. "Where is it you're going?" the elder Sammon asked, frowning. "Back to war?"

"Not exactly," Fadil said, wondering if he should tell his father that the Trofts had left. Probably not, he decided regretfully. The invaders would be back—everyone he'd spoken to agreed on that. Best not to confuse the issue while his father wasn't thinking straight. "But it is related to our defense," he continued. "Anyway, I just wanted to say good-bye, and to tell you that the doctors say you're doing well. Another two or three weeks and you should be completely healed."

Daulo smiled weakly. "Three more weeks, is it?" he murmured. "I must have been hurt more badly than I thought."

Fadil swallowed hard. He'd been hurt, all right. In fact, he'd nearly died in that first failed attack against the Trofts. Even now, there was some serious reconstruction going on within his right shoulder and arm. "There were others hurt worse than you who are also going to be fine," he assured his father. "And before that you'll be well enough for me to take you home." Assuming, he added silently, that the Trofts didn't launch their next attack before then.

"Good." Daulo's eyes flicked upward to the feeding tube attached to his arm. "I do so dislike hospital food."

"I'll get you home as soon as I can," Fadil promised. "Until then, you just rest, do what they tell you, and concentrate on getting well." He looked at the bedside clock. "I need to go now, Father. Farewell."

"And to you, my son," Daulo said. His left arm twitched, and Fadil reached down to take his father's hand. "Whatever you're doing, I know you'll make our family proud."

"I'll do my best," Fadil promised. Giving his father's hand a final squeeze, he turned and walked away.

Daulo's breathing had settled into the steady rhythm of sleep even before Fadil had made it out of earshot.

Miron Akim was waiting in the treatment center's anteroom when Fadil arrived. "You said your farewells?" Akim asked, gesturing Fadil to the chair in front of him.

"To my father, yes," Fadil said, settling gingerly into the chair. This was it, he knew, an unpleasant tingling sensation running up his spine. This was his last chance to turn back. "I was wondering if I might also be permitted to say good-bye to Merrick Moreau and his mother."

Akim shook his head. "Unfortunately, neither is available at the moment."

"Because the Shahni have sent them home?" Fadil asked.

For the first time in their admittedly brief acquaintance Akim actually seemed taken aback. "Why do you say such an outrageous thing?" he asked cautiously.

"Because I've noticed their absence these past few days," Fadil said. "Yet there's no report of their deaths, which would certainly be on public record with so distinguished a pair of warriors."

"Perhaps they've simply been assigned to a different area," Akim suggested.

"Perhaps," Fadil said. "But I note also the absence of Carsh Zoshak and your son Siraj Akim. From that I deduce that Merrick Moreau and his mother didn't simply flee Qasama, but have been sent back to their home for some other purpose."

Akim eyed him in silence for a few heartbeats. "They're off Qasama," he conceded at last. "That's all you need to know." He raised his eyebrows slightly. "It's also far more than you *should* know."

"I understand," Fadil said. "Please forgive any impertinence. I mention it only to remind you that I *am* able to think deeply and logically, and am therefore worthy to participate in this experiment."

"An experiment which may seriously and permanently damage you," Akim reminded him in turn. "I'm required by law to confirm your acceptance of that risk this one final time."

Fadil suppressed a grimace. The drugs and medicines the Qasaman scientists and doctors had so painstakingly developed over the centuries were highly useful, both to individuals and to the society as a whole. But each of those drugs also carried its own set of risks, risks that increased in direct proportion to its power. Fadil's family had historically chosen to err on the side of caution, avoiding all but necessary medical drugs.

But Qasama was at war, and the alien antipersonnel missiles targeted the very radio signals that her defenders needed to coordinate both attack and defense. Somewhere, Fadil knew, there had to be a solution to that problem. But so far none of the techs had been able to come up with one.

It was time to try something more drastic. And since the true experts were far too valuable to risk this way, someone else would have to step up to that duty. Someone who was otherwise expendable to the war effort.

Someone like Fadil Sammon.

"I understand fully the risks inherent in the use of chemicals of mental stimulation," he said, quoting the words of the formal agreement. "I accept those risks, and am prepared to proceed."

"Then proceed you will," Akim said. Standing up, he opened the door to the treatment room proper and gestured.

Fadil stood up, feeling a slight trembling in his arms and legs. The die was cast, and there was no turning back. Whatever happened over the next few hours and days, whether his gamble succeeded or failed, he would willingly bear the cost.

And win or lose, at least the people of Qasama would never again look quite so condescendingly upon villagers. That alone made the risk worthwhile.

Squaring his shoulders, he followed Akim through the doorway.

CHAPTER TWENTY-TWO

"One minute," Khatir called from the pilot's seat.

"Acknowledged," Jin said. It was an unnecessary announcement, really, given that all five of the ship's complement had been gathered here in the transport's command room for the past half hour.

Surreptitiously, she looked around at each of the others, wondering what was going on behind all those dark eyes. Carsh Zoshak had taken the news of his new assignment very well, almost eagerly. But over the course of the past five days he'd grown quieter and more distant. Perhaps he was having second thoughts.

Siraj Akim didn't need to have second thoughts. It had been clear from the beginning that his first thoughts were bad enough. The fact that it was his own father who'd come up with this gamble was probably at the heart of his attitude, and Jin had never quite decided whether Moffren Omnathi signing off on it had made Siraj's discomfiture better or worse. Still, he was polite enough, and followed Jin's orders without question or argument.

Ghofl Khatir, in contrast, had not only started the mission eagerly but had managed to hold on to that cheery outlook. Talkative by nature, he nevertheless seldom spoke to Jin herself unless required to by his duties. Her best guess was that he was mostly excited by the chance to actually fly a starship, even if it was one his own people hadn't designed or built.

And then there was the young woman Rashida Vil. She said little to anyone, maintaining a rigid professionalism at all times that Jin sometimes found almost painful to watch. Perhaps as a female pilot from a male-dominated world she felt she had to continually prove herself and her abilities.

It was a challenge, and an attitude, with which Jin could definitely sympathize.

"Here we go," Khatir said, resettling his hands on the control yoke.

Jin grimaced. Because looming on the horizon was the biggest wild card of all: the leaders and people of the Cobra Worlds. What would they say, she wondered uneasily, when she landed a stolen Troft vehicle full of Qasamans on the Capitalia landing field and asked for help? Would they ignore her? Would they cry treason and try to lock her up? They'd nearly done that the last time she'd come back from Qasama, and she hadn't brought any visitors with her that time.

Or would they actually see the logic and humanity in her plea?

On the control board, the timer ran down and the stars burst into view through the command room viewport. A hundred thousand kilometers directly in front of them, a glorious visual symphony in white and blue and brown, was Jin's home.

It was only as she tore her eyes from the planet itself that she saw the ring of ships floating in a lazy orbital ring above Aventine's equator.

The Troft attack had already begun.

For a long minute no one spoke. Jin stared at the fleet, her heart aching, her stomach wanting to be sick. It was over. Aventine had been invaded, and her mission was over before it had even begun. There would be no help for Qasama from here. The people of the Cobra Worlds were in their own war for survival.

Beside her, Zoshak stirred. "What now?" he asked.

"We go back," Siraj said before Jin could find an answer. "It was a fool's notion to hope for any help from here anyway. We go back, and we fight the invaders with whatever strength we have, until that strength is gone."

"You can't win a war of attrition," Jin told him, trying desperately to think. But her brain was as frozen as her heart. "Neither can we. We have to come up with something else."

"Like what?" Siraj countered. "Unless you're prepared to run that gauntlet—"

"Signal!" Khatir snapped, swinging around to the communications part of his board. "We're being hailed."

"I'll take it," Rashida said, her voice glacially calm. "What do you want me to say?"

Jin pursed her lips. "Let's start by finding out what they want," she told the younger woman as Khatir half turned in his seat and tossed translator earphones to

Zoshak and Siraj. "As far as they're concerned we're just the latest in a long line of transports coming from Qasama."

"Should I transmit the clearance codes we used to leave Qasama?" Rashida asked.

"Let's wait until someone asks," Jin said. "There might be different codes for landing on Aventine that we didn't get."

Rashida nodded and keyed the transmitter. [The signal, it is acknowledged,] she said in flawless cattertalk. [Assistance, how may we render it?]

[Your cargo bay, analysis shows it to be empty,] a Troft voice came back. [The predators, why have you none?]

Jin winced. So the Troft ship out there had decided to take the time to give their harmless little transport a deep scan. "Tell them—"

Rashida silenced her with an upraised hand. [The predators, all died en route,] she said. [A disease, it was apparently brought aboard.]

Zoshak nudged Jin's side. "How good are these sensors of theirs?" he murmured. "Will they be able to tell we're not Trofts?"

"I don't know," Jin murmured back. "Probably depends on how much effort they're willing to put into this."

[The message, it is understood,] the Troft replied. There was a short pause. [Jasmine Jin Moreau, is there word from her?]

Jin felt her heart seize up in her chest. So it really *was* over. The ship had scanned them and had spotted the humans. Now, they wouldn't even have the option of returning to Qasama.

And then, suddenly the obvious fact struck her. *How had the Trofts come up with her name?*

She frowned, peering at the display. The only ship close enough for that kind of scan appeared to be a simple freighter, not any kind of warship. More than that, as near as she could tell from the cattertalk curlies on the hull, it was not only a freighter, but a *Tlossie* freighter. A ship from one of the Cobra Worlds' longtime trading partners.

Abruptly, she realized that all four Qasamans were looking expectantly at her. "What kind of signal are they using?" she asked quietly.

Khatir took a quick look at his board. "It looks like a tight beam."

[Jasmine Jin Moreau, is there word from her?] the Troft asked again.

Jin braced herself. [Jasmine Jin Moreau, it is I,] she called toward the microphone.

If the Troft in the other ship was surprised to hear from Jin herself, it didn't show in his voice. [The news from Qasama, what is it?] he asked.

The news from Qasama? What in the Worlds did he mean by that? [The battle, it has been won,] Jin said cautiously.

[Yet the war, it has been lost?]

[The war, it is not yet over,] Jin corrected.

There was a long silence. [Then our mission, it has failed,] the Troft said sadly.

"What mission?" Siraj muttered.

[Your pardon, I crave it,] Jin said. [Your mission, what is its purpose and meaning?]

[The mission, it is of no matter,] the Troft said. [Its failure, that is all I need know.]

Jin felt her mouth fall open as the last piece finally fell into place. [The message, from *you* it came,] she said. [To Qasama, you wished me to go.]

"*They* sent you the message?" Siraj demanded, his eyes wide with disbelief.

"Apparently so," Jin said as it all suddenly made sense. "Disguised to look like it came from someone on Qasama, of course, in case it was intercepted."

"But why?" Zoshak demanded.

Jin lifted a finger and switched back to cattertalk. [Your mission, I understand it now,] she said. [War with Aventine, your demesne-lord does not wish. Yet a stand against the attacking demesnes, he dare not take alone. A victory against them, one must first exist.]

"I'll be damned," Khatir murmured.

[The truth, you speak it,] the Troft said. [A stand, other demesne-lords wish to make. But a stand against a victorious army, one cannot be made.]

[The reality, I understand it,] Jin said grimly. [But hope, do not abandon it.] "Djinni Khatir, what's our fuel situation?"

Again, Khatir studied his displays. "We're down about one-third," he reported.

Jin did a quick calculation. Probably enough, but better to err on the safe side. [Refueling, our transport needs,] she said. [Extra fuel, can you supply it?]

There was a pause. [To return to Qasama, enough exists.]

[The truth, you speak it,] Jin agreed. [But Qasama, we do not yet return there. Extra fuel, can you supply it?]

[This fuel, to what use?]

Jin smiled tightly. [Victory against the attacking demesne-lords, its use will be.]

There was another pause. Jin could feel the eyes of the Qasamans on her; deliberately, she kept her own gaze on the Troft ship on the display. [Your course, you will hold it,] the Troft said at last. [To your side, we will come.]

[Our gratitude, you have it,] Jin said. [Your arrival, we will await it.]

There was a click from the speaker. Jin gestured, and Rashida flicked off their own transmitter. "Is this making of rash promises a general trait of your people?" Khatir asked mildly. "Or is it just you personally?"

"I've made no rash promises," Jin assured him. "To anyone," she added, looking at Siraj Akim. "I promised Miron Akim that I would return with help. And I will." She gestured toward the besieged world hanging in space in the distance. "I simply came to the wrong place to get it."

"I thought Aventine was the capital and most powerful of your worlds," Akim said, frowning.

"It is," Jin said, nodding. "It has one and a quarter million inhabitants, about eighty-five percent of our total population. If the Trofts have any tactical sense at all, this is where they'll throw the bulk of their forces."

"Obviously, they have," Khatir said, waving at the distant ring of ships.

"But there's another world out there," Jin continued. "A world named Caelian, with a little over four thousand colonists. Tactically and strategically speaking, it's a completely insignificant place. I can't imagine any competent military commander putting more than a token force there, if that much."

"And you expect all four thousand to rise to our aid?" Siraj scoffed.

"Not at all," Jin said. "The point is that among those four thousand colonists are seven hundred Cobras."

And suddenly, the atmosphere in the control room was charged with electricity. The Qasamans sat up a little straighter, flicking glances back and forth between them, and Jin could see in their faces a sense of understanding and a freshly renewed hope.

As well as a freshly renewed fear.

She couldn't blame them. They had grown up hating and fearing the Cobra Worlds, the people in general and the Cobras in particular. Now, suddenly, their leaders had ordered that those very Cobras be asked for help.

Would the ultimate result of that plea be Qasama's salvation? Or was it a pact with the devil that would lead to their ruin?

It was a question none of them could answer. Including Jin herself.

Typically, it was Khatir who broke the silence. "So what are we doing here?" he asked. "Let's get this ship fueled, and go find some demon warriors."

"I just hope some of them will be willing to come to Qasama to fight," Siraj added doubtfully.

"I know at least one who will," Jin told him, a sudden pang in her heart. "My husband is there. Along with my daughter."

Siraj snorted. "*One* Cobra? Yes, that will certainly bring us victory."

Zoshak stirred. "If he fights as do Jasmine and Merrick Moreau," he said quietly, "it very well might."

"There will be more," Jin promised.

And she meant it. Whatever it took, she *would* assemble a fighting force to take back with them.

Because the Tlossies were right. They needed a clear-cut human victory if they were to have any hope of rallying support among the other Troft demesnes. From the number of sentry ships encircling Aventine, it was clear that victory wasn't going to be achieved there. Not any time soon.

Perhaps that was only fitting. The war had begun on Qasama. One way or another, it was going to end there.

The following is an excerpt from:

COBRA GUARDIAN

COBRA WAR BOOK II

TIMOTHY ZAHN

Available from Baen Books
January 2011
hardcover

CHAPTER ONE

The first indication that it was going to be one of those days was when the cooker burned the leftover pizza Lorne Broom had planned to have for breakfast.

"Oh, for—" he choked off the curse before it could get out past his throat, old habits of propriety kicking in as he glared at the cooker. This was the third time this month the stupid thing had gone gunnybags on him, and with everything else weighing on his shoulders he had precious little patience left for balky appliances.

Or, better even than a curse, he could deal with the balky cooker once and for all. A single, full-power fingertip laser blast into the cooker's core would turn the thing into a conversation-piece paperweight. A shot with his arcthrower would send the cooker beyond paperweight status into a slagged heap that even the revivalist Earth artist Salvador Dali would have been proud of. Even better, a blast from his antiarmor laser—

Lorne took a deep breath, forcing down the surge of frustration. A blast from his antiarmor laser would not only blow a hole through the cooker, but also through the kitchen wall, the wall behind that, and possibly the wall beyond that into the building corridor. At that point, he could say good-bye not only to the cooker, but to his damage deposit as well.

With a sigh, he unloaded the burned pizza and pushed the cooker back into its niche at the back of the counter. The depressing fact was that Cobra salaries had been on a steady downward slide for the past two years, and even with the extra hazard pay he got out here at the edge of Aventine's expansion area, he simply couldn't afford to dump uncooperative appliances. Not when there was still a chance they could be repaired.

Unfortunately, he couldn't afford to dump a ruined meal, either.

He picked away as much of the blackened cheese as he could without giving up on the meal entirely. Then, taking the plate over to the breakfast nook, he keyed his computer for the news feed and sat down to eat.

The news, as usual, was right up there with the quality of his meal. The late-year election season was heating up, and puff ads by incumbents and hopefuls were starting to crowd out the usual selection of business and service commercials. Viminal, the latest addition to the Cobra Worlds, announced that its population had just passed the twenty-two thousand mark, and Governor Conzjuaraz was taking the opportunity to remind Aventinians that there was a world's worth of good land out there going cheap.

And right at the end, almost as an afterthought, came a report that there'd been another spine leopard attack at the edge of a settlement out past Mayring in Willaway Province. Five of the big predators had been involved, killing three settlers and injuring eight others. The local Cobras were already on the hunt in hopes of catching and killing the family-pack before it struck again.

The report was only an hour old, but already two of Aventine's most outspoken politicians had jumped on it with their usual and predictable stances as the news switched over into commentary. Governor Ellen Hoffman had gotten on record first, pointing to the incident as proof that the government needed to budget more money for Cobra recruitment and training. Senior Governor Tomo Treakness was right behind her, sympathizing with the victims while at the same time managing to imply it was partially their fault for moving out into the planet's wilderness areas in the first place instead of filling up the cities and farms the way good sociable people were apparently supposed to. He also made it clear that he would vigorously oppose pouring more money into the MacDonald and Sun Centers, declaring that the incident proved that an expansion of the Cobra program wasn't the solution.

By the time Lorne finally turned off the feed in disgust, the worst taste in his mouth was no longer that of burned pizza.

He loaded the dishes in the washer for later, giving the cooker a baleful look as he did so and wondering once again how long he could keep his shaky finances a secret from the rest of his family. His brother Merrick, who had been assigned to the small Cobra contingent in Capitalia, was paid even less than Lorne was, but the

Cobra barracks attached to the MacDonald Center had rooms that went for a quarter of the price of even Lorne's miniscule apartment. Besides that, Merrick had parents and grandparents right there in the city with him, whose houses he could go to for meals on a regular basis. Especially since with his gourmet skills he could bargain for those meals with the offer to cook them.

Someday, Lorne vowed to himself, he really should learn how to cook something.

He was fastening his tunic and heading for the door when his comm buzzed. He pulled it out, frowning at the ID as he keyed it on. What in the Worlds was Commandant Yoshio Ishikuma calling for when Lorne would be there in another fifteen minutes? Keying it on, he held it to his ear. "Broom."

"You left your apartment yet?" Ishikuma asked.

"Just heading out now," Lorne assured him.

"Well, when you hit the door, break left instead of right," Ishikuma said. "There's an aircar coming in from the Dome to get you."

Lorne felt his stomach close into a hard knot around his breakfast. "What's happened?"

"No idea," Ishikuma said. "But they're not coming with an armed guard, so whatever you've been doing in your off-hours you can relax about."

"Like we actually have any off-hours," Lorne said, trying to sound his usual flippant self even as his stomach tightened another couple of turns. Had something happened to his father or sister on Caelian? On that hellworld, death could come in a splintered heartbeat, and from any of a hundred different directions.

Or could someone have found out where Lorne's mother and Merrick had disappeared to?

"Just remember that it could always be worse," Ishikuma said. "You could be on burial duty in Hunter's Crossing."

"Yes, I heard about that," Lorne said grimly. "We sending anyone to help in the hunt?"

"So far, they haven't asked," Ishikuma said. "But it might not matter. If Willaway is getting an uptick in spiny activity, we could see the same thing here by the end of next week. So whatever the fancy desks in Capitalia want with you, close it down fast and get your tail back out here."

"Don't worry," Lorne promised. He pulled open the building's front door and turned left toward the airfield eight blocks away. "By the way, if they're calling me in to tell me they want to shower us with new funding, how much do we want?"

"Chin-deep ought to do it," Ishikuma said. "No need to be greedy."

"Chin-deep it is," Lorne agreed. "See you soon."

"Just watch your back," Ishikuma warned. "These days, every Cobra in the Worlds has a bull's-eye tattooed there."

"Understood," Lorne said. "I'll be back as soon as I can." He keyed off the comm and picked up his pace.

It was definitely going to be one of those days.

The aircar waiting on the field had Directorate markings on it, which meant the vehicle and its driver were attached to the fifteen most powerful people in the Cobra Worlds. Given the violent political polarizations currently swirling around those fifteen people, Lorne expected the driver to present as neutral and nonaligned an attitude as it was possible for a human being to achieve.

Sure enough, the other greeted Lorne with exactly the correct degree of cool courtesy as he ushered him into the passenger section. He quickly and efficiently got the vehicle into the air, and then spent the next two and a half hours saying absolutely nothing.

They put down in the private landing terrace behind the Dome, the two-decades-old governmental building that had been named after the much larger and more dramatic structure in the main governmental center of the distant Dominion of Man. Lorne had always thought the name here to be more than a little pretentious, given that the Dominion held sway over seventy worlds—possibly more than that now—while the Cobra Worlds numbered a paltry and underdeveloped five.

Still, it could have been worse. They could have named the center after one of the previous governor-generals, very few of whom had been worth naming anything significant after. At least, not as Lorne read his family's history.

The driver had called ahead, and there was a young woman with a red-and-white shoulder band waiting when Lorne emerged from the aircar. "Cobra Lorne Broom?" she asked briskly.

"Yes," Lorne confirmed, slightly taken aback by her open face and genuinely pleasant smile. Either her job was secure enough that she didn't have to worry about keeping her head below the political firestorms, or else she hadn't been at the Dome long enough to have learned the driver's studied caution and neutrality.

"Welcome to the Dome," she said, holding out her hand. "I'm Nissa Gendreves, secondary assistant to Governor-General Chintawa."

"Nice to meet you," Lorne said, taking her hand in a brief handshake. The woman had a good, firm grip. "What exactly does a secondary assistant do?"

"All the unpaid, unglamorous, and dirty jobs no one else wants," she said straightforwardly and unapologetically, her friendly smile going a little dry. "Though I think that in this particular case someone must have slipped up." She gestured to a door behind her, flanked by two Cobras in semidress uniforms. "If you'll follow me, the governor-general is waiting."

She led the way through the door into a nicely appointed hallway filled with other governmental types. The older ones—the governors, syndics, and top bureaucrats—mostly moved at sedate walks, as befit their noble status and venerable ages. Those of Nissa's age or slightly older moved much faster on apparently less dignified errands. Most of the latter group, Lorne noted, had assistant or aide shoulder bands of various colors. "What did you mean that someone must have slipped up?" he asked as they headed toward the center of the building.

"I meant that acting as your escort is hardly one of the dirty jobs," Nissa said. "You're something of a celebrity, you know. Or at least your family is."

"Was," Lorne corrected. "Not so much anymore."

"Perhaps, but they certainly were once," Nissa conceded. "I read about your mother when I was a little girl, the first female Cobra and all. Even if the Qasaman mission didn't come out the way everyone hoped, she was still the first woman to step up and take the challenge. That makes her someone special."

"I've always thought so," Lorne murmured, wondering what Nissa would say if he told her that the official history of the Qasaman mission was pretty much a complete and bald-faced fabrication. Wondered what her response would be if he told her that his mother had actually succeeded in every damn thing they'd sent her to Qasama to accomplish, and a whole lot more.

But it wasn't worth the effort. Nissa was young and idealistic, and that sort of revelation would either upset her or simply convince her that Lorne was a biased and untrustworthy observer. Nissa had passed through the Worlds' school system, and as he himself had learned, that system never let truth get in the way of the official line. "So what am I doing here?" he asked instead.

"I really don't know," she said. "But Governor-General Chintawa seemed very anxious to see you."

"So it's just the governor-general who's waiting for me?" Lorne probed gently.

"I don't know—he didn't have me on conference call," Nissa said dryly. "Come on, Cobra Broom. I know your family was well-known for its political machinations, but pumping me for information isn't going to get you anywhere."

"Yes, I can see that," Lorne said, pushing back a fresh flicker of annoyance.

Still, that one, at least, *did* have a certain ring of truth to it.

There was a secretary and another pair of Cobra guards stationed outside Chintawa's private office. The former looked up and silently nodded Nissa toward the door, while the latter moved a step farther apart to indicate their own acceptance of the visitors' right to pass unchallenged. One of the Cobras caught Lorne's eye and gave him a microscopic nod of acknowledgment as Nissa led the way between them and pushed open the door.

Lorne had visited the governor-general's official office once or twice, that large and photogenic chamber where public business, meetings, and interviews took place. He'd never before seen Chintawa's private office, though, and his first impression as he followed Nissa in was that a Willaway windstorm must have swept through overnight. The oversized desk was almost literally covered with scattered stacks of papers, though none of the stacks seemed to be more than a few pages deep. The floor-to-ceiling shelves were crammed with books, awards, and dozens of small mementos Chintawa had collected during his years on the political scene, all arranged haphazardly without any of the calculated symmetry or eye appeal of the similar shelves in the official office. There were no windows, but across from the shelves was a group of nine displays, all of them set to different news channels with the volume down and simul transcriptions crawling across the pictures. Directly across from the desk, where it was the first thing Chintawa would see when he lifted his head from his papers or his computer, was a full-wall montage of scenes from different parts of the five Cobra Worlds.

"Cobra Broom," Chintawa said, smiling as he looked up. "Good of you to come. Please, sit down." He gestured to a chair at the corner of his desk. "Can Nissa get you some refreshment?"

"No, thank you," Lorne said as he crossed to the indicated chair and sat down.

Chintawa nodded to Nissa. "Dismissed."

"Yes, sir." Nissa's eyes flicked once to Lorne, and then she was gone.

"Impressive young lady," Chintawa commented as the door closed behind her with a solid-sounding thunk. "I'm sure you didn't get much of a feel for her on the short walk from the landing terrace, but she really is quite bright."

"Well read, too," Lorne murmured. "She was telling me all about my family history."

"Now, now—you're way too young to go all cynical on me," Chintawa chided mildly. "Anyway, she's young yet. Idealistic. Believes what she reads in school. She'll learn." He leaned back in his chair. "But I didn't ask you here to talk about your family's past. I brought you here to talk about your family's present."

Lorne frowned. "Excuse me?"

"Specifically," Chintawa continued, "I want to know where your mother is."

Lorne felt his heart seize up inside his ceramic-laminated rib cage. Had Chintawa somehow found out about his mother and brother's quiet and incredibly illegal trip to Qasama? "She's somewhere in the wilderness out past Pindar," he said, managing with a supreme effort to keep his voice steady. "Didn't Merrick tell Commandant Dreysler that when he requested temporary leave?"

"Yes, he did," Chintawa said, eyeing Lorne closely. "And at the time I was willing to let it slide."

"What do you mean?" Lorne asked, and immediately cursed himself for doing so. Now he was going to have to hear Chintawa's answer, and he was pretty sure he wasn't going to like it.

He was right. "Please, Broom," Chintawa scoffed. "Jin Moreau Broom, the first woman Cobra, who single-handedly took down a traitorous Qasaman and his Troft allies, suddenly going all to pieces in the Esserling scrubland just because her husband and daughter have gone off on a visit to Caelian?" He snorted. "You forget that as governor-general I have access to *genuine* Cobra Worlds' history."

"We really should see about getting that published someday," Lorne said stiffly. "As to Mom being upset about Dad and Jody going to Caelian, I didn't realize Cobras weren't allowed to be concerned about their loved ones."

"Of course she's allowed to be concerned," Chintawa said. "But going off to commune with nature simply isn't her style."

"People's styles change."

"Not that much they don't," Chintawa said flatly. "More significantly, people worried about their loved ones don't deliberately go incommunicado for days at a time. We've tried both their comms—repeatedly—and get nothing but their voice stacks."

"Maybe they just don't feel like talking to anyone in the Dome."

"Or maybe they aren't out crying in the wilderness at all," Chintawa countered brusquely. "They're with your great-uncle Corwin, aren't they?"

Lorne blinked, the sheer unexpectedness of the question bringing his mad scramble for a good defensible position to a skidding halt. "*What*?" he asked.

"No games," Chintawa said sternly. "I've been keeping track of Corwin Moreau's work over the years. I know that right now he's trying to develop a type of bone laminate that might ease some of the long-term anemia and arthritis problems. The fact that your mother and brother have suddenly disappeared tells me he's reached the point where he's ready to do some field tests with actual Cobras."

"That's ridiculous," Lorne said with as much dignity as he could drum up on the spur of the moment. It *was* ridiculous, actually—Uncle Corwin had been working on and off on the Cobra medical problems for most of Lorne's lifetime, and as far as Lorne knew he'd never gotten any traction with any of them.

But Chintawa obviously didn't know that. And in fact, the more Lorne thought about it, the more he realized the governor-general's suspicions made for a much better cover story than even the one he, Merrick, Jody, and their dad had come up with.

"It's not ridiculous, and I frankly don't care what any of them is doing," Chintawa said. "The point is that I need your mother here, and I need her here now."

"What for?"

"Something important and confidential," Chintawa said. "Also something I think will help put your family in a better light than it's been in for the past several years." He smiled faintly. "She's not in trouble, if that's what you're wondering."

If you only knew, Lorne thought grimly. "It would certainly be nice to have the record set at least a little straighter," he said, "though it would probably be terribly confusing to people like Nissa. You say you need her right now?"

"By noon tomorrow, actually," Chintawa said. "If absolutely necessary I could probably postpone the ceremony a couple of days."

Lorne frowned. "Ceremony?"

Chintawa smiled faintly. "You'll know when your mother knows," he said. "Until then, it's my prerogative to be mysterious."

"In that case, it's my prerogative to take my leave," Lorne said, standing up. "If I hear from her, I'll be sure and let her know you're looking for her."

"Just a minute," Chintawa said, his voice darkening as he also stood up. "That's it?"

"What do you want me to say?" Lorne countered. "That I'll bring my mother in whether she wants to be here or not? I can't promise that. If you want to tell me something that'll sweeten the pot, I'll be happy to hear it."

"You want the pot sweetened?" Chintawa rumbled. "Fine. Tell her that if she isn't here, other people will get all the credit and she'll get nothing. *And* they'll get to put their own spin on it, which will leave the Moreau name right where it is. In the historical gutter."

Lorne snorted. "With all due respect, sir, my family stopped caring about who got credit for what a long time ago. And unless you're planning to nominate my mother for sainthood, it's going to take more than anything you can do to put our family name back where it deserves."

"Certainly not if you aren't willing to make some effort of your own," Chintawa ground out. "If you can't see that, why should I waste my time trying to help?"

"I don't know," Lorne said sarcastically. This was probably not the direction his mother or father would take the conversation, and certainly not where Uncle Corwin would go. But he didn't have their verbal finesse, and he simply couldn't think of anything else to try. "Maybe because you see some political gain in it for yourself?"

Chintawa's face darkened like an approaching thunderstorm. "How in the Worlds did you grow up in the Moreau family without learning anything about politics?" he demanded. "It's not a zero-sum game, you know. What's gain for me can also be gain for you."

"And all you need for that gain is to put my mother up on a stage like your private sock puppet?" Lorne suggested.

Chintawa muttered something under his breath. "Get out of here," he ordered. "Just get out."

"As you wish, Governor-General Chintawa," Lorne said formally, starting to breathe again as he stood up.

It had actually worked. He'd made Chintawa so mad at him that he didn't even want to see Lorne's mother anymore.

Now if Chintawa would just stay this mad long enough for Lorne to get out of Capitalia and back to DeVegas Province, this whole thing might blow over. Or at least quiet down long enough for his mother and brother to finish up their mysterious errand on Qasama and get back home.

He'd made it halfway to the office door when Chintawa cleared his throat. "And where exactly do you think you're going?"

Lorne stopped but didn't turn around. "I'm going back to my duty station," he said over his shoulder. "As per your orders."

"I've given you no such orders," Chintawa said. "But since you bring it up, let's do that, shall we? You're hereby relieved of all other duties and tasked with the job of finding Cobra Jasmine Moreau Broom and bringing her to the Dome."

Lorne turned around, feeling his mouth drop open. "*What*?"

"You heard me," Chintawa said. The thunderstorm of anger had passed, leaving frozen ground behind it. "Until your mother is standing in front of me, you're not going back to Archway or anywhere else."

"This is ridiculous," Lorne protested. "I have work to do."

"Then you'd better persuade your mother to come in, hadn't you?" Chintawa said. "Otherwise, you'd better get used to living in your parents' house again."

"This is illegal and out of channels. Sir," Lorne bit out. "Barring a declared state of emergency, you can't counteract standing orders and assignments."

"You're welcome to appeal to Commandant Dreysler," Chintawa said. "But I can tell you right now that the orders will be cut before you even reach his office."

For a long moment the two men locked eyes. "Fine," Lorne said stiffly. It was clear that Chintawa had his mind made up. It was also clear that Lorne himself didn't have the faintest idea of what to do now.

But he knew who might. "I'll need a way to get to Uncle Corwin's house," he continued. "Cobra pay doesn't stretch far enough to cover car rentals."

Chintawa reached over and touched a switch on his intercom. "Nissa, come in here, please."

He straightened up again, and the staring contest resumed. Thirty-two seconds later by Lorne's nanocomputer clock, the door opened and Nissa stepped inside. "Yes, sir?" she asked, a slight frown creasing her forehead as her eyes flicked back and forth between the two men.

"Until further notice, you're assigned to Cobra Broom," Chintawa told her. "Check out a car and take him anywhere in or around Capitalia he wants to go. If he wants to leave the city, call Ms. Oomara first and have her clear it with me."

"Yes, sir," Nissa said, her forehead clearing as she apparently decided whatever was happening was none of her business. "Cobra Broom?"

Lorne held his glare another second and a half. Then, turning away from Chintawa, he stalked across the room, past the girl, and out the door.

It was going to be one of those days, all right. And then some.

Corwin Moreau listened silently as Lorne described the morning's events, occasionally nodding in reaction to something his great-nephew said, his fingertips occasionally rubbing gently at the arm of his chair in response to some inner thoughts or musings of his own.

"And so I came here," Lorne finished, looking briefly over at Aunt Thena, who had listened to the tale in the same silence as her husband. "It might not have been very smart, but I couldn't think of anything else to do."

"No, you did fine," Corwin assured him, looking questioningly at Thena. She gave a slight shrug in return. "Is the young lady still waiting out there? We should at least invite her in for lunch."

"I don't know if she's there or not," Lorne said. "Probably not—I told her I'd be here for a while, and she told me she has family a couple of blocks away. Maybe that's why Chintawa gave her the job of carting me around in the first place. He probably figured I'd go to ground here, and she might as well have someplace of her own to wait for me."

"Or else she got the job because he thought you might open up to someone who wasn't a hardened politician," Thena offered. "It's an old trick, and not beneath Chintawa's dignity."

"Certainly not if lying isn't," Lorne growled.

Corwin cocked an eyebrow at him. "What did he lie about?"

"Oh, come on," Lorne scoffed. "This whole secret ceremony thing? How obvious can a lie get?"

"Well, that's the point, isn't it?" Corwin said thoughtfully. "It's such an obviously ridiculous cover story that one has to wonder whether it might actually be true."

Lorne frowned. "Have you heard something?"

"No, not a whisper," Corwin said. "But I'm hardly in the official gossip ring these days."

"Besides being obvious, the story's also pointless," Thena added. "As a Cobra, your mother is still a reservist, and hence subject to immediate call-up by the governor-general for any reason. He can order her to appear at the Dome, or order you to go get her, with no explanation needed."

"Maybe," Lorne said. "But right now it doesn't really matter why he wants her. What we need is a way to stall him off. And I can tell you right now, he didn't look to be in a stalling mood."

"Not if he's willing to pull a Cobra in from frontier duty," Corwin agreed heavily. "Especially right after a major spine leopard attack in the same general region. Any chance he could be persuaded to accept the story that she and Merrick are off on a retreat somewhere?"

"No," Lorne said. "And in fact, he pointed out the logical flaw in it: that they wouldn't go off without leaving some way of contacting them."

"Yes, that was always the weak spot," Corwin said heavily. "I should have come up with something better."

"You didn't have much time," Thena pointed out. "Besides, there was no way to guess that anyone would take more than a passing interest in their absence."

"I suppose," Corwin conceded. "So now what?"

"Well, we can't pretend they're hiding here," Thena said slowly. "If Chintawa is determined enough to get a search warrant, a few patrollers could pop that balloon within half an hour."

"So again, they're somewhere else," Corwin said. "Someplace where Lorne presumably can try to call them."

"Right now?" Lorne asked, pulling out his comm.

"Yes, this would be good," Corwin confirmed, looking at his watch. "You've been here just long enough to have consulted with us, and for us to have decided together that this is worth breaking into her solitude. Go ahead—your mother first."

Lorne nodded and punched in his mother's number. "I presume this is purely for the benefit of anyone who might decide to pull my comm records later?"

"Correct." Corwin hesitated. "It'll also put all the rest of us in a slightly better legal position should the worst-case scenario happen."

Lorne felt his throat tighten. That scenario being if his mother and brother got caught sneaking back onto Aventine from Qasama and were brought up on charges of treason.

At which point, of course, all of Uncle Corwin's caution would go scattering to the four winds, because Lorne was absolutely not going to hunker down behind legal excuses while two of his family stood in the dock. He would be right up there with them, as would his father and sister. And probably Uncle Corwin and Aunt Thena, too.

At which point Chintawa and the Directorate would have to decide whether they really wanted to risk the kind of political fallout that could come of prosecuting the whole family.

Lorne almost hoped they did. He would use the occasion to make sure the true story of his mother's original mission to Qasama got brought up into the open from the shallow grave where Uncle Corwin's political enemies had buried it.

"Hello, this is Jasmine," his mother's voice came in his ear. "I'm not available right now, but if you'd care to leave a message . . . "

Lorne waited for the greeting to run its course, recorded a short message telling her to call as soon as it was convenient, and keyed off. "Now Merrick?" he asked.